ANN M. MARTIN

BABY-SITTERS LITTLE SISTER®

KAREN'S ROLLER SKATES

A GRAPHIC NOVEL BY
KATY FARINA
WITH COLOR BY BRADEN LAMB

graphix

An Imprint of

SCHOLASTIC

This book is in loving memory
of my grandmother Adele Read Martin
August 2, 1894 – April 18, 1988
A. M. M.

For my parents, who were always there to
make scrapes, sickness, and broken bones feel better
K. F.

Text copyright © 2020 by Ann M. Martin
Art copyright © 2020 by Katy Farina

Library of Congress Control Number: 2019945281

ISBN 978-1-338-35616-8 (hardcover)
ISBN 978-1-338-35614-4 (paperback)

10 9 8 7 6 5 4 3 2 1   20 21 22 23 24

Printed in Malaysia   108
First edition, July 2020

Edited by Cassandra Pelham Fulton and David Levithan
Book design by Phil Falco and Shivana Sookdeo
Penciling assistance from Kendra Wells
Publisher: David Saylor

CHAPTER 1

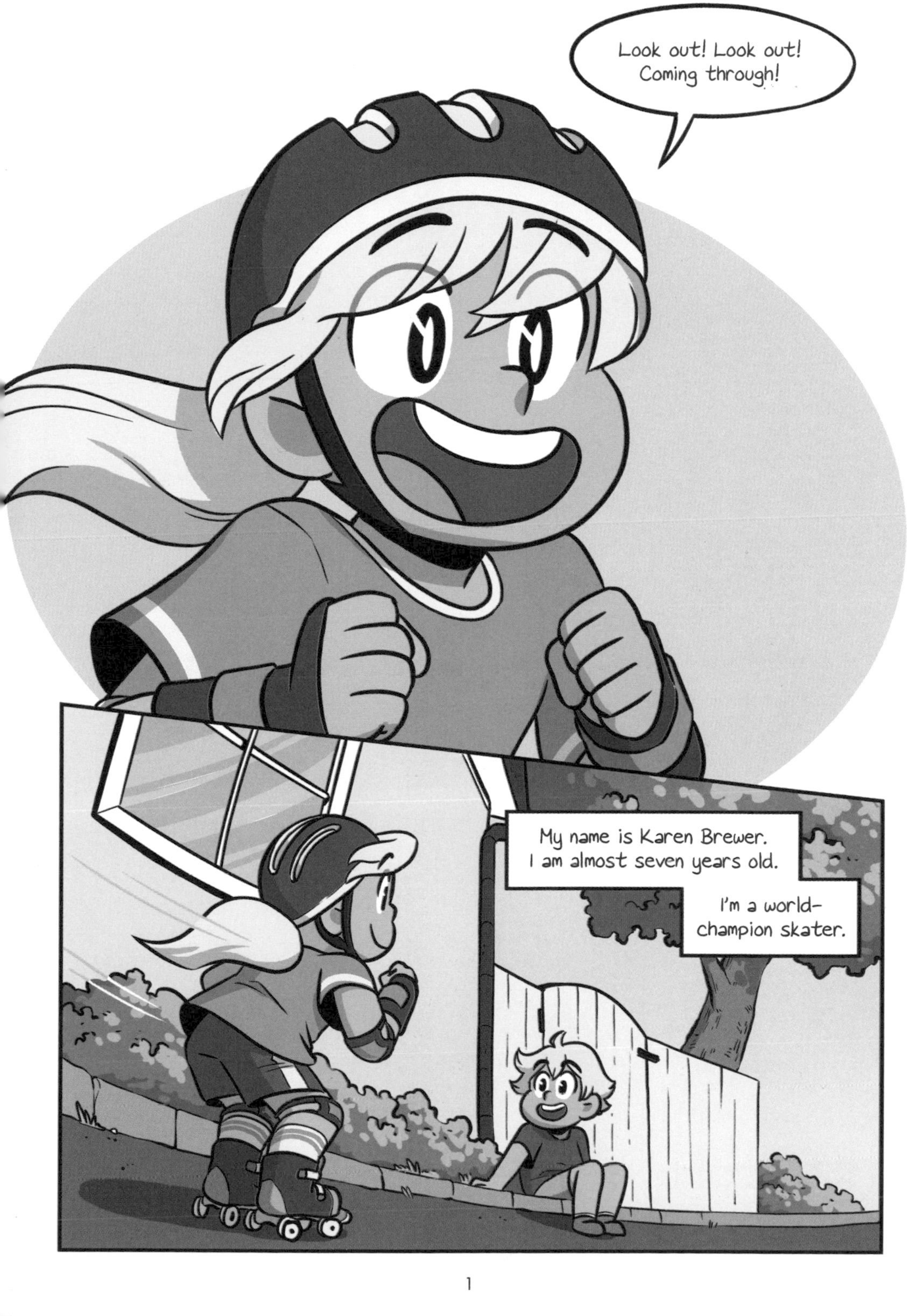
Look out! Look out! Coming through!
My name is Karen Brewer. I am almost seven years old.
I'm a world-champion skater.

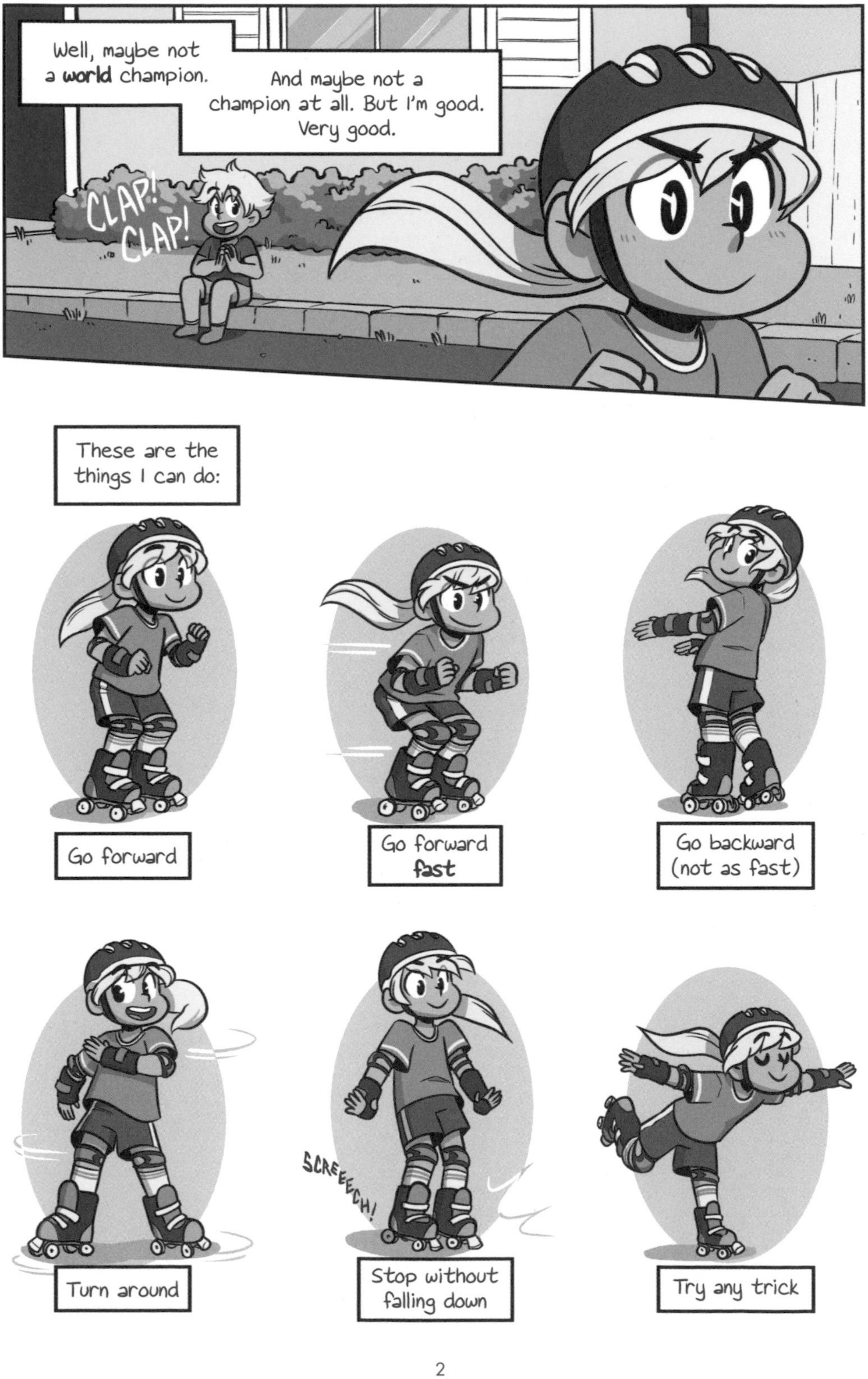
Well, maybe not a **world** champion.
And maybe not a champion at all. But I'm good. Very good.
CLAP! CLAP!
These are the things I can do:
Go forward
Go forward **fast**
Go backward (not as fast)
Turn around
SCREEECH!
Stop without falling down
Try any trick

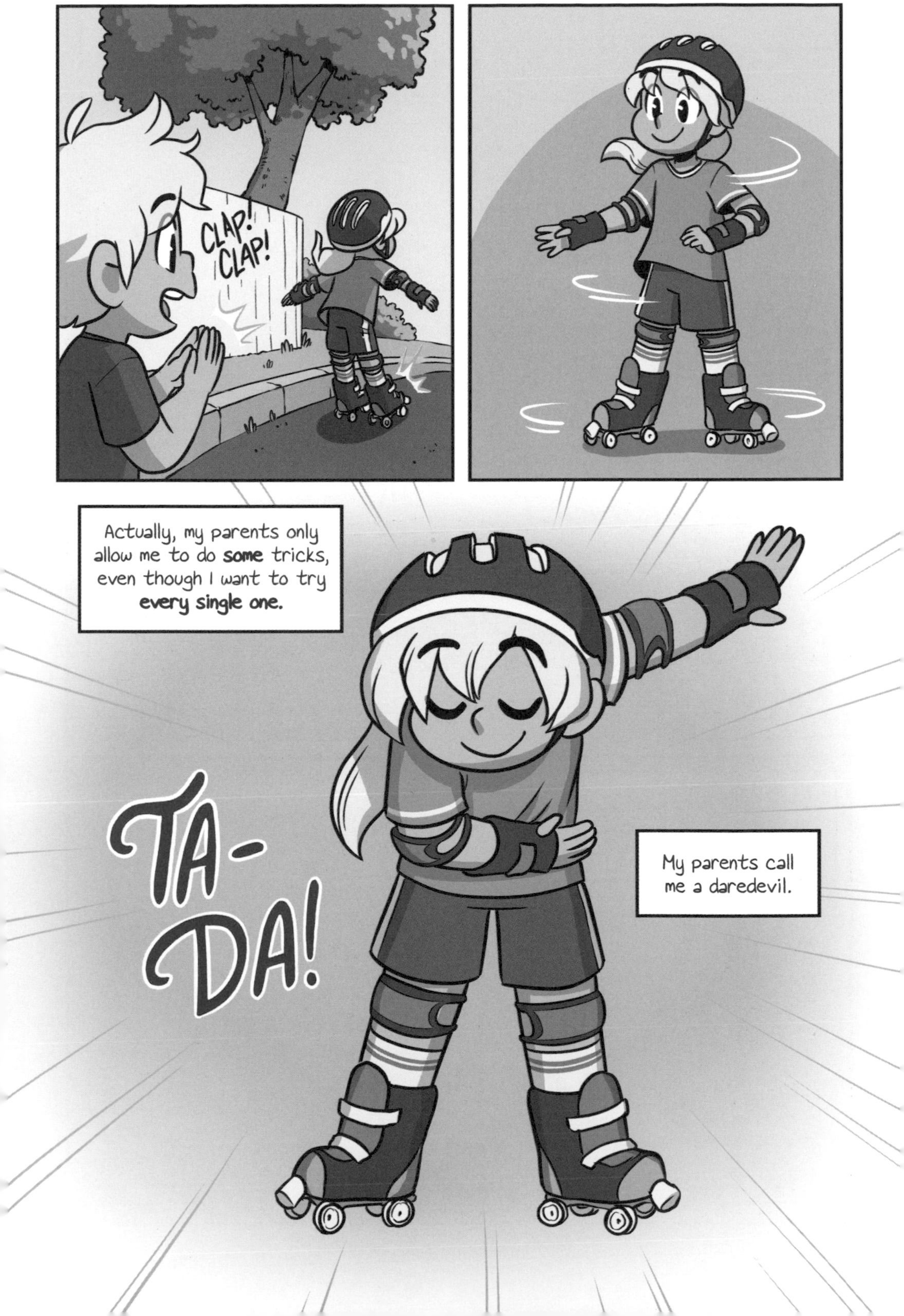
CLAP! CLAP!
Actually, my parents only allow me to do **some** tricks, even though I want to try **every single one.**
TA-DA!
My parents call me a daredevil.

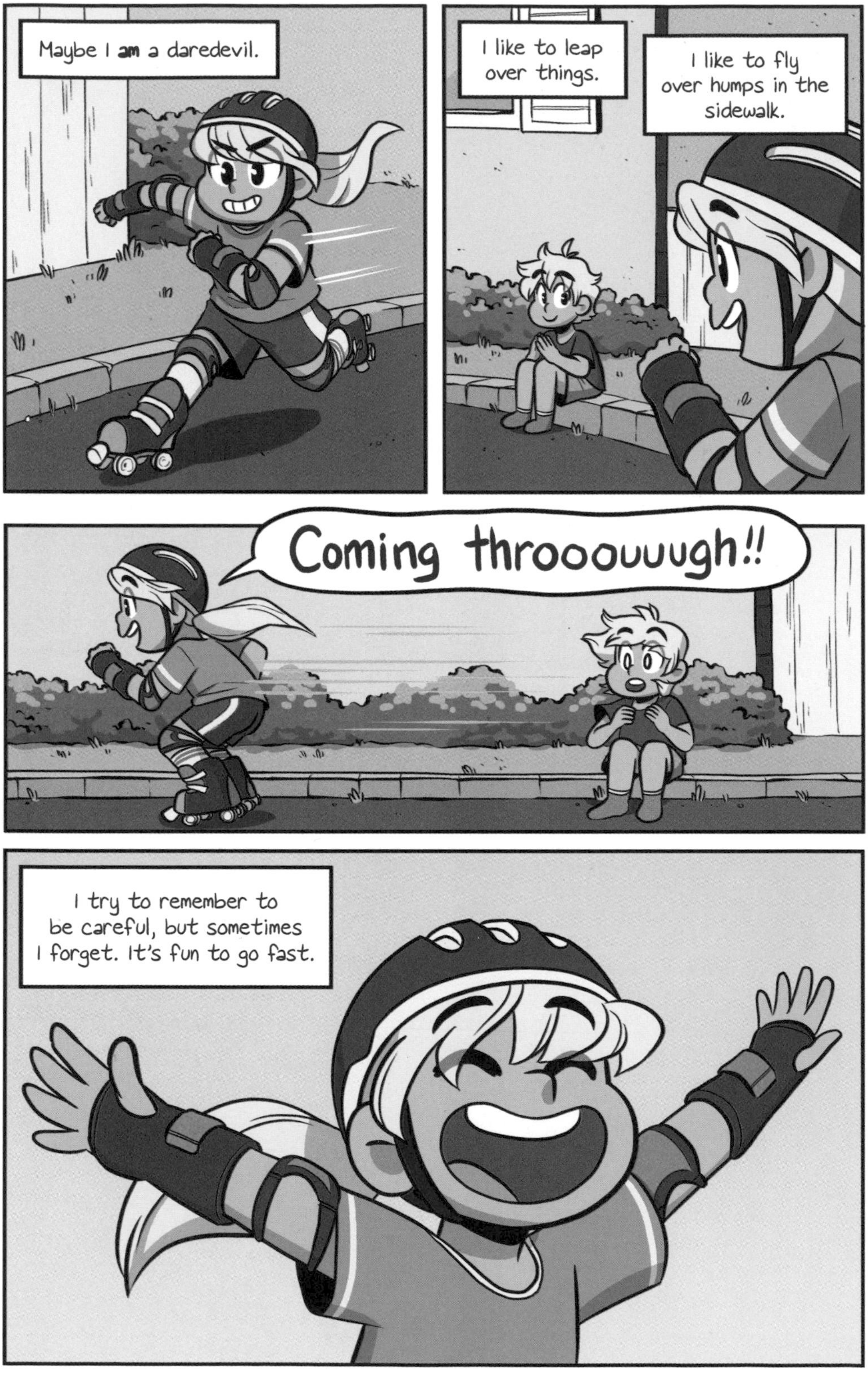

Maybe I **am** a daredevil.
I like to leap over things.
I like to fly over humps in the sidewalk.
Coming throooouuugh!!
I try to remember to be careful, but sometimes I forget. It's fun to go fast.

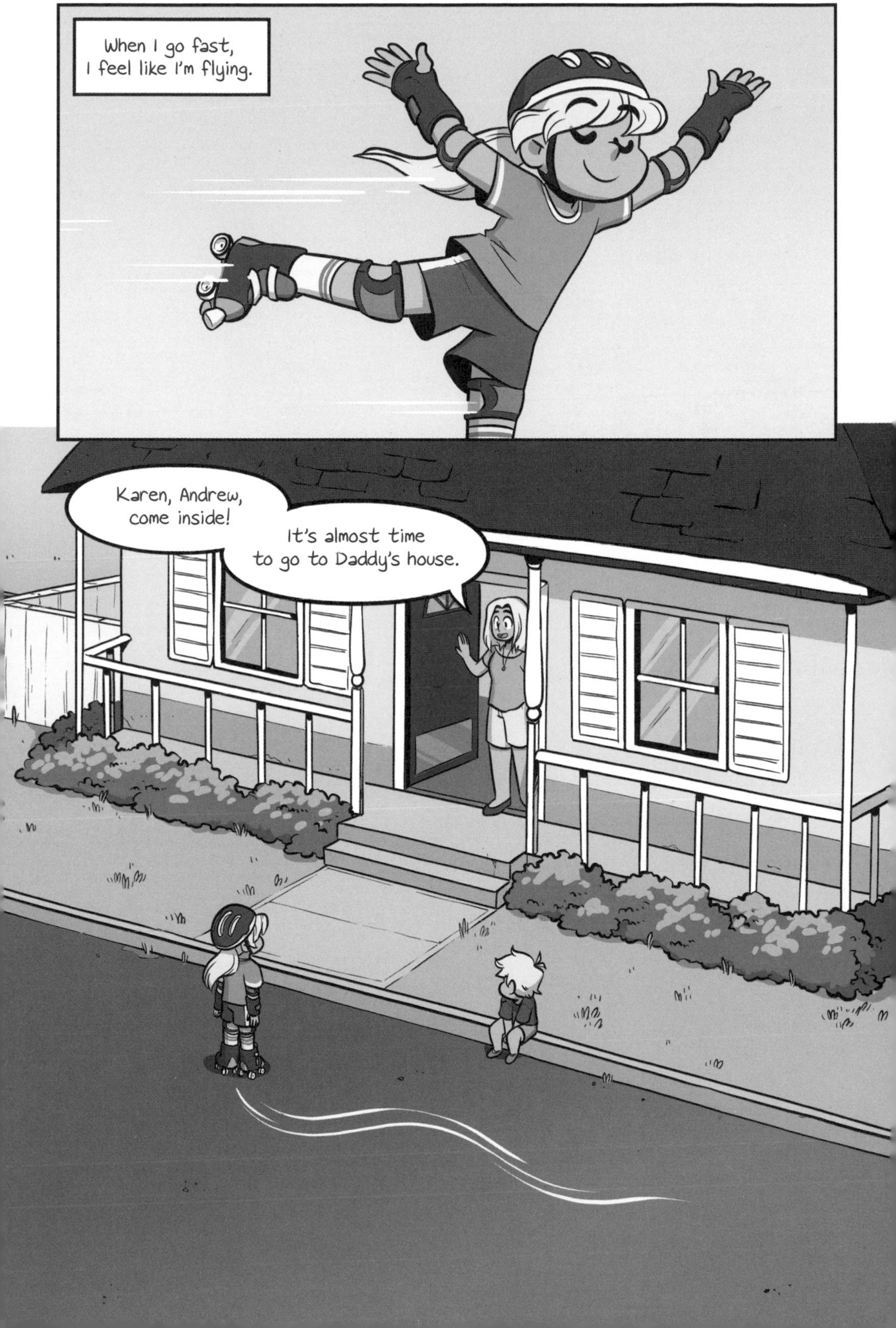
When I go fast, I feel like I'm flying.
Karen, Andrew, come inside!
It's almost time to go to Daddy's house.

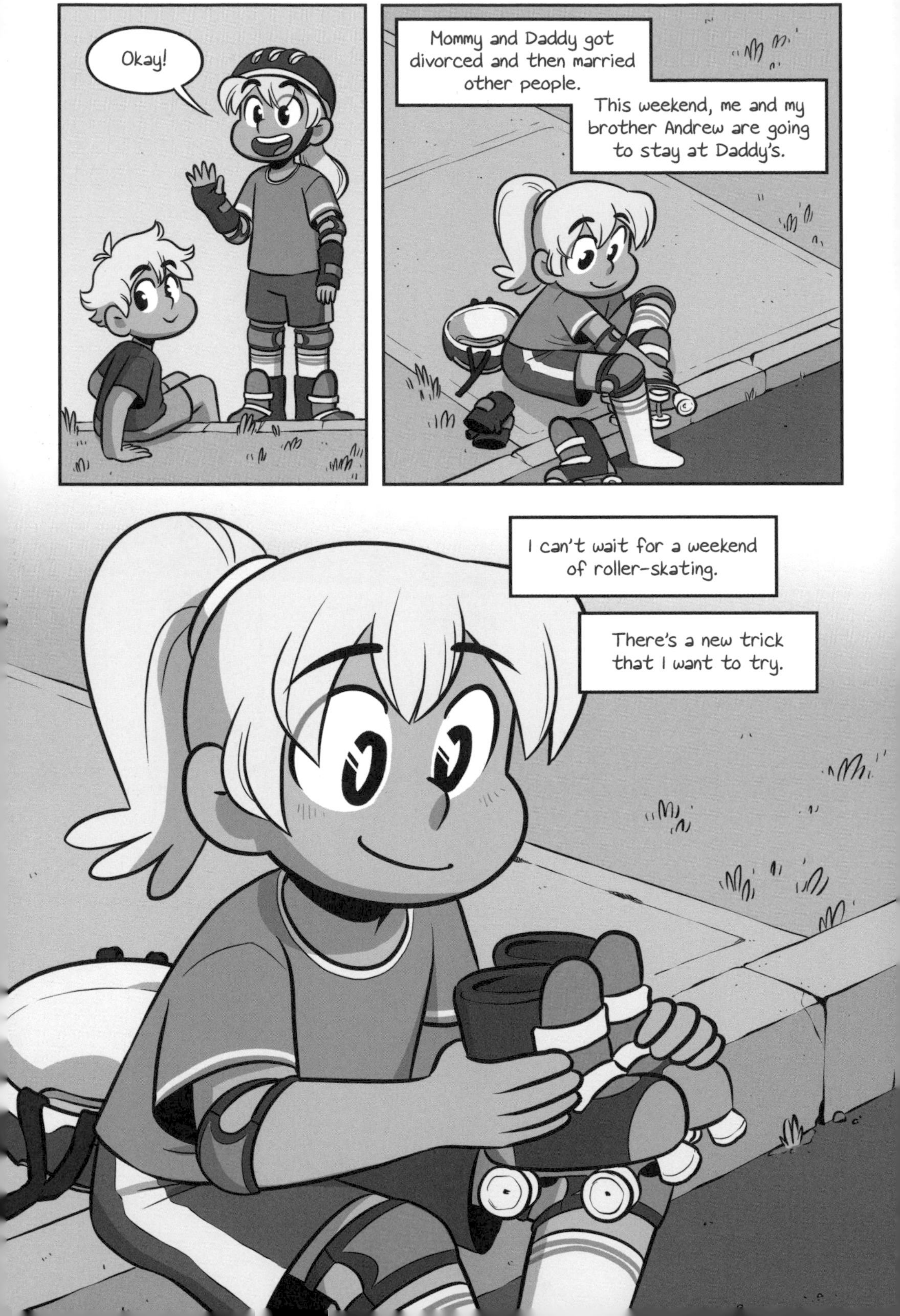
Okay!
Mommy and Daddy got divorced and then married other people.
This weekend, me and my brother Andrew are going to stay at Daddy's.
I can't wait for a weekend of roller-skating.
There's a new trick that I want to try.

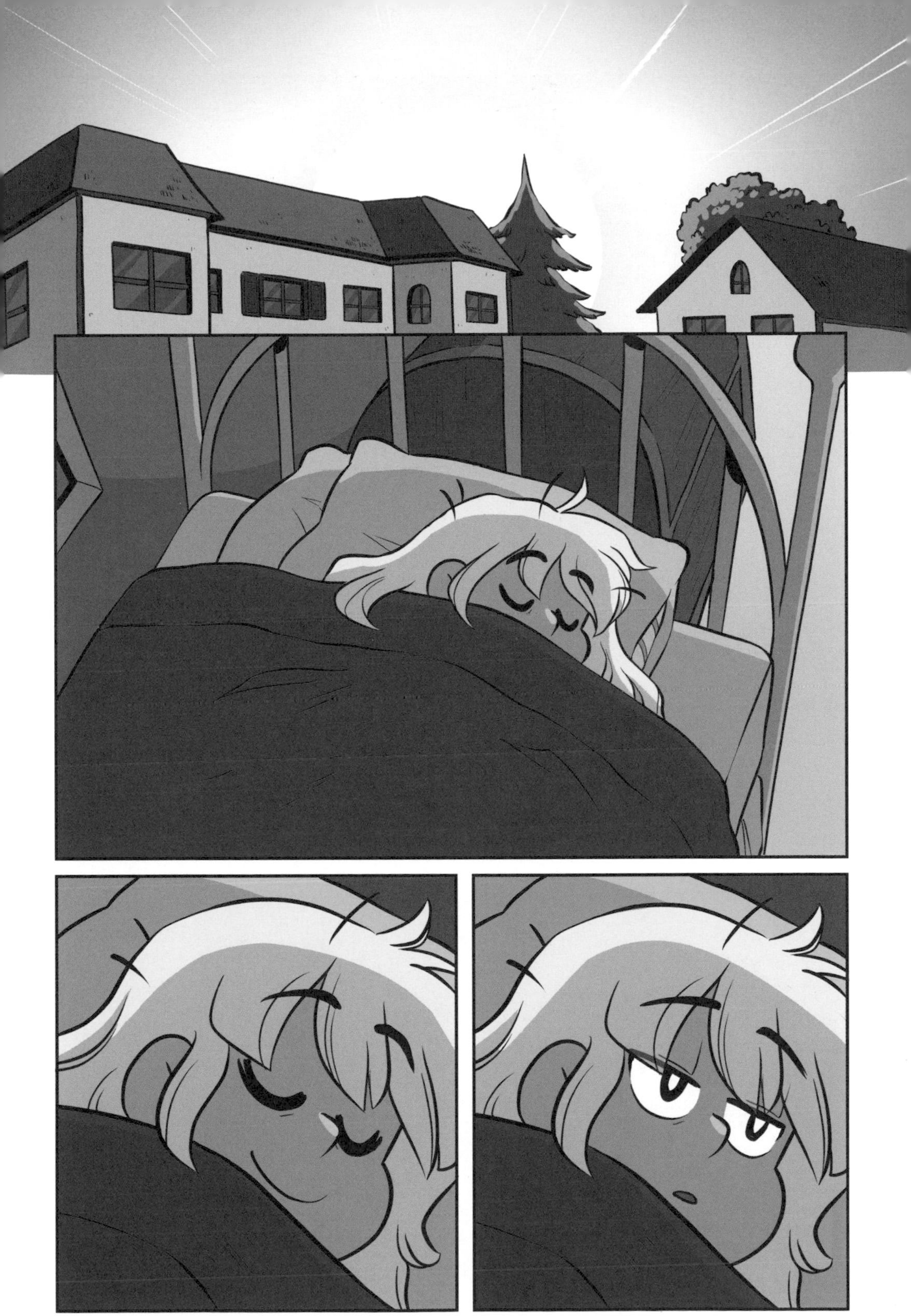

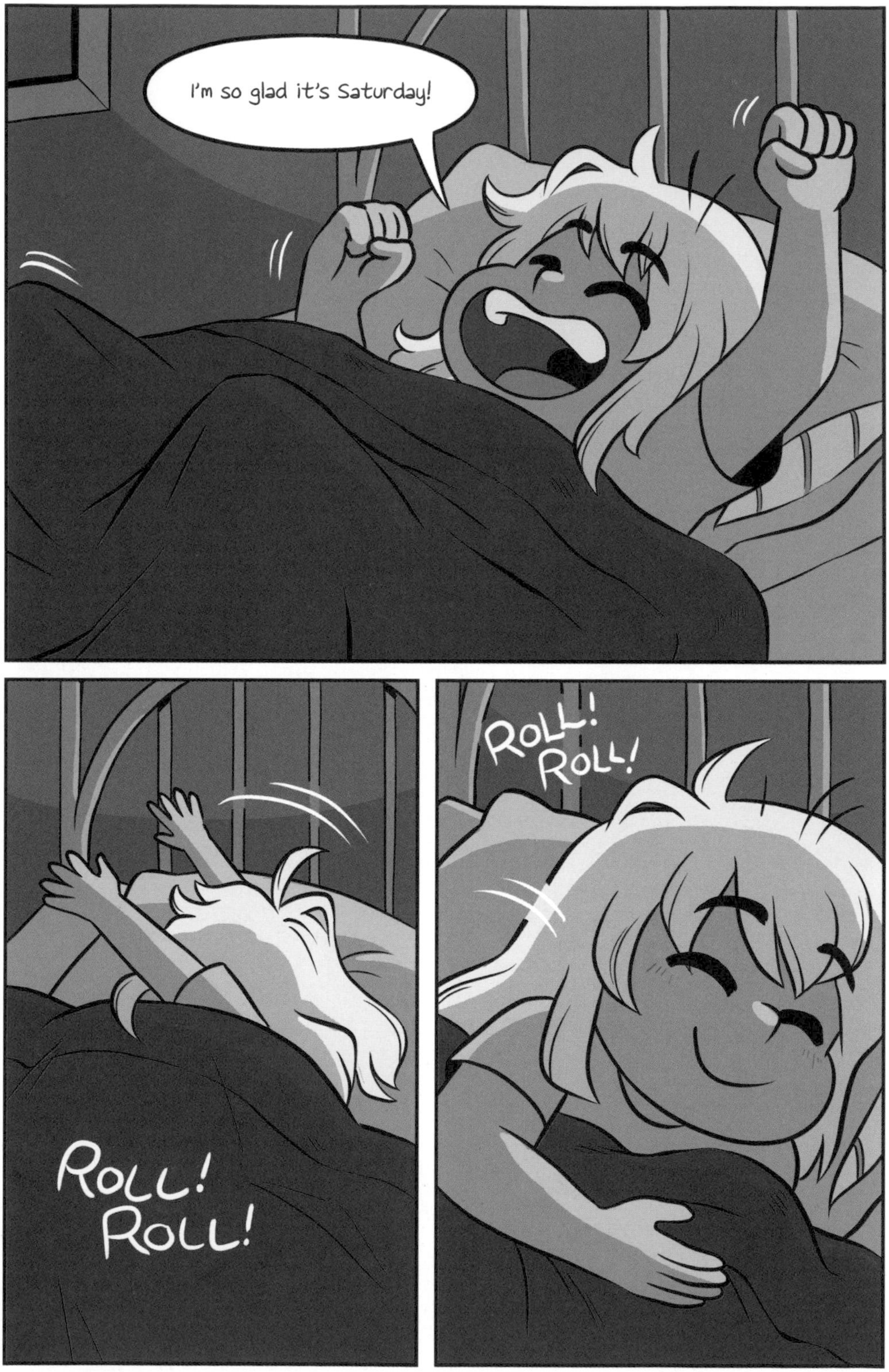
I'm so glad it's Saturday!
ROLL! ROLL!
ROLL! ROLL!

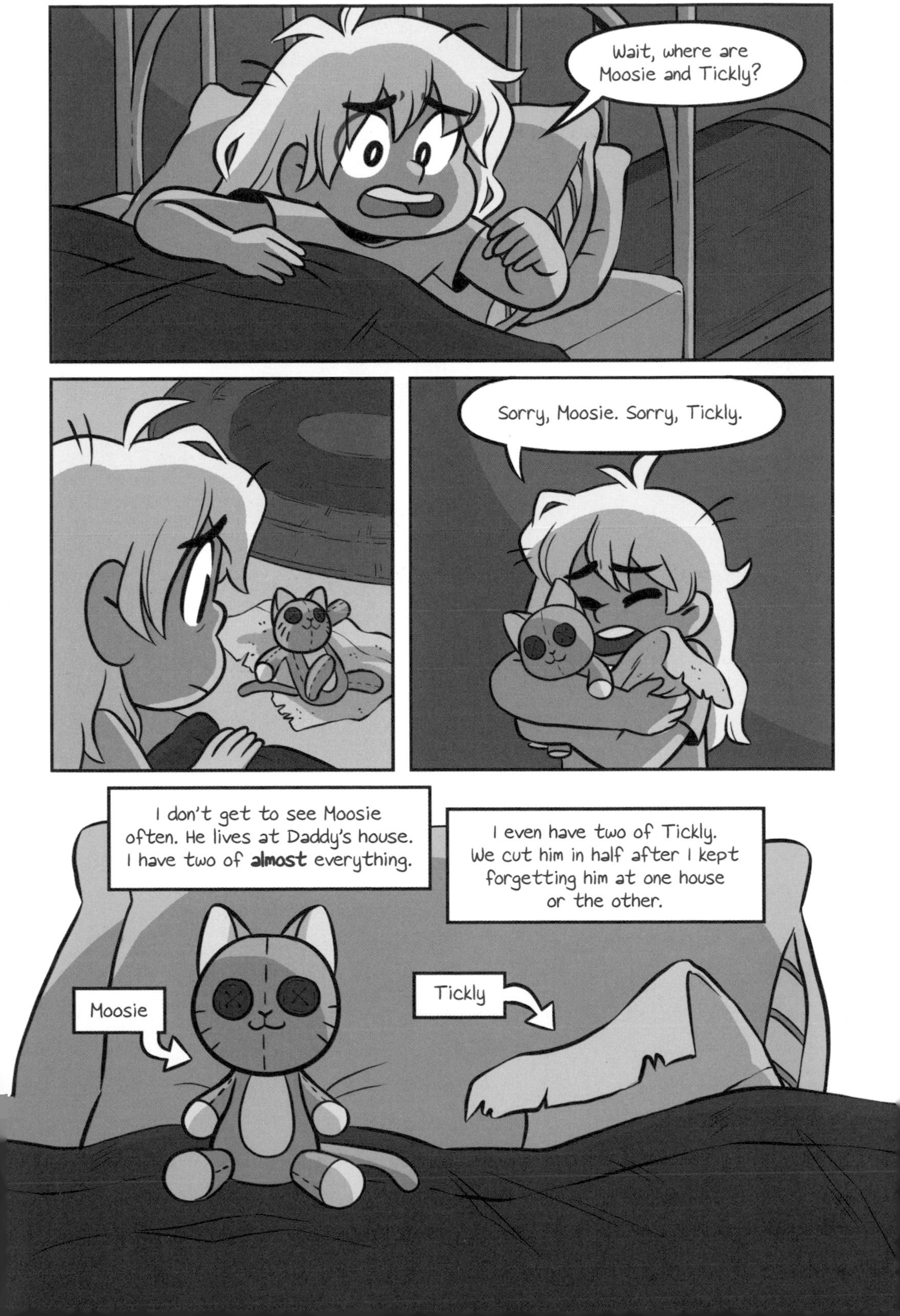

Wait, where are Moosie and Tickly?
Sorry, Moosie. Sorry, Tickly.
I don't get to see Moosie often. He lives at Daddy's house. I have two of **almost** everything.
I even have two of Tickly. We cut him in half after I kept forgetting him at one house or the other.
Moosie
Tickly

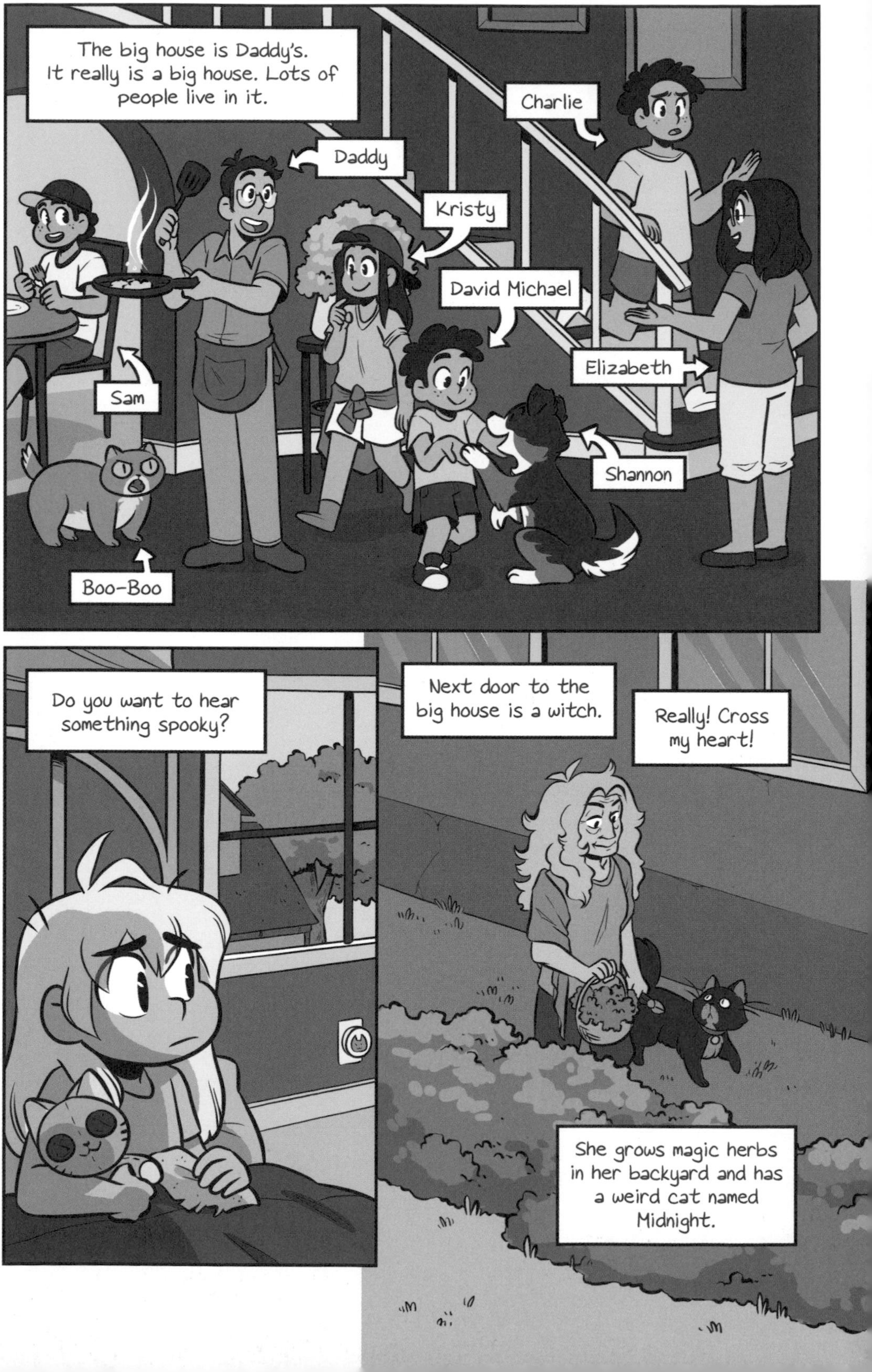
The big house is Daddy's.
It really is a big house. Lots of people live in it.
Charlie
Daddy
Kristy
David Michael
Elizabeth
Sam
Shannon
Boo-Boo
Do you want to hear something spooky?
Next door to the big house is a witch.
Really! Cross my heart!
She grows magic herbs in her backyard and has a weird cat named Midnight.

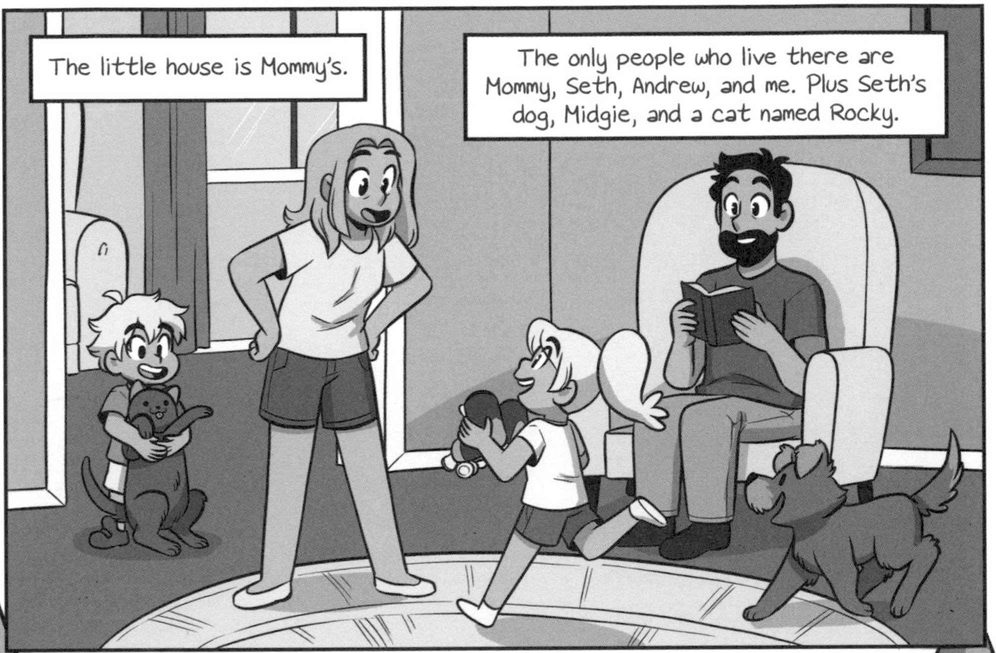
The little house is Mommy's.
The only people who live there are Mommy, Seth, Andrew, and me. Plus Seth's dog, Midgie, and a cat named Rocky.

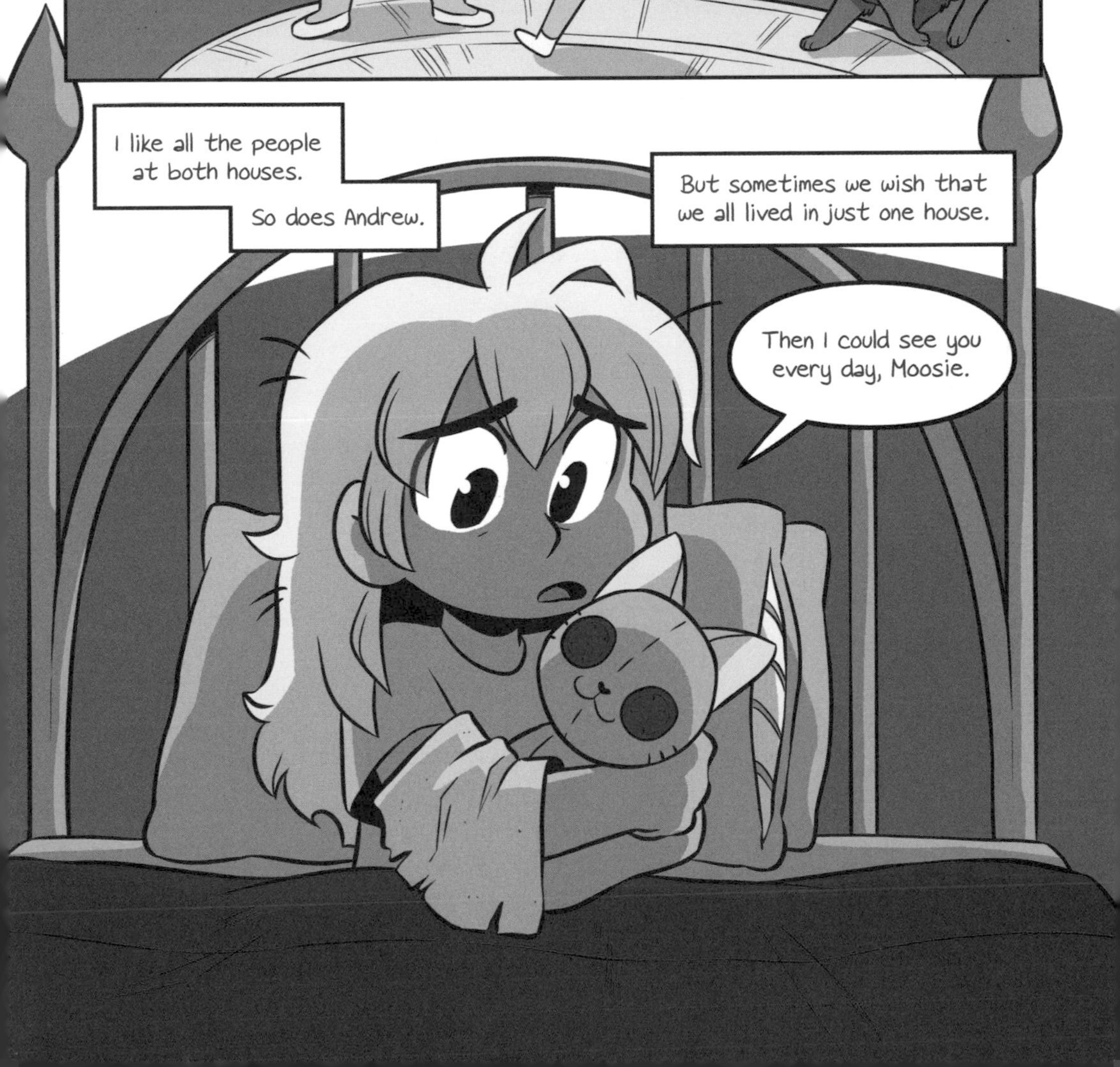
I like all the people at both houses.
So does Andrew.
But sometimes we wish that we all lived in just one house.
Then I could see you every day, Moosie.

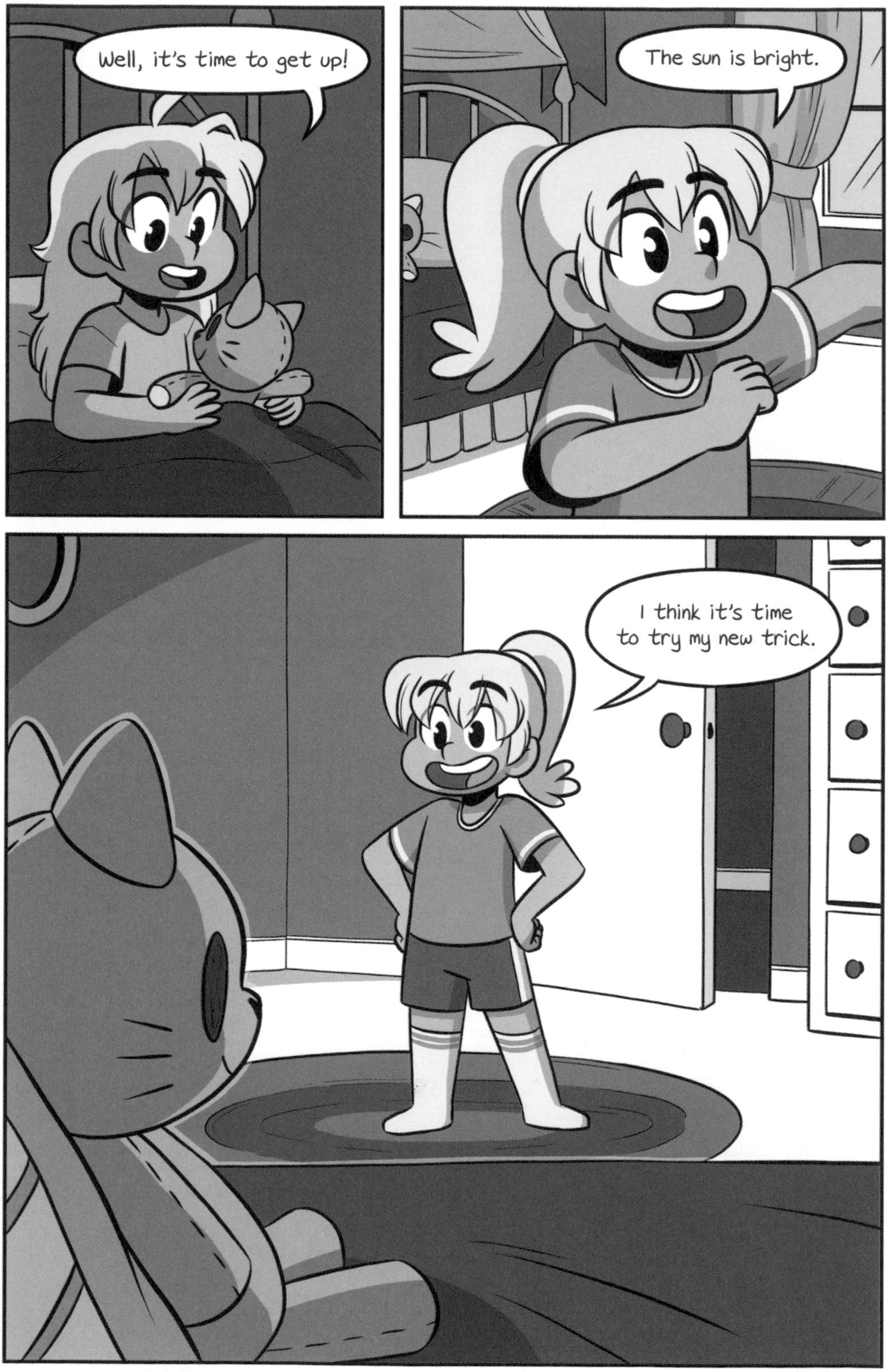
Well, it's time to get up!
The sun is bright.
I think it's time
to try my new trick.

CHAPTER 2

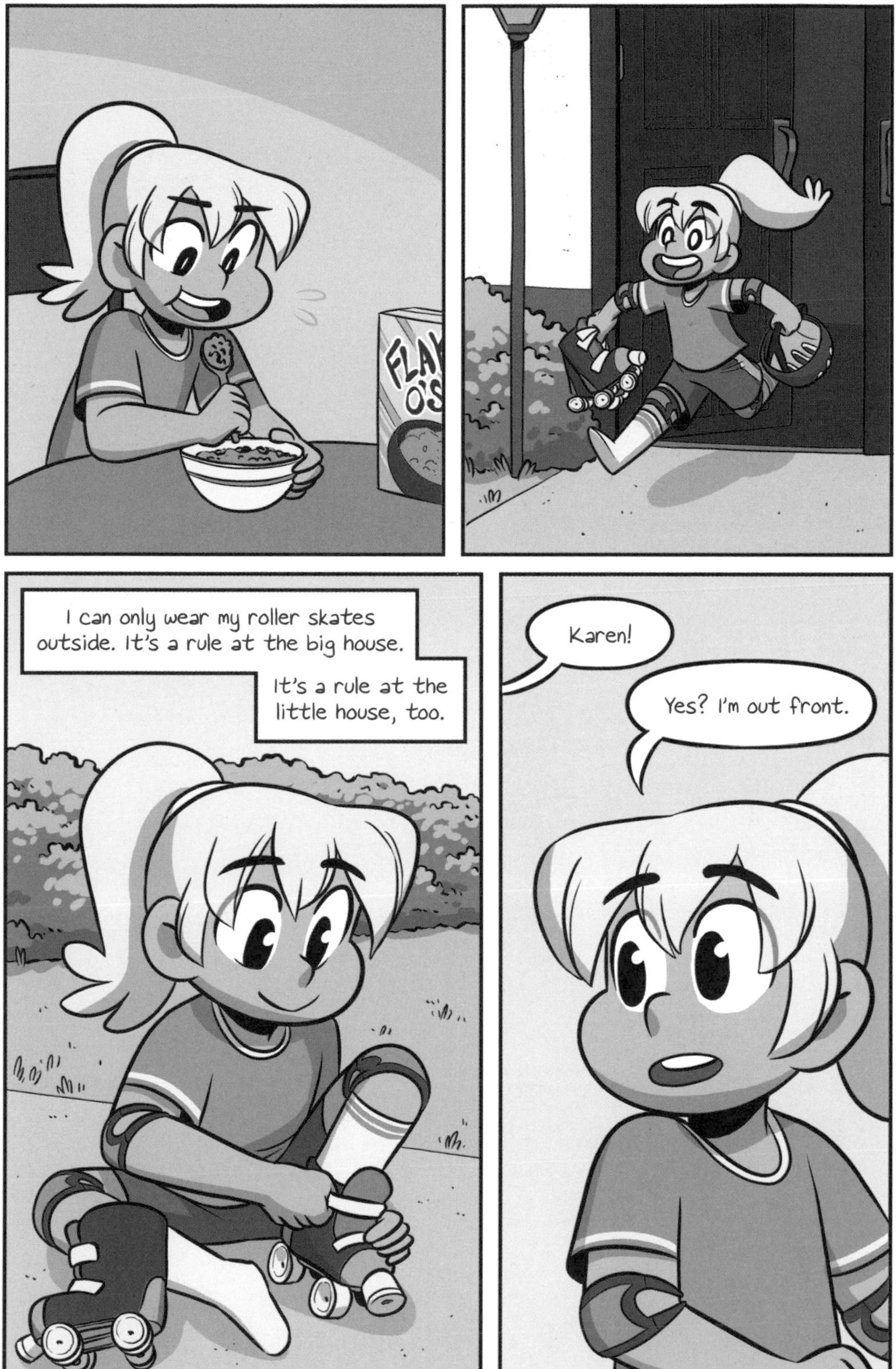
FLAKY O'S
I can only wear my roller skates outside. It's a rule at the big house.
It's a rule at the little house, too.
Karen!
Yes? I'm out front.

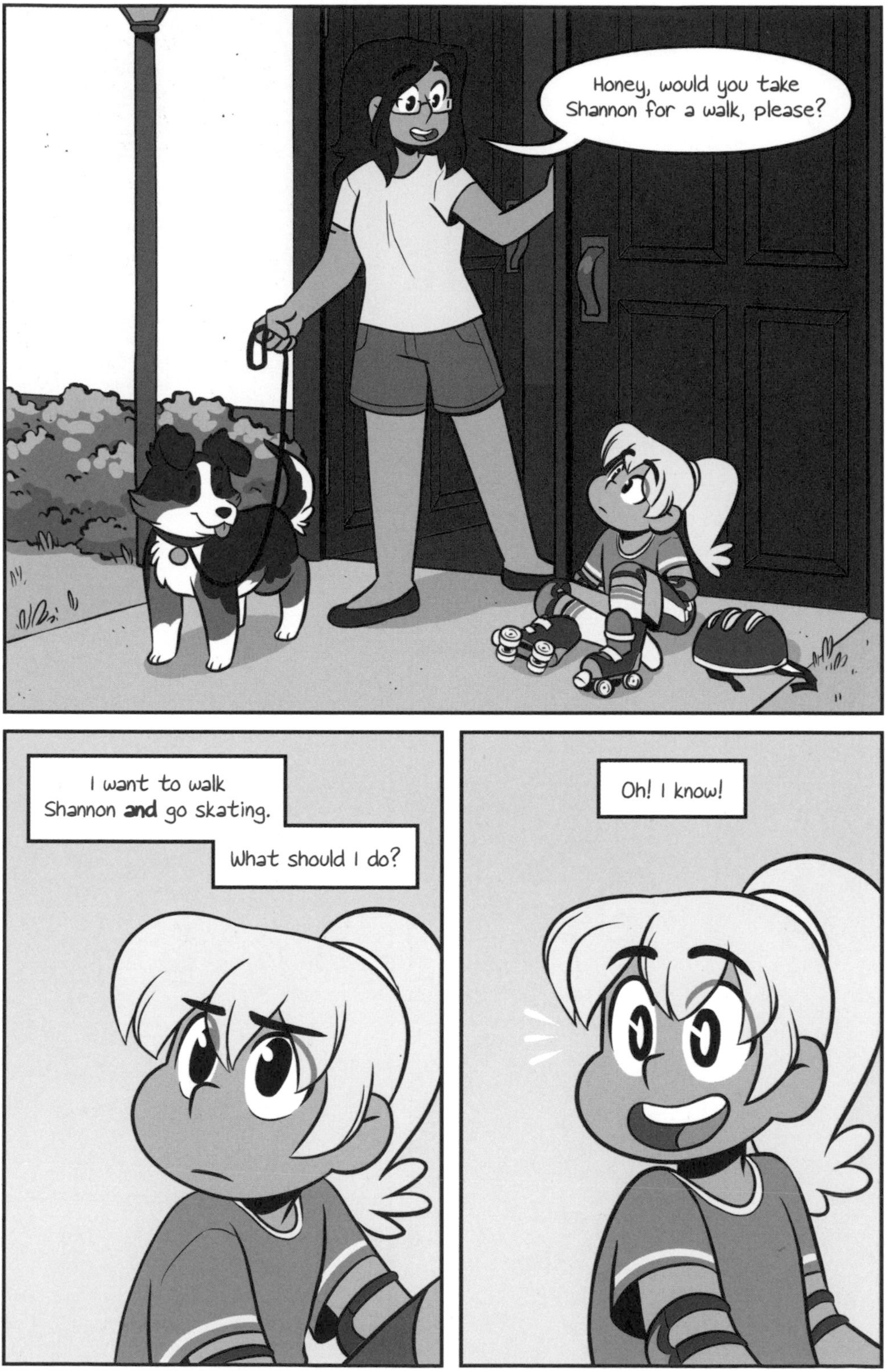
Honey, would you take Shannon for a walk, please?
I want to walk Shannon **and** go skating.
What should I do?
Oh! I know!

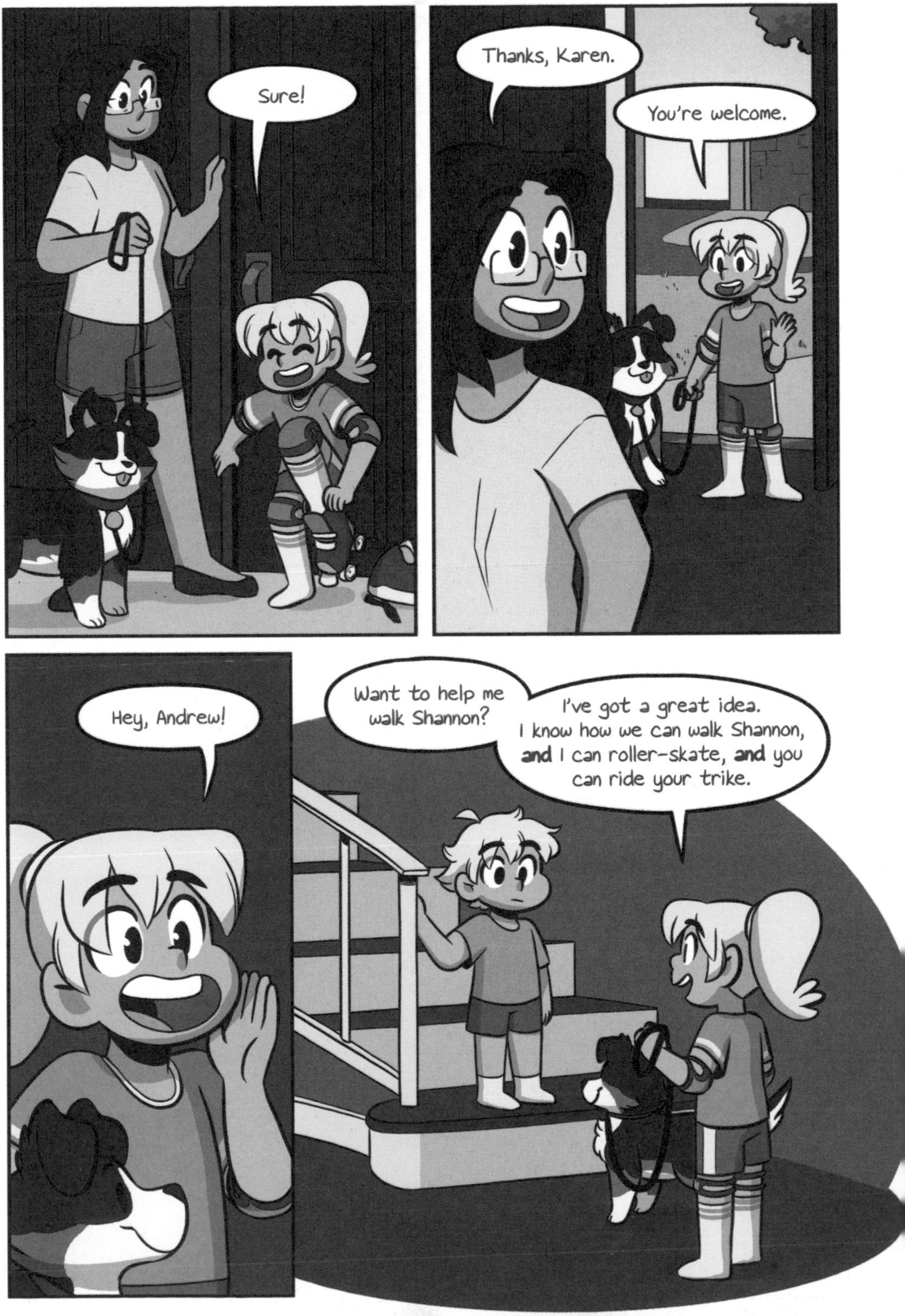
Sure!
Thanks, Karen.
You're welcome.
Hey, Andrew!
Want to help me walk Shannon?
I've got a great idea. I know how we can walk Shannon, **and** I can roller-skate, **and** you can ride your trike.

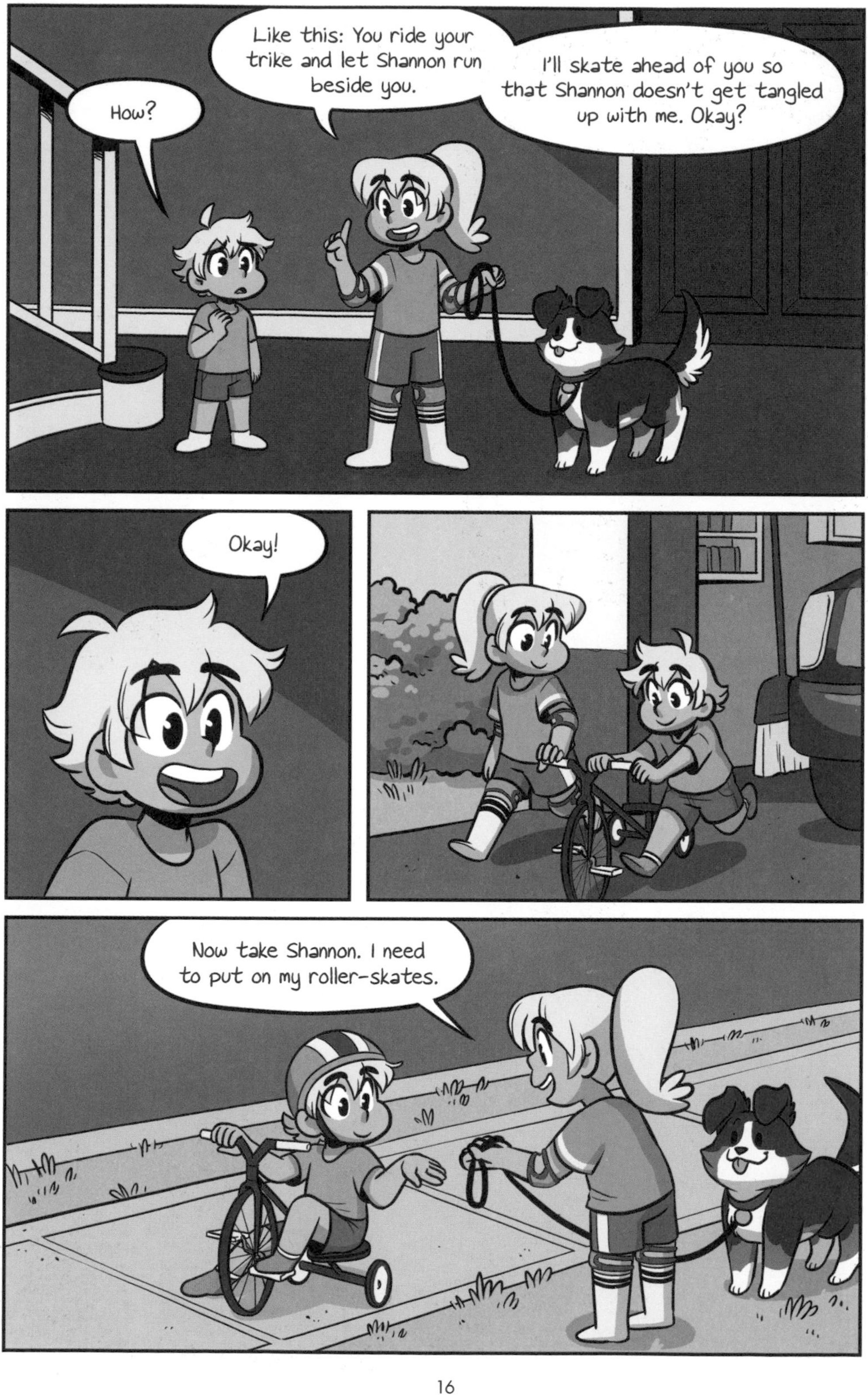
How?
Like this: You ride your trike and let Shannon run beside you.
I'll skate ahead of you so that Shannon doesn't get tangled up with me. Okay?
Okay!
Now take Shannon. I need to put on my roller-skates.

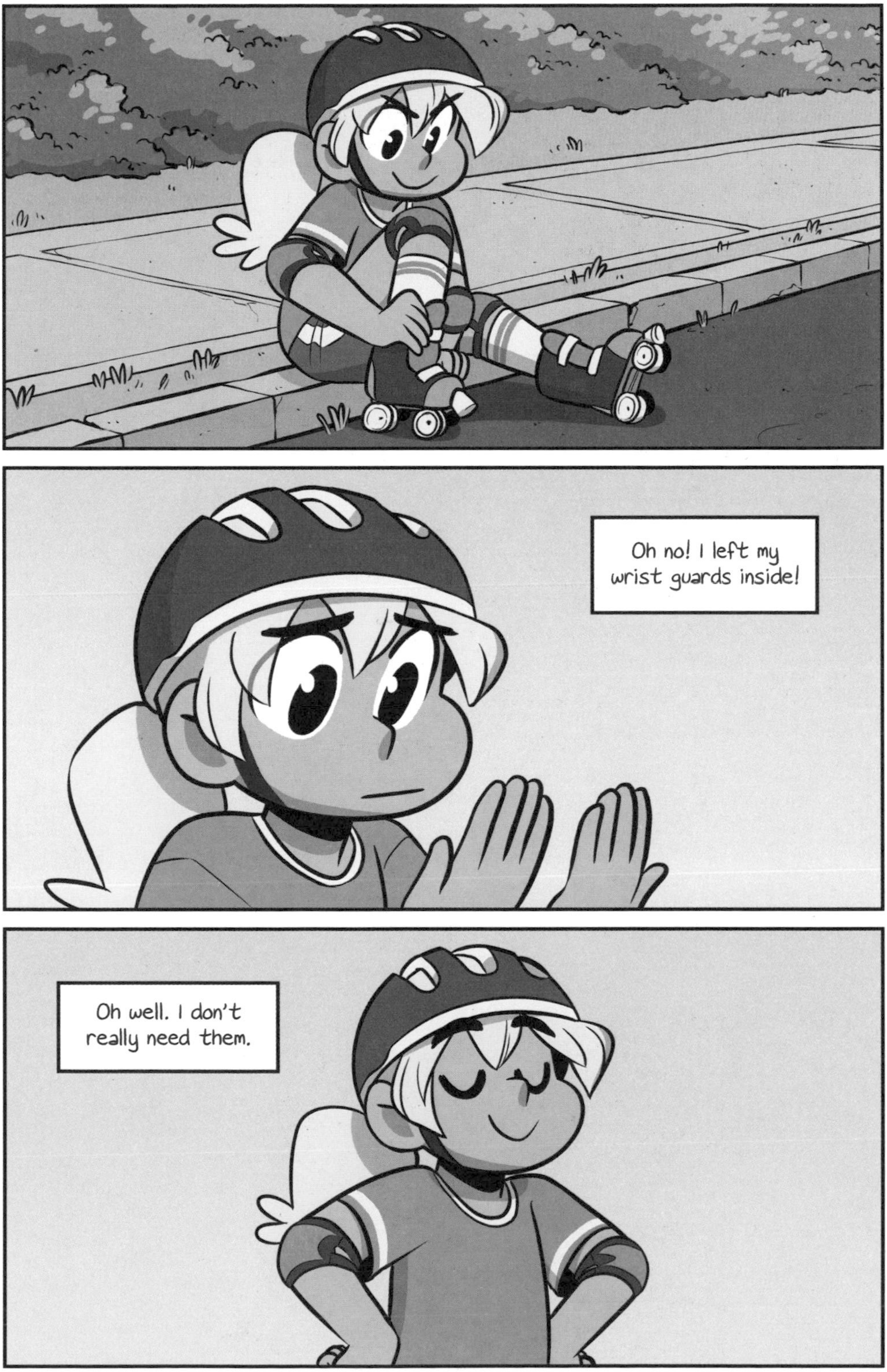
Oh no! I left my wrist guards inside!
Oh well. I don't really need them.

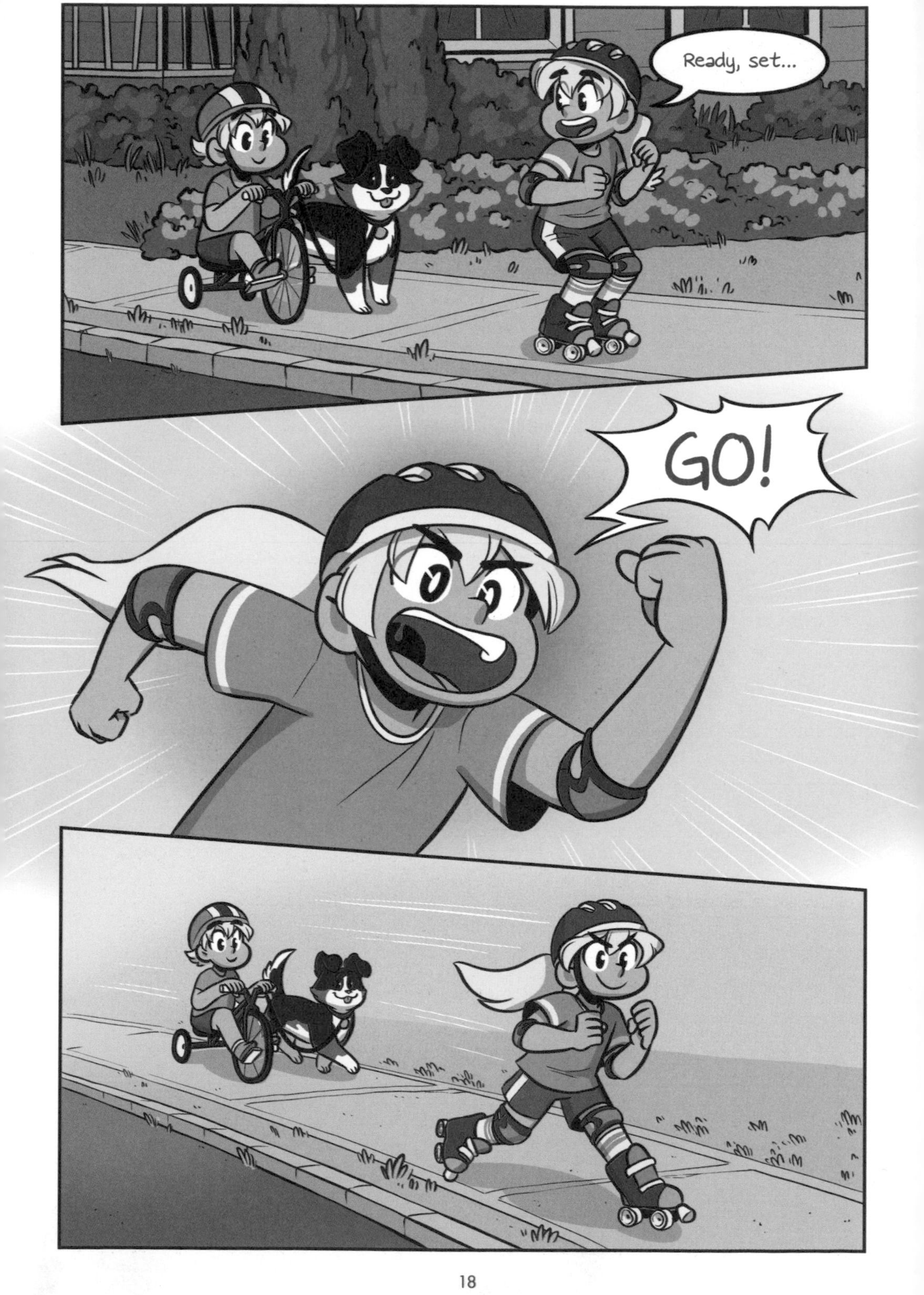

Ready, set...
GO!

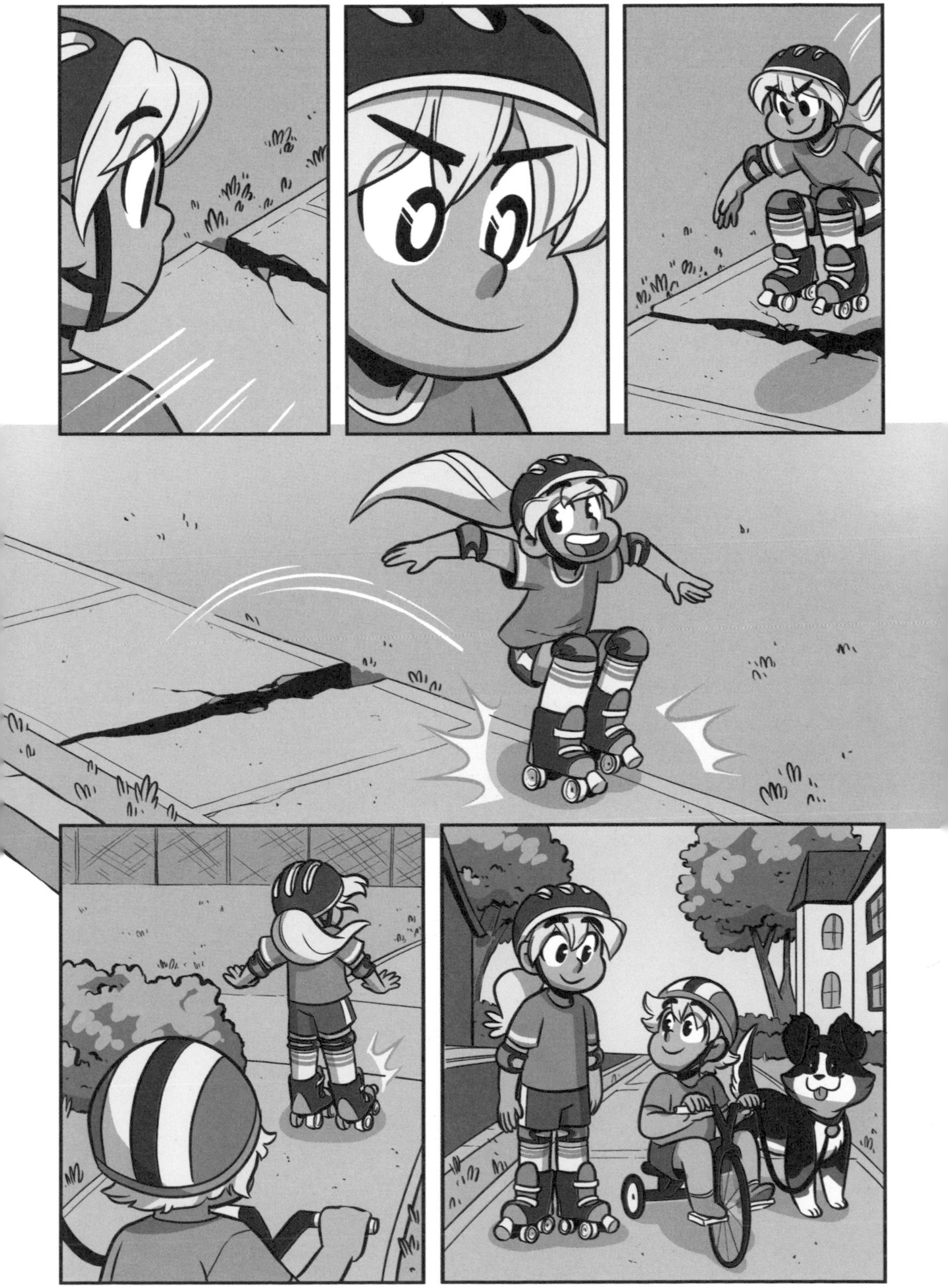

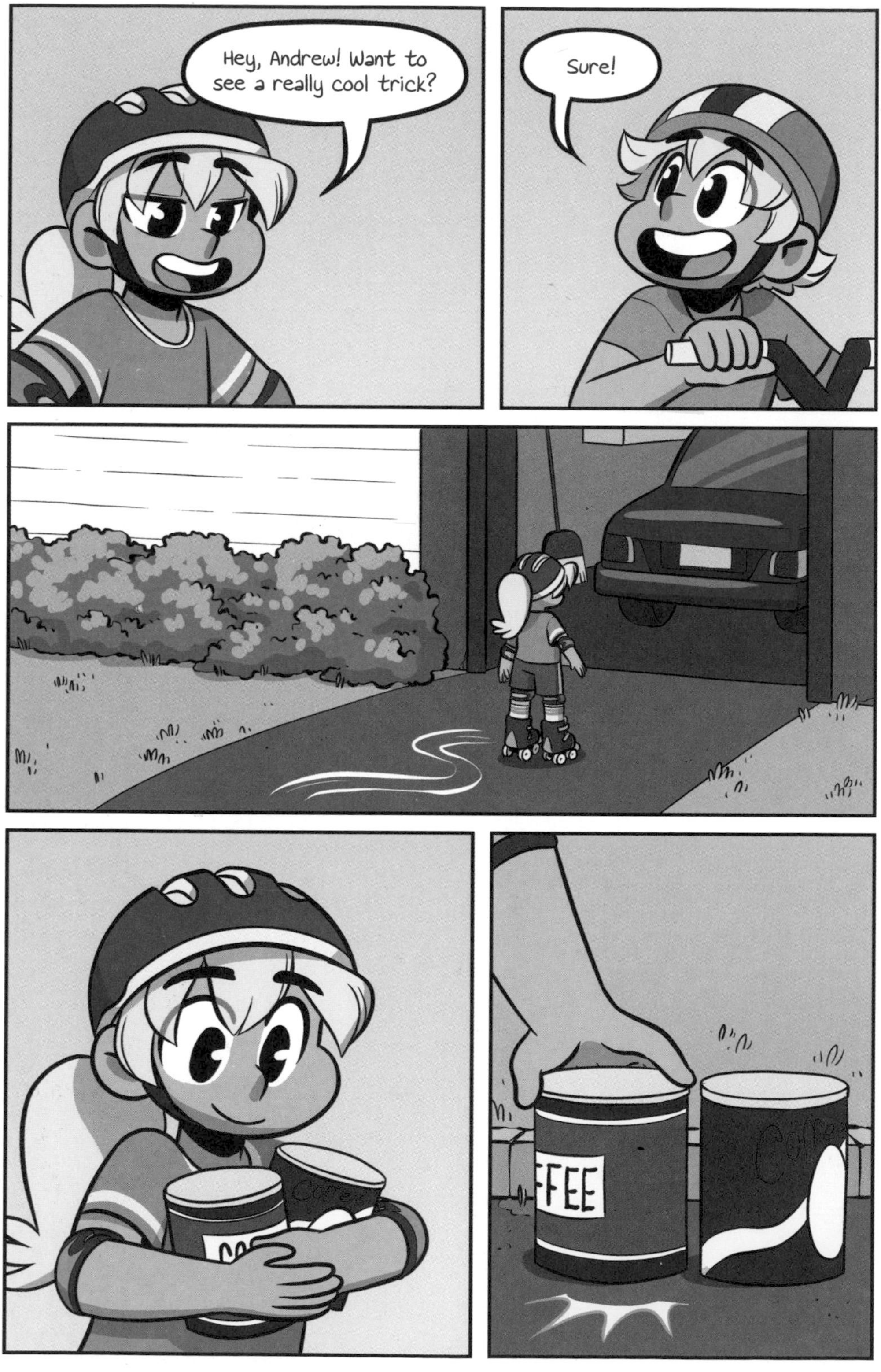
Hey, Andrew! Want to see a really cool trick?
Sure!
FFEE

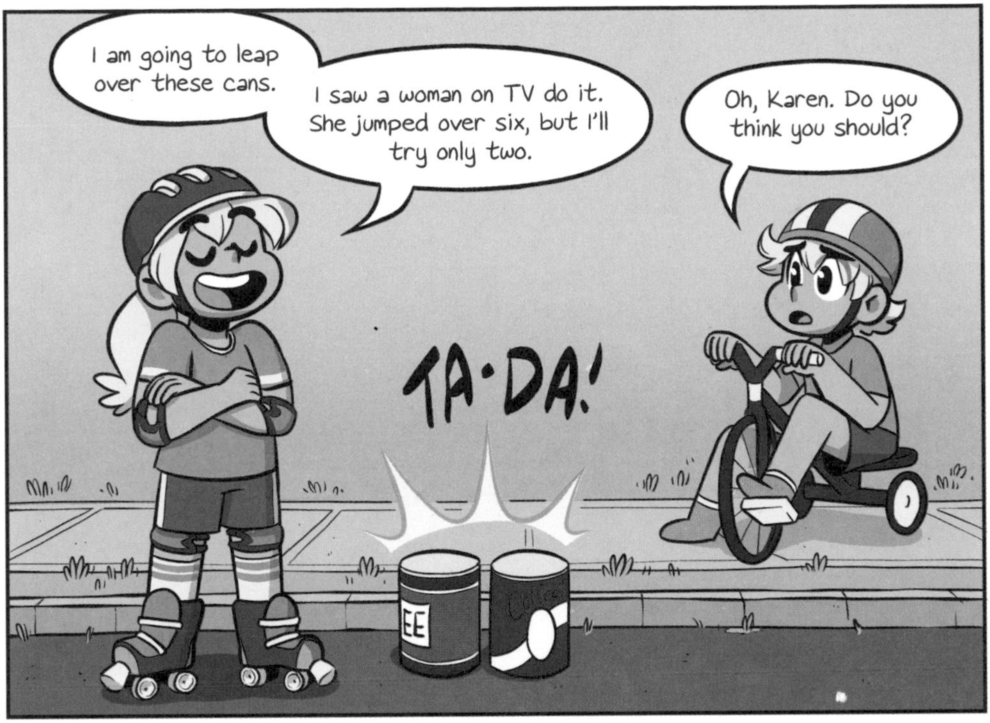
I am going to leap over these cans.
I saw a woman on TV do it. She jumped over six, but I'll try only two.
Oh, Karen. Do you think you should?
TA-DA!

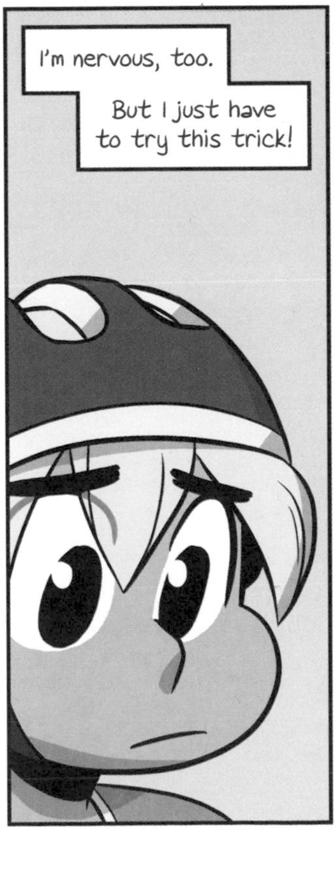
I'm nervous, too.
But I just have to try this trick!

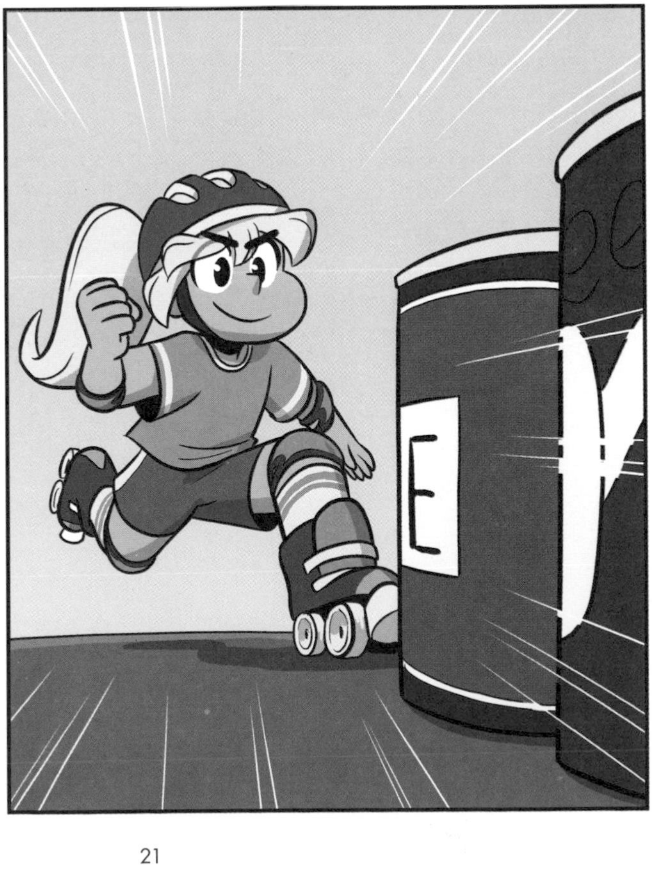

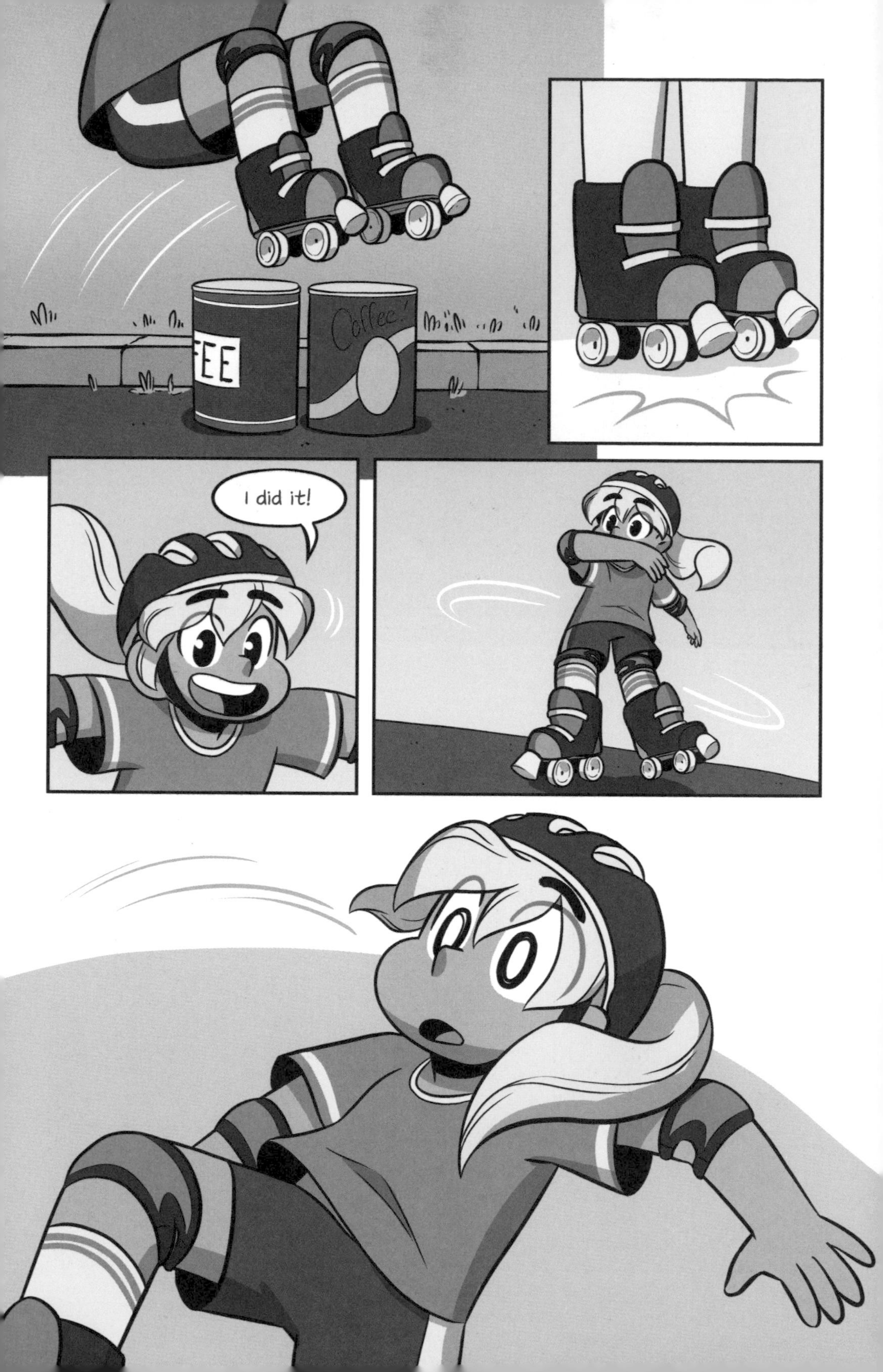
FEE
Coffee!
I did it!

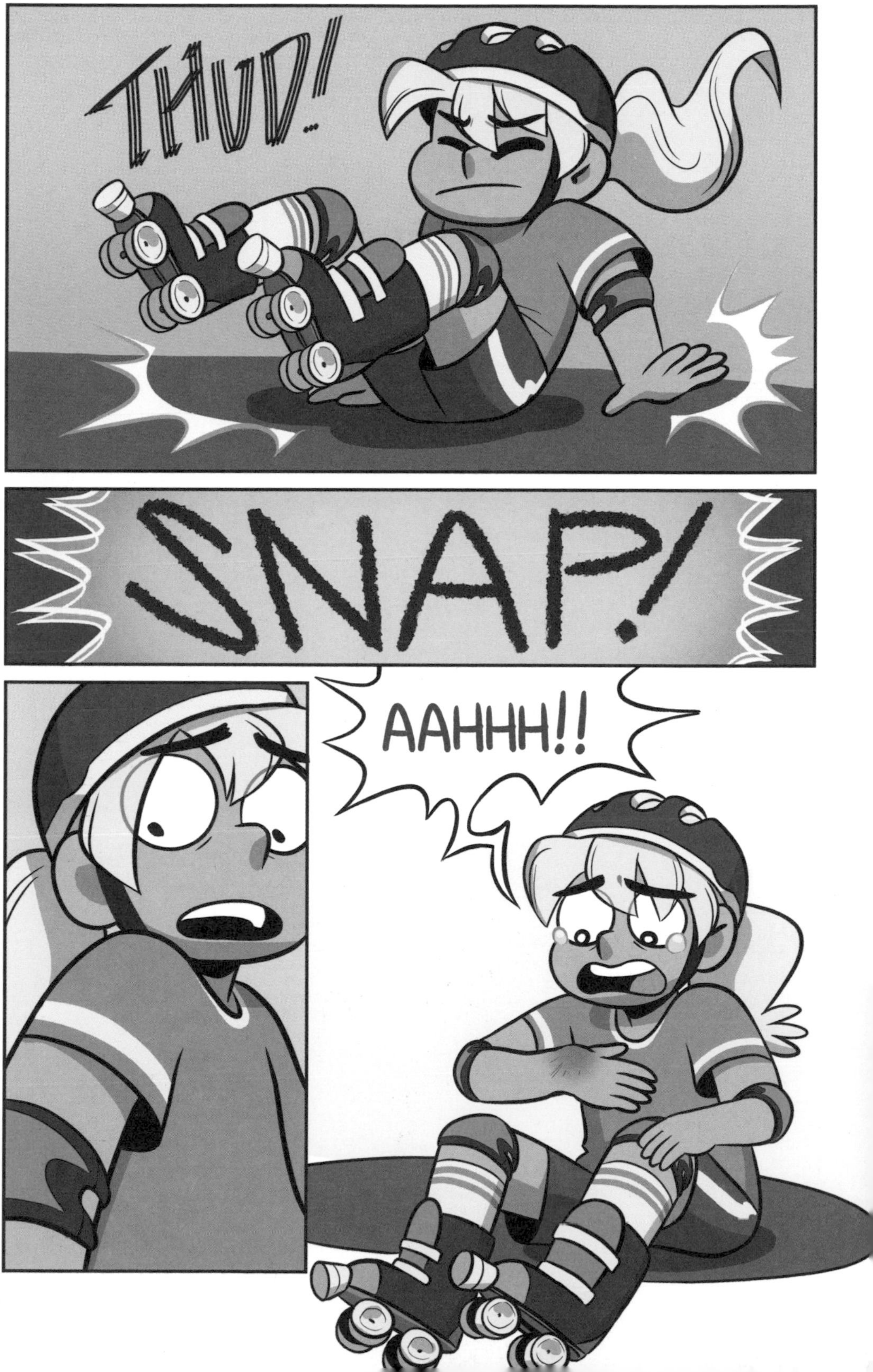
THUD!...
SNAP!
AAHHH!!

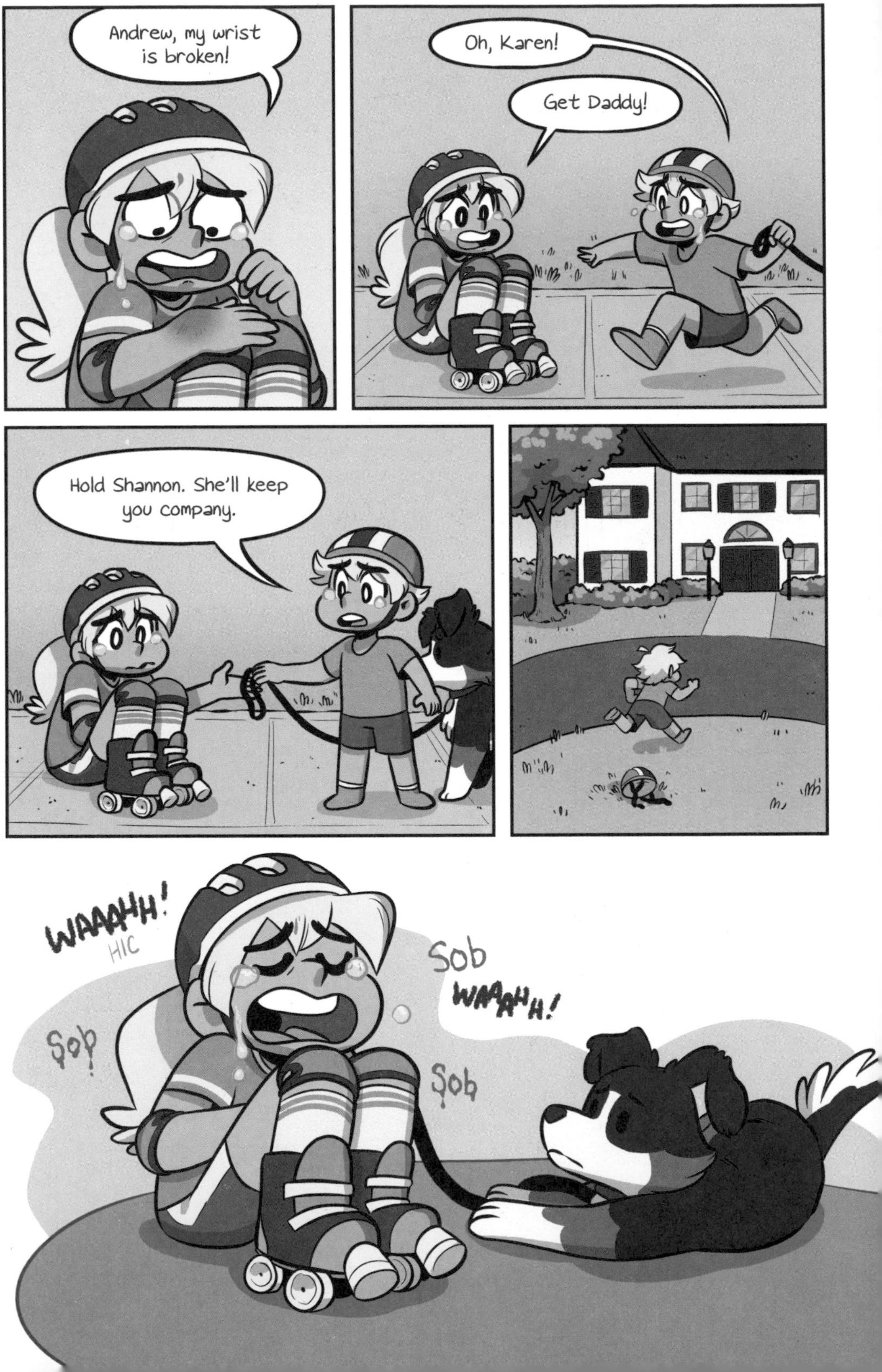
Andrew, my wrist is broken!
Oh, Karen!
Get Daddy!
Hold Shannon. She'll keep you company.
WAAAHH!
HIC
Sob
WAAAHH!
Sob
Sob

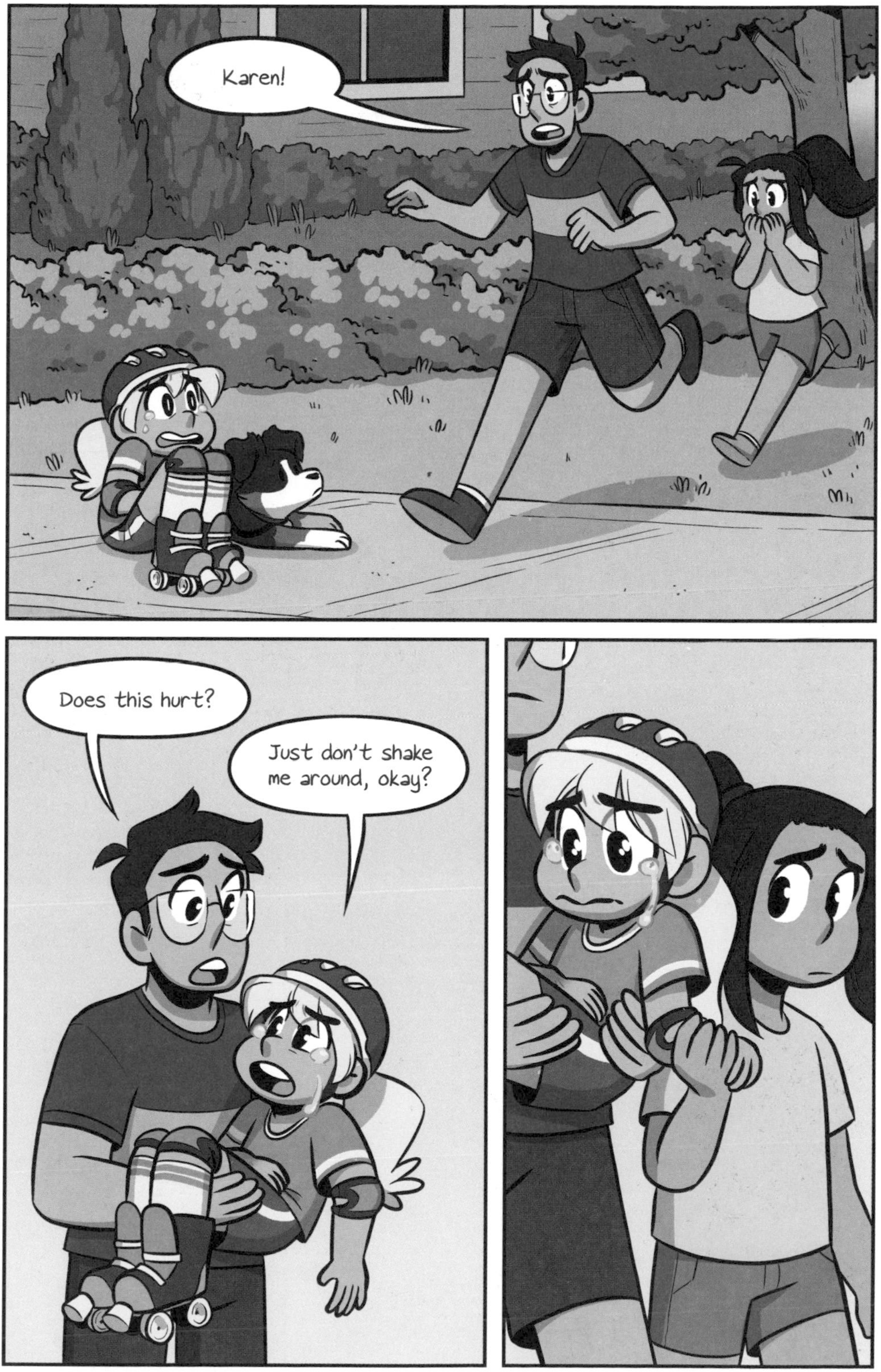
Karen!
Does this hurt?
Just don't shake me around, okay?

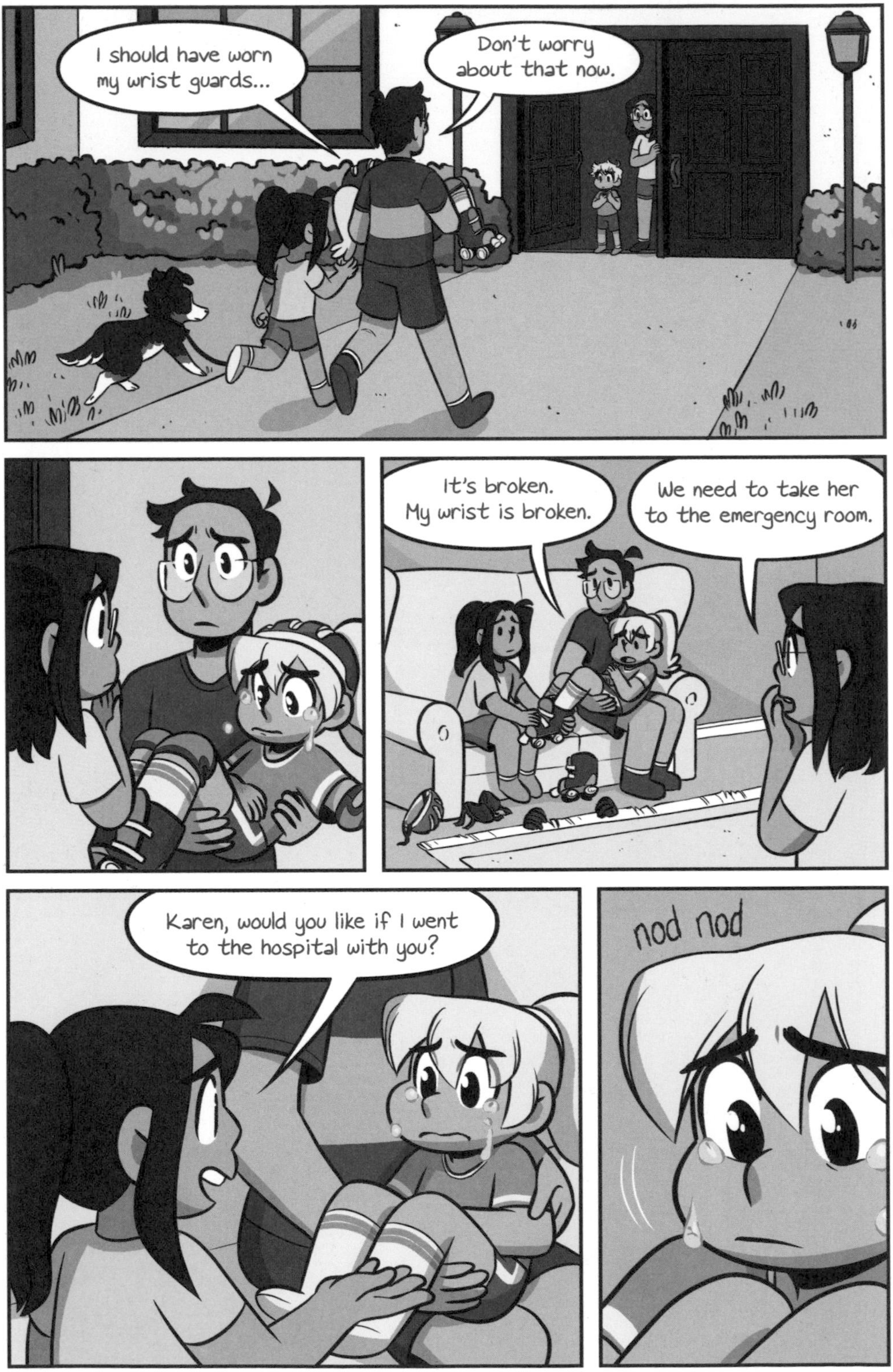
I should have worn my wrist guards...
Don't worry about that now.
It's broken. My wrist is broken.
We need to take her to the emergency room.
Karen, would you like if I went to the hospital with you?
nod nod

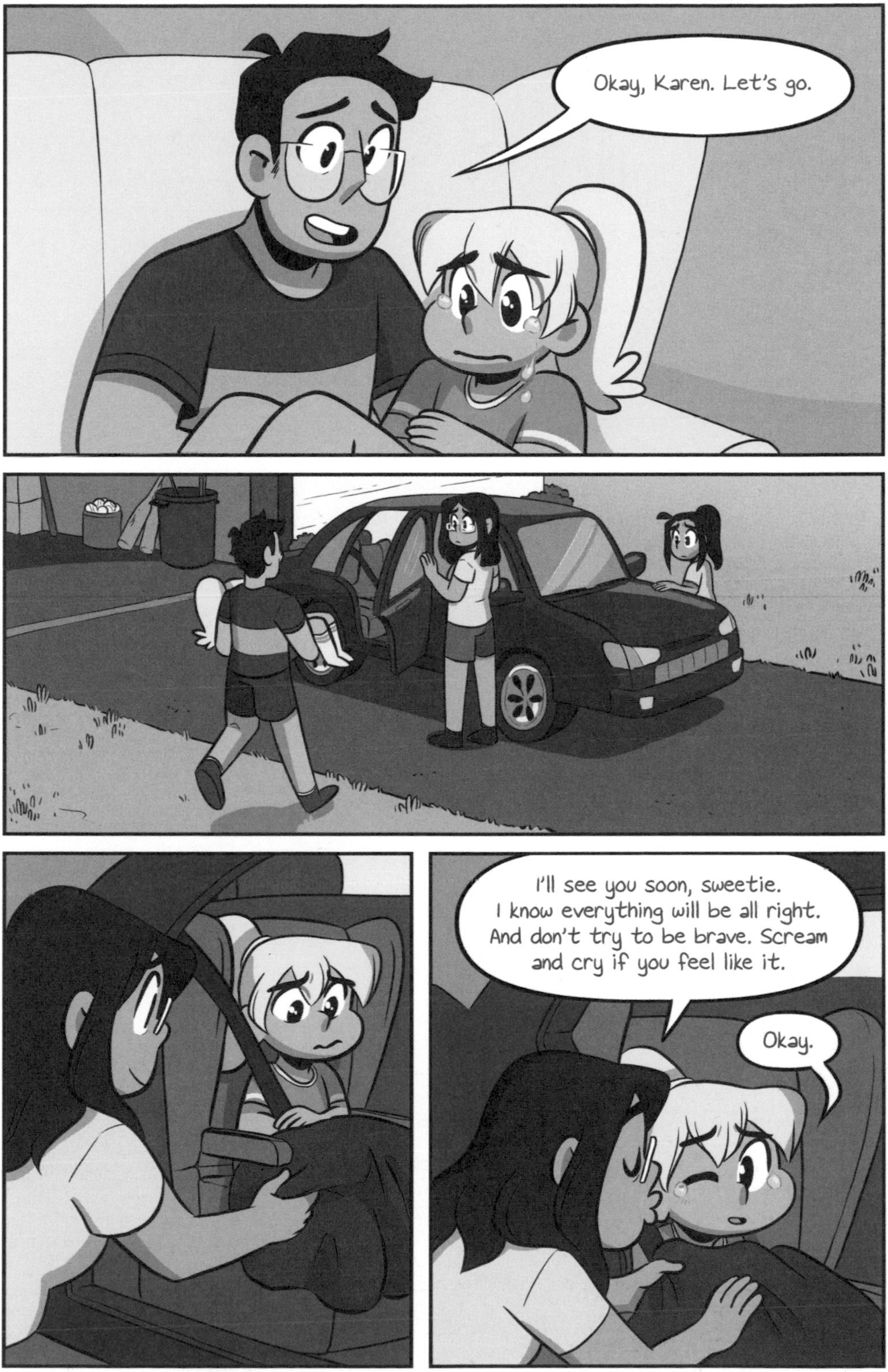
Okay, Karen. Let's go.
I'll see you soon, sweetie. I know everything will be all right. And don't try to be brave. Scream and cry if you feel like it.
Okay.

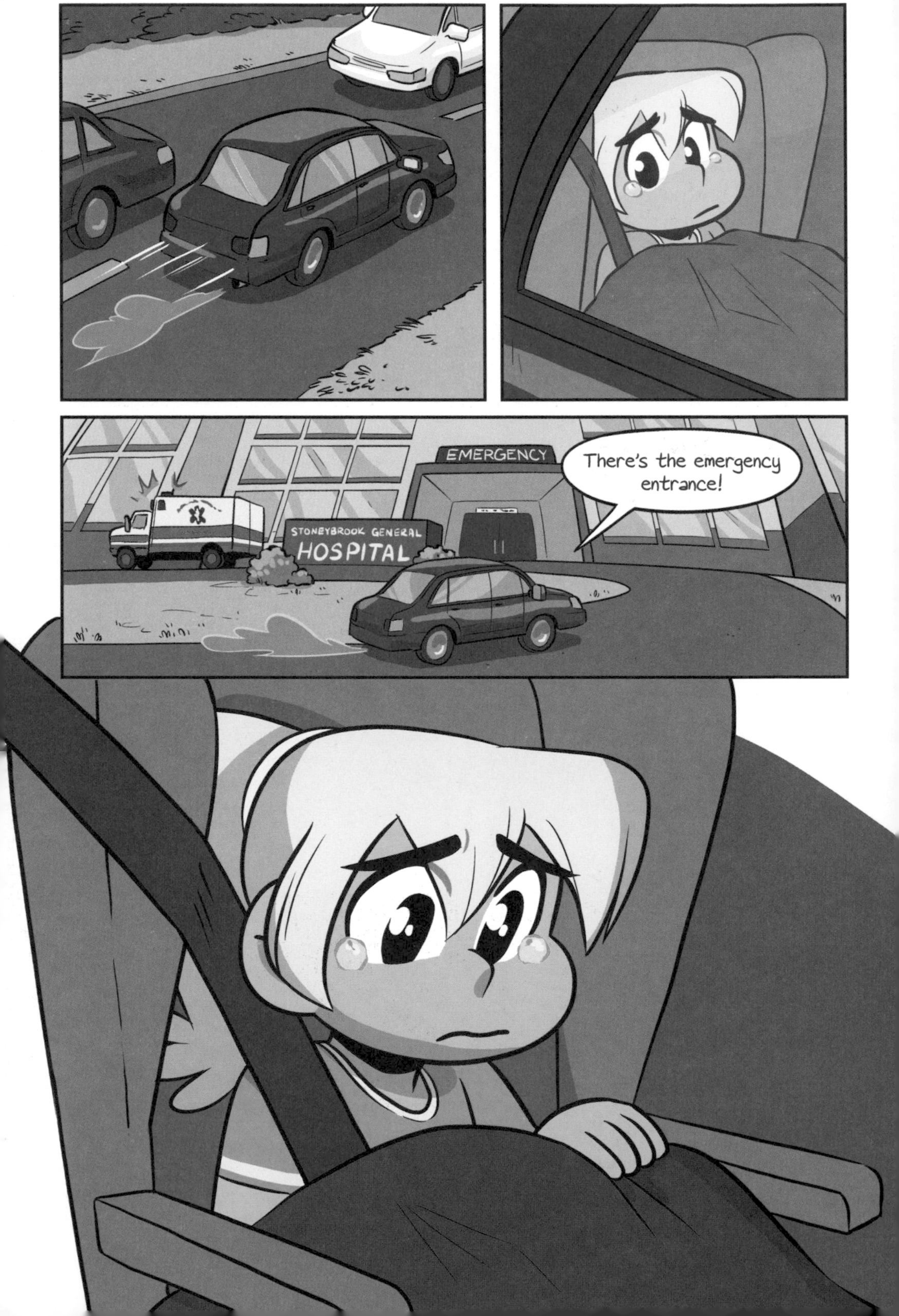
EMERGENCY
STONEYBROOK GENERAL
HOSPITAL
There's the emergency entrance!

CHAPTER 3

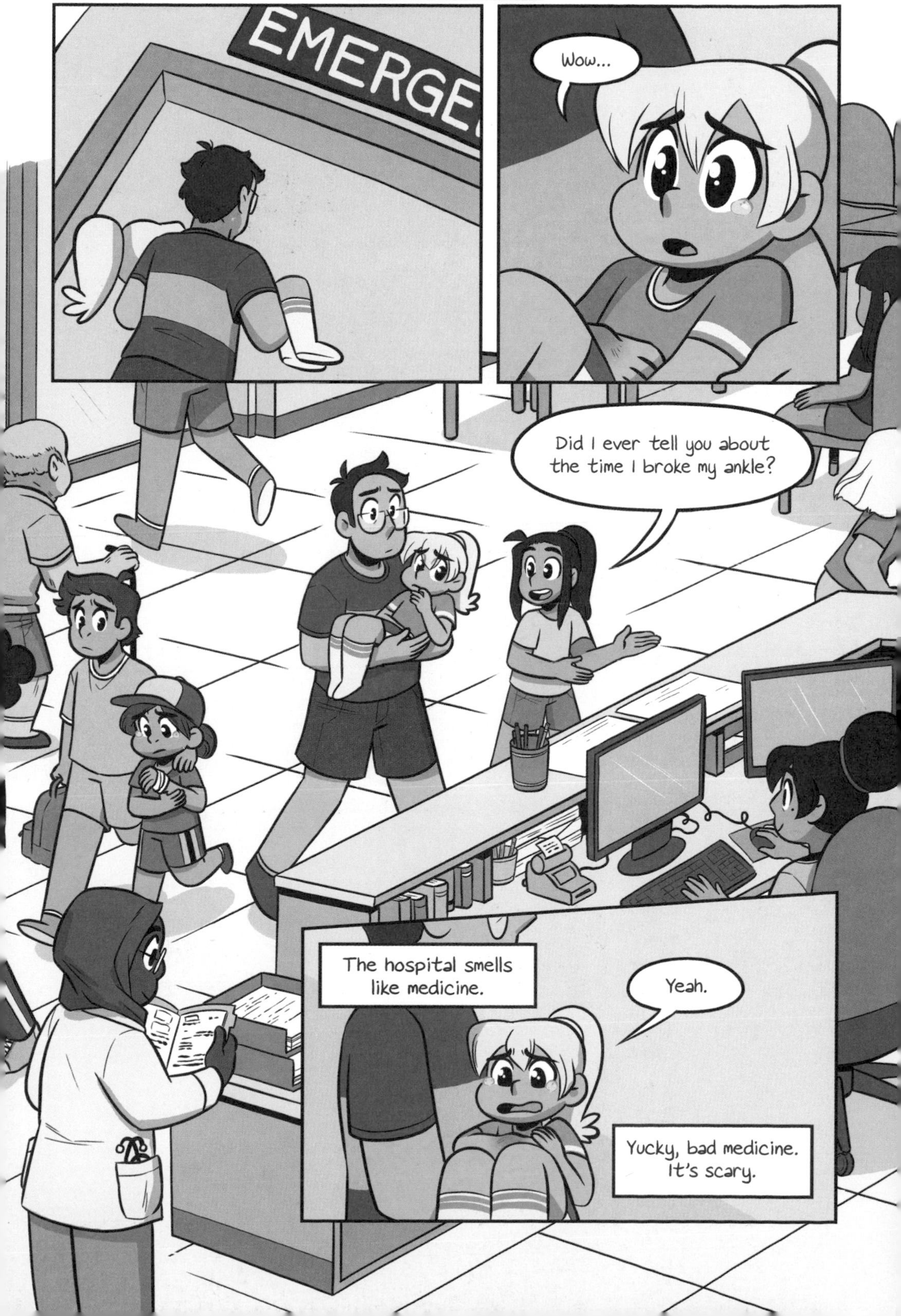
EMERGE
Wow...
Did I ever tell you about the time I broke my ankle?
The hospital smells like medicine.
Yeah.
Yucky, bad medicine. It's scary.

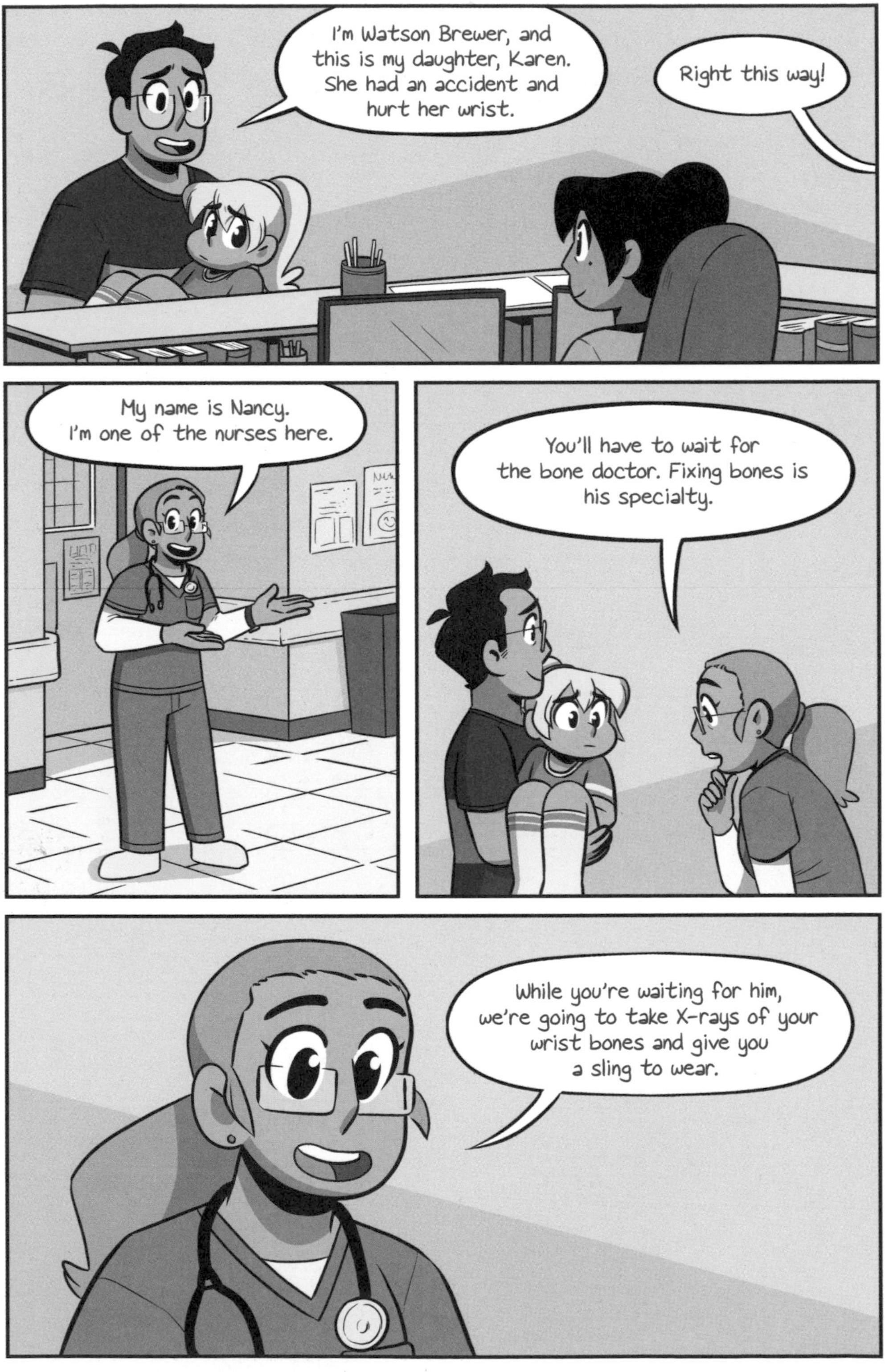
I'm Watson Brewer, and this is my daughter, Karen. She had an accident and hurt her wrist.
Right this way!
My name is Nancy. I'm one of the nurses here.
You'll have to wait for the bone doctor. Fixing bones is his specialty.
While you're waiting for him, we're going to take X-rays of your wrist bones and give you a sling to wear.

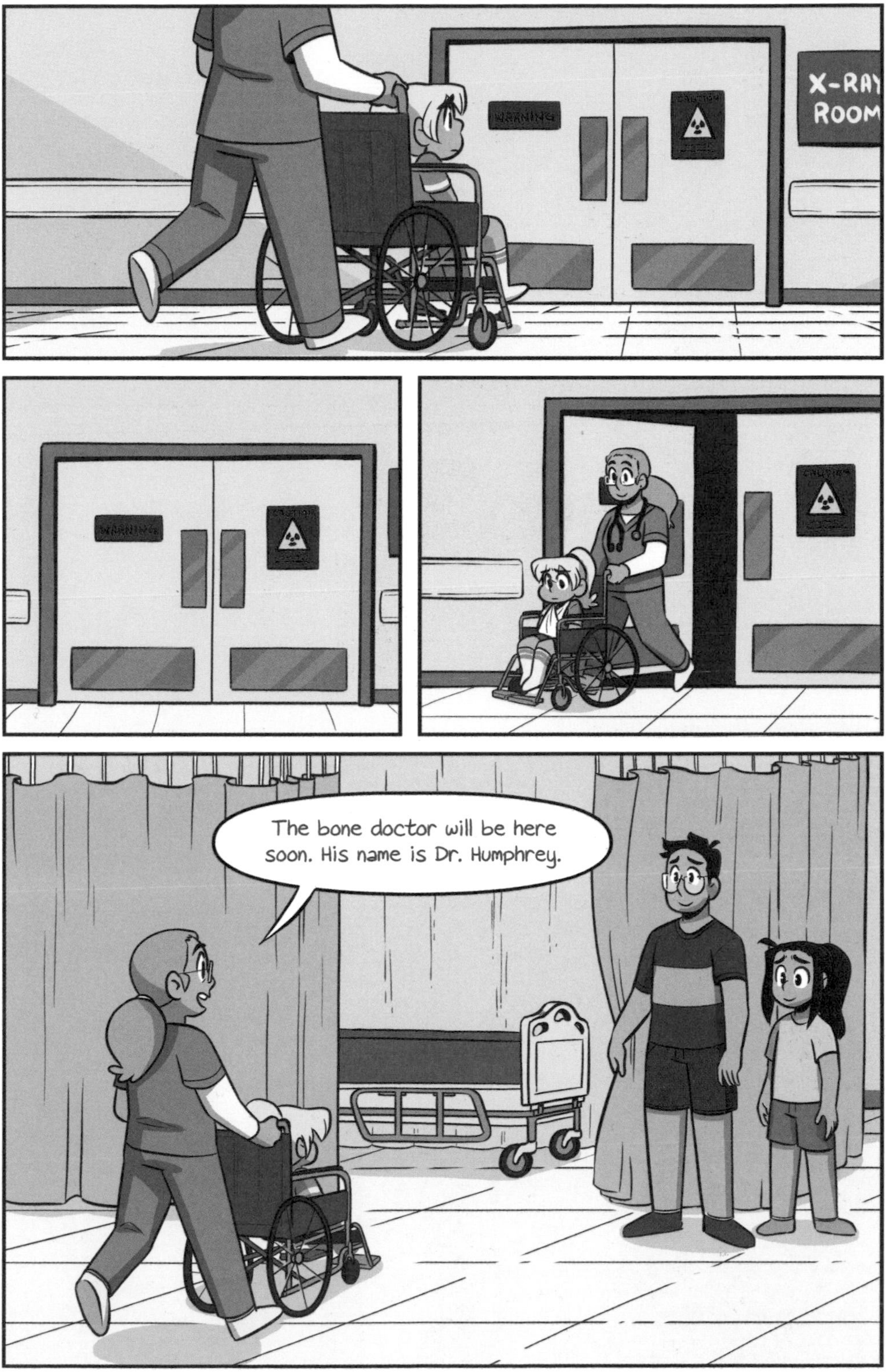
X-RAY
ROOM
WARNING
The bone doctor will be here soon. His name is Dr. Humphrey.

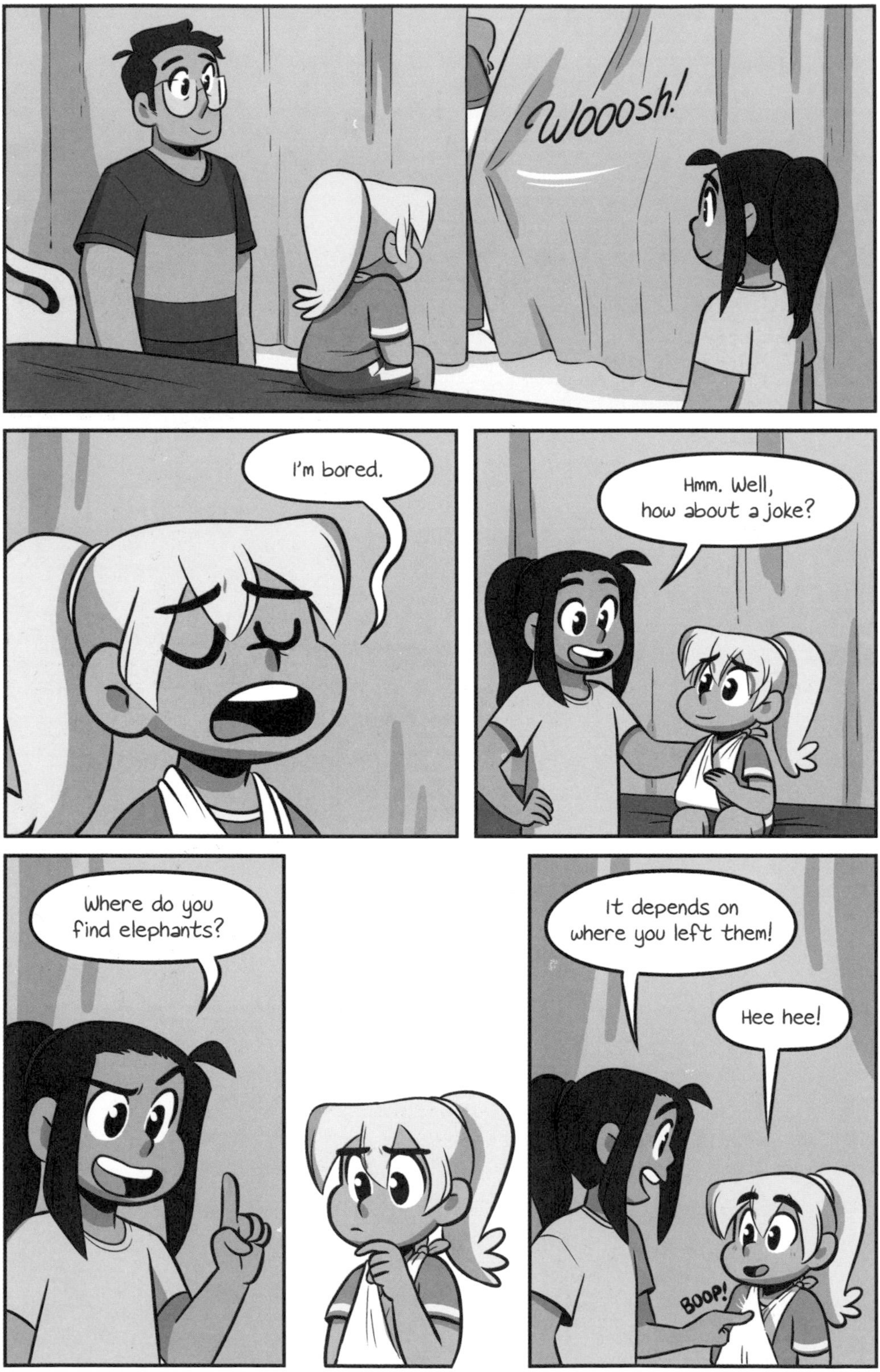
Wooosh!
I'm bored.
Hmm. Well, how about a joke?
Where do you find elephants?
It depends on where you left them!
Hee hee!
BOOP!

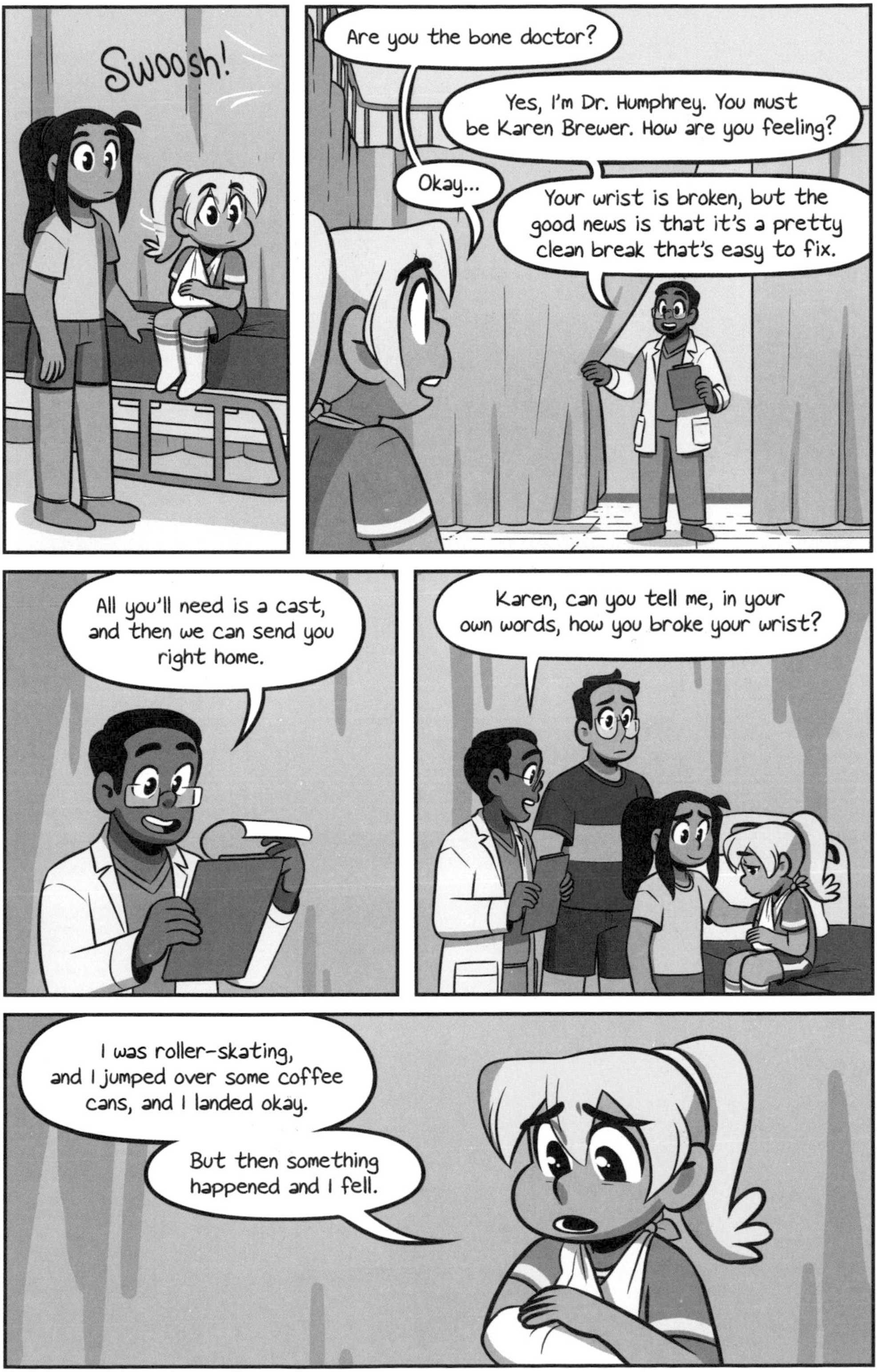
Swoosh!
Are you the bone doctor?
Yes, I'm Dr. Humphrey. You must be Karen Brewer. How are you feeling?
Okay...
Your wrist is broken, but the good news is that it's a pretty clean break that's easy to fix.
All you'll need is a cast, and then we can send you right home.
Karen, can you tell me, in your own words, how you broke your wrist?
I was roller-skating, and I jumped over some coffee cans, and I landed okay.
But then something happened and I fell.

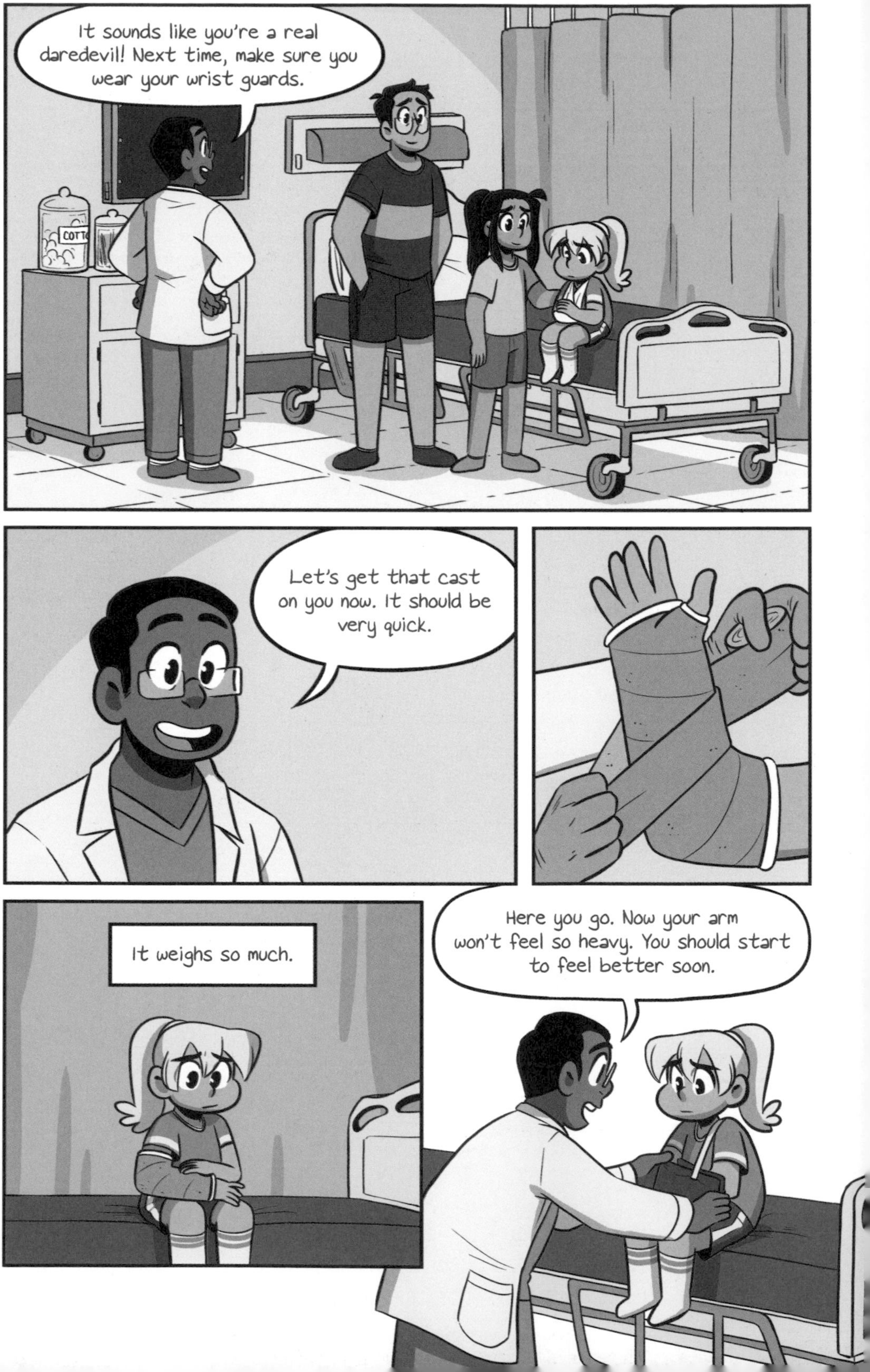
It sounds like you're a real daredevil! Next time, make sure you wear your wrist guards.
COTT
Let's get that cast on you now. It should be very quick.
It weighs so much.
Here you go. Now your arm won't feel so heavy. You should start to feel better soon.

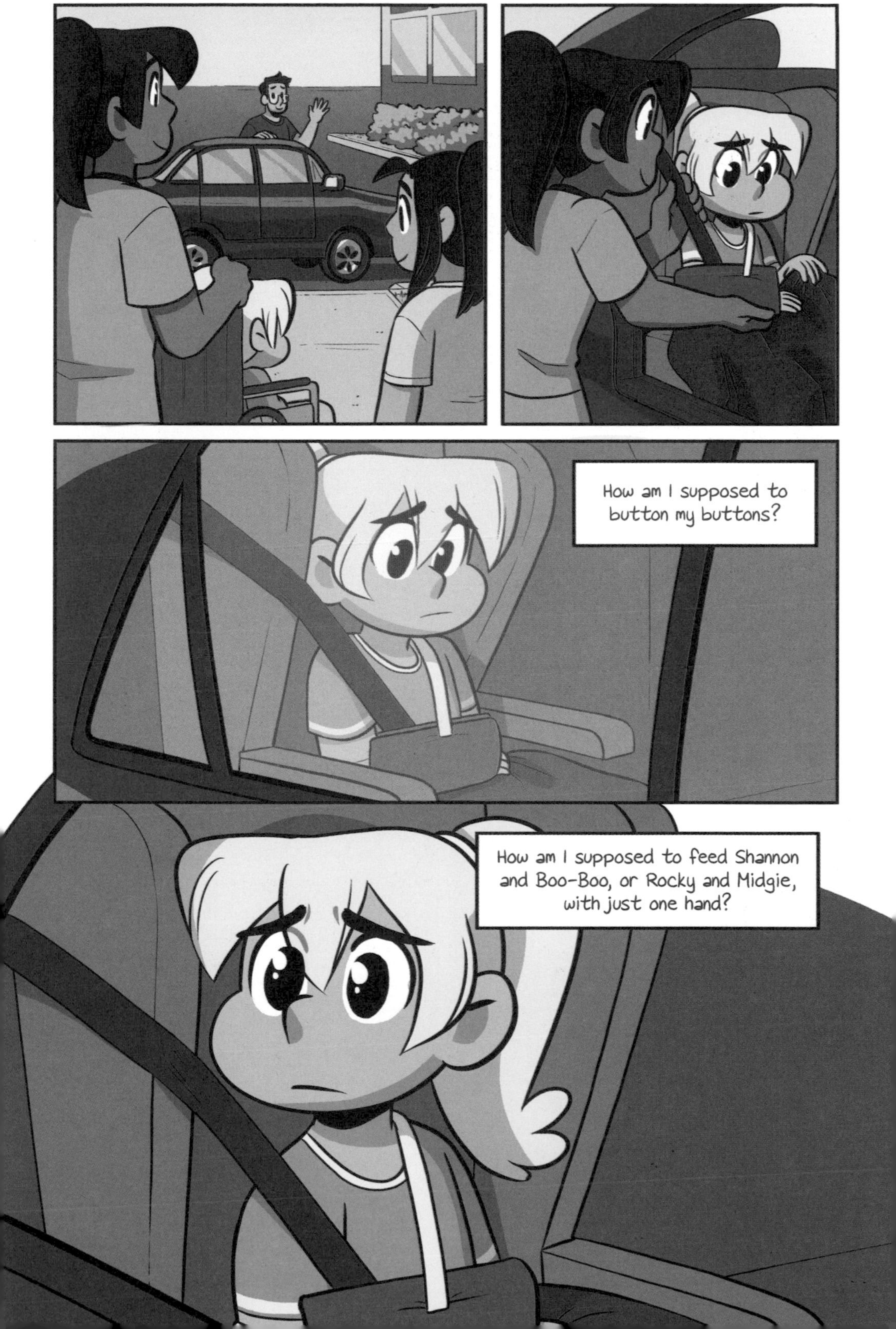
How am I supposed to button my buttons?
How am I supposed to feed Shannon and Boo-Boo, or Rocky and Midgie, with just one hand?

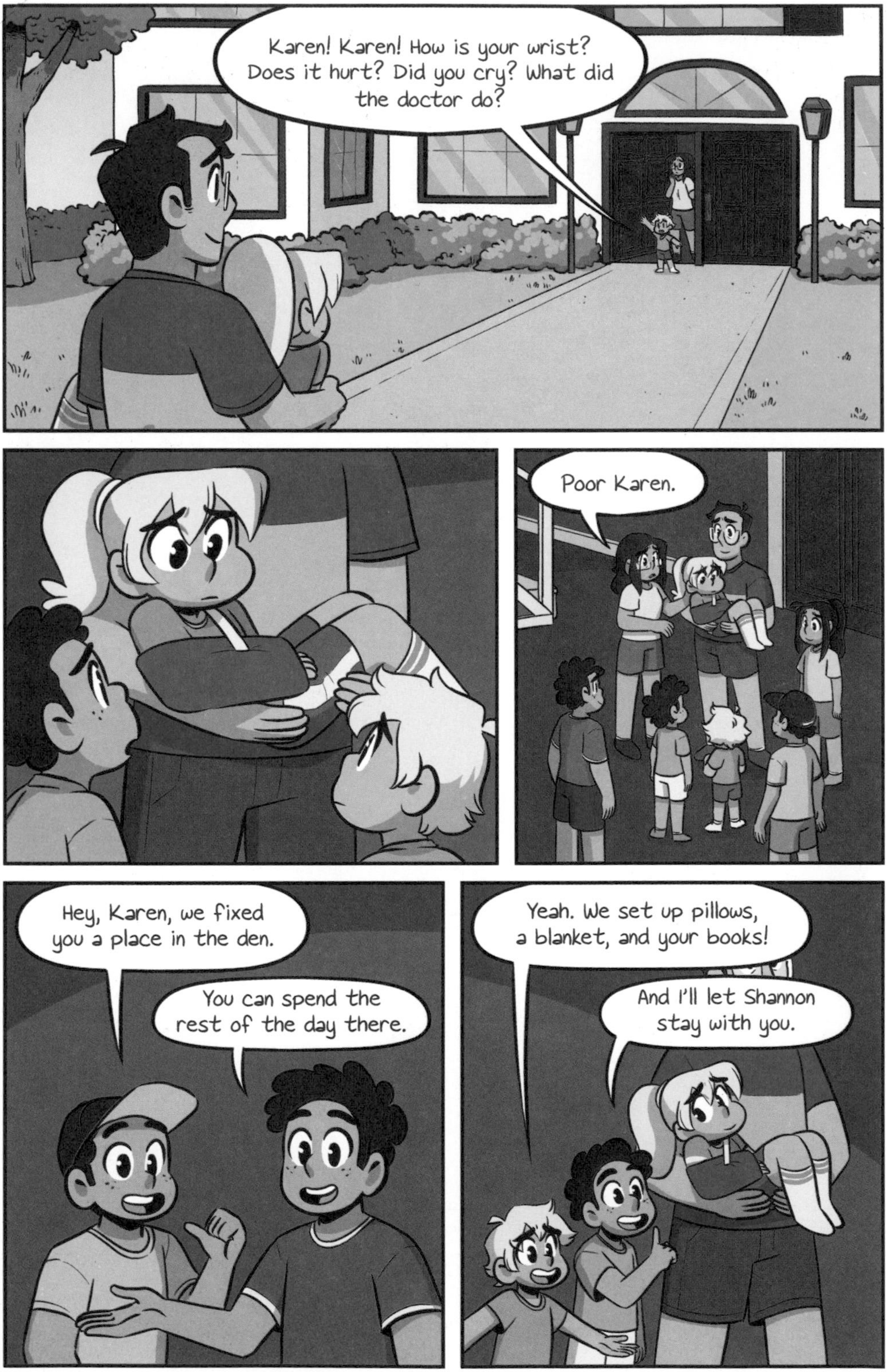
Karen! Karen! How is your wrist? Does it hurt? Did you cry? What did the doctor do?
Poor Karen.
Hey, Karen, we fixed you a place in the den.
You can spend the rest of the day there.
Yeah. We set up pillows, a blanket, and your books!
And I'll let Shannon stay with you.

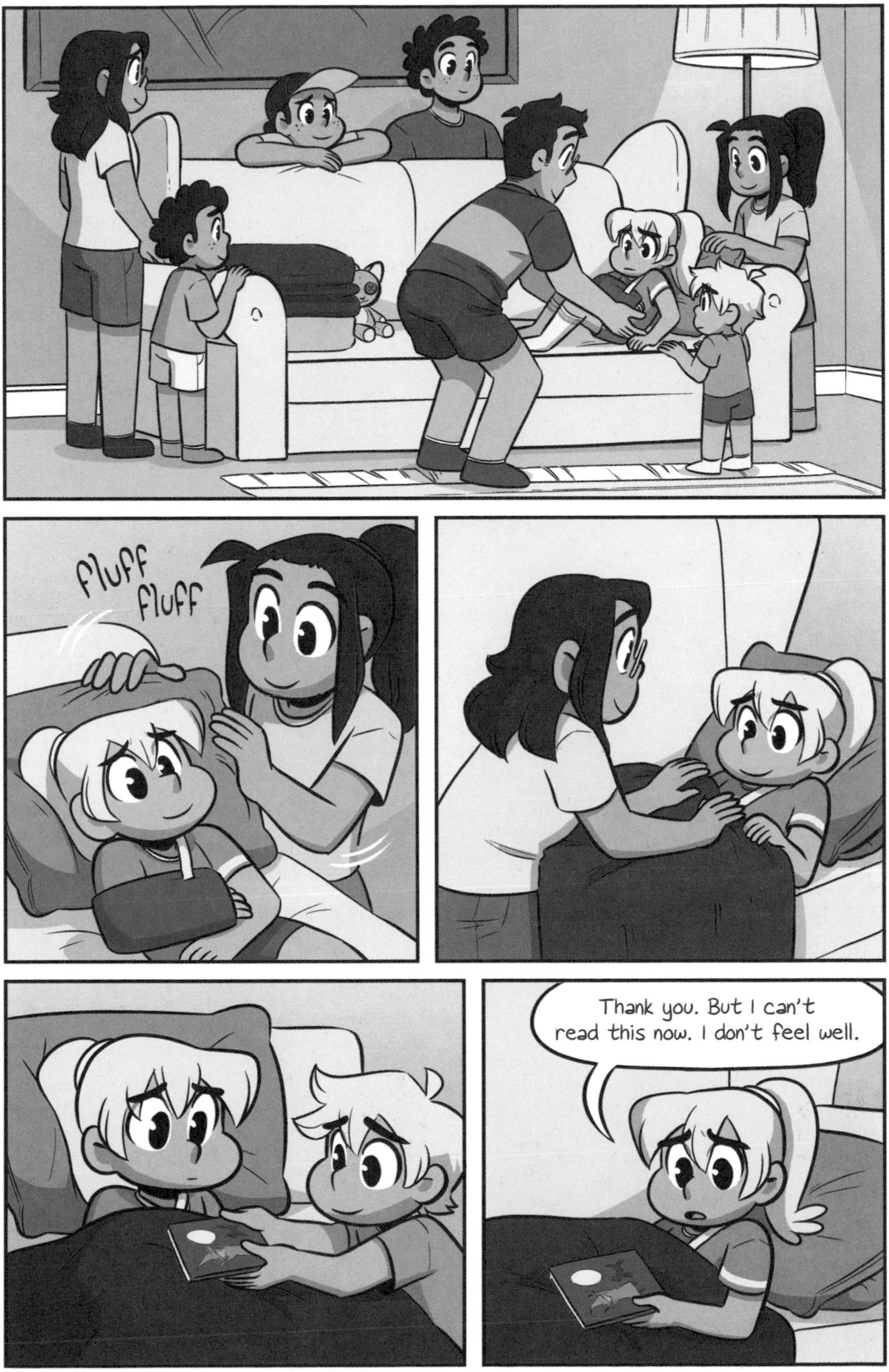
fluff
fluff
Thank you. But I can't read this now. I don't feel well.

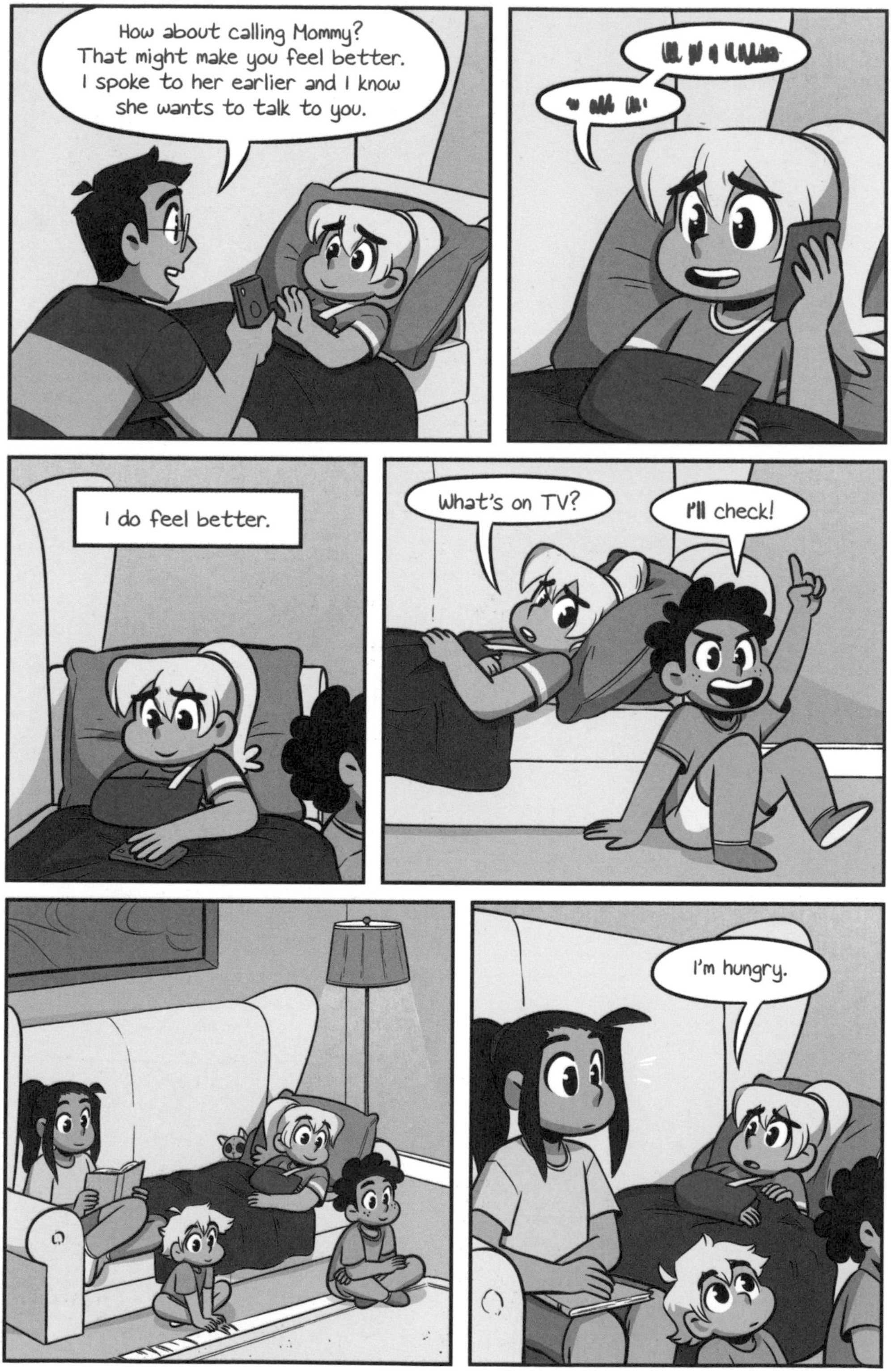
How about calling Mommy? That might make you feel better. I spoke to her earlier and I know she wants to talk to you.
I do feel better.
What's on TV?
I'll check!
I'm hungry.

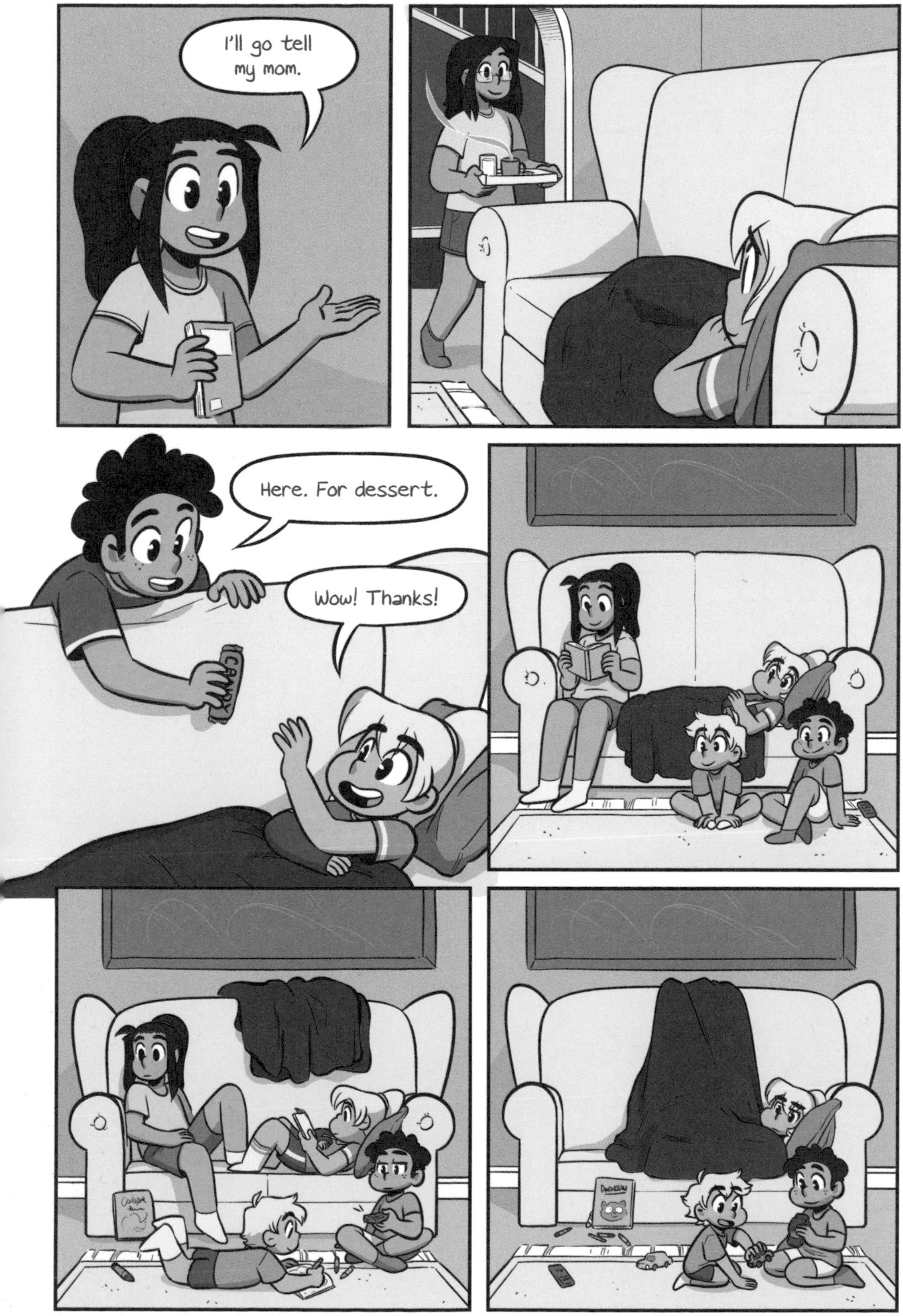
I'll go tell my mom.
Here. For dessert.
CANDY
Wow! Thanks!

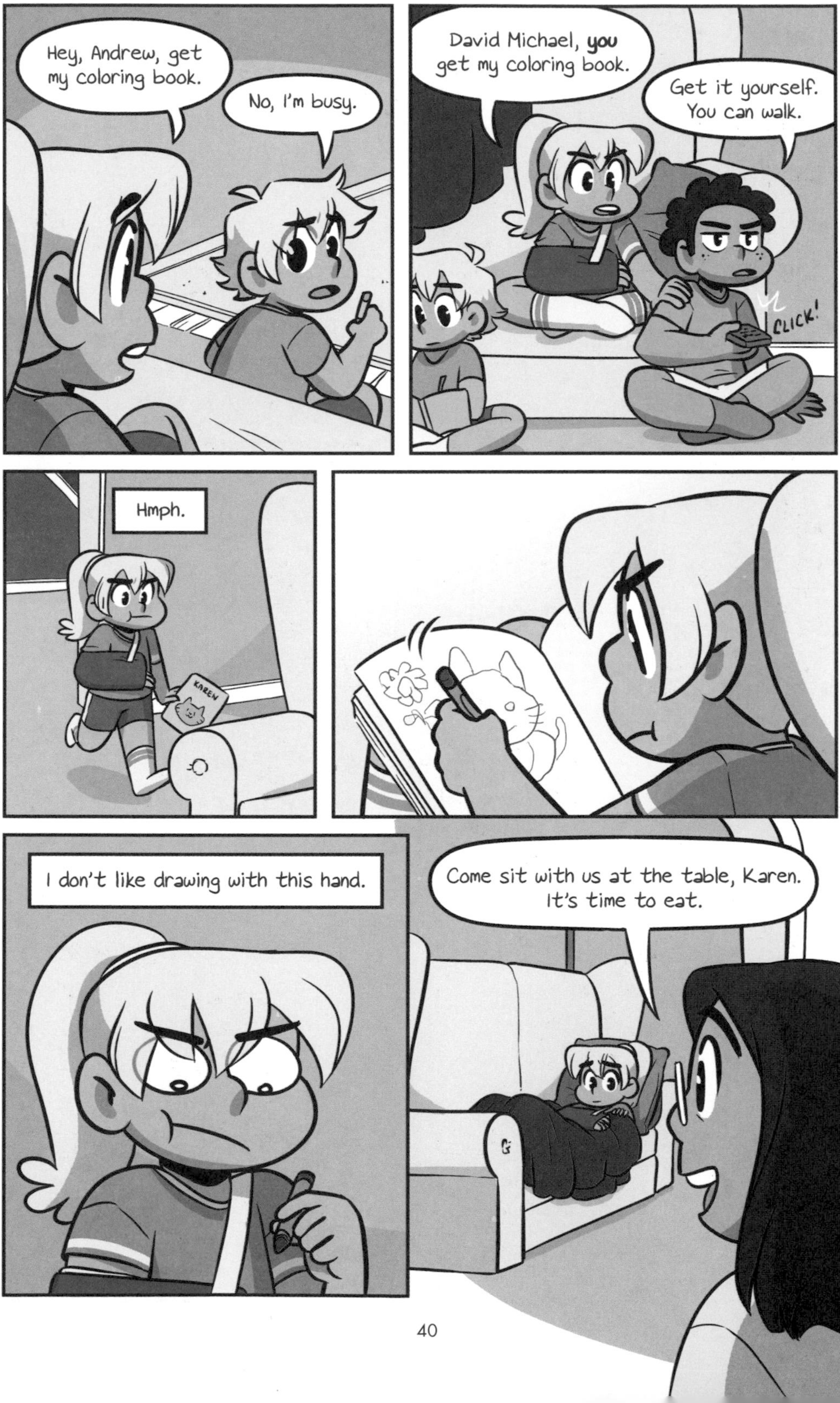
Hey, Andrew, get my coloring book.
No, I'm busy.
David Michael, **you** get my coloring book.
Get it yourself. You can walk.
CLICK!
Hmph.
KAREN
I don't like drawing with this hand.
Come sit with us at the table, Karen. It's time to eat.

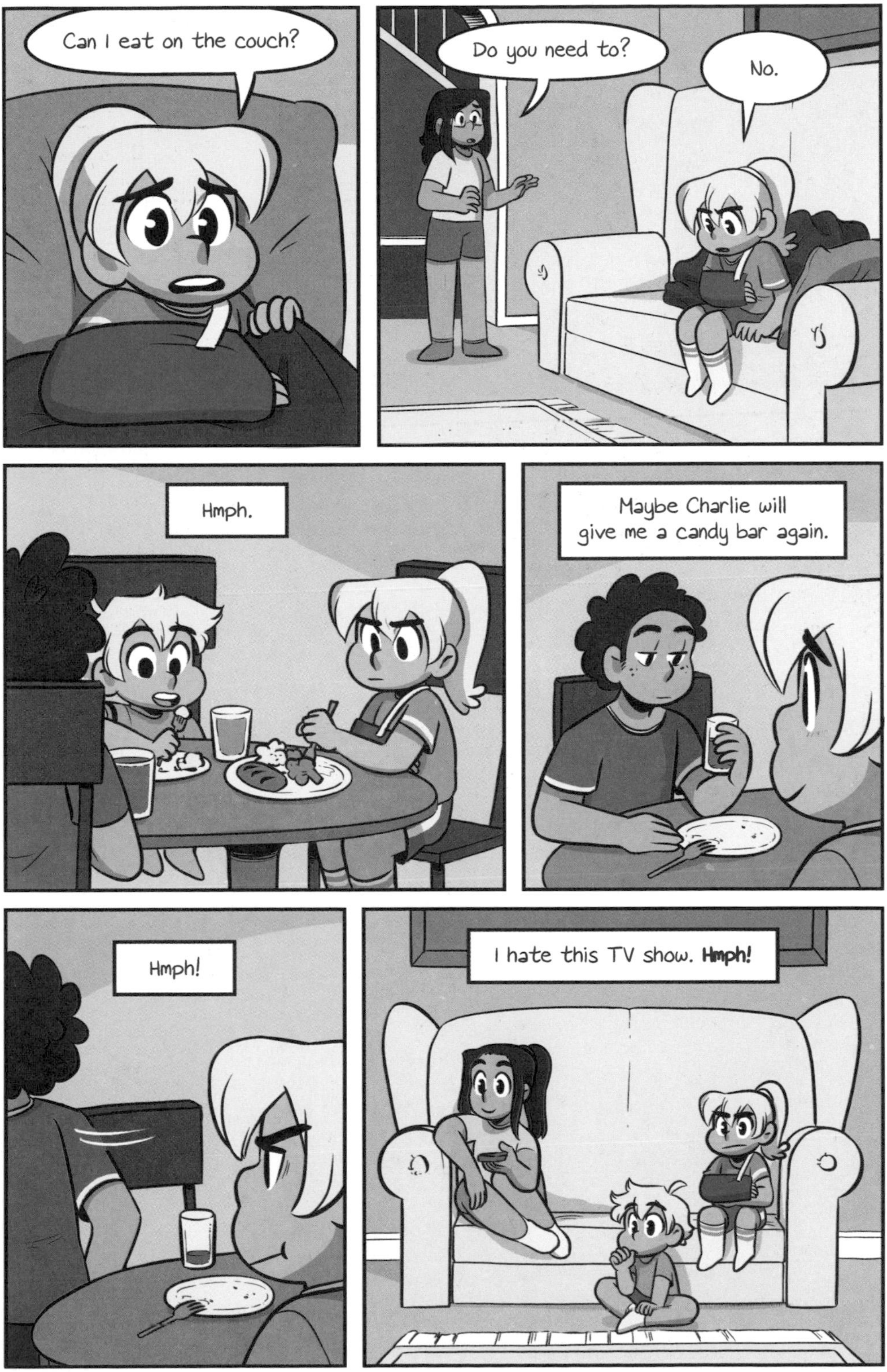
Can I eat on the couch?
Do you need to?
No.
Hmph.
Maybe Charlie will give me a candy bar again.
Hmph!
I hate this TV show. **Hmph!**

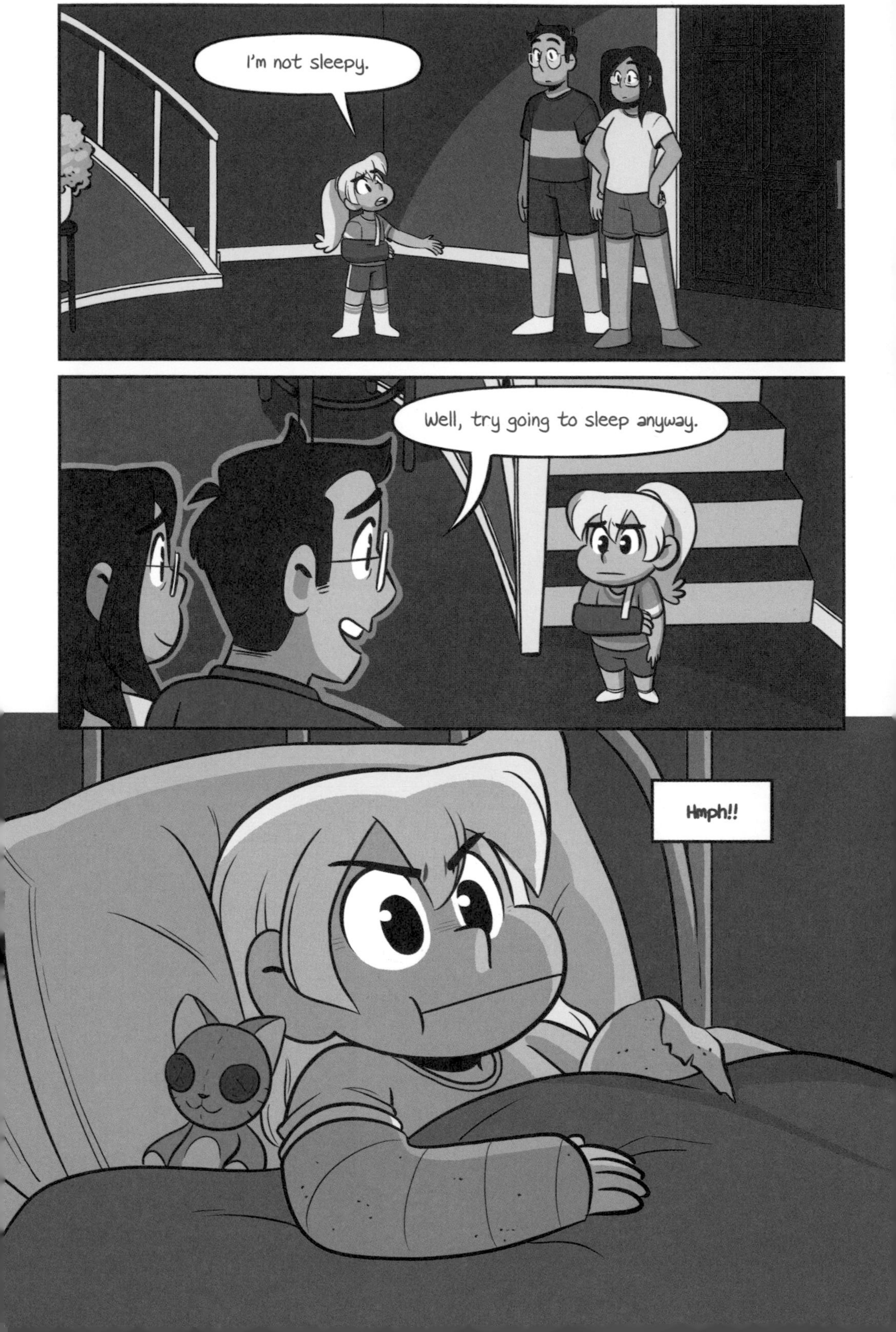
I'm not sleepy.
Well, try going to sleep anyway.
Hmph!!

CHAPTER 4

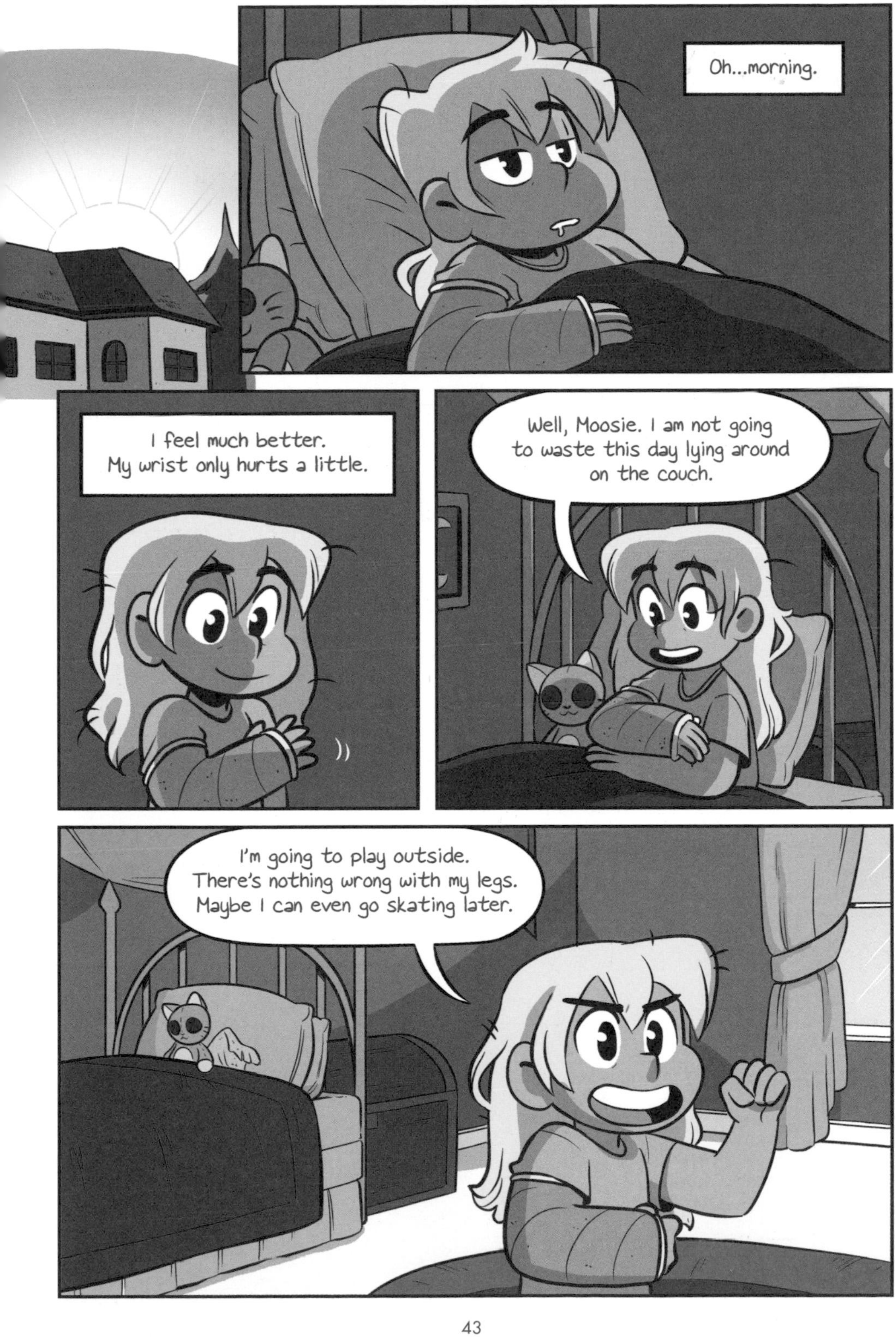
Oh...morning.
I feel much better.
My wrist only hurts a little.
Well, Moosie. I am not going to waste this day lying around on the couch.
I'm going to play outside.
There's nothing wrong with my legs.
Maybe I can even go skating later.

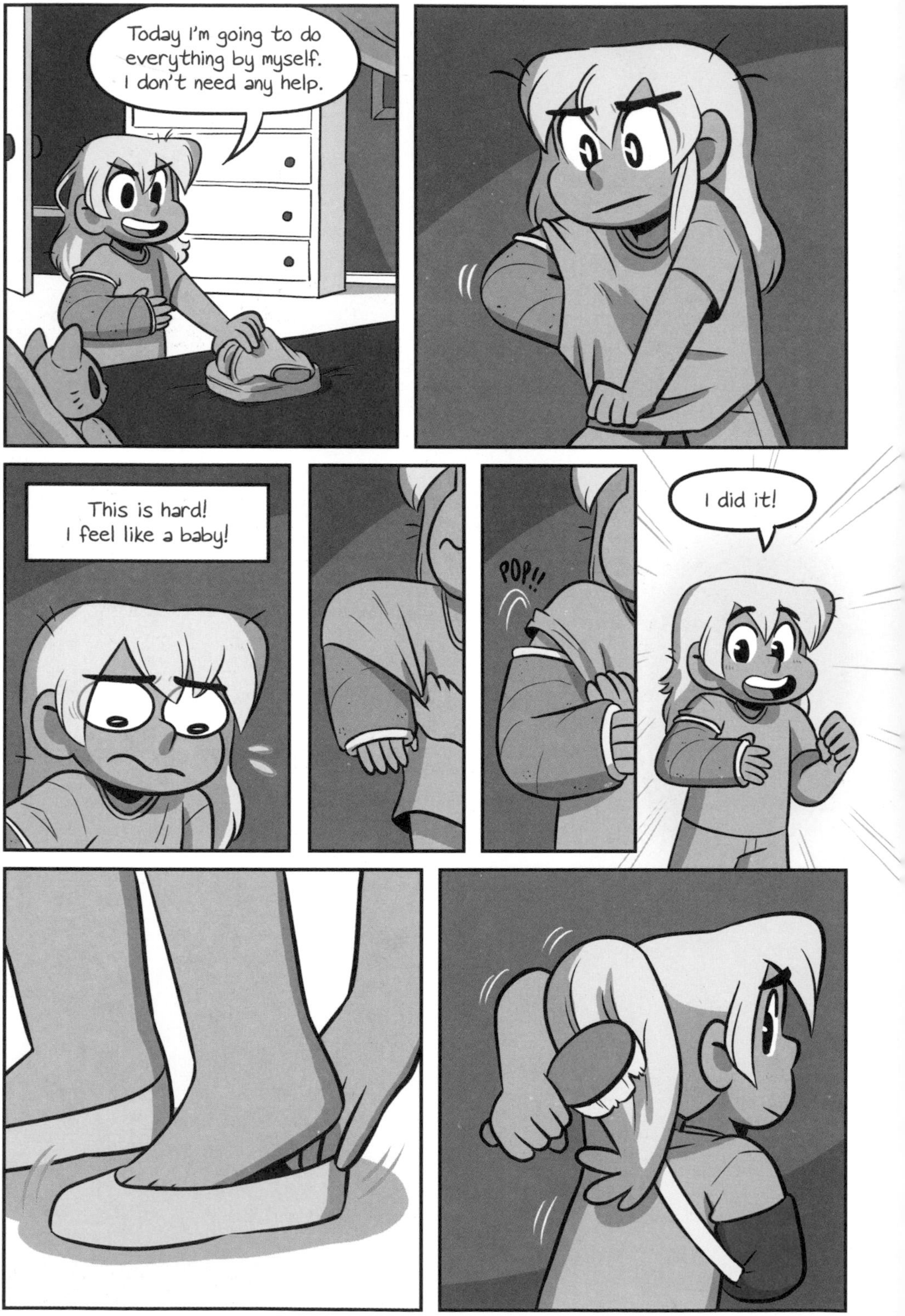
Today I'm going to do everything by myself. I don't need any help.
This is hard! I feel like a baby!
POP!!
I did it!

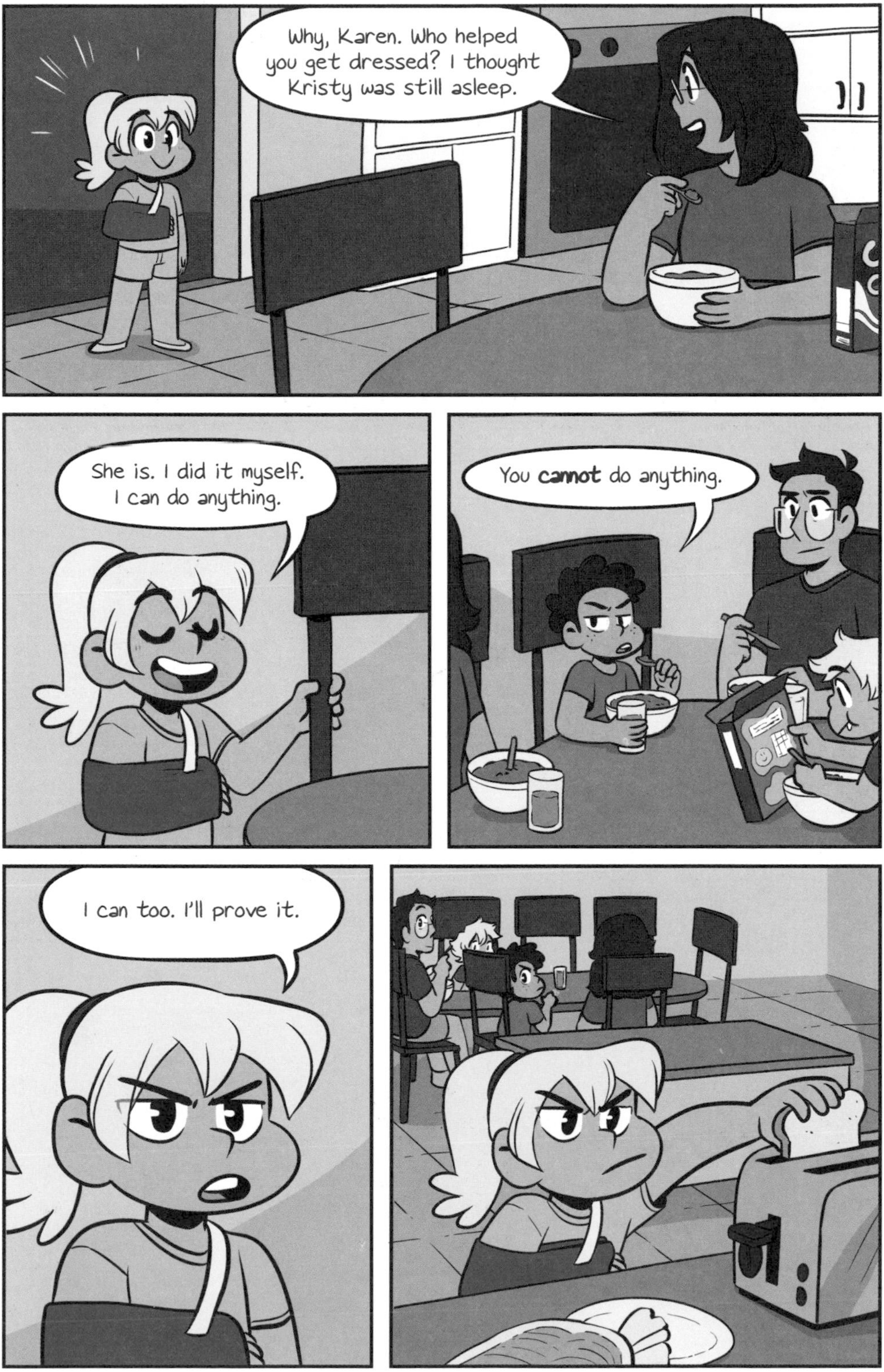
Why, Karen. Who helped you get dressed? I thought Kristy was still asleep.
She is. I did it myself. I can do anything.
You **cannot** do anything.
I can too. I'll prove it.

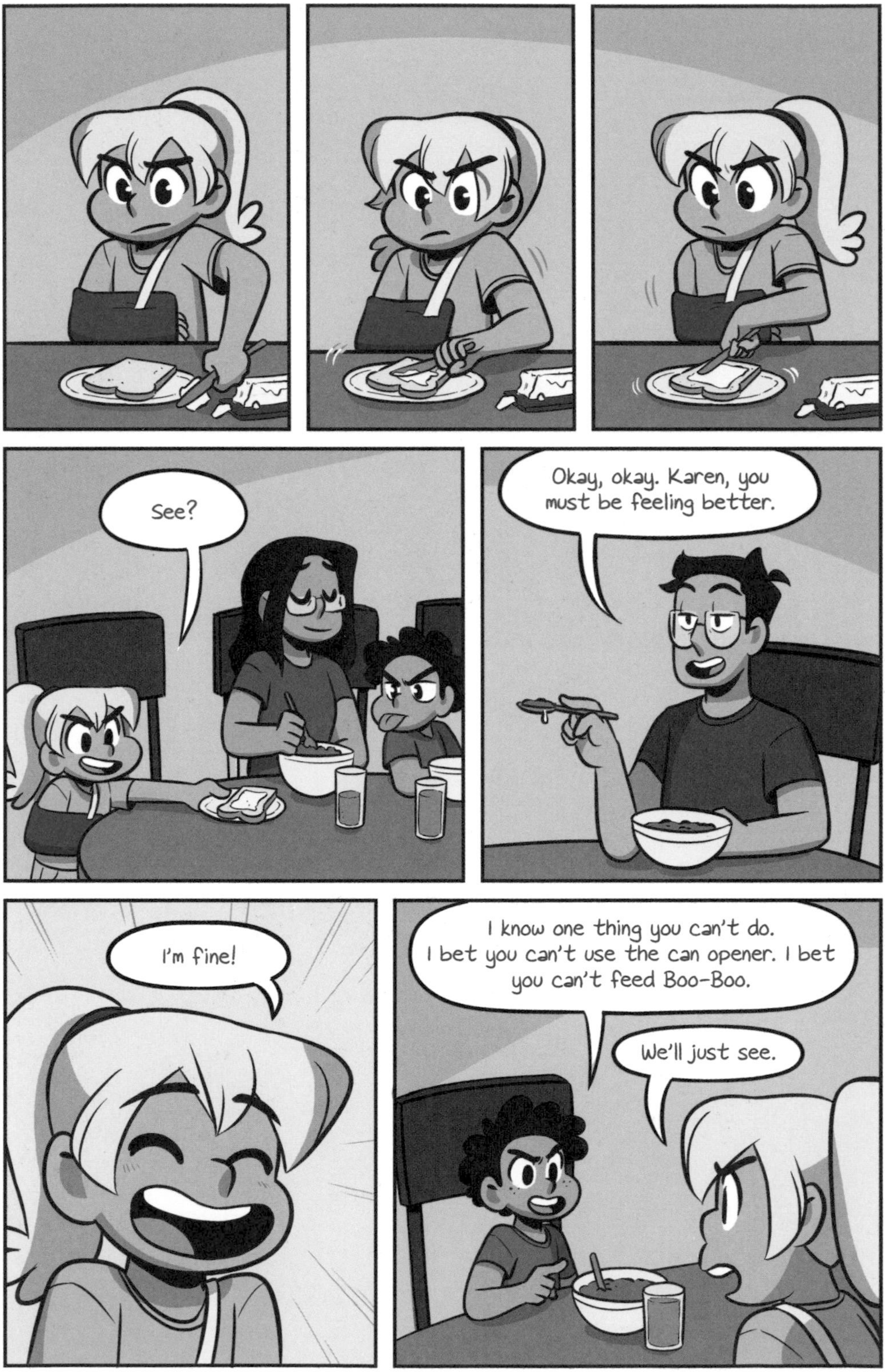
See?
Okay, okay. Karen, you must be feeling better.
I'm fine!
I know one thing you can't do. I bet you can't use the can opener. I bet you can't feed Boo-Boo.
We'll just see.

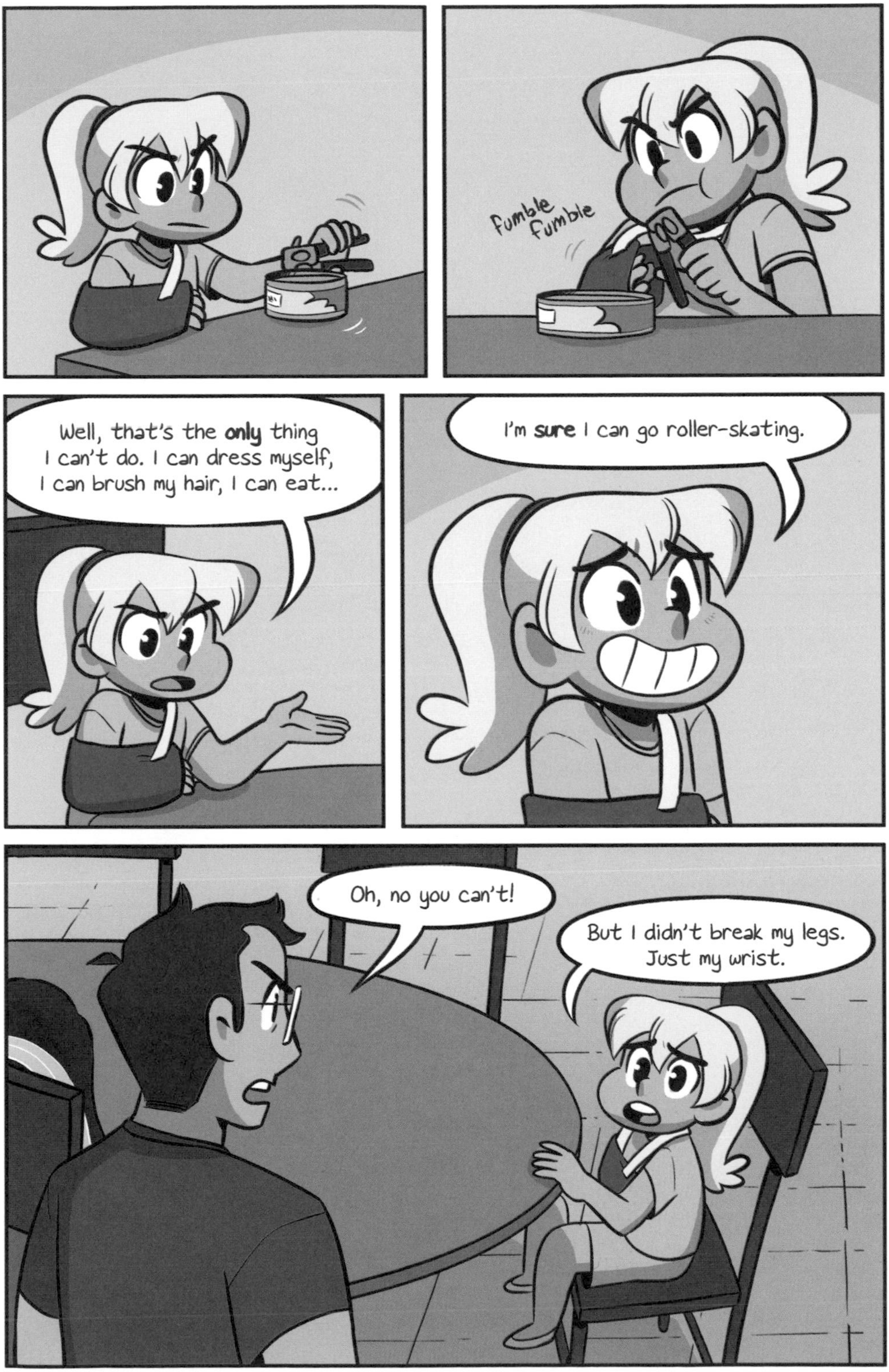
fumble fumble
Well, that's the **only** thing I can't do. I can dress myself, I can brush my hair, I can eat...
I'm **sure** I can go roller-skating.
Oh, no you can't!
But I didn't break my legs. Just my wrist.

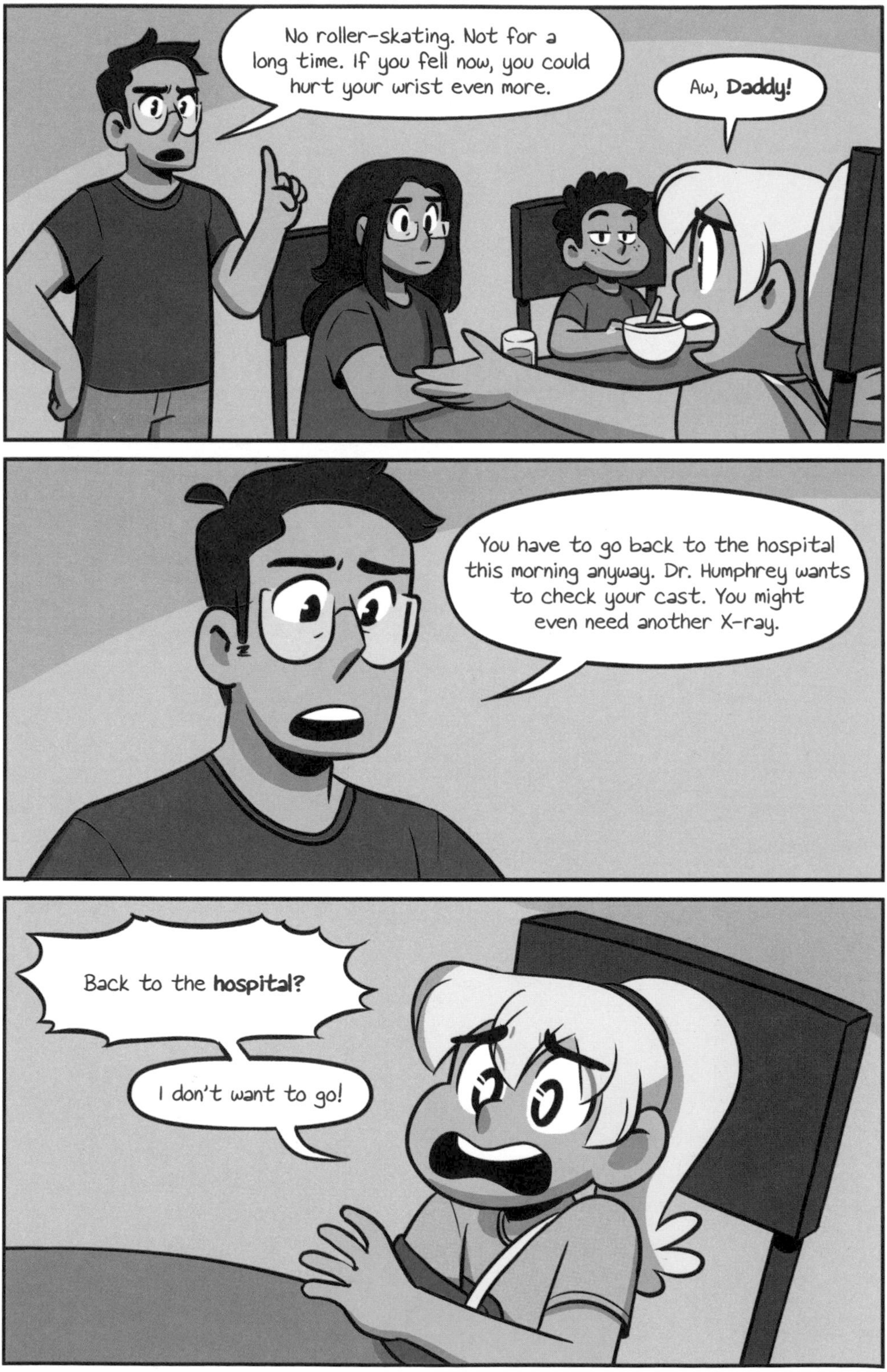
No roller-skating. Not for a long time. If you fell now, you could hurt your wrist even more.
Aw, **Daddy!**
You have to go back to the hospital this morning anyway. Dr. Humphrey wants to check your cast. You might even need another X-ray.
Back to the **hospital?**
I don't want to go!

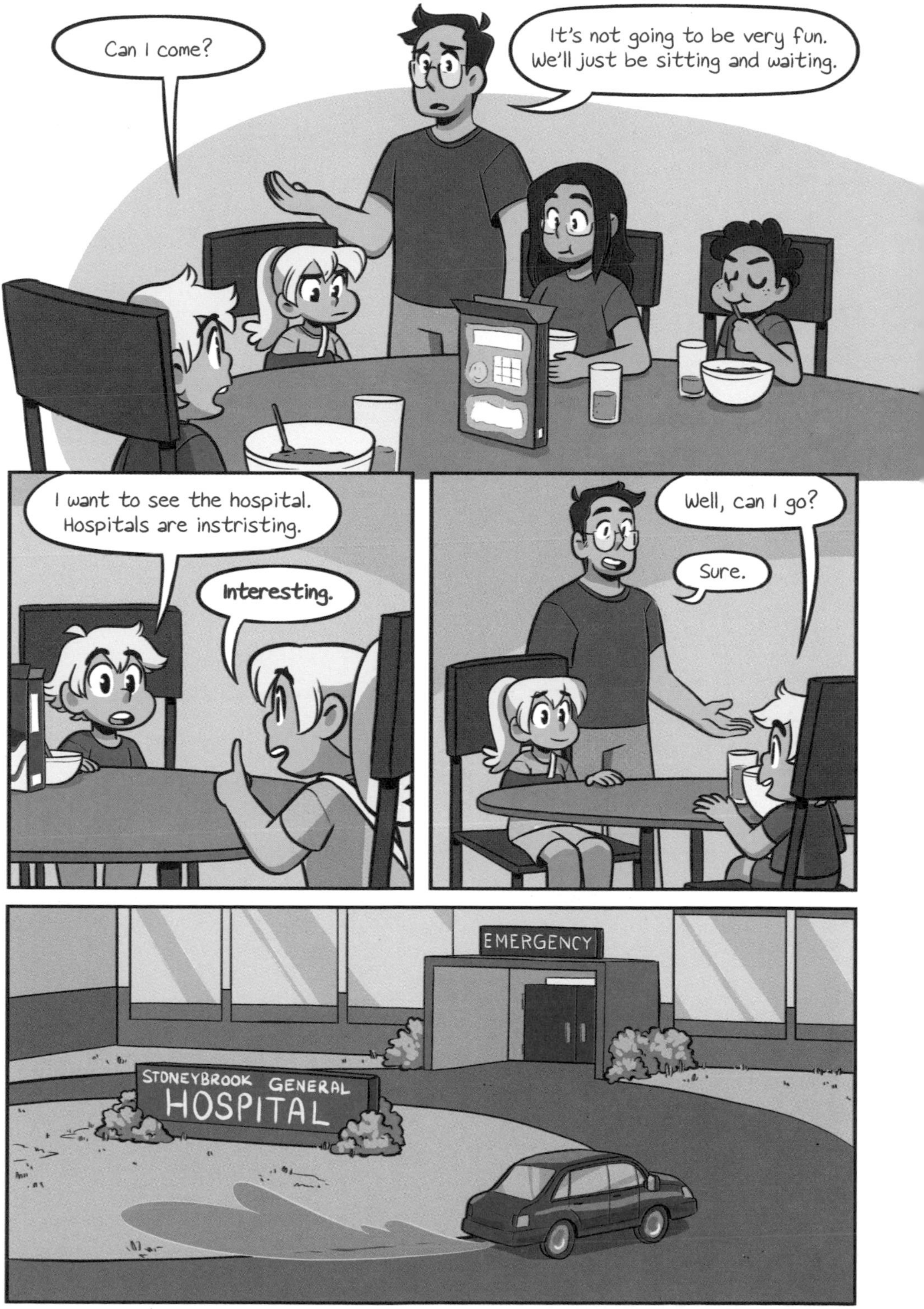
Can I come?
It's not going to be very fun. We'll just be sitting and waiting.
I want to see the hospital. Hospitals are instristing.
Interesting.
Well, can I go?
Sure.
EMERGENCY
STONEYBROOK GENERAL HOSPITAL

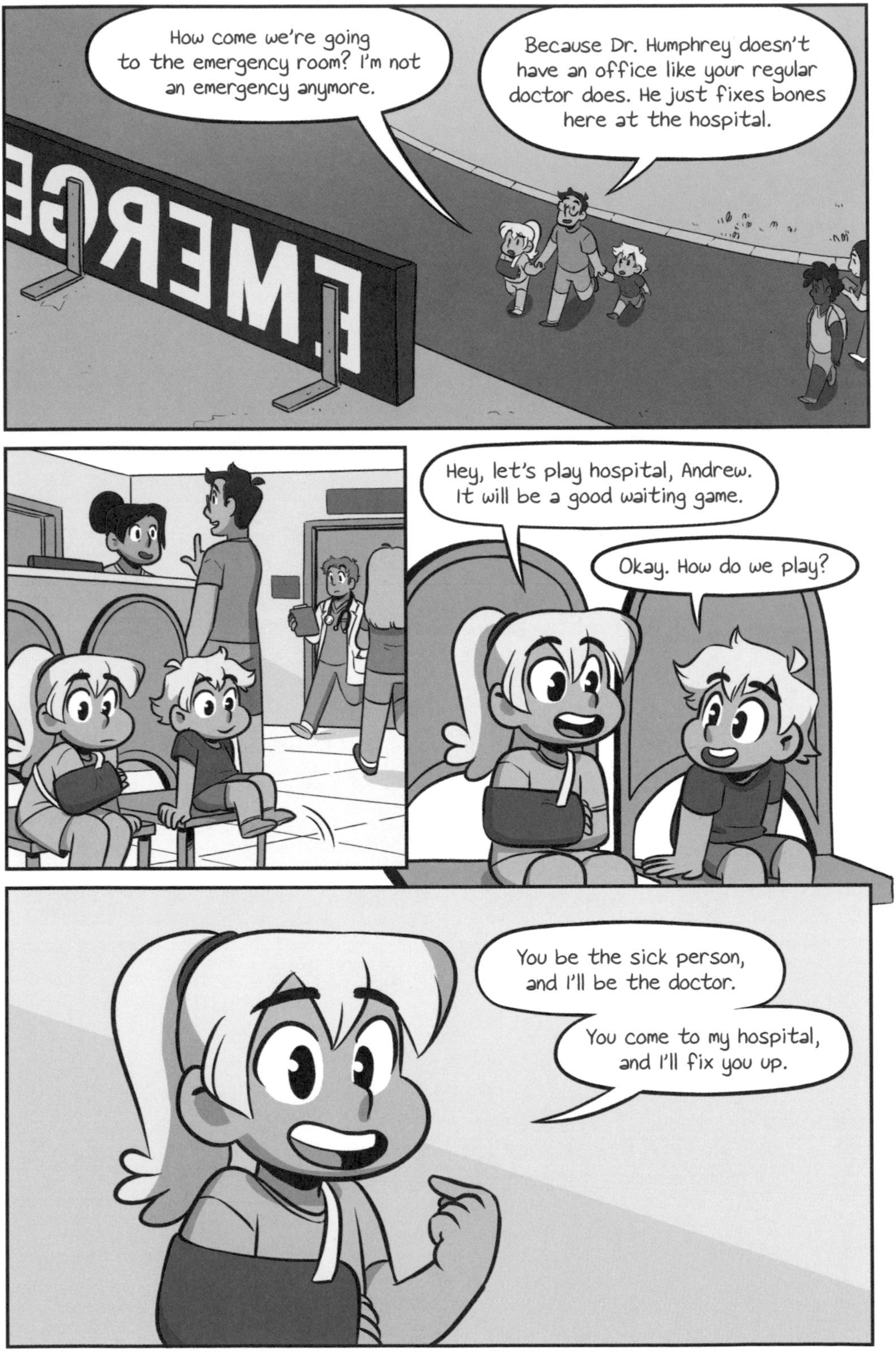
How come we're going to the emergency room? I'm not an emergency anymore.
Because Dr. Humphrey doesn't have an office like your regular doctor does. He just fixes bones here at the hospital.
EMERGE
Hey, let's play hospital, Andrew. It will be a good waiting game.
Okay. How do we play?
You be the sick person, and I'll be the doctor.
You come to my hospital, and I'll fix you up.

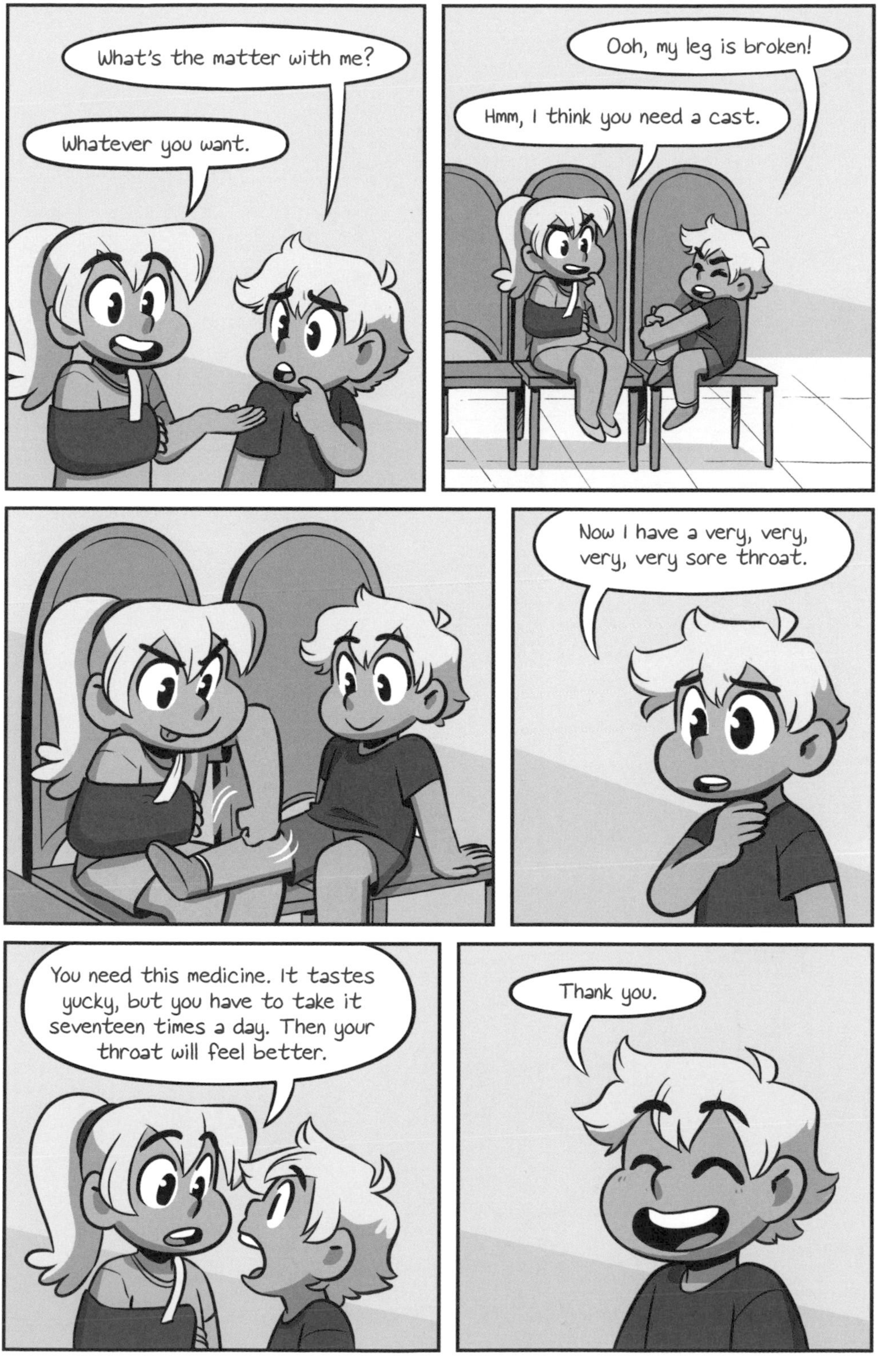
What's the matter with me?
Whatever you want.
Ooh, my leg is broken!
Hmm, I think you need a cast.
Now I have a very, very, very, very sore throat.
You need this medicine. It tastes yucky, but you have to take it seventeen times a day. Then your throat will feel better.
Thank you.

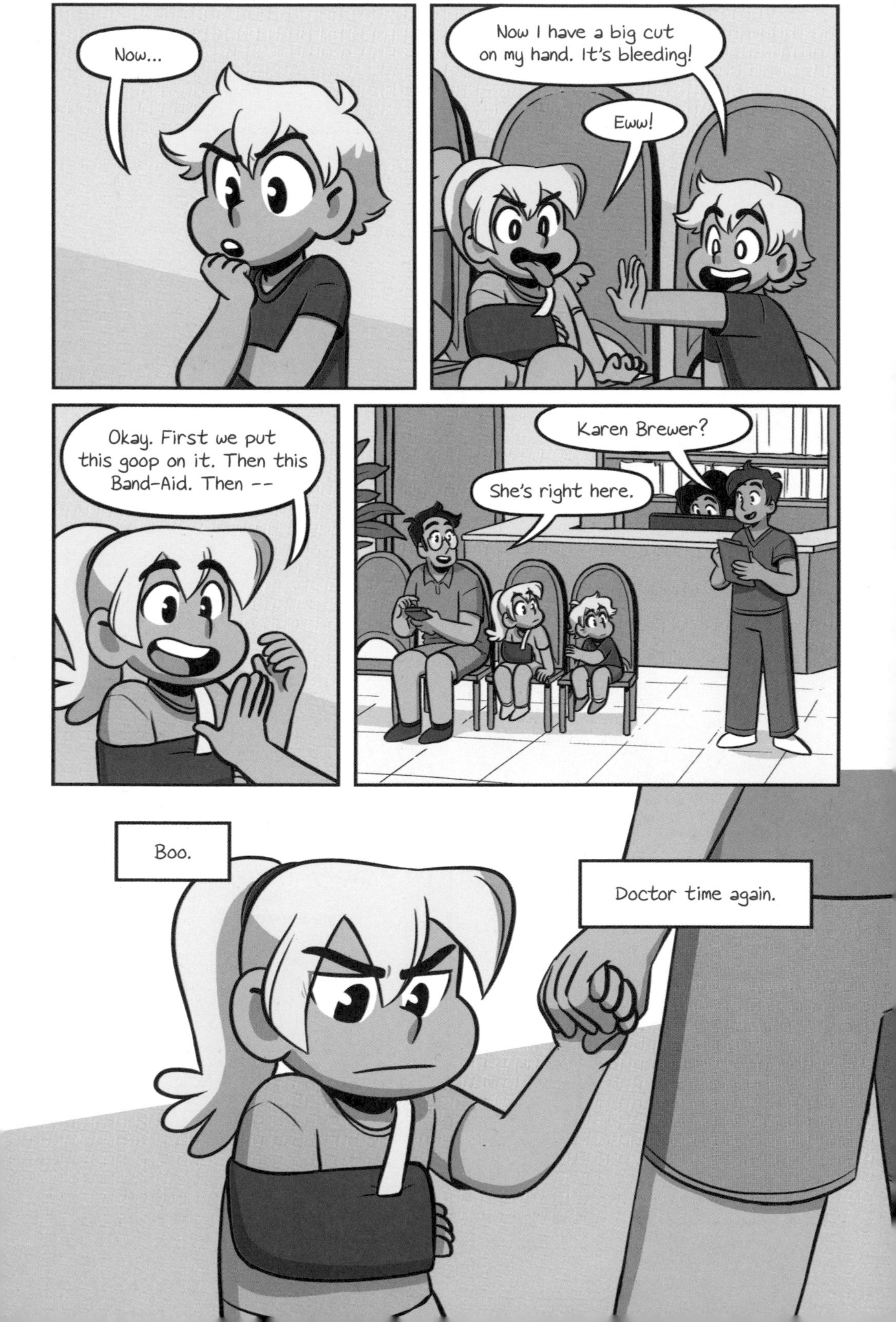
Now...
Now I have a big cut on my hand. It's bleeding!
Eww!
Okay. First we put this goop on it. Then this Band-Aid. Then --
Karen Brewer?
She's right here.
Boo.
Doctor time again.

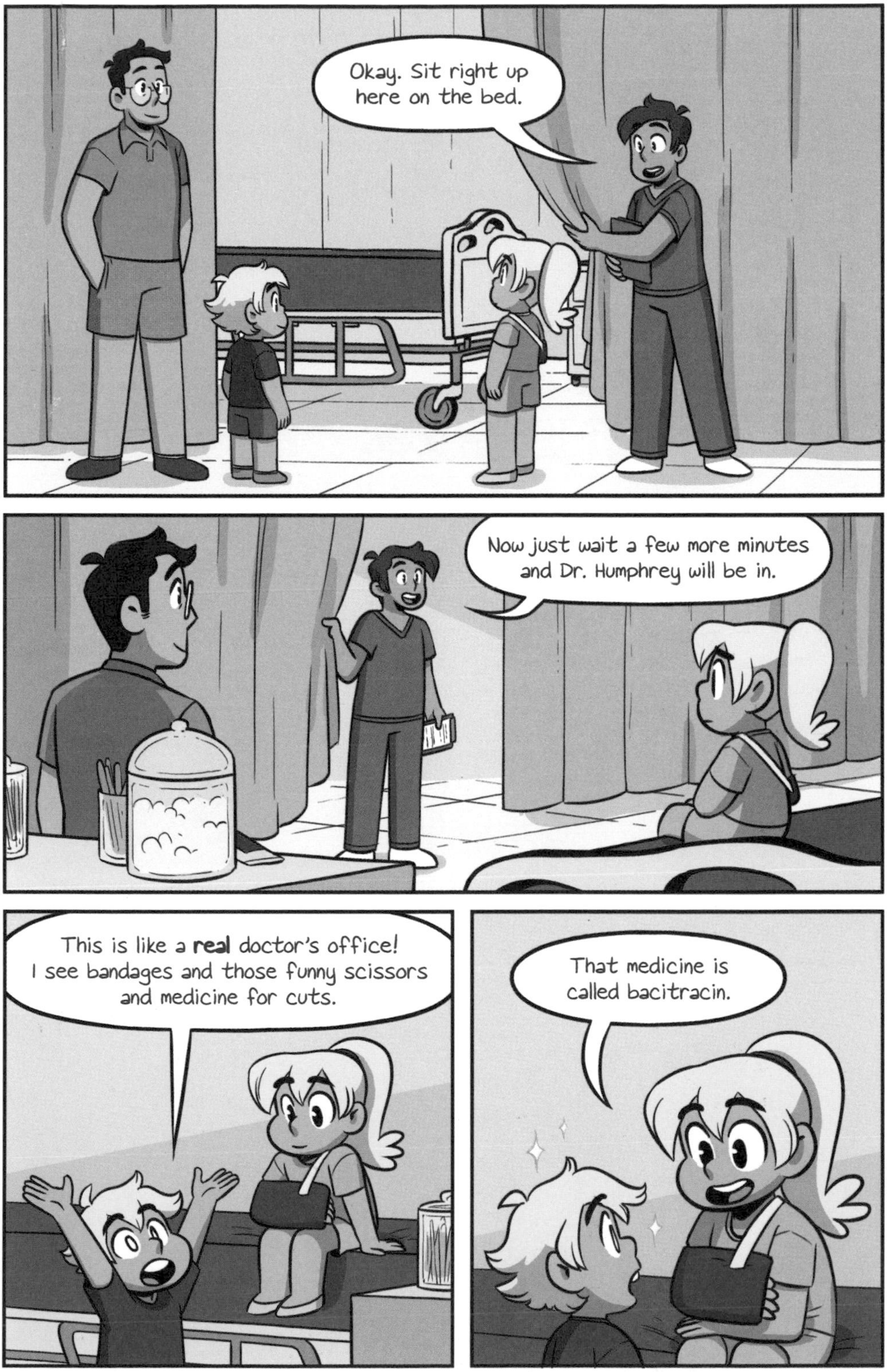
Okay. Sit right up here on the bed.
Now just wait a few more minutes and Dr. Humphrey will be in.
This is like a **real** doctor's office! I see bandages and those funny scissors and medicine for cuts.
That medicine is called bacitracin.

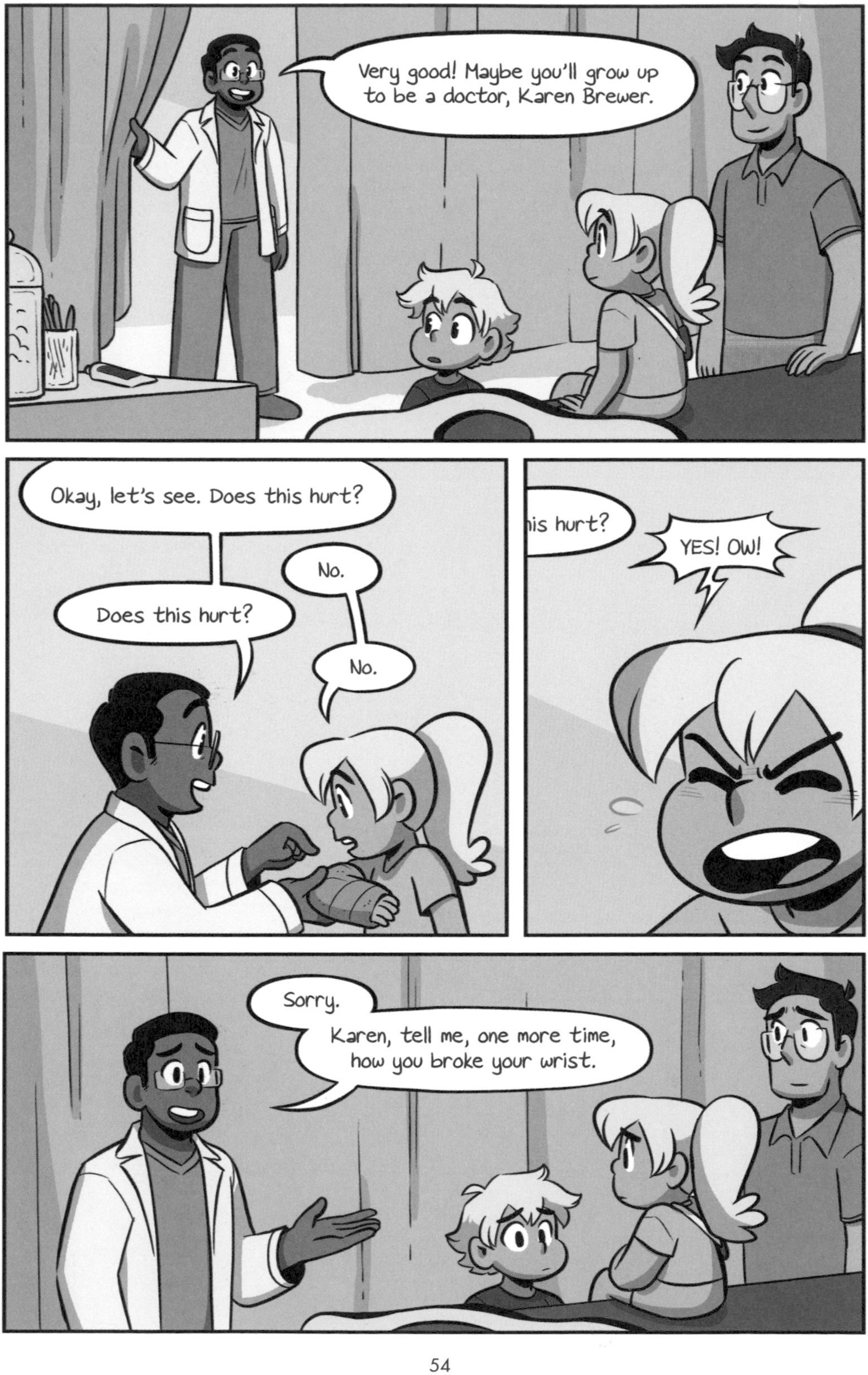
Very good! Maybe you'll grow up to be a doctor, Karen Brewer.
Okay, let's see. Does this hurt?
No.
Does this hurt?
No.
is hurt?
YES! OW!
Sorry.
Karen, tell me, one more time, how you broke your wrist.

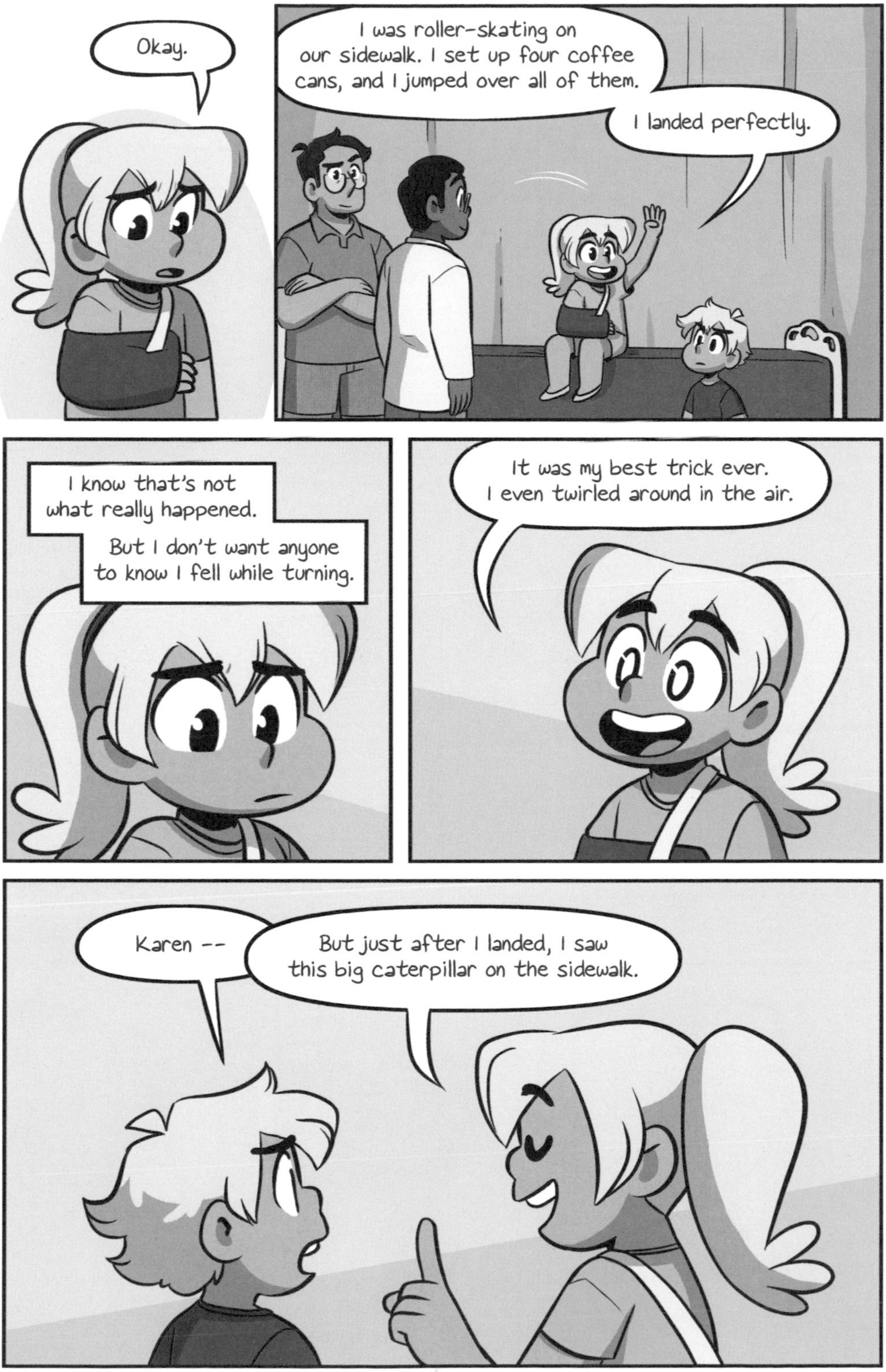
Okay.
I was roller-skating on our sidewalk. I set up four coffee cans, and I jumped over all of them.
I landed perfectly.
I know that's not what really happened.
But I don't want anyone to know I fell while turning.
It was my best trick ever. I even twirled around in the air.
Karen --
But just after I landed, I saw this big caterpillar on the sidewalk.

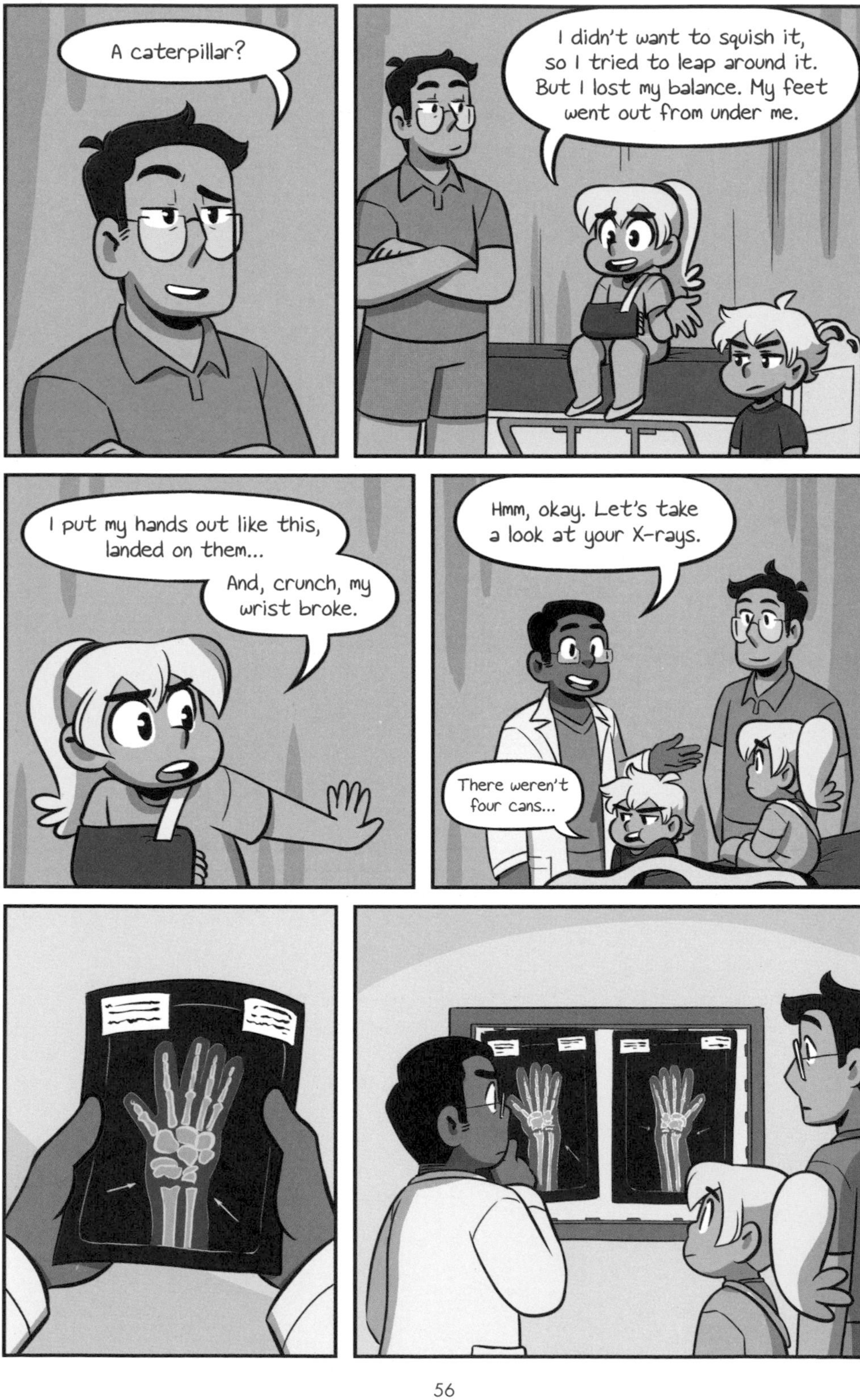
A caterpillar?
I didn't want to squish it, so I tried to leap around it. But I lost my balance. My feet went out from under me.
I put my hands out like this, landed on them...
And, crunch, my wrist broke.
Hmm, okay. Let's take a look at your X-rays.
There weren't four cans...

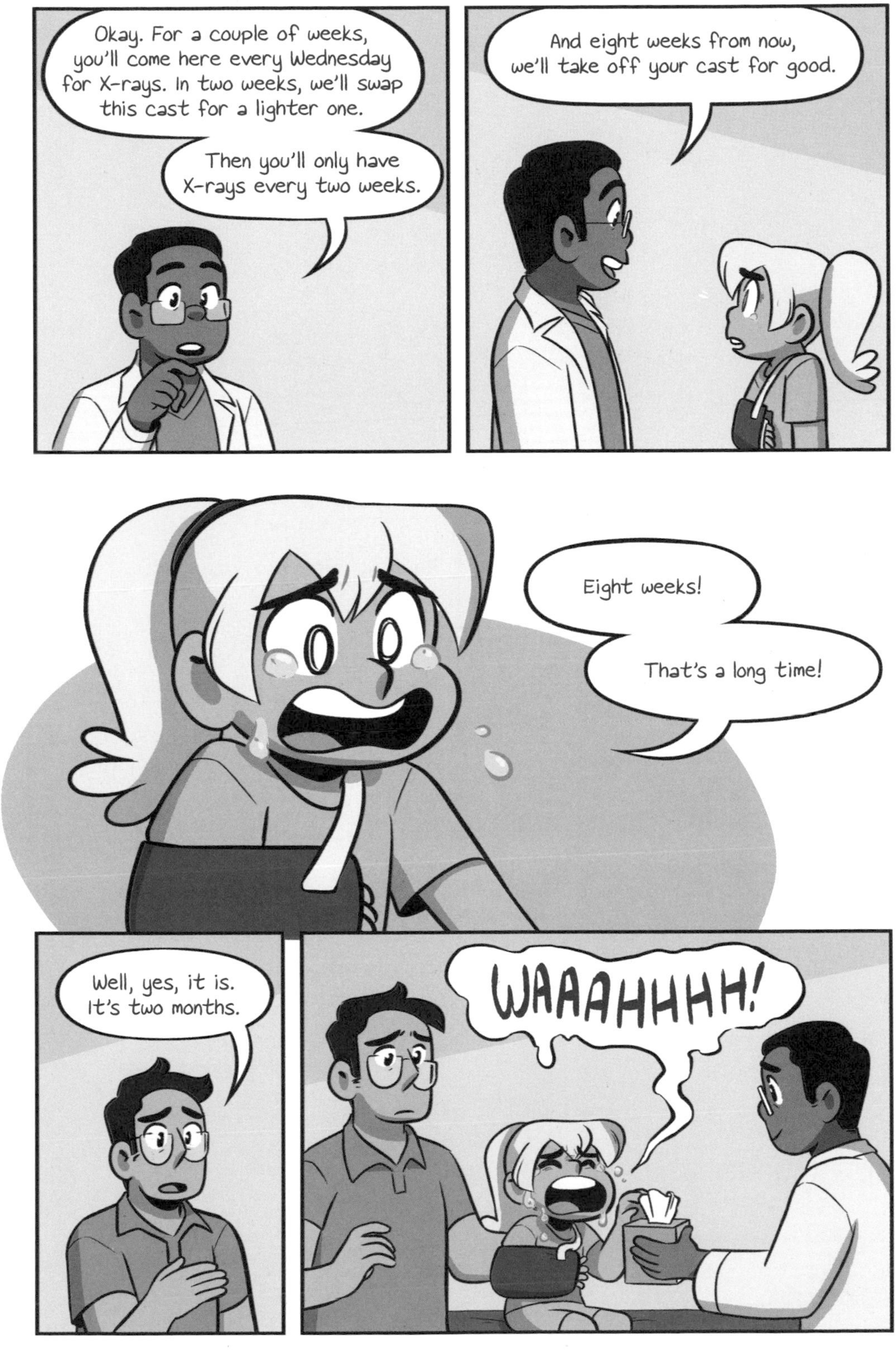
Okay. For a couple of weeks, you'll come here every Wednesday for X-rays. In two weeks, we'll swap this cast for a lighter one.
Then you'll only have X-rays every two weeks.
And eight weeks from now, we'll take off your cast for good.
Eight weeks!
That's a long time!
Well, yes, it is. It's two months.
WAAAHHHH!

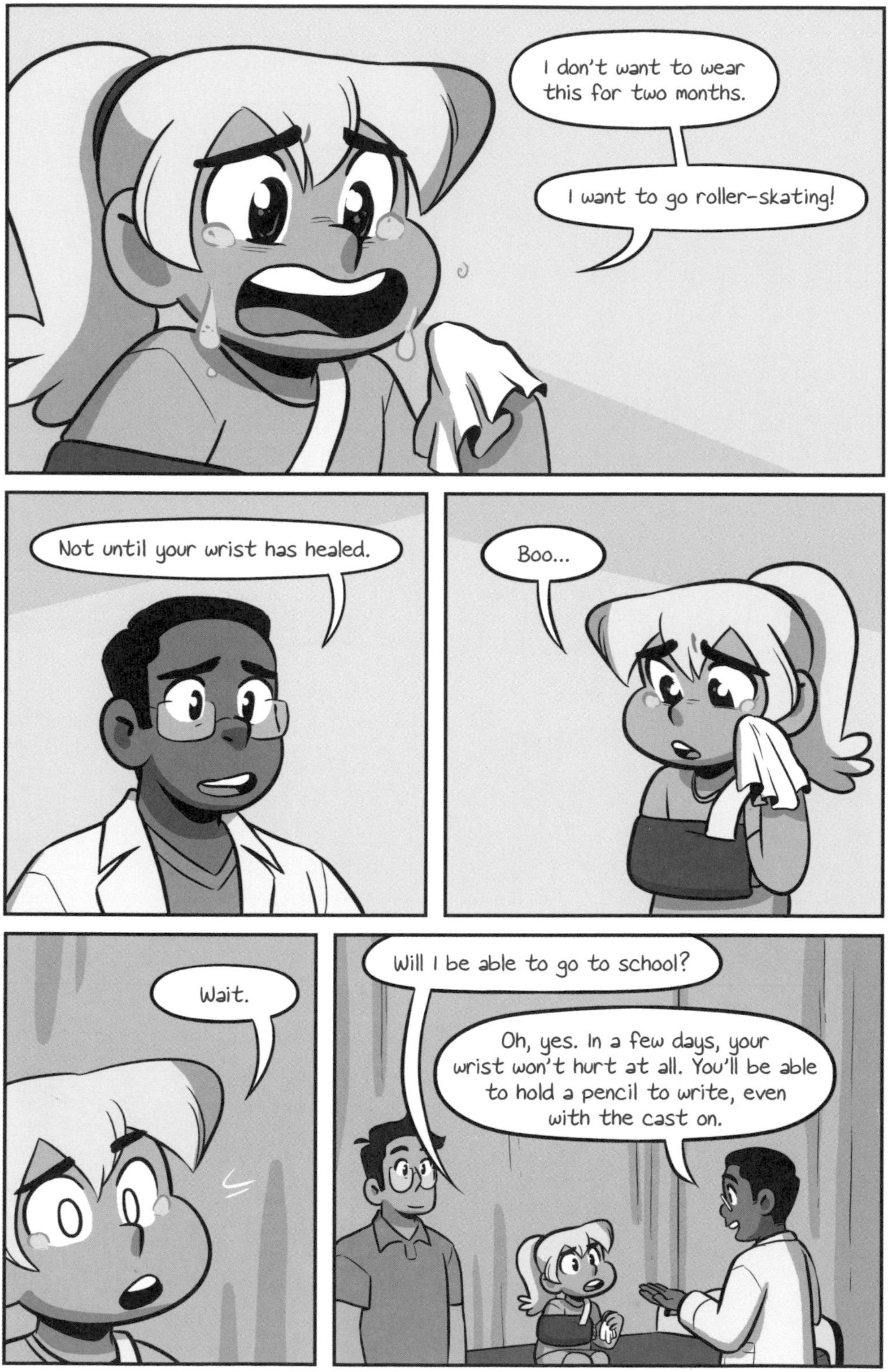
I don't want to wear this for two months.
I want to go roller-skating!
Not until your wrist has healed.
Boo...
Wait.
Will I be able to go to school?
Oh, yes. In a few days, your wrist won't hurt at all. You'll be able to hold a pencil to write, even with the cast on.

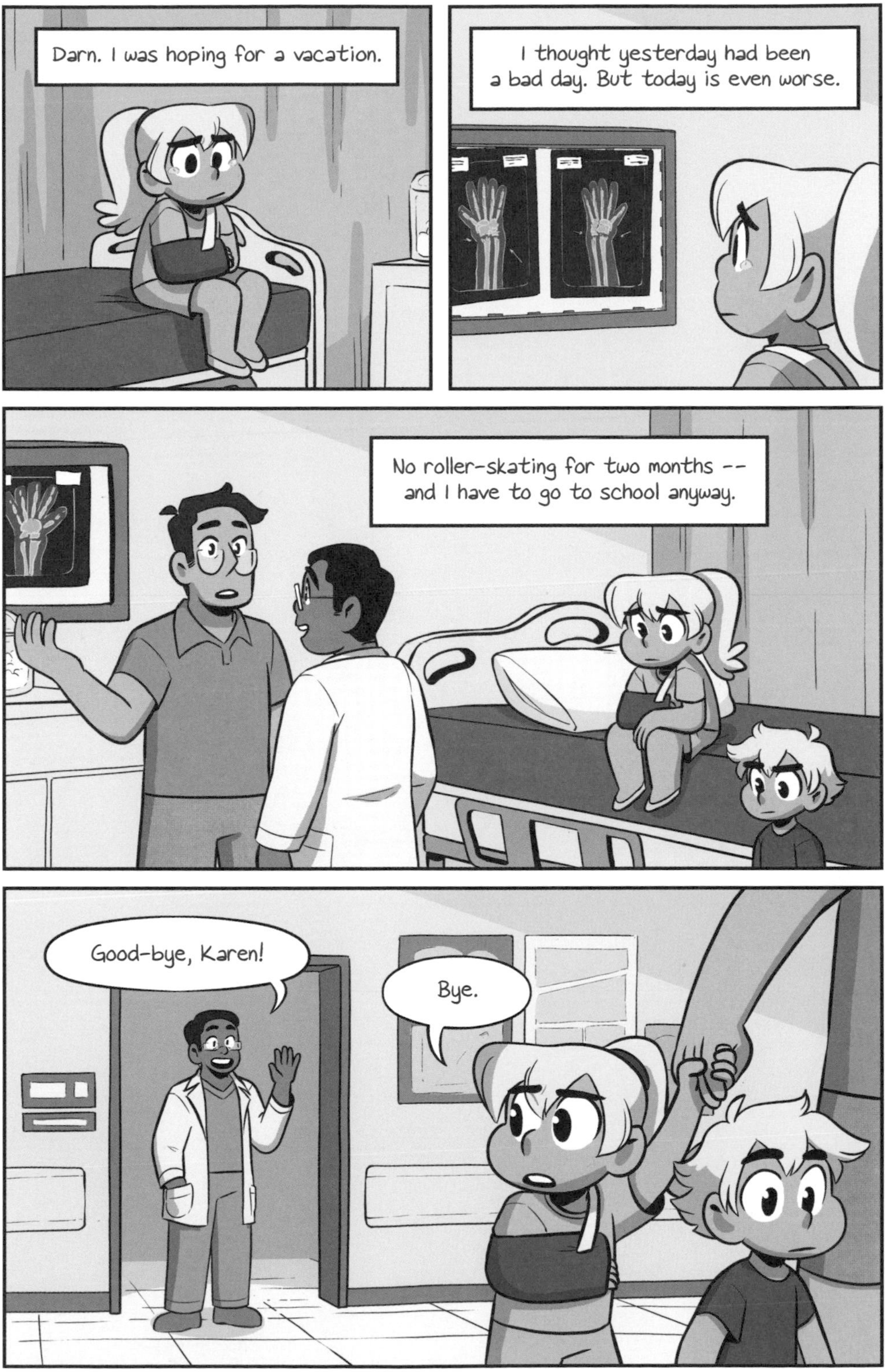
Darn. I was hoping for a vacation.
I thought yesterday had been a bad day. But today is even worse.
No roller-skating for two months -- and I have to go to school anyway.
Good-bye, Karen!
Bye.

CHAPTER 5

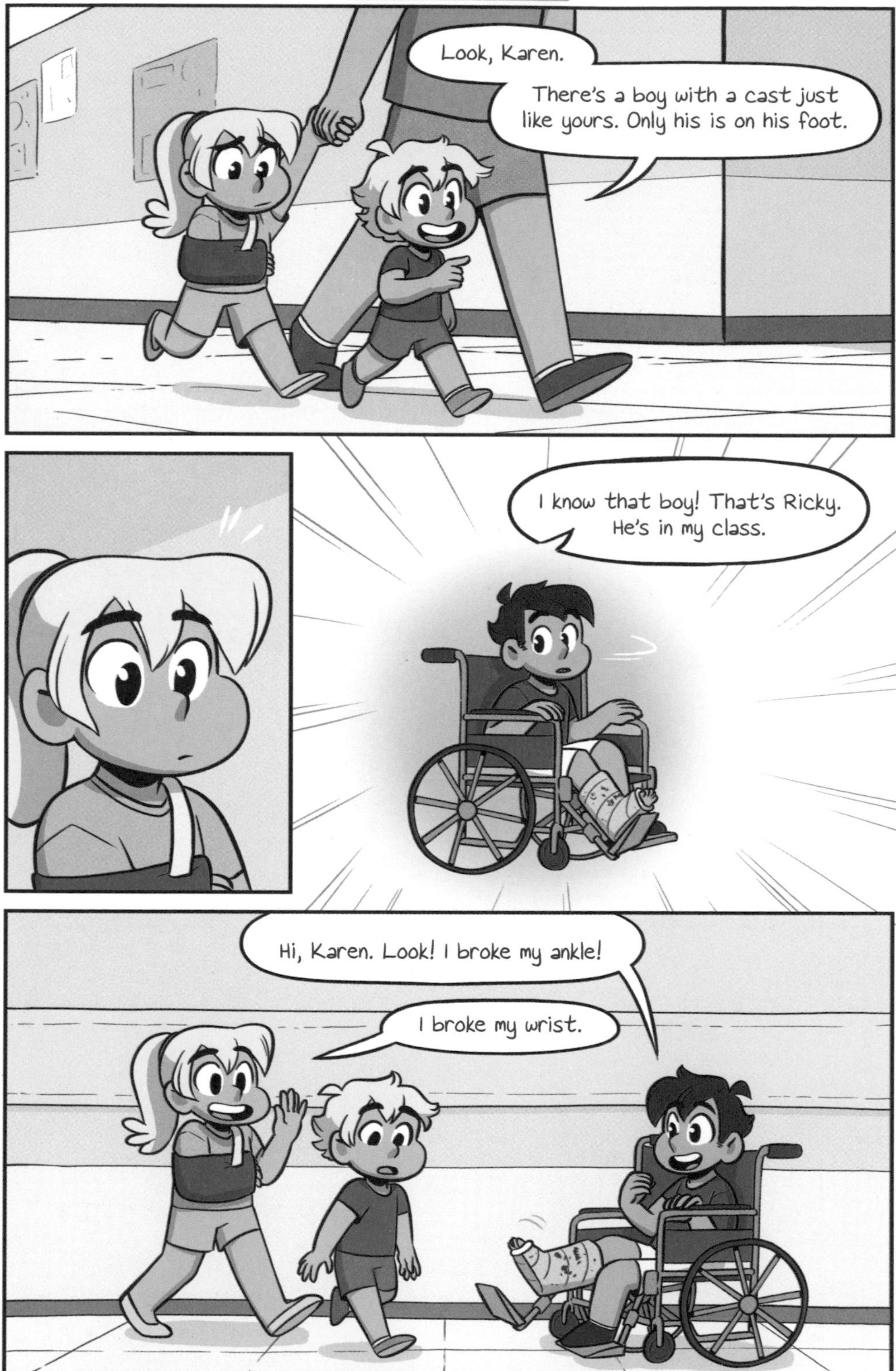
Look, Karen.
There's a boy with a cast just like yours. Only his is on his foot.
I know that boy! That's Ricky. He's in my class.
Hi, Karen. Look! I broke my ankle!
I broke my wrist.

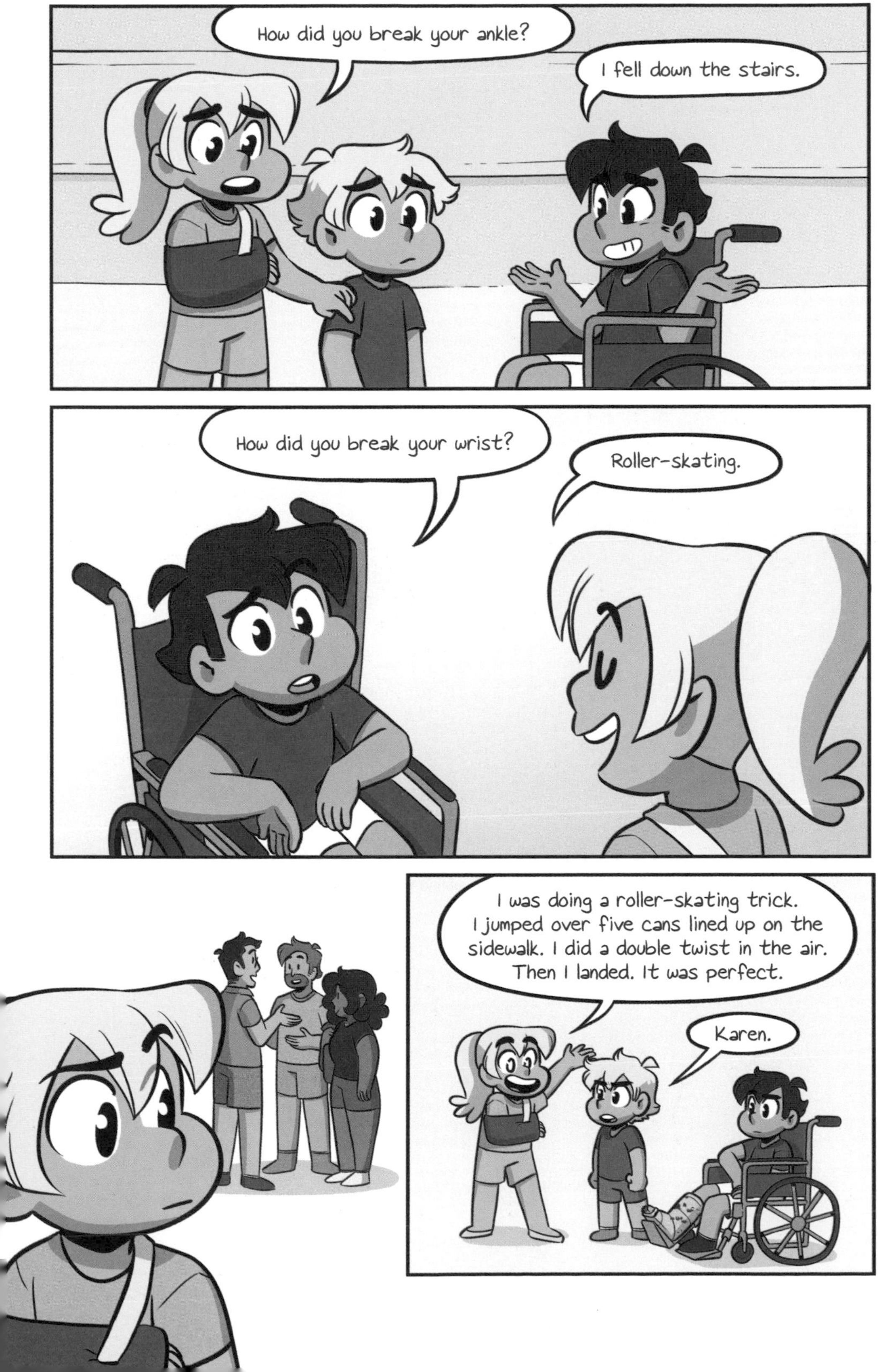
How did you break your ankle?
I fell down the stairs.
How did you break your wrist?
Roller-skating.
I was doing a roller-skating trick. I jumped over five cans lined up on the sidewalk. I did a double twist in the air. Then I landed. It was perfect.
Karen.

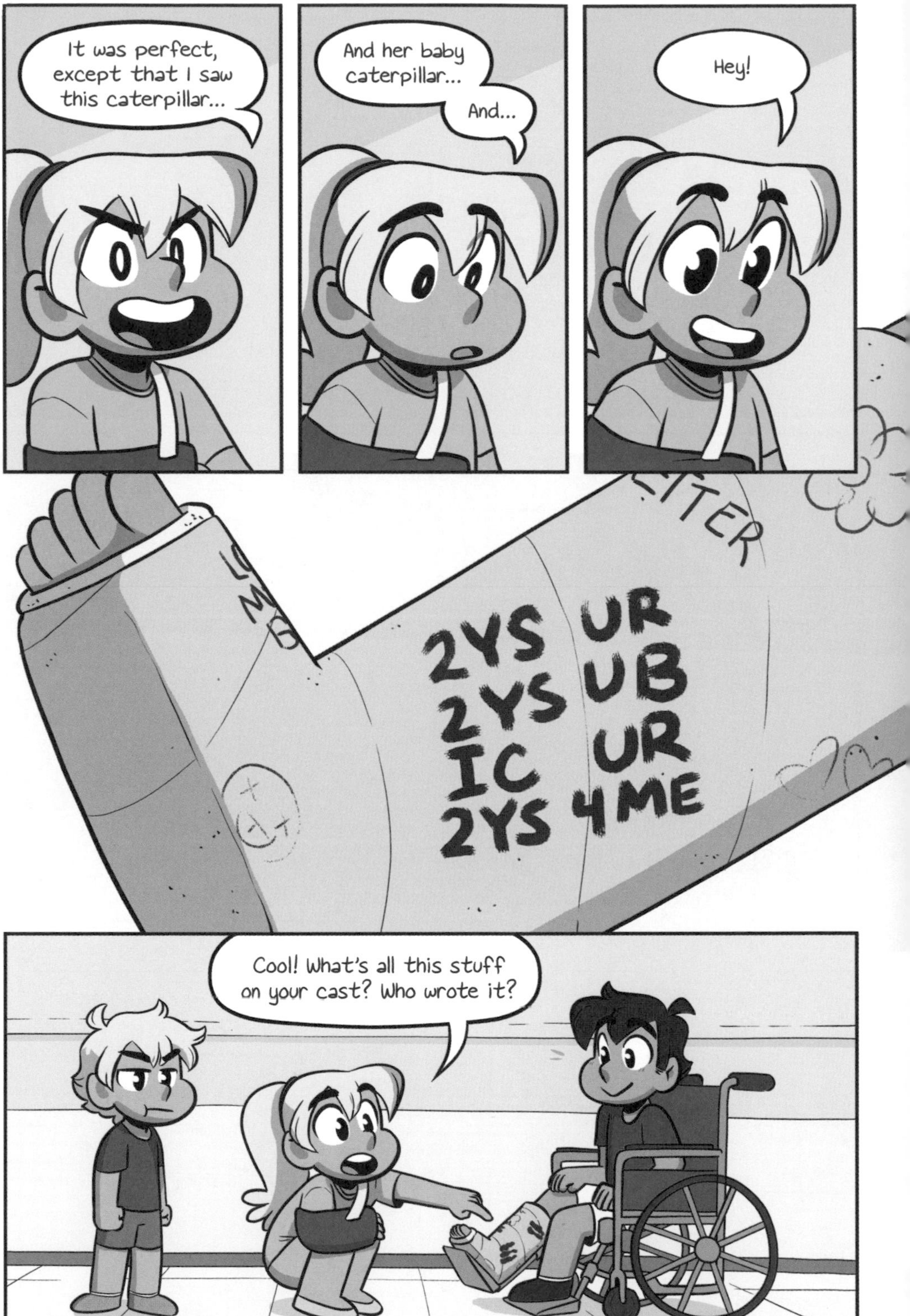
It was perfect, except that I saw this caterpillar...
And her baby caterpillar...
And...
Hey!
2YS UR
2YS UB
IC UR
2YS 4ME
Cool! What's all this stuff on your cast? Who wrote it?

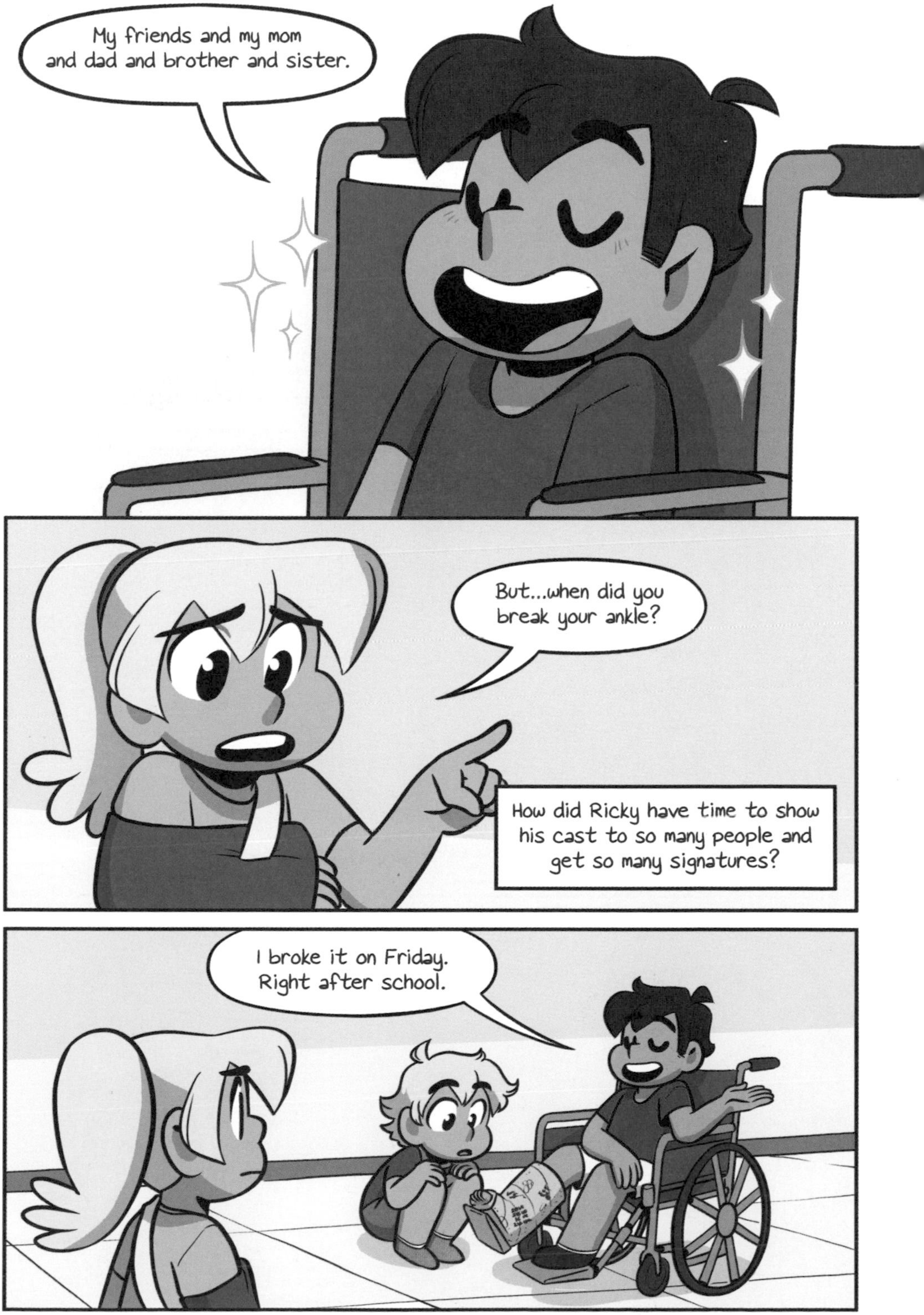
My friends and my mom and dad and brother and sister.
But...when did you break your ankle?
How did Ricky have time to show his cast to so many people and get so many signatures?
I broke it on Friday. Right after school.

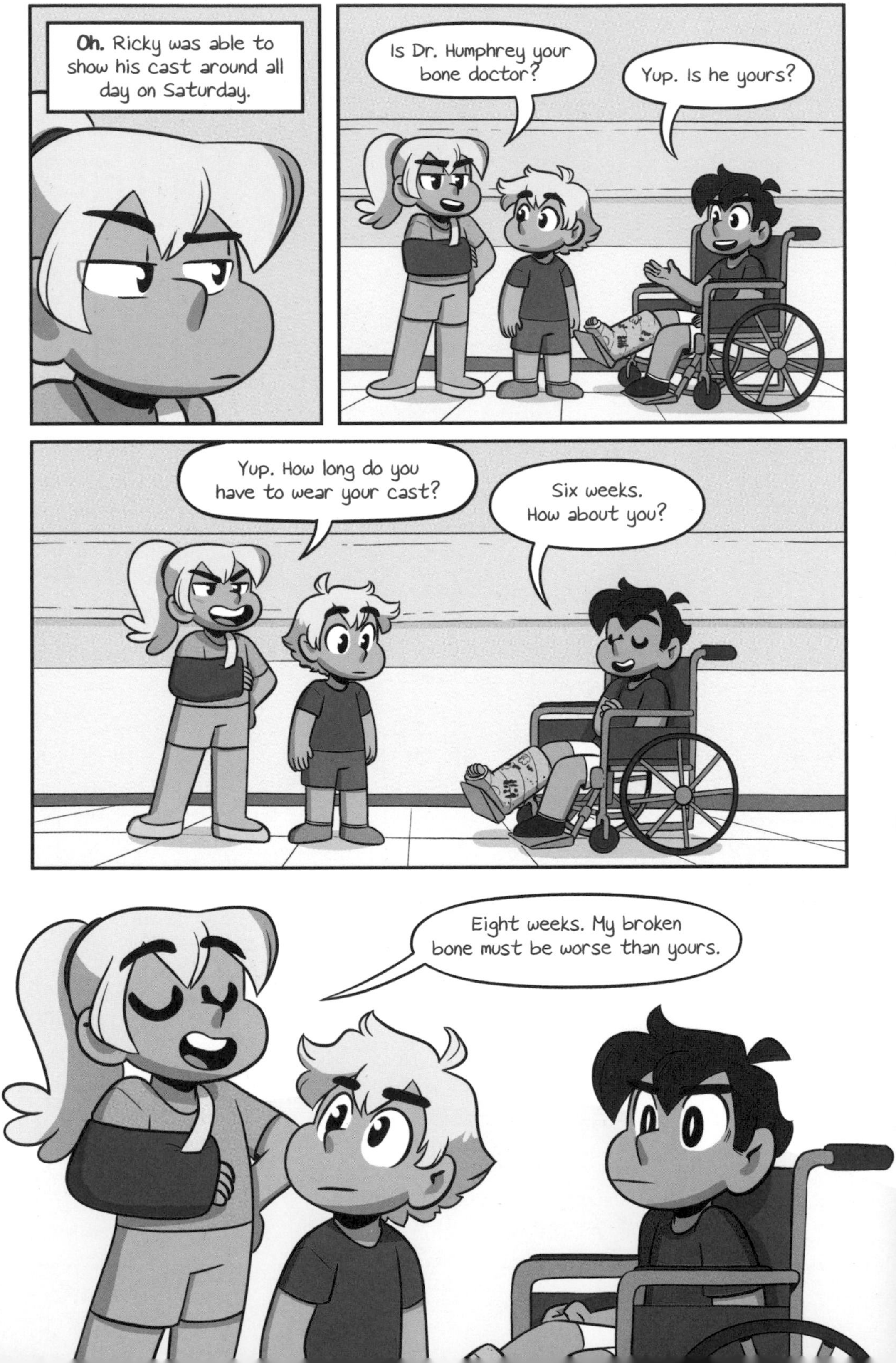
Oh. Ricky was able to show his cast around all day on Saturday.
Is Dr. Humphrey your bone doctor?
Yup. Is he yours?
Yup. How long do you have to wear your cast?
Six weeks. How about you?
Eight weeks. My broken bone must be worse than yours.

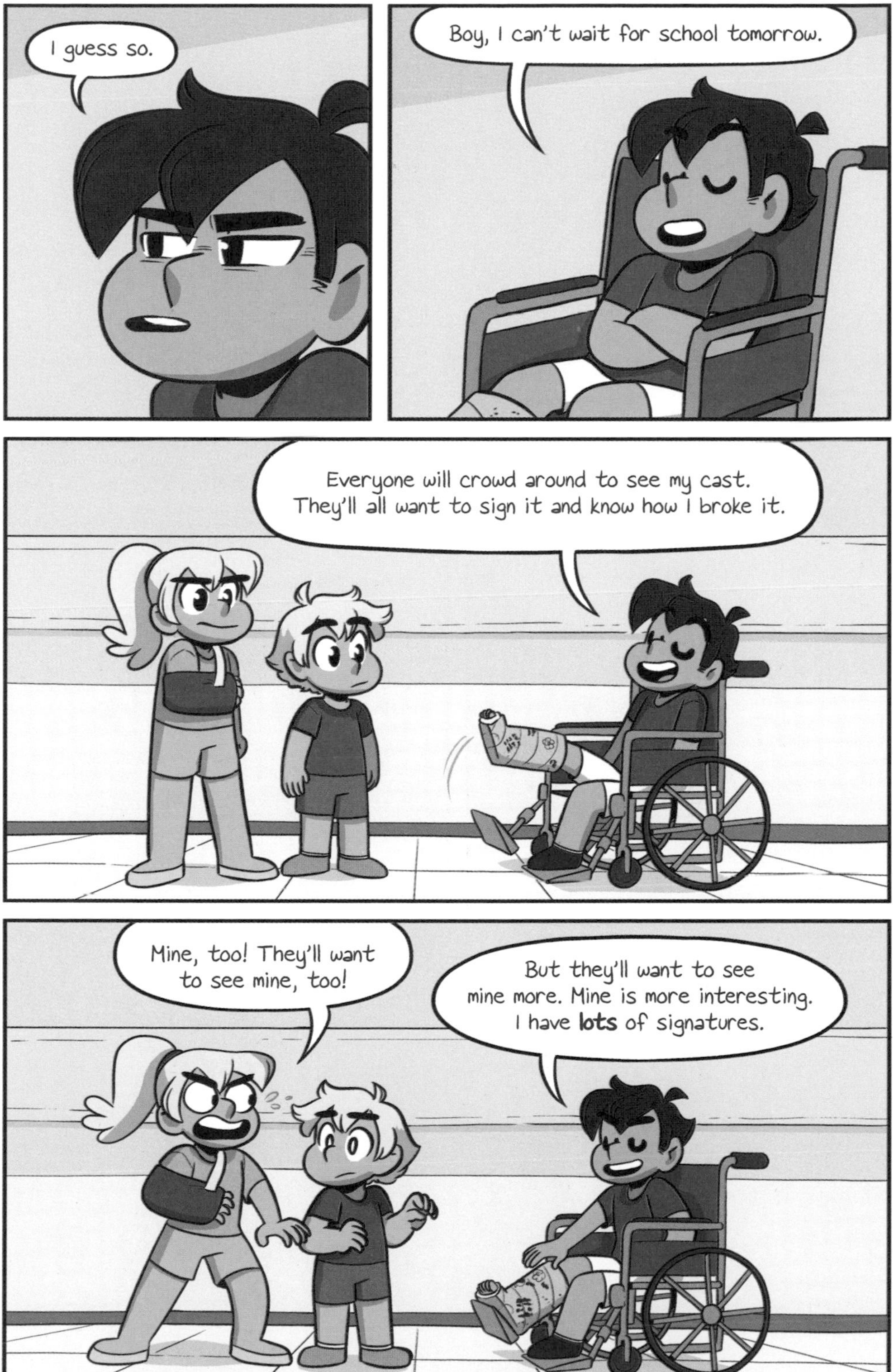
I guess so.
Boy, I can't wait for school tomorrow.
Everyone will crowd around to see my cast. They'll all want to sign it and know how I broke it.
Mine, too! They'll want to see mine, too!
But they'll want to see mine more. Mine is more interesting. I have **lots** of signatures.

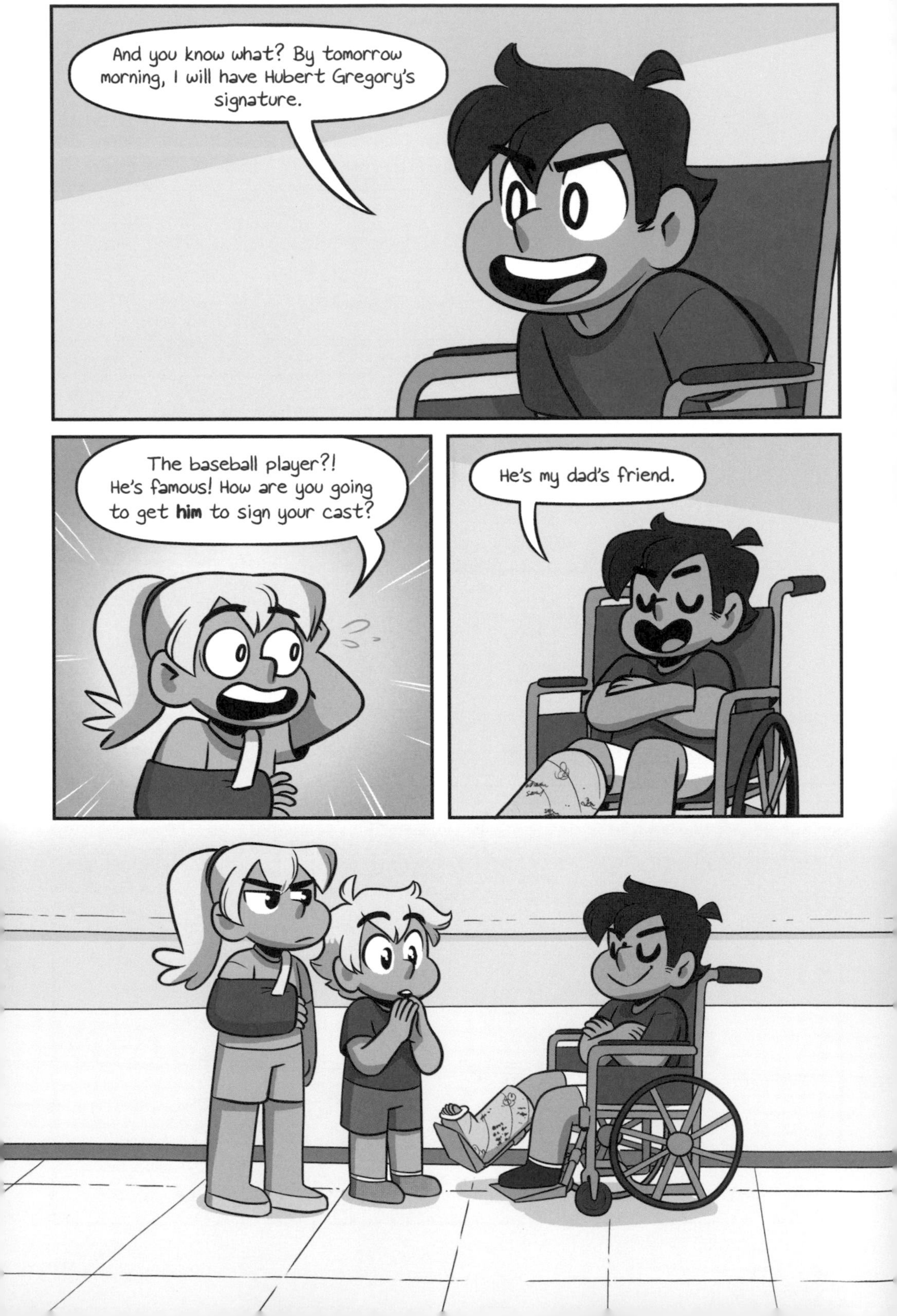
And you know what? By tomorrow morning, I will have Hubert Gregory's signature.
The baseball player?! He's famous! How are you going to get **him** to sign your cast?
He's my dad's friend.

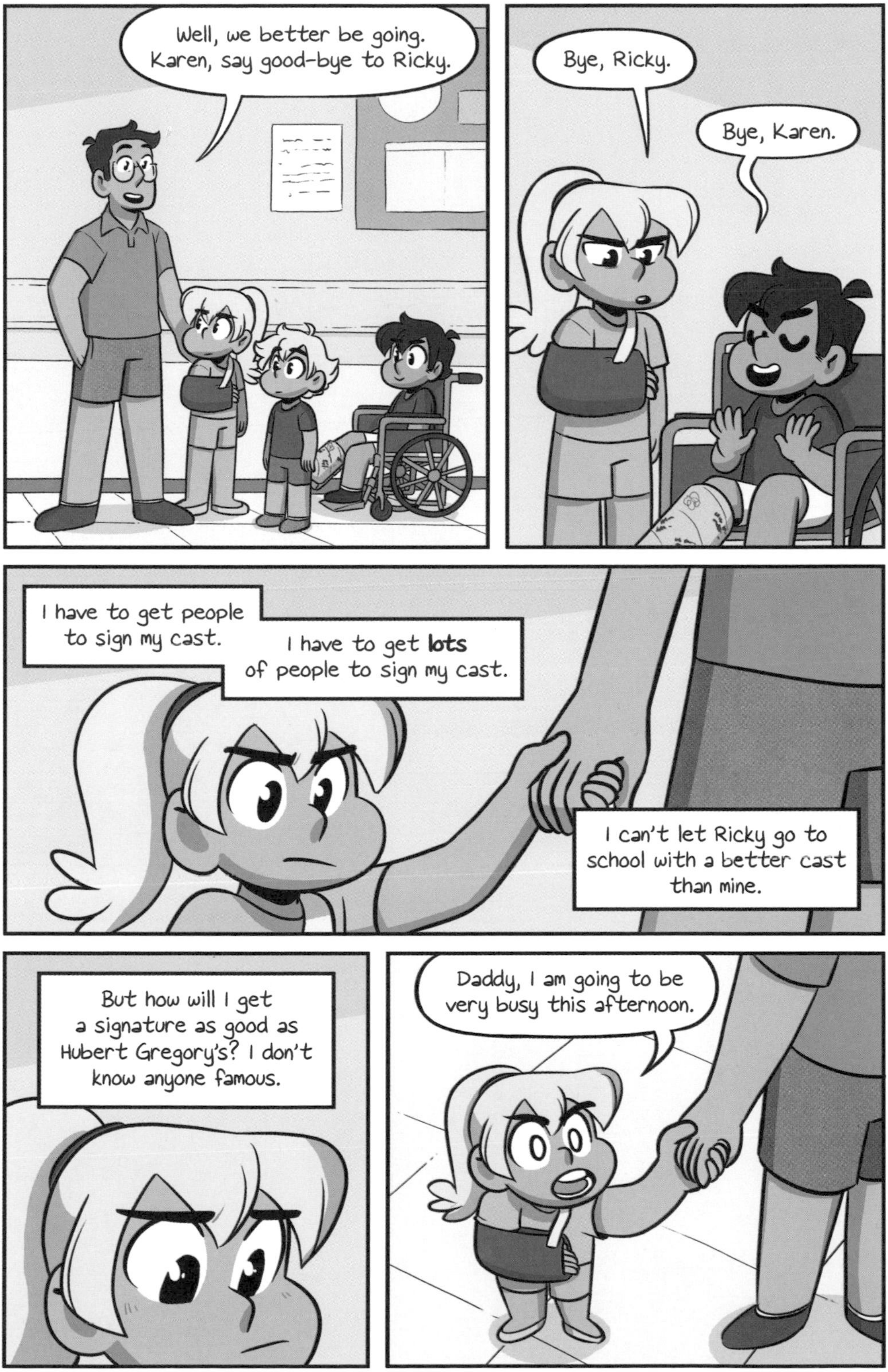

Well, we better be going. Karen, say good-bye to Ricky.
Bye, Ricky.
Bye, Karen.
I have to get people to sign my cast.
I have to get **lots** of people to sign my cast.
I can't let Ricky go to school with a better cast than mine.
But how will I get a signature as good as Hubert Gregory's? I don't know anyone famous.
Daddy, I am going to be very busy this afternoon.

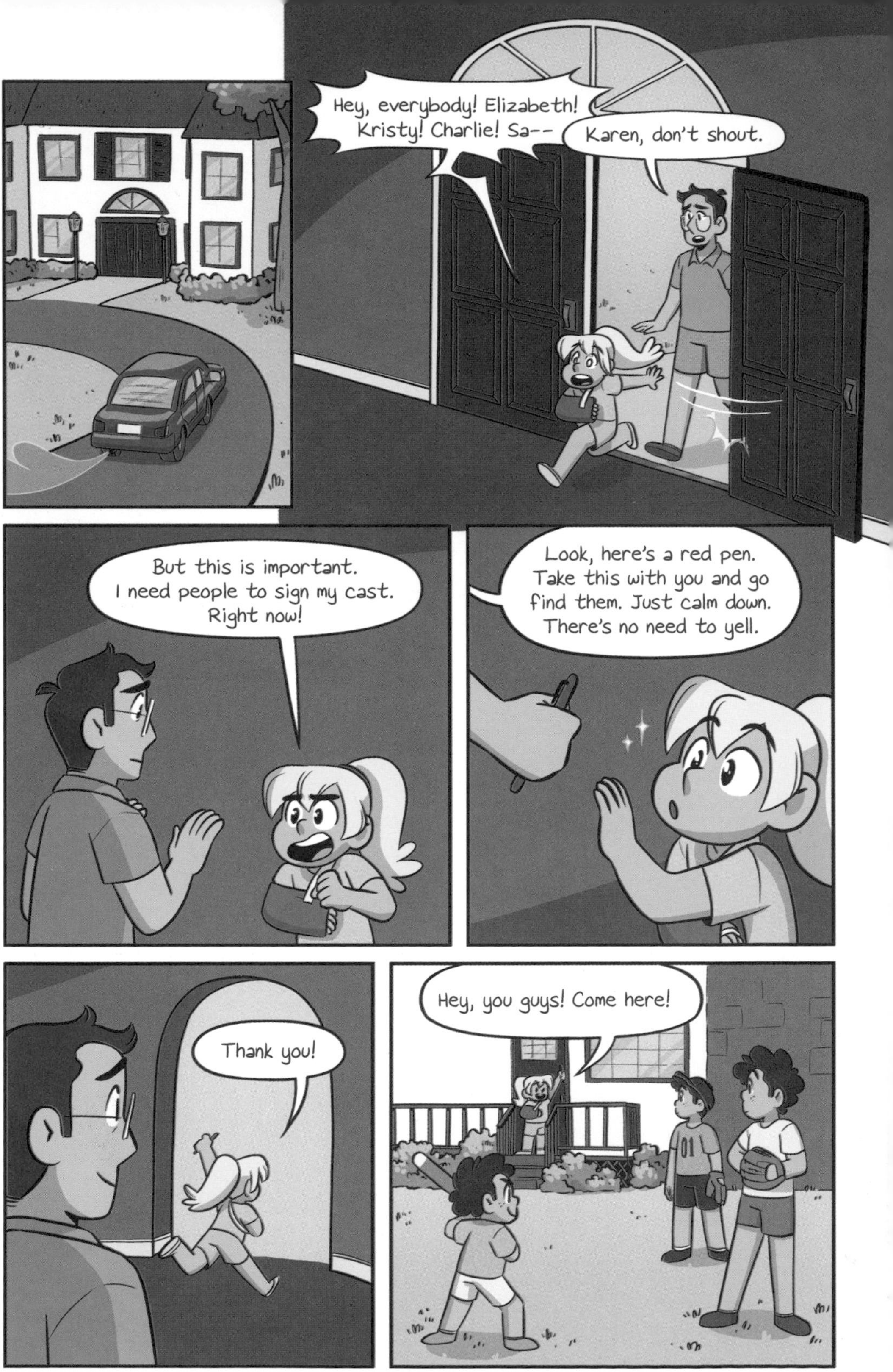
Hey, everybody! Elizabeth! Kristy! Charlie! Sa--
Karen, don't shout.
But this is important. I need people to sign my cast. Right now!
Look, here's a red pen. Take this with you and go find them. Just calm down. There's no need to yell.
Thank you!
Hey, you guys! Come here!

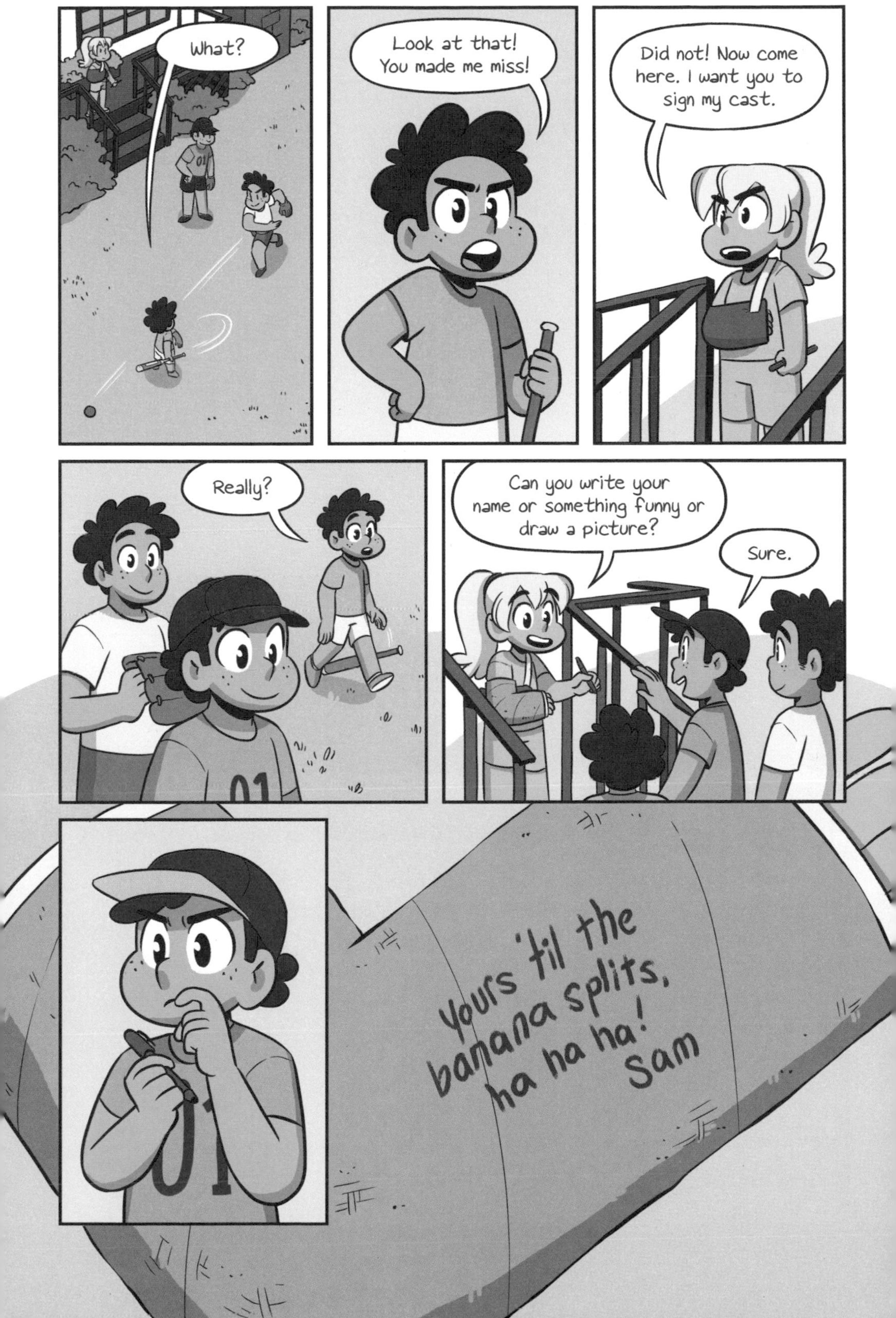
What?
Look at that! You made me miss!
Did not! Now come here. I want you to sign my cast.
Really?
Can you write your name or something funny or draw a picture?
Sure.
Yours 'til the banana splits, ha ha ha! Sam

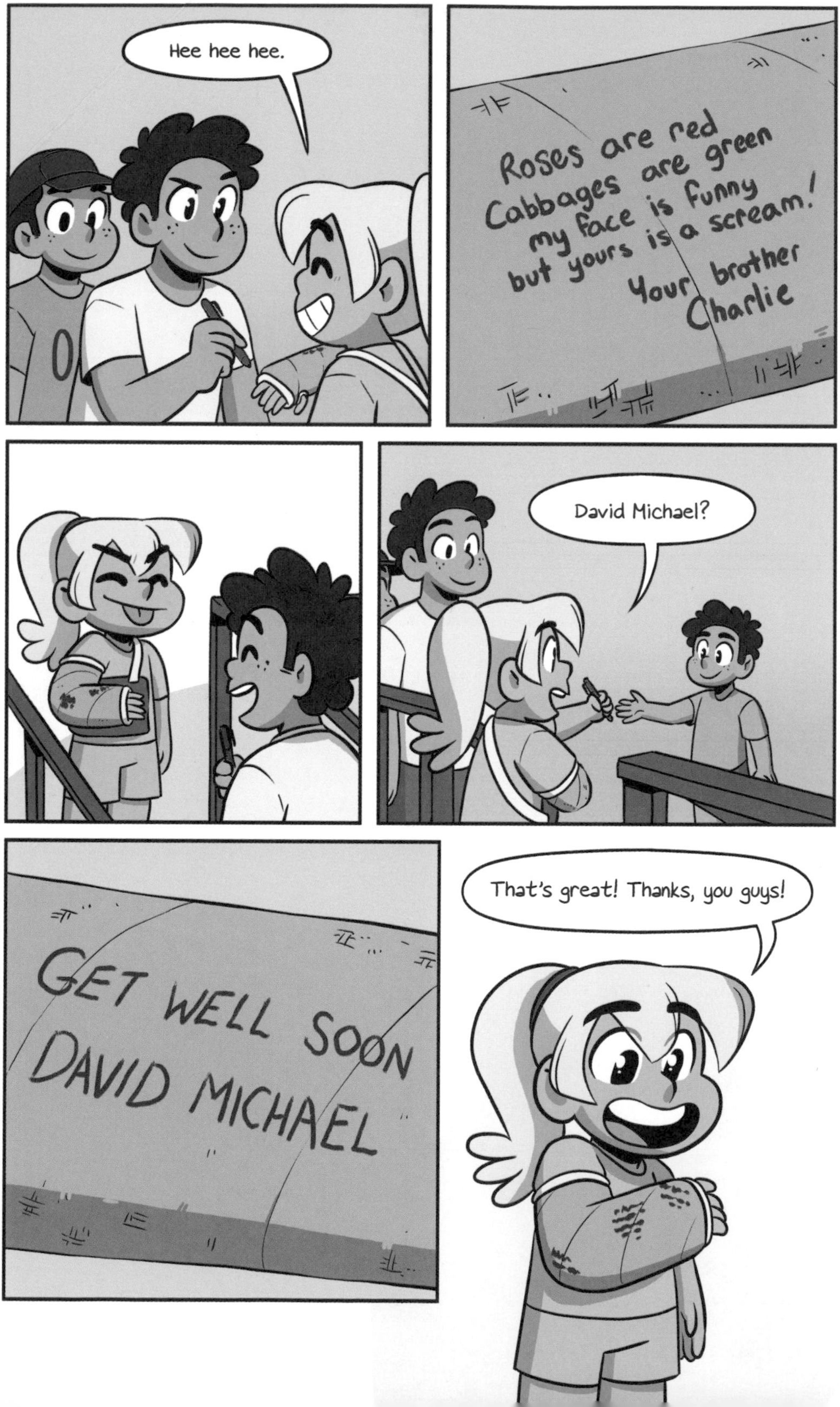
Hee hee hee.
Roses are red
Cabbages are green
my face is funny
but yours is a scream!
Your brother
Charlie
David Michael?
GET WELL SOON
DAVID MICHAEL
That's great! Thanks, you guys!

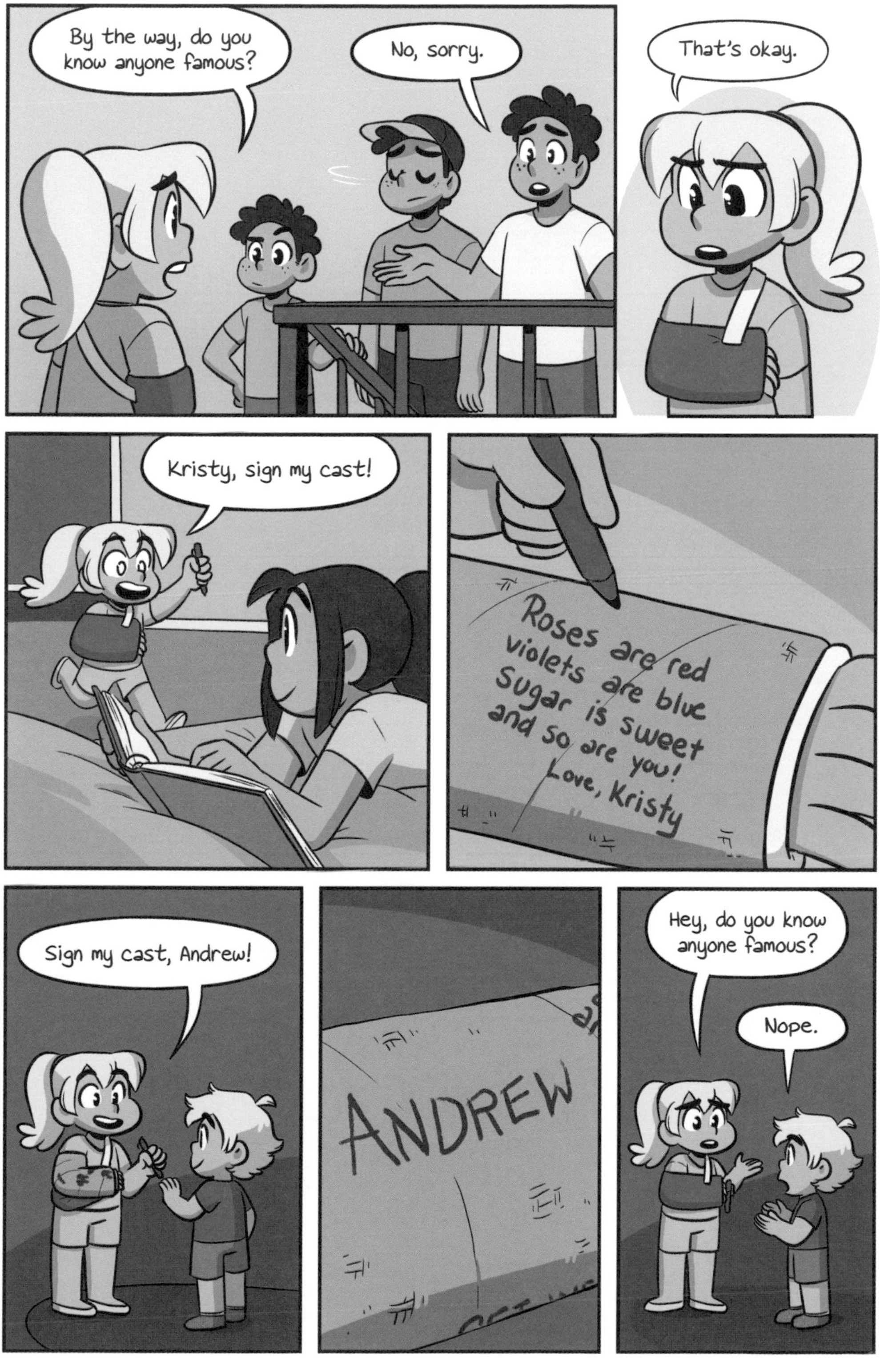
By the way, do you know anyone famous?
No, sorry.
That's okay.
Kristy, sign my cast!
Roses are red violets are blue Sugar is sweet and so are you! Love, Kristy
Sign my cast, Andrew!
ANDREW
Hey, do you know anyone famous?
Nope.

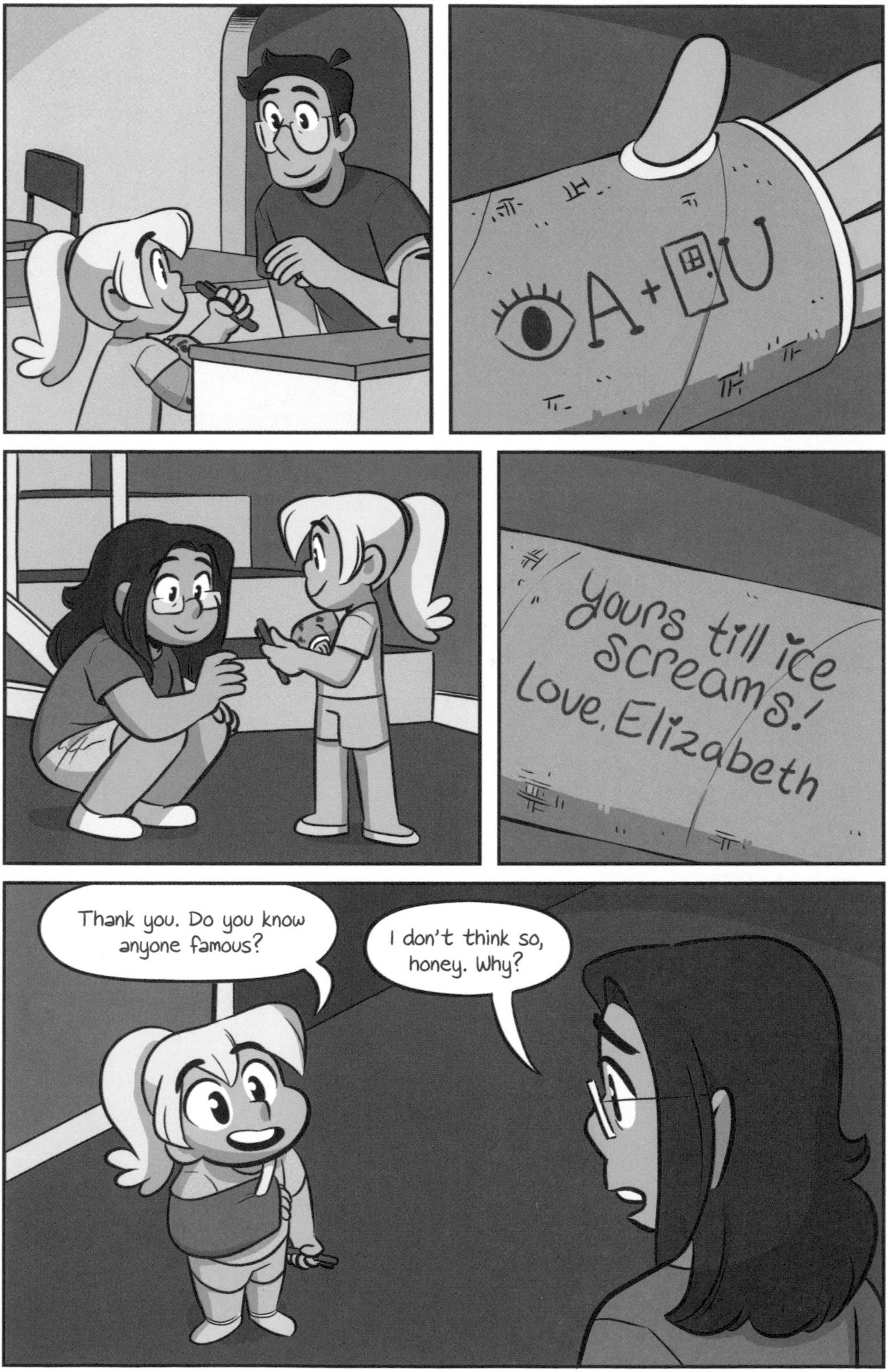
A + U
Yours till ice screams!
Love, Elizabeth
Thank you. Do you know anyone famous?
I don't think so, honey. Why?

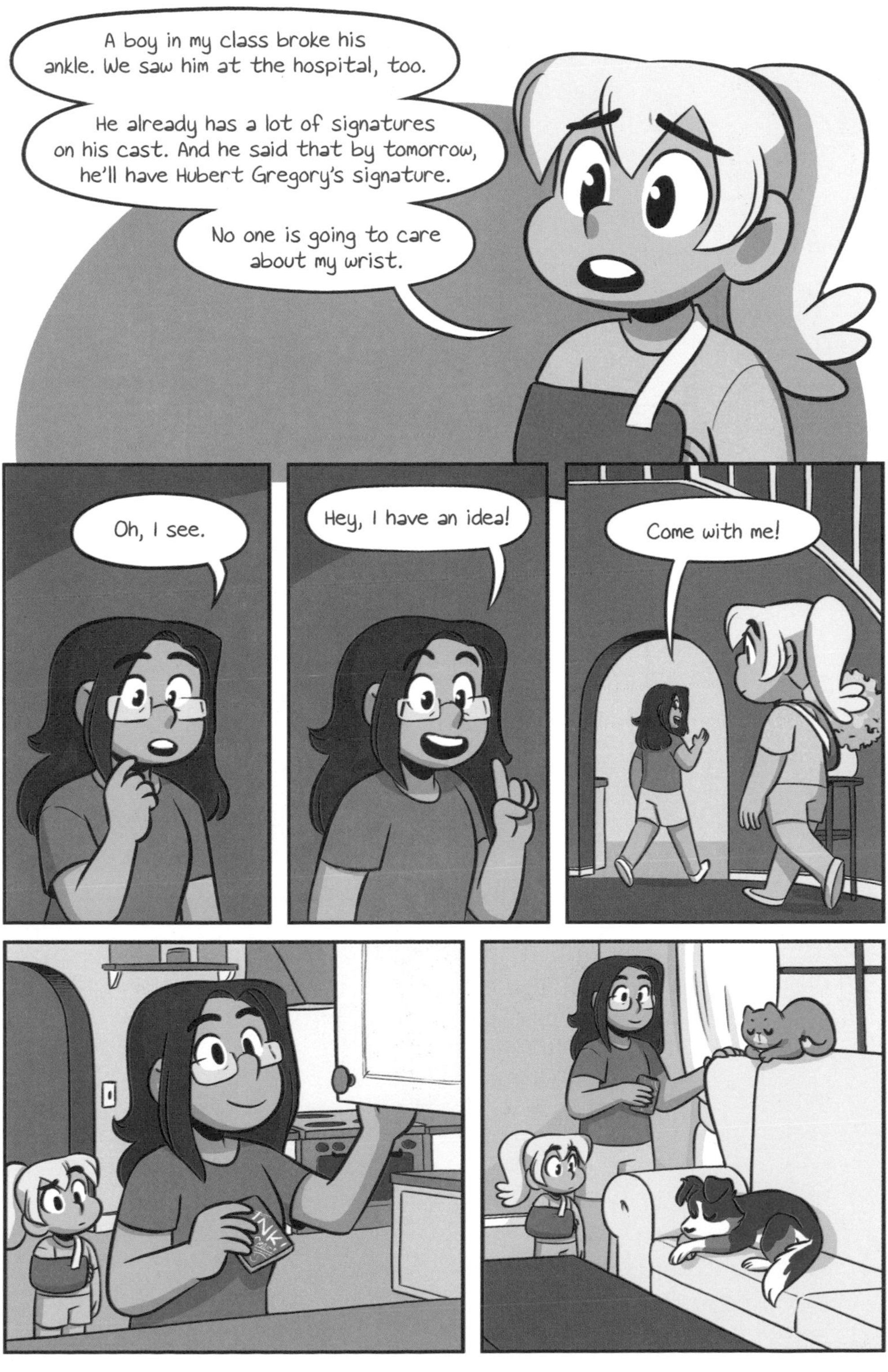
A boy in my class broke his ankle. We saw him at the hospital, too.
He already has a lot of signatures on his cast. And he said that by tomorrow, he'll have Hubert Gregory's signature.
No one is going to care about my wrist.
Oh, I see.
Hey, I have an idea!
Come with me!
INK

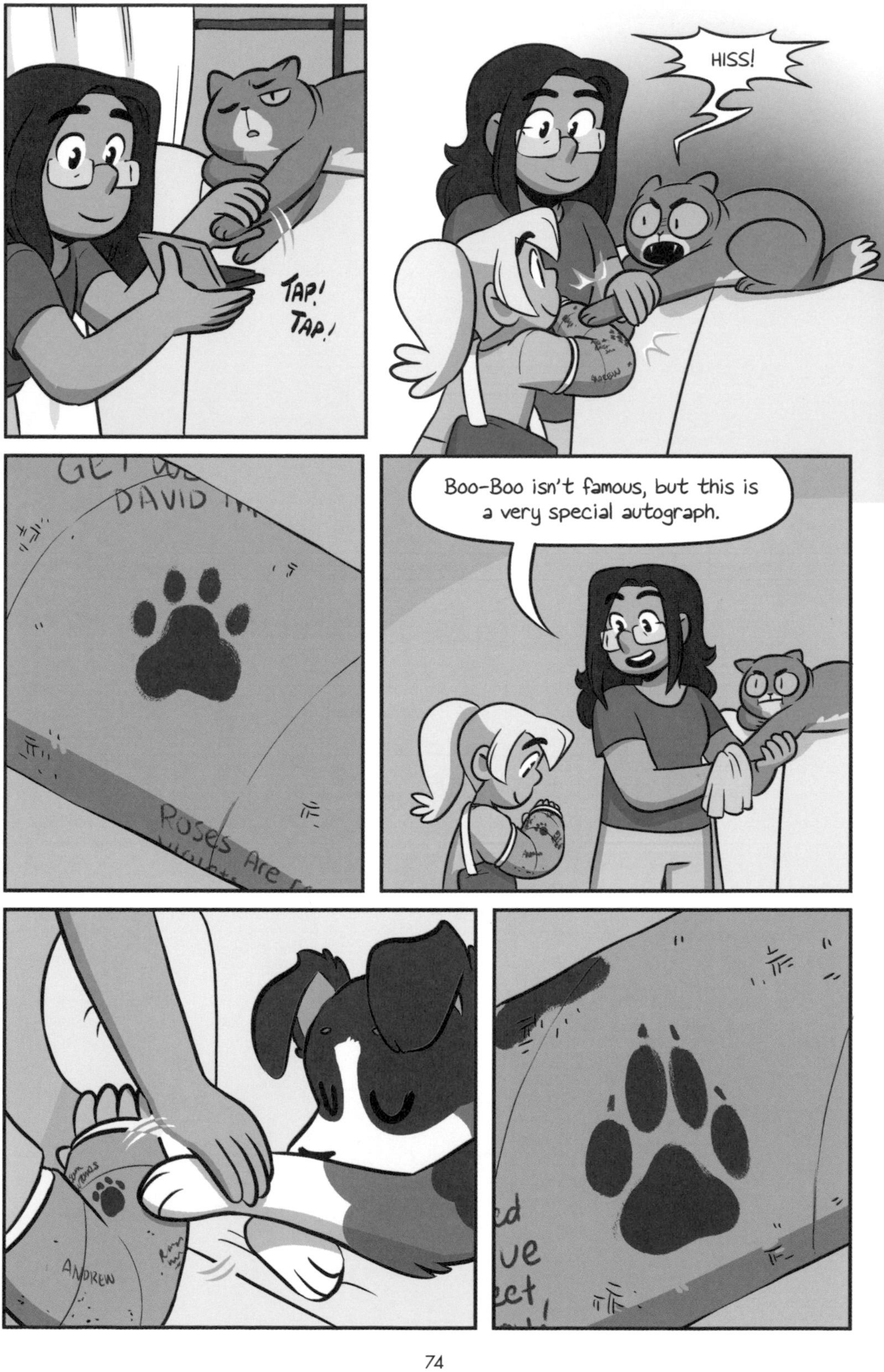

TAP! TAP!
HISS!
Boo-Boo isn't famous, but this is a very special autograph.

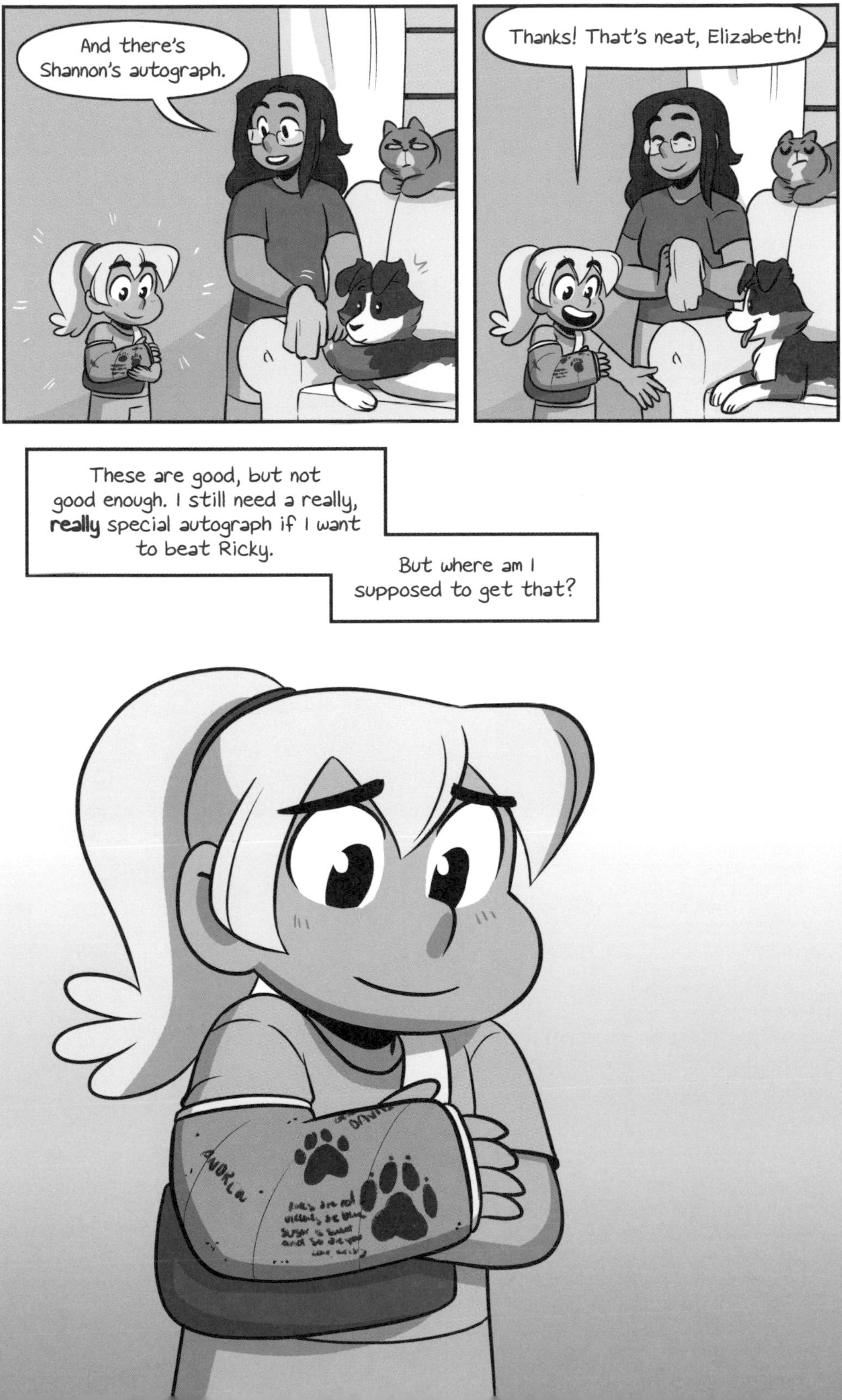
And there's Shannon's autograph.
Thanks! That's neat, Elizabeth!
These are good, but not good enough. I still need a really, **really** special autograph if I want to beat Ricky.
But where am I supposed to get that?

CHAPTER 6

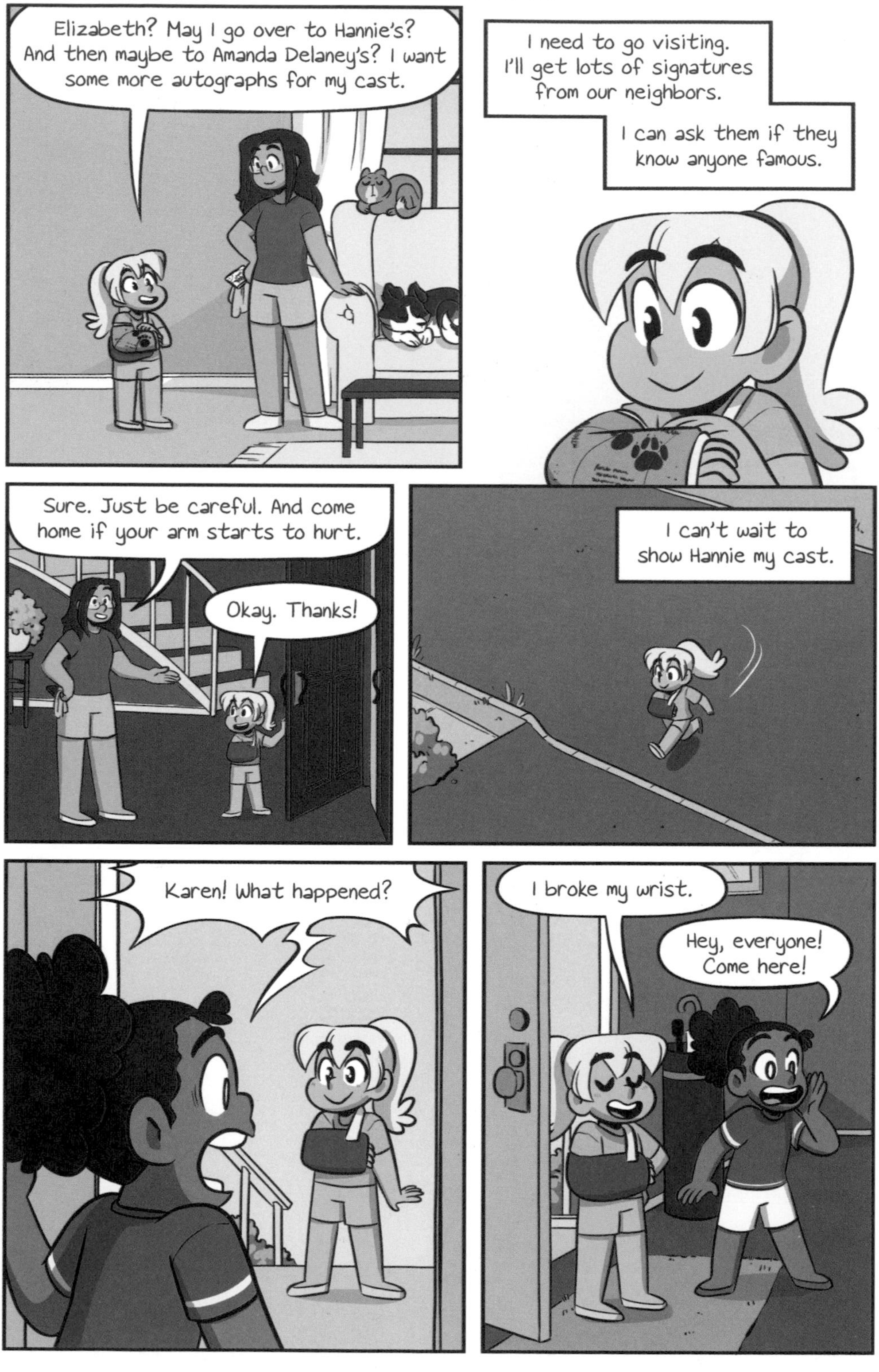

Elizabeth? May I go over to Hannie's? And then maybe to Amanda Delaney's? I want some more autographs for my cast.
I need to go visiting. I'll get lots of signatures from our neighbors.
I can ask them if they know anyone famous.
Sure. Just be careful. And come home if your arm starts to hurt.
Okay. Thanks!
I can't wait to show Hannie my cast.
Karen! What happened?
I broke my wrist.
Hey, everyone! Come here!

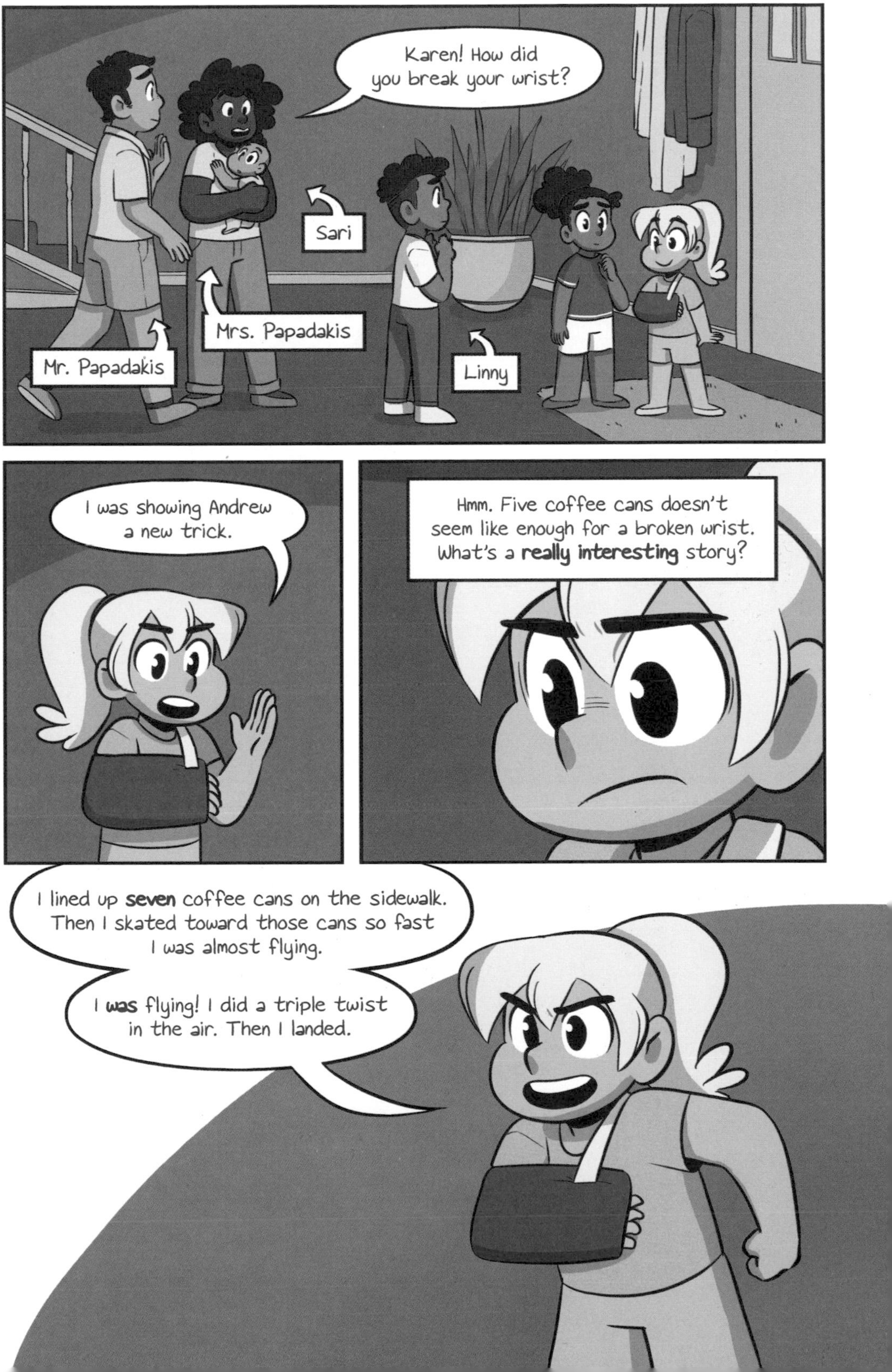

Karen! How did you break your wrist?
Sari
Mrs. Papadakis
Mr. Papadakis
Linny
I was showing Andrew a new trick.
Hmm. Five coffee cans doesn't seem like enough for a broken wrist. What's a **really interesting** story?
I lined up **seven** coffee cans on the sidewalk. Then I skated toward those cans so fast I was almost flying.
I **was** flying! I did a triple twist in the air. Then I landed.

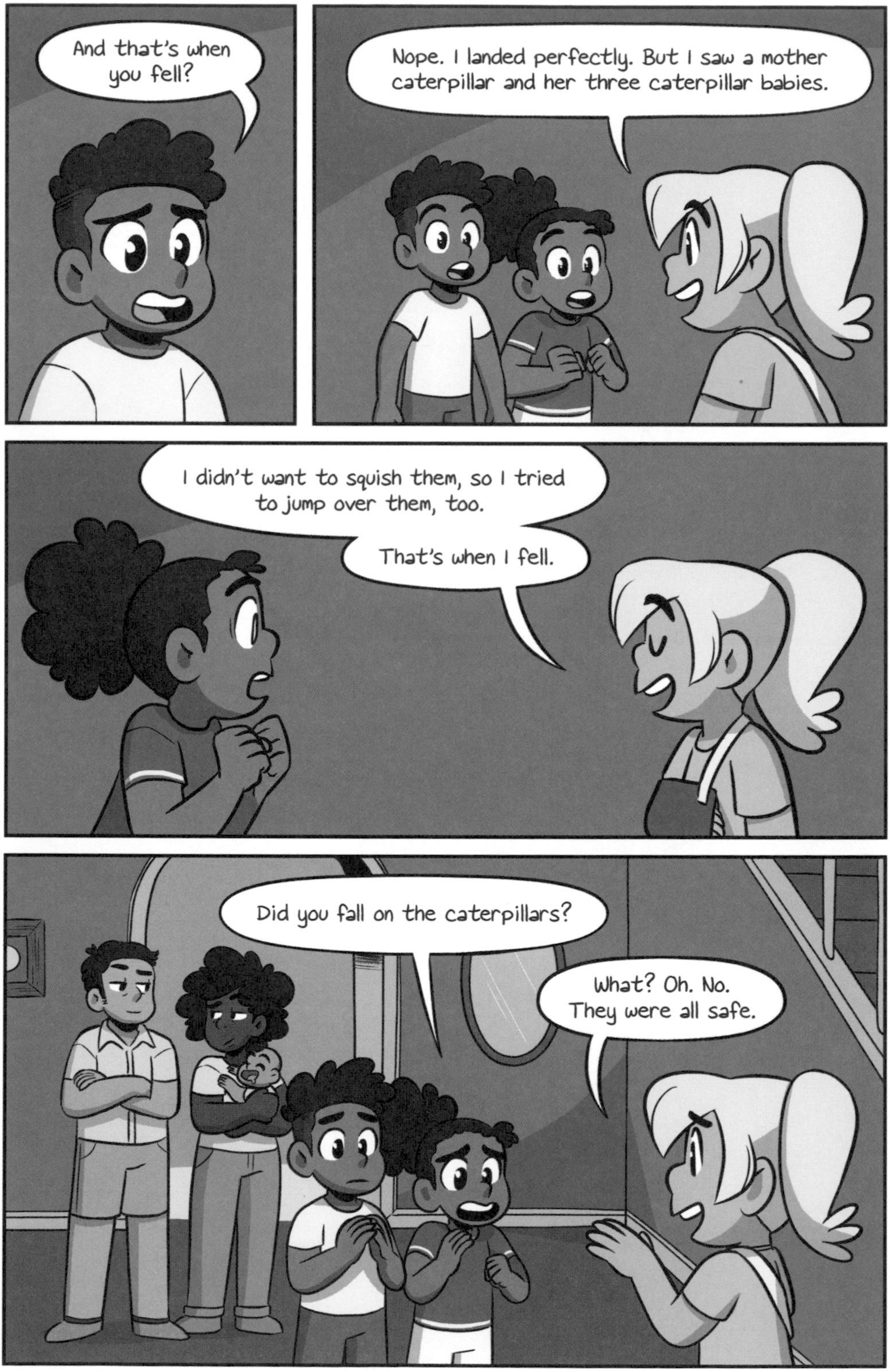
And that's when you fell?
Nope. I landed perfectly. But I saw a mother caterpillar and her three caterpillar babies.
I didn't want to squish them, so I tried to jump over them, too.
That's when I fell.
Did you fall on the caterpillars?
What? Oh. No. They were all safe.

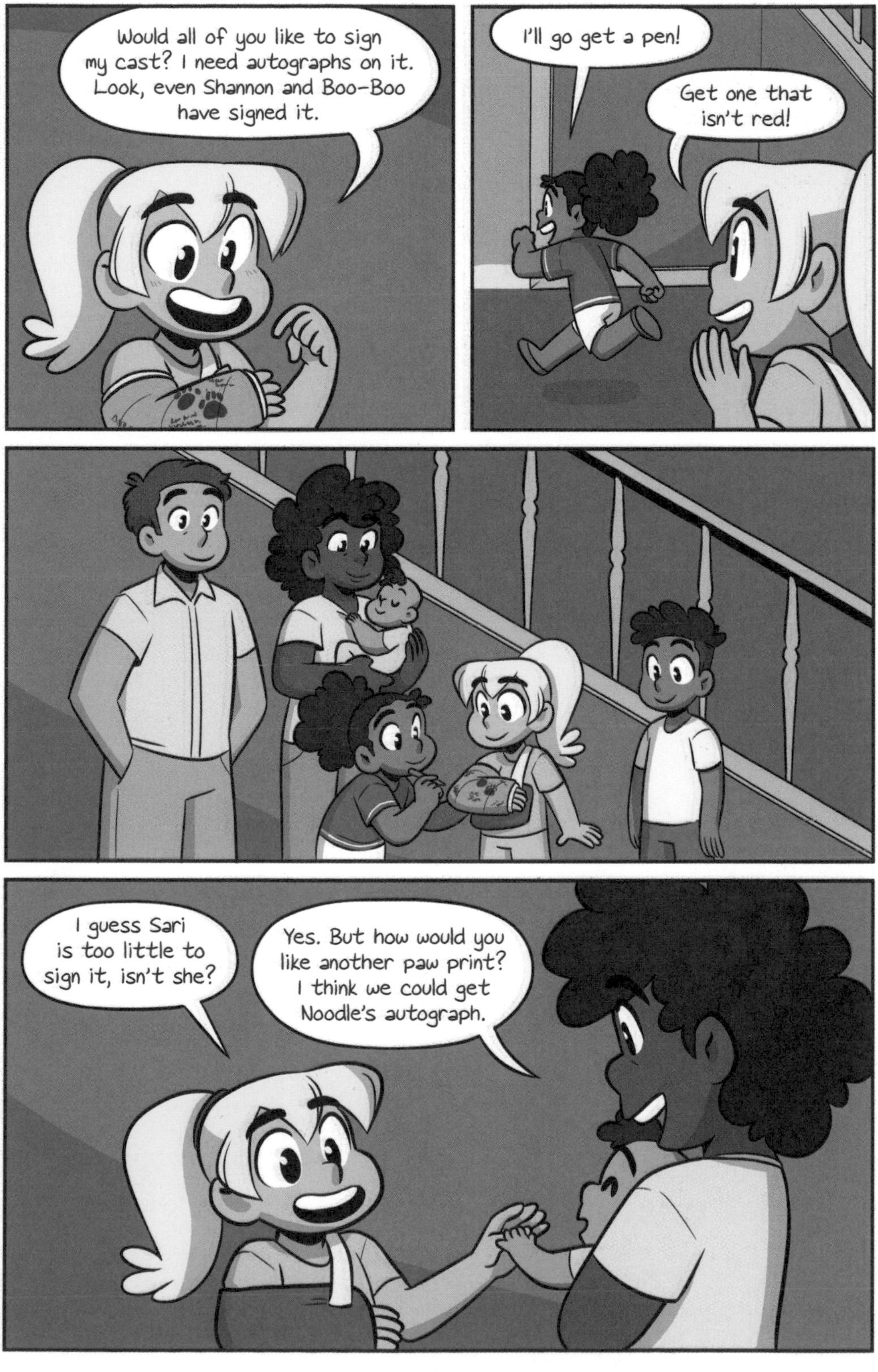
Would all of you like to sign my cast? I need autographs on it. Look, even Shannon and Boo-Boo have signed it.
I'll go get a pen!
Get one that isn't red!
I guess Sari is too little to sign it, isn't she?
Yes. But how would you like another paw print? I think we could get Noodle's autograph.

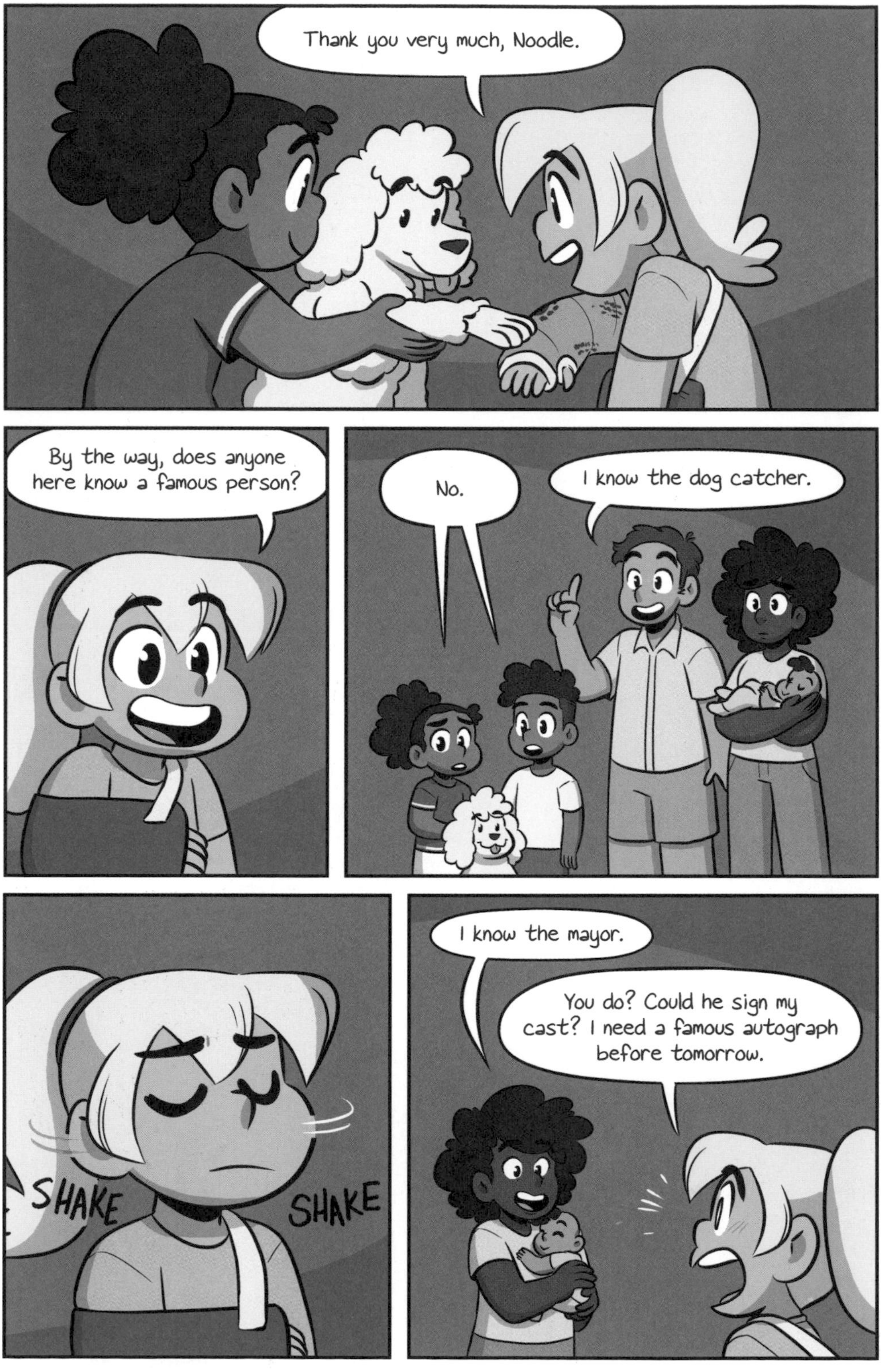
Thank you very much, Noodle.
By the way, does anyone here know a famous person?
No.
I know the dog catcher.
SHAKE
SHAKE
I know the mayor.
You do? Could he sign my cast? I need a famous autograph before tomorrow.

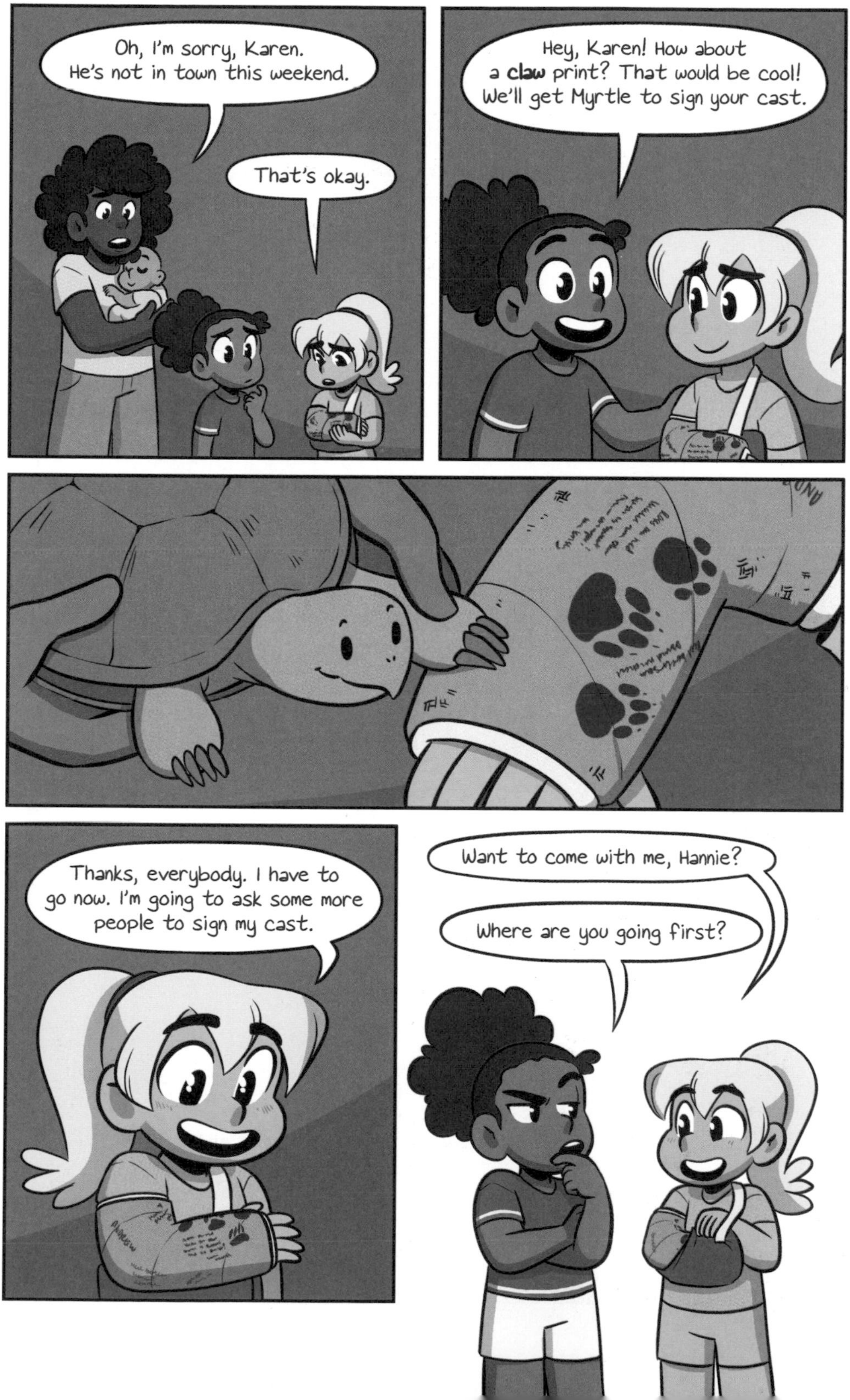
Oh, I'm sorry, Karen. He's not in town this weekend.
That's okay.
Hey, Karen! How about a **claw** print? That would be cool! We'll get Myrtle to sign your cast.
Thanks, everybody. I have to go now. I'm going to ask some more people to sign my cast.
Want to come with me, Hannie?
Where are you going first?

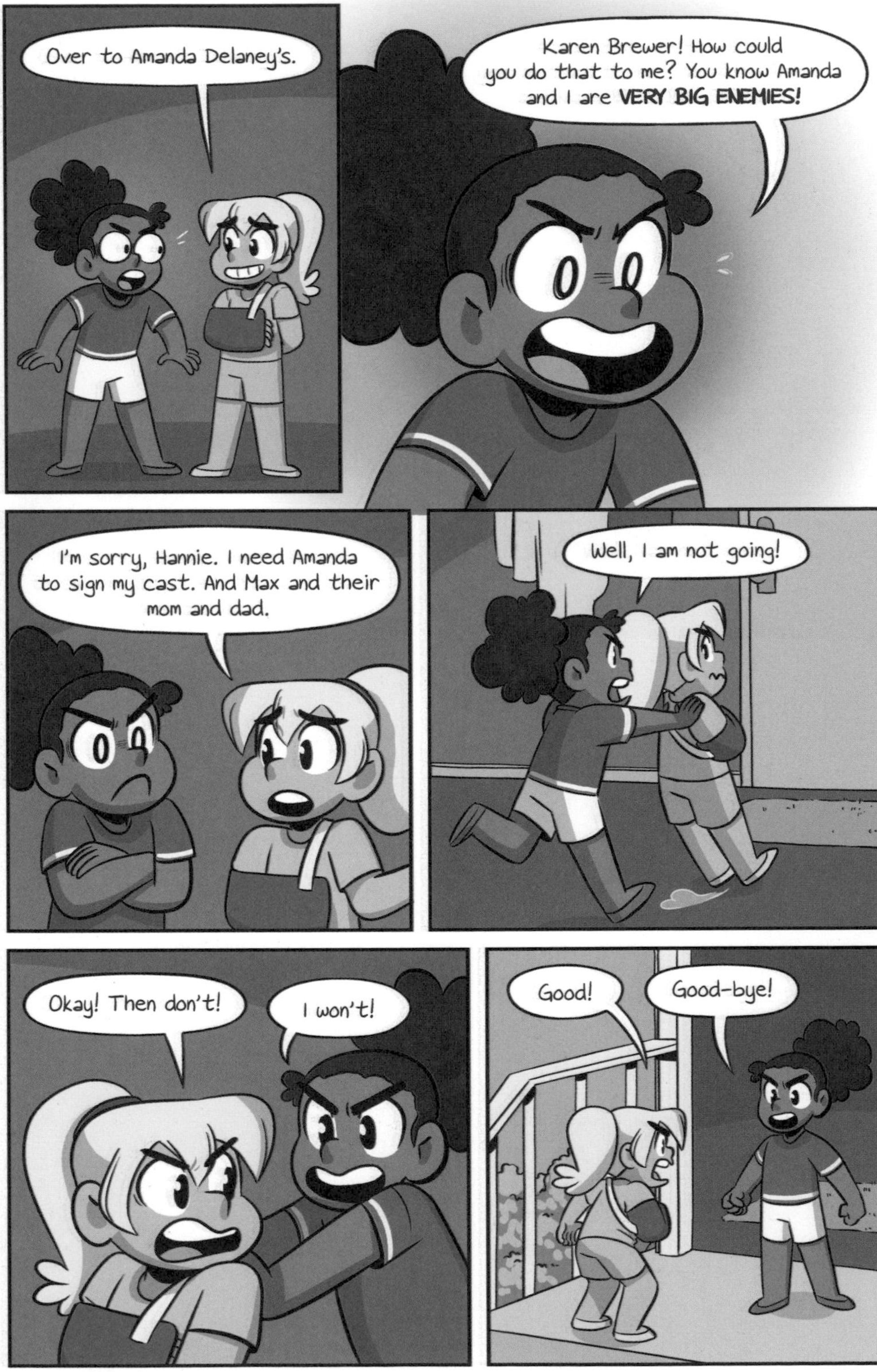
Over to Amanda Delaney's.
Karen Brewer! How could you do that to me? You know Amanda and I are **VERY BIG ENEMIES!**
I'm sorry, Hannie. I need Amanda to sign my cast. And Max and their mom and dad.
Well, I am not going!
Okay! Then don't!
I won't!
Good!
Good-bye!

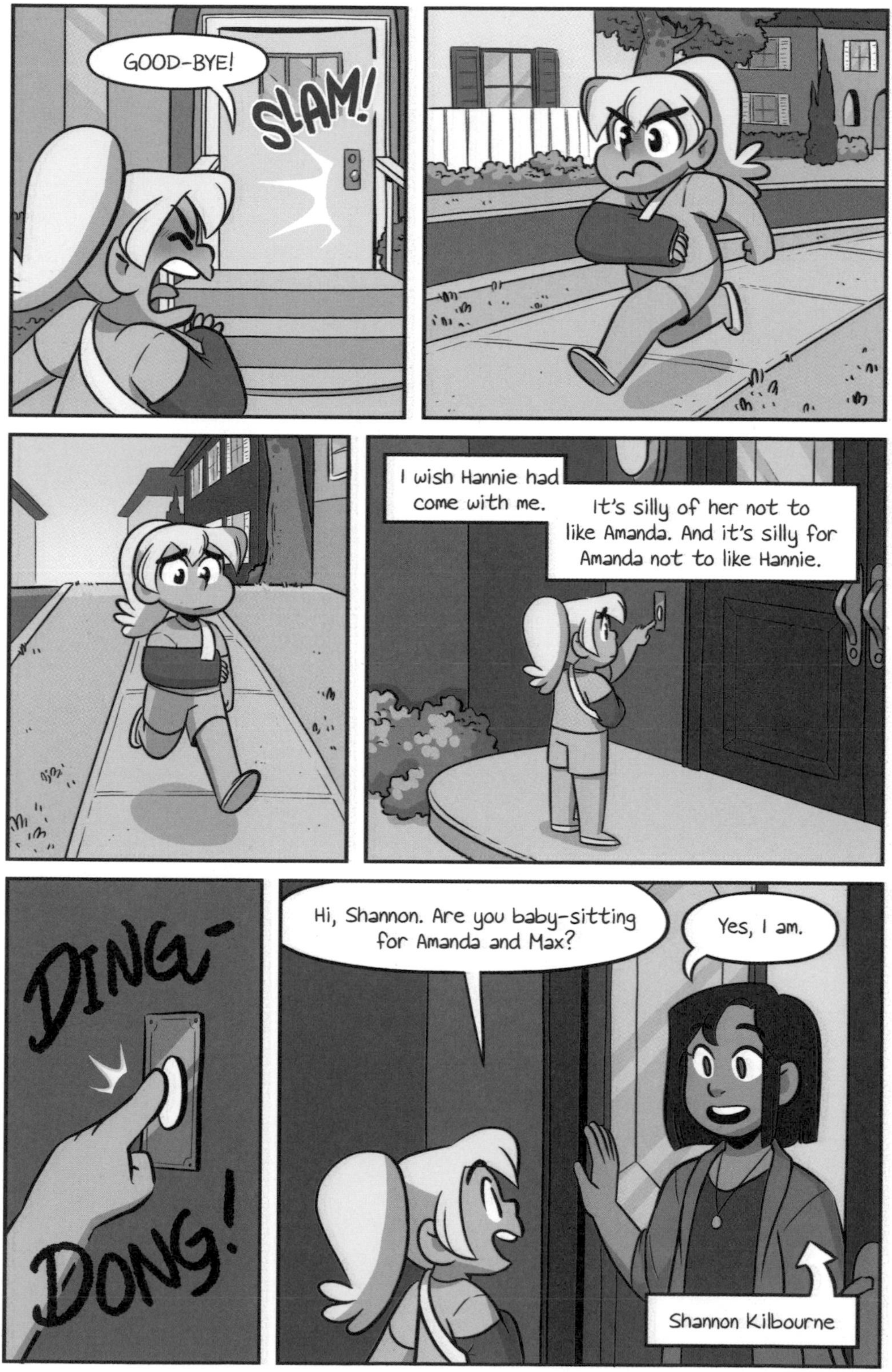
GOOD-BYE!
SLAM!
I wish Hannie had come with me.
It's silly of her not to like Amanda. And it's silly for Amanda not to like Hannie.
DING-DONG!
Hi, Shannon. Are you baby-sitting for Amanda and Max?
Yes, I am.
Shannon Kilbourne

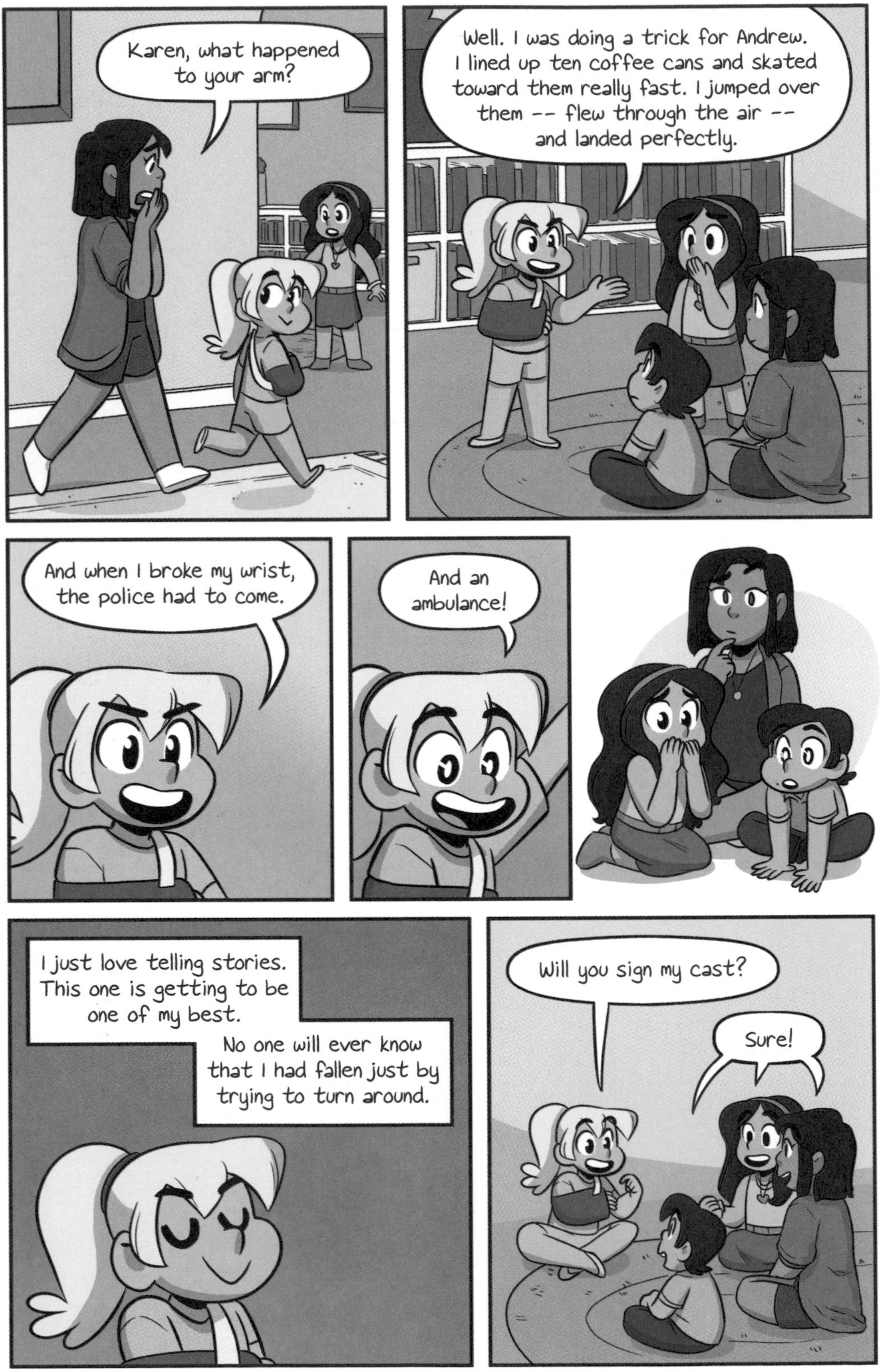

Karen, what happened to your arm?
Well. I was doing a trick for Andrew. I lined up ten coffee cans and skated toward them really fast. I jumped over them -- flew through the air -- and landed perfectly.
And when I broke my wrist, the police had to come.
And an ambulance!
I just love telling stories. This one is getting to be one of my best.
No one will ever know that I had fallen just by trying to turn around.
Will you sign my cast?
Sure!

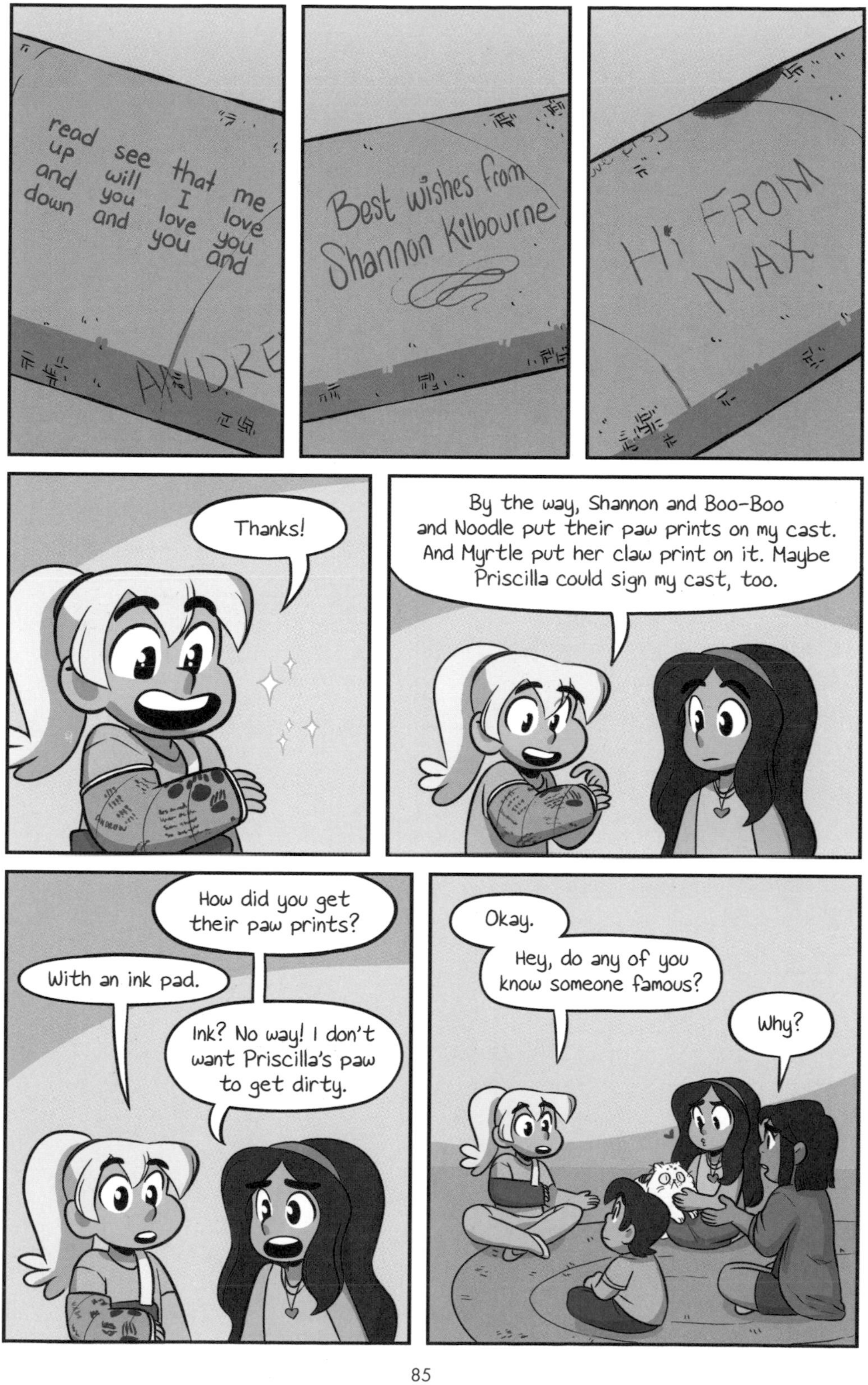

read up and down
see that I love you and
will you love you
me love you and
ANDRE
Best wishes from Shannon Kilbourne
Hi FROM MAX
Thanks!
By the way, Shannon and Boo-Boo and Noodle put their paw prints on my cast. And Myrtle put her claw print on it. Maybe Priscilla could sign my cast, too.
How did you get their paw prints?
With an ink pad.
Ink? No way! I don't want Priscilla's paw to get dirty.
Okay.
Hey, do any of you know someone famous?
Why?

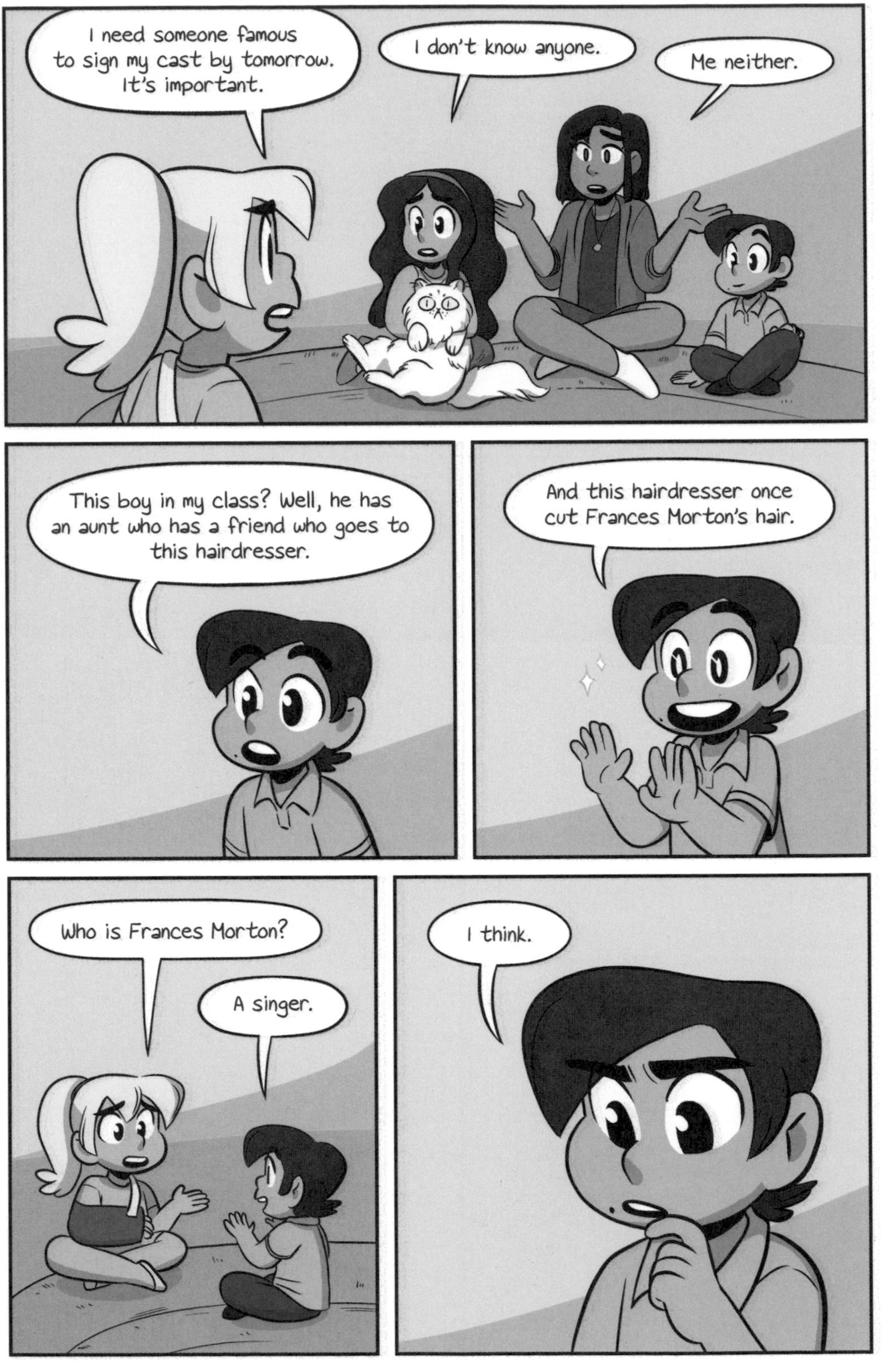
I need someone famous to sign my cast by tomorrow. It's important.
I don't know anyone.
Me neither.
This boy in my class? Well, he has an aunt who has a friend who goes to this hairdresser.
And this hairdresser once cut Frances Morton's hair.
Who is Frances Morton?
A singer.
I think.

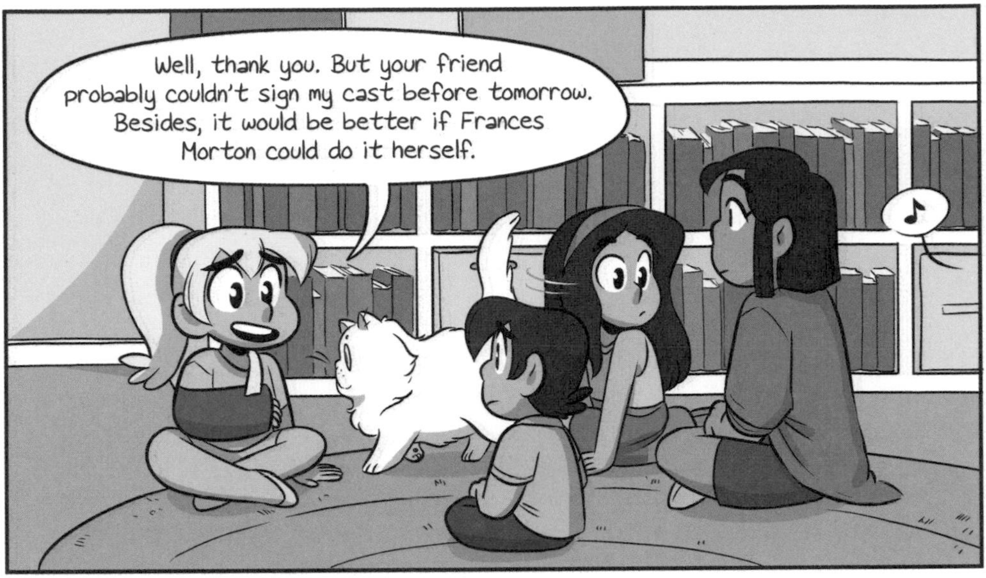
Well, thank you. But your friend probably couldn't sign my cast before tomorrow. Besides, it would be better if Frances Morton could do it herself.

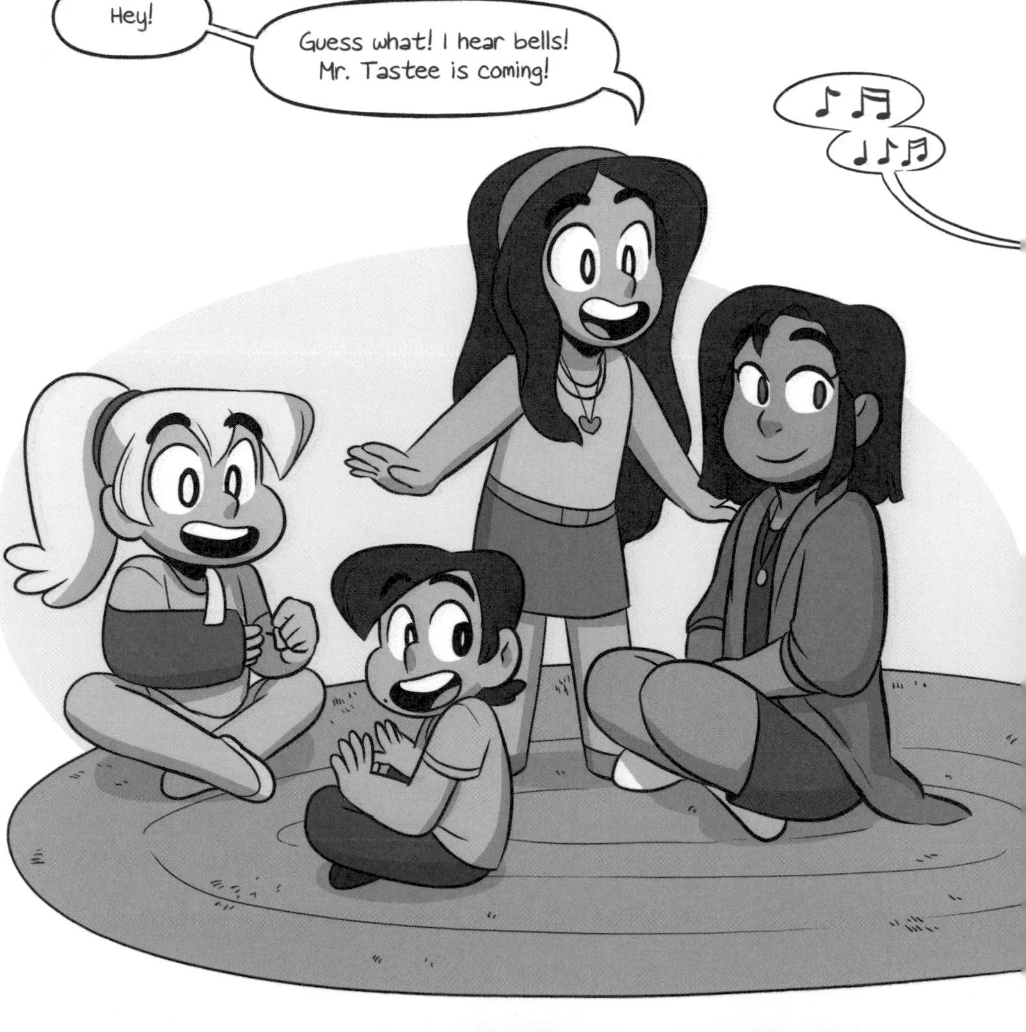
Hey!
Guess what! I hear bells! Mr. Tastee is coming!

CHAPTER 7

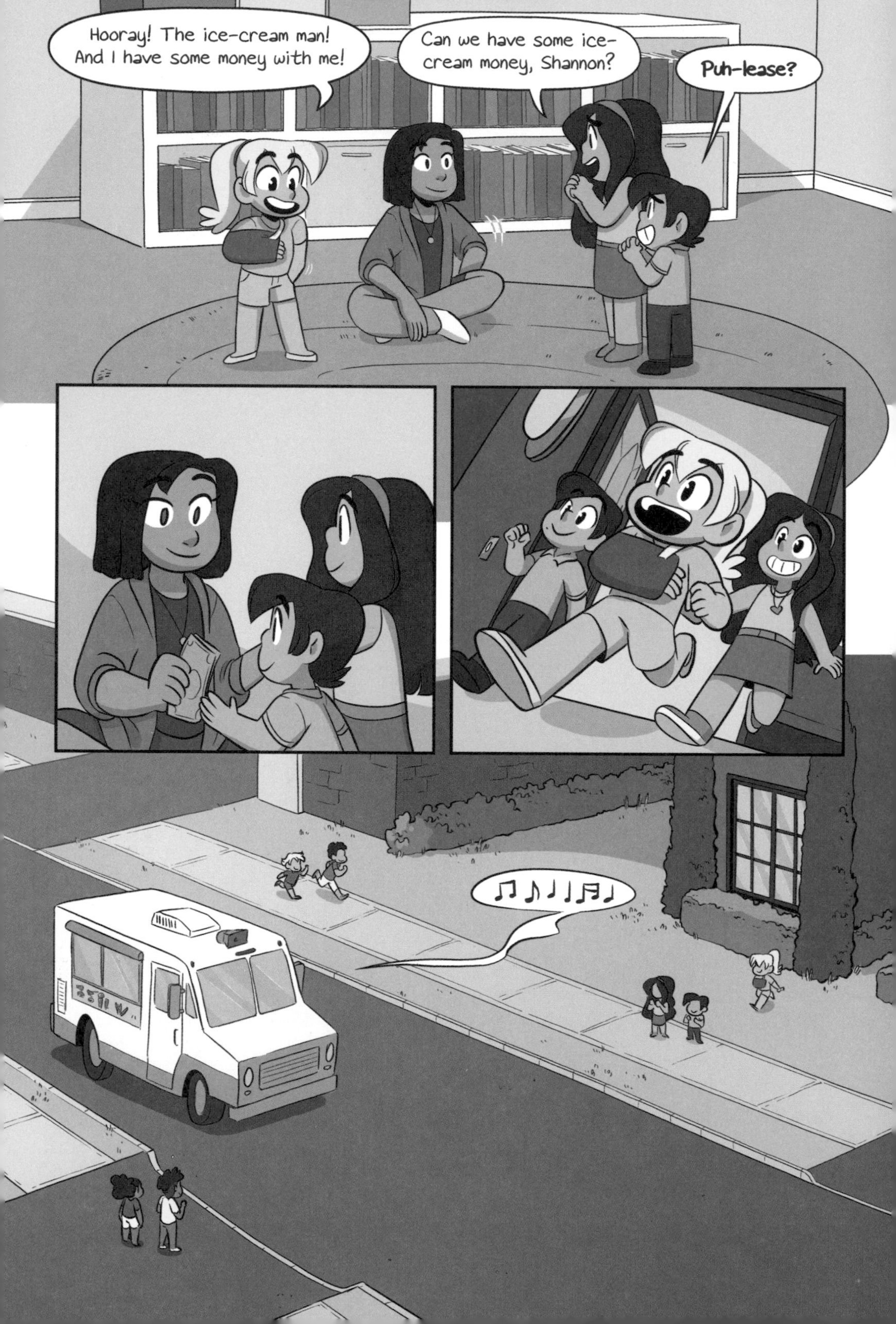
Hooray! The ice-cream man! And I have some money with me!
Can we have some ice-cream money, Shannon?
Puh-lease?

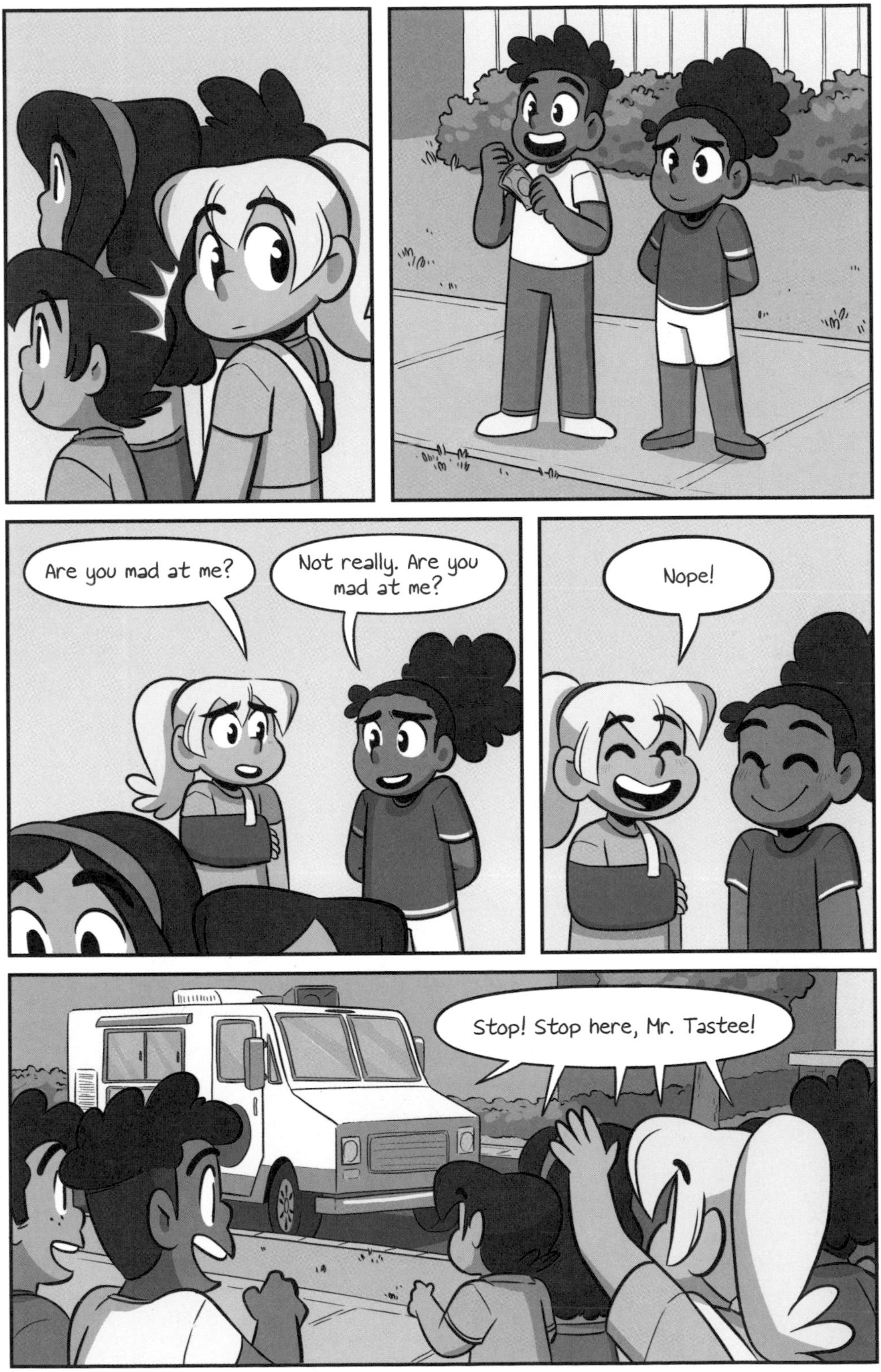

Are you mad at me?
Not really. Are you mad at me?
Nope!
Stop! Stop here, Mr. Tastee!

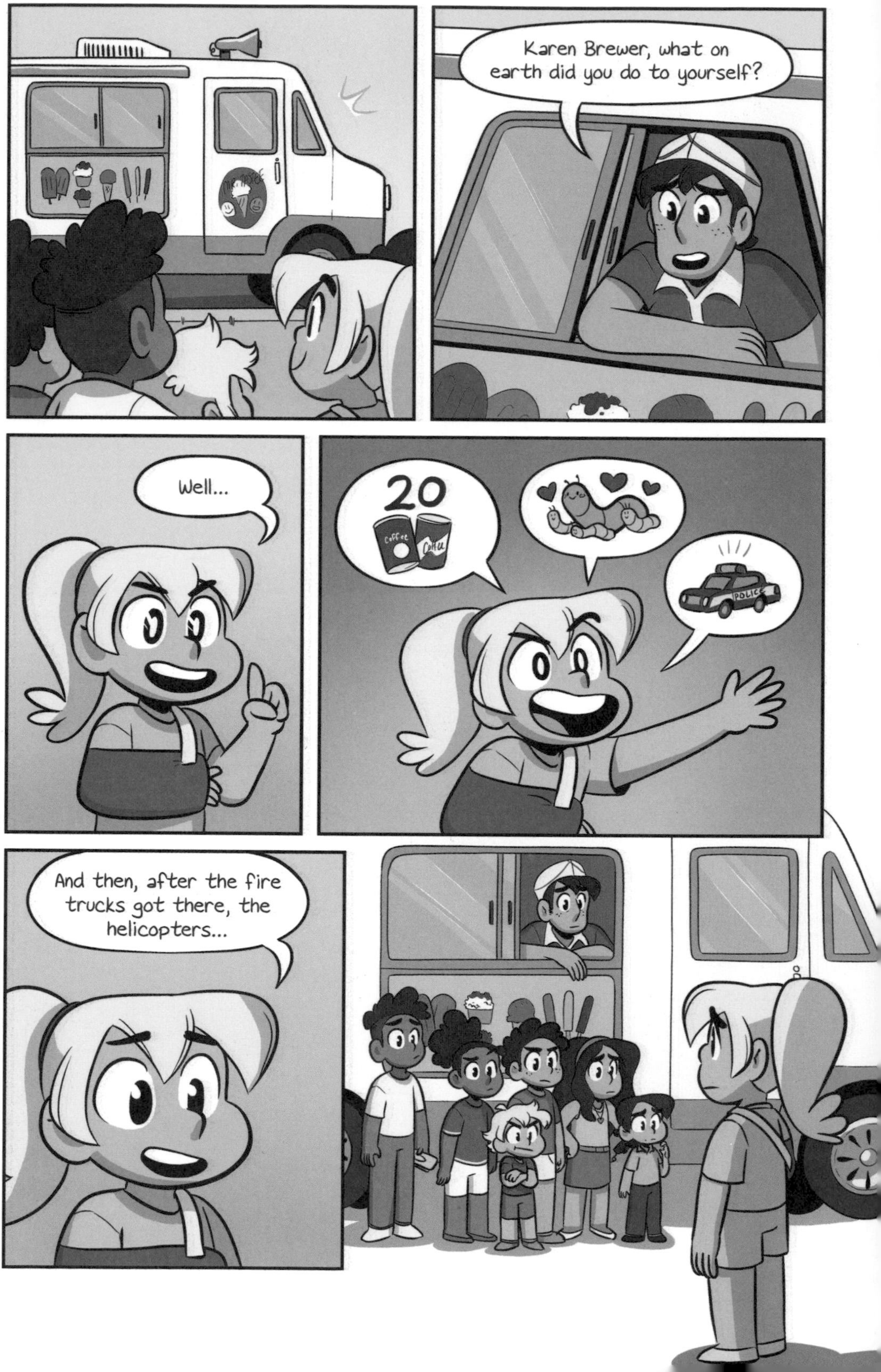
Karen Brewer, what on earth did you do to yourself?
Well...
20
Coffee
Coffee
POLICE
And then, after the fire trucks got there, the helicopters...

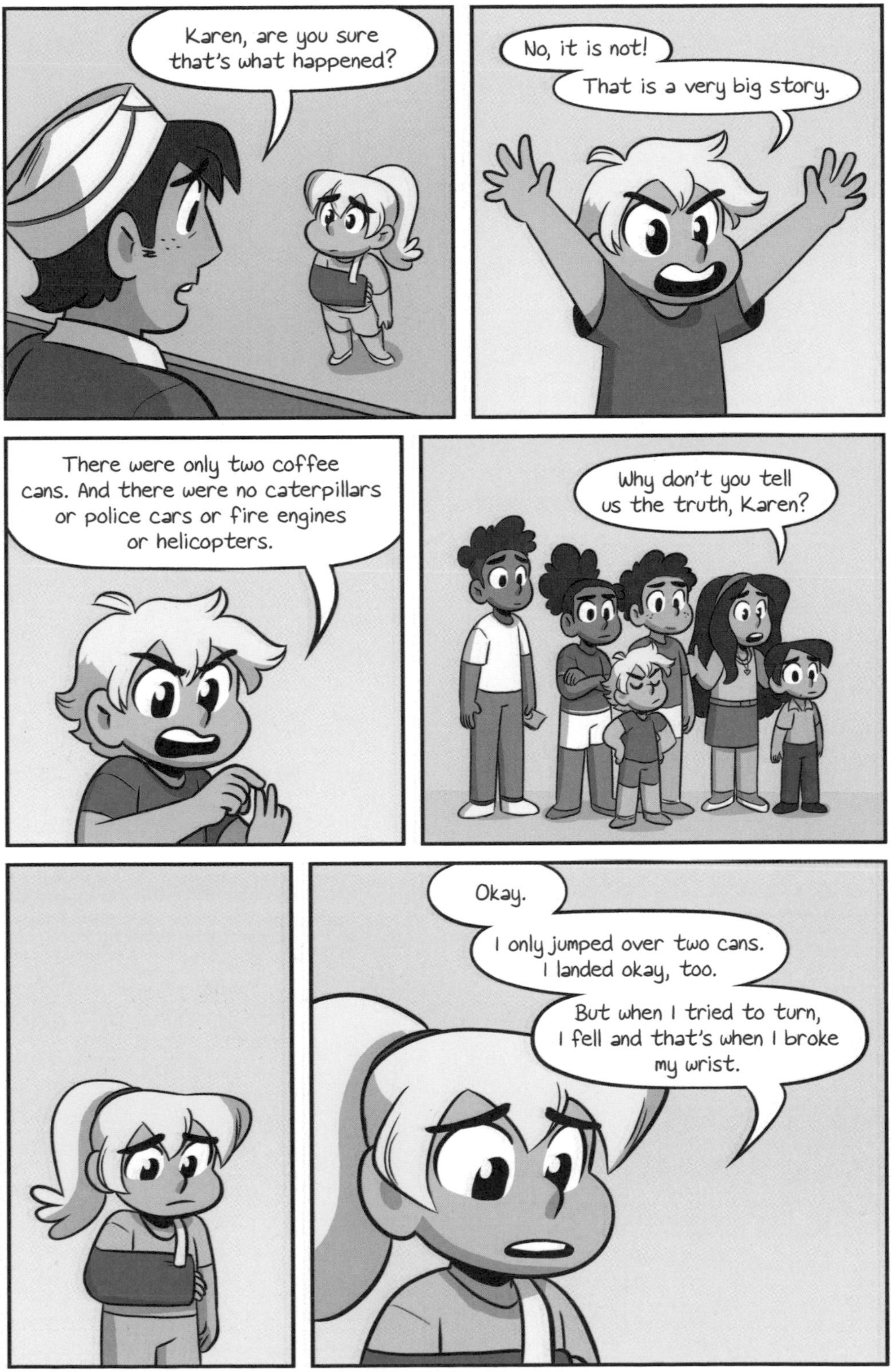
Karen, are you sure that's what happened?
No, it is not!
That is a very big story.
There were only two coffee cans. And there were no caterpillars or police cars or fire engines or helicopters.
Why don't you tell us the truth, Karen?
Okay.
I only jumped over two cans. I landed okay, too.
But when I tried to turn, I fell and that's when I broke my wrist.

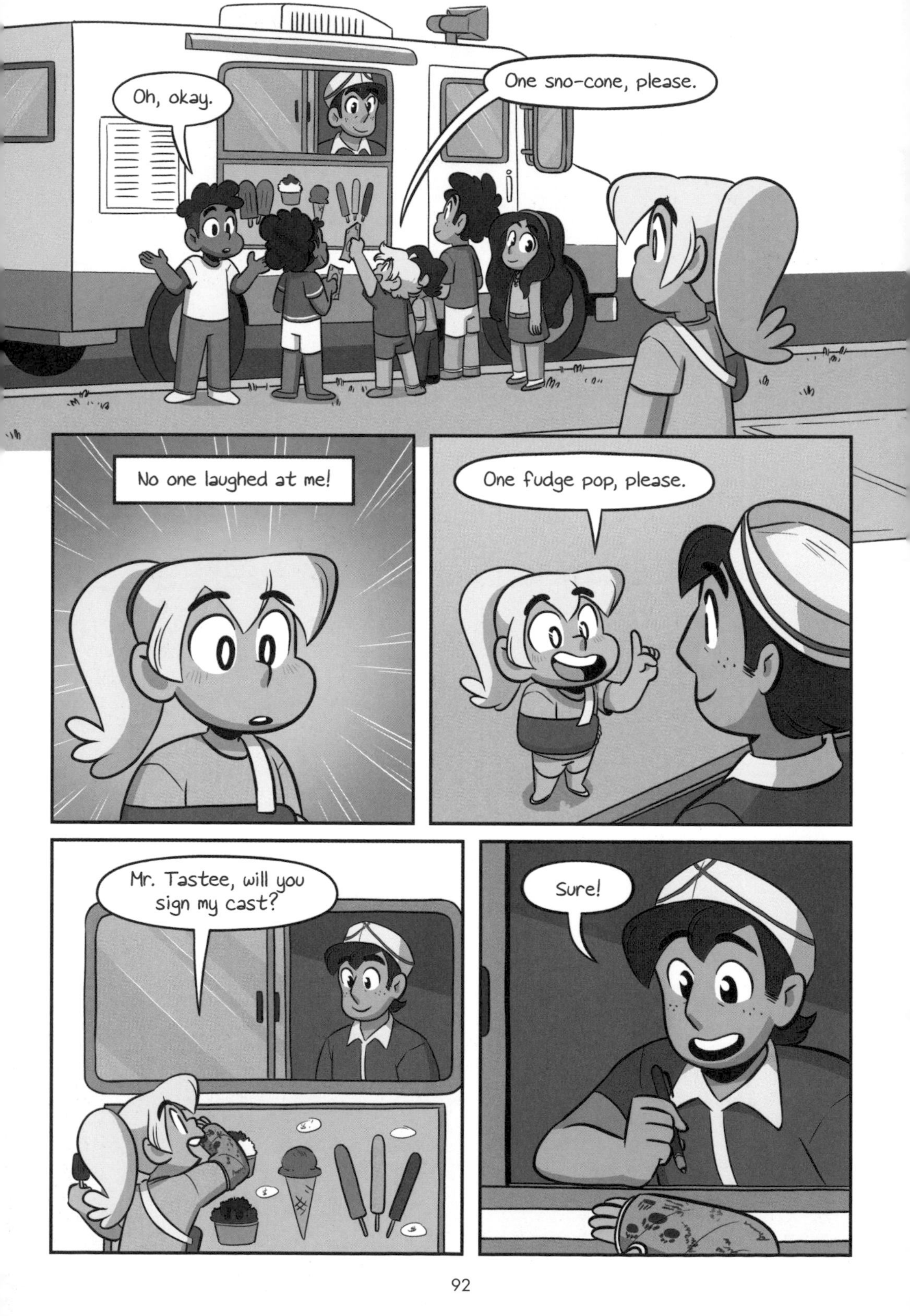
Oh, okay.
One sno-cone, please.
No one laughed at me!
One fudge pop, please.
Mr. Tastee, will you sign my cast?
Sure!

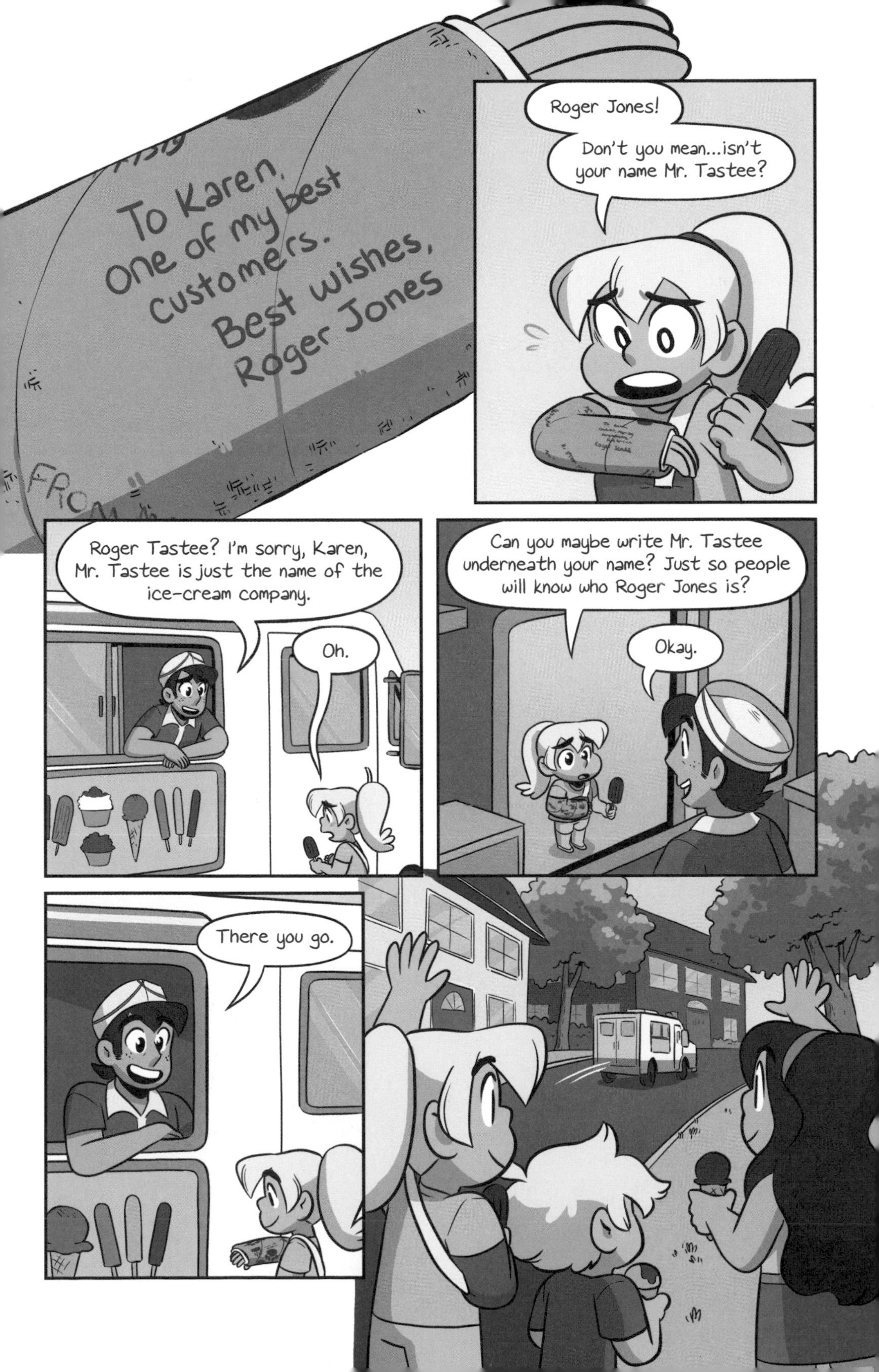
To Karen,
One of my best customers.
Best wishes,
Roger Jones
FROM
Roger Jones!
Don't you mean...isn't your name Mr. Tastee?
Roger Tastee? I'm sorry, Karen, Mr. Tastee is just the name of the ice-cream company.
Oh.
Can you maybe write Mr. Tastee underneath your name? Just so people will know who Roger Jones is?
Okay.
There you go.

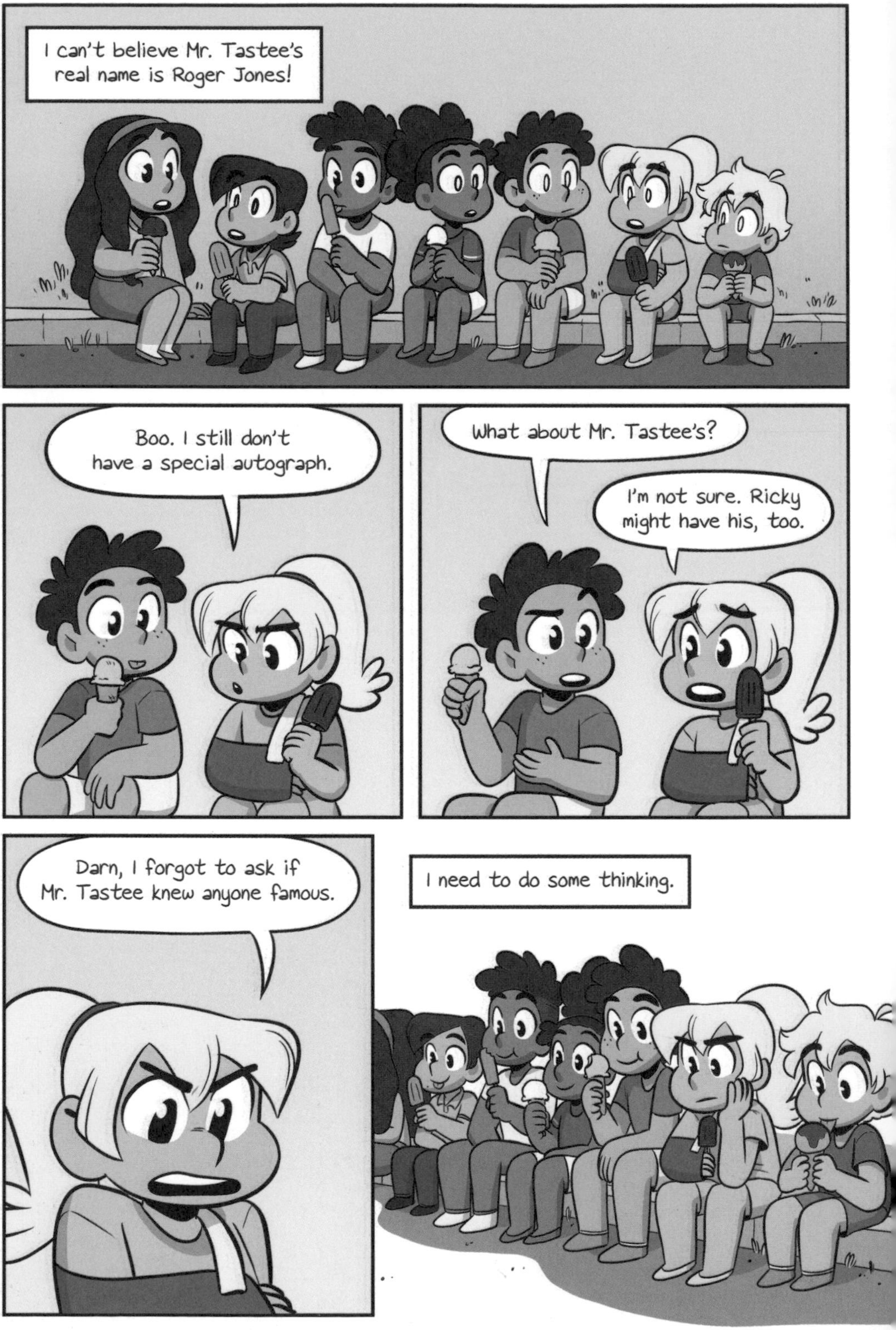
I can't believe Mr. Tastee's real name is Roger Jones!
Boo. I still don't have a special autograph.
What about Mr. Tastee's?
I'm not sure. Ricky might have his, too.
Darn, I forgot to ask if Mr. Tastee knew anyone famous.
I need to do some thinking.

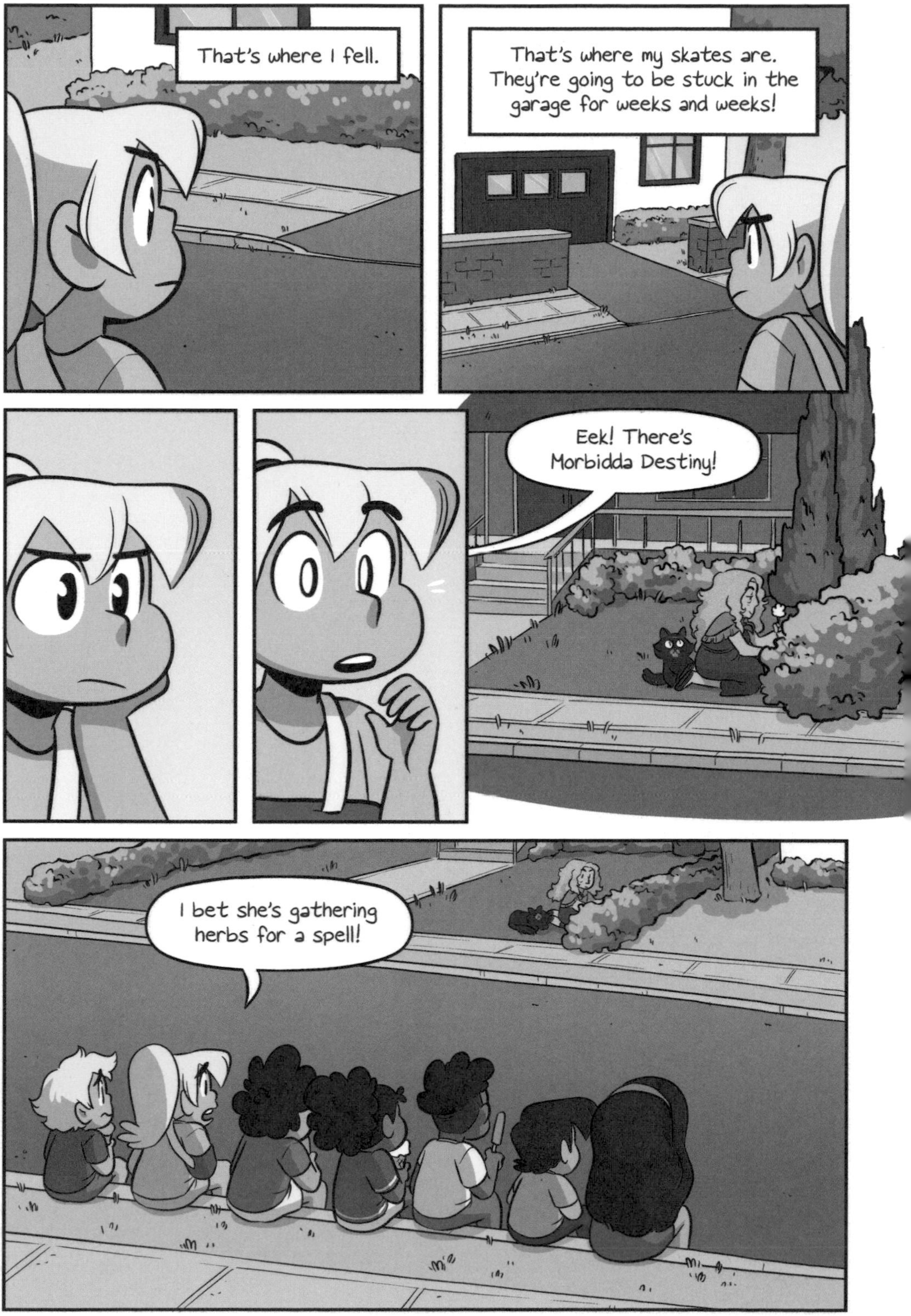
That's where I fell.
That's where my skates are. They're going to be stuck in the garage for weeks and weeks!
Eek! There's Morbidda Destiny!
I bet she's gathering herbs for a spell!

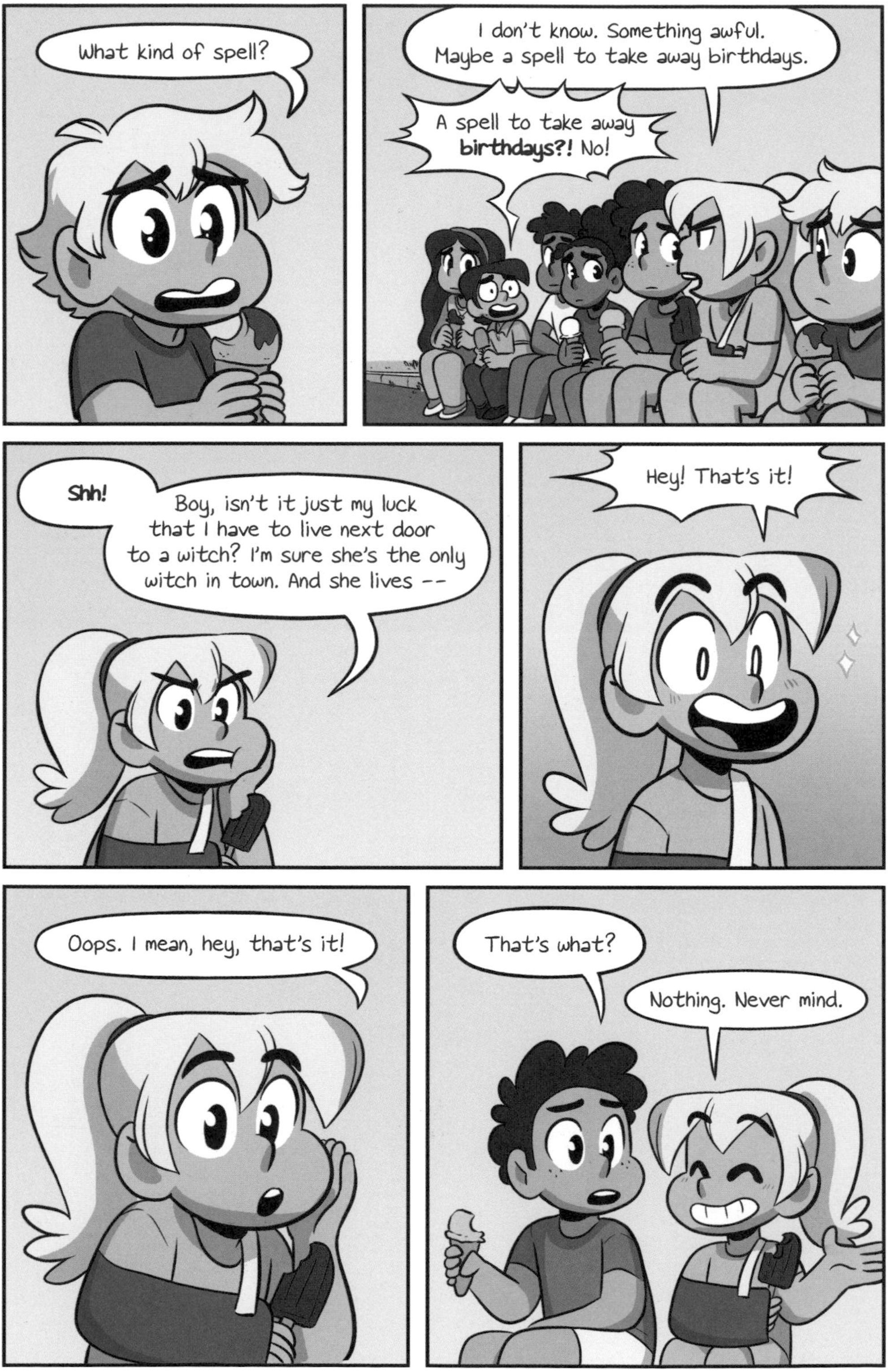
What kind of spell?
I don't know. Something awful. Maybe a spell to take away birthdays.
A spell to take away **birthdays?!** No!
Shh!
Boy, isn't it just my luck that I have to live next door to a witch? I'm sure she's the only witch in town. And she lives --
Hey! That's it!
Oops. I mean, hey, that's it!
That's what?
Nothing. Never mind.

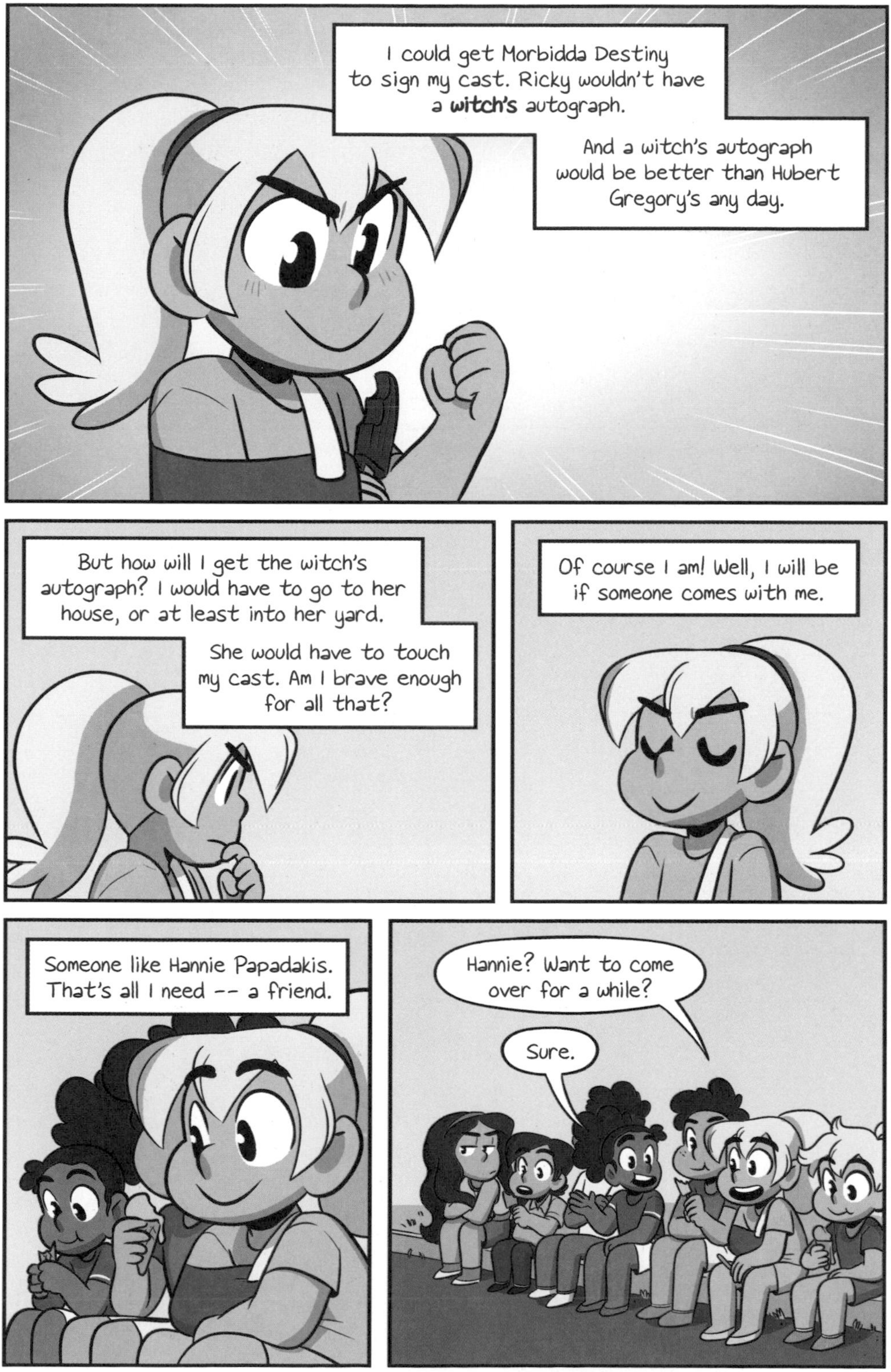
I could get Morbidda Destiny to sign my cast. Ricky wouldn't have a **witch's** autograph.
And a witch's autograph would be better than Hubert Gregory's any day.
But how will I get the witch's autograph? I would have to go to her house, or at least into her yard.
She would have to touch my cast. Am I brave enough for all that?
Of course I am! Well, I will be if someone comes with me.
Someone like Hannie Papadakis. That's all I need -- a friend.
Hannie? Want to come over for a while?
Sure.

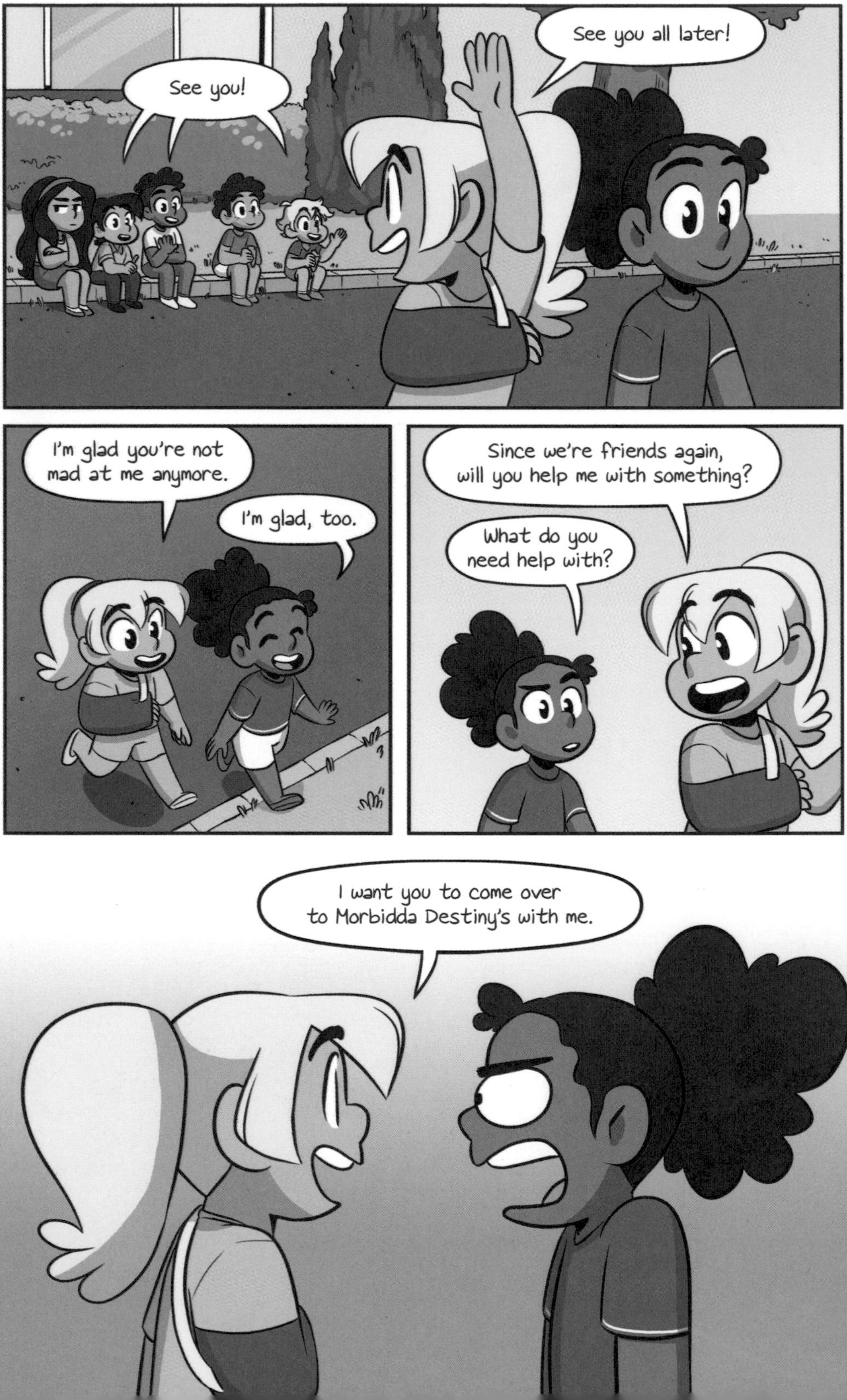
See you!
See you all later!
I'm glad you're not mad at me anymore.
I'm glad, too.
Since we're friends again, will you help me with something?
What do you need help with?
I want you to come over to Morbidda Destiny's with me.

CHAPTER 8

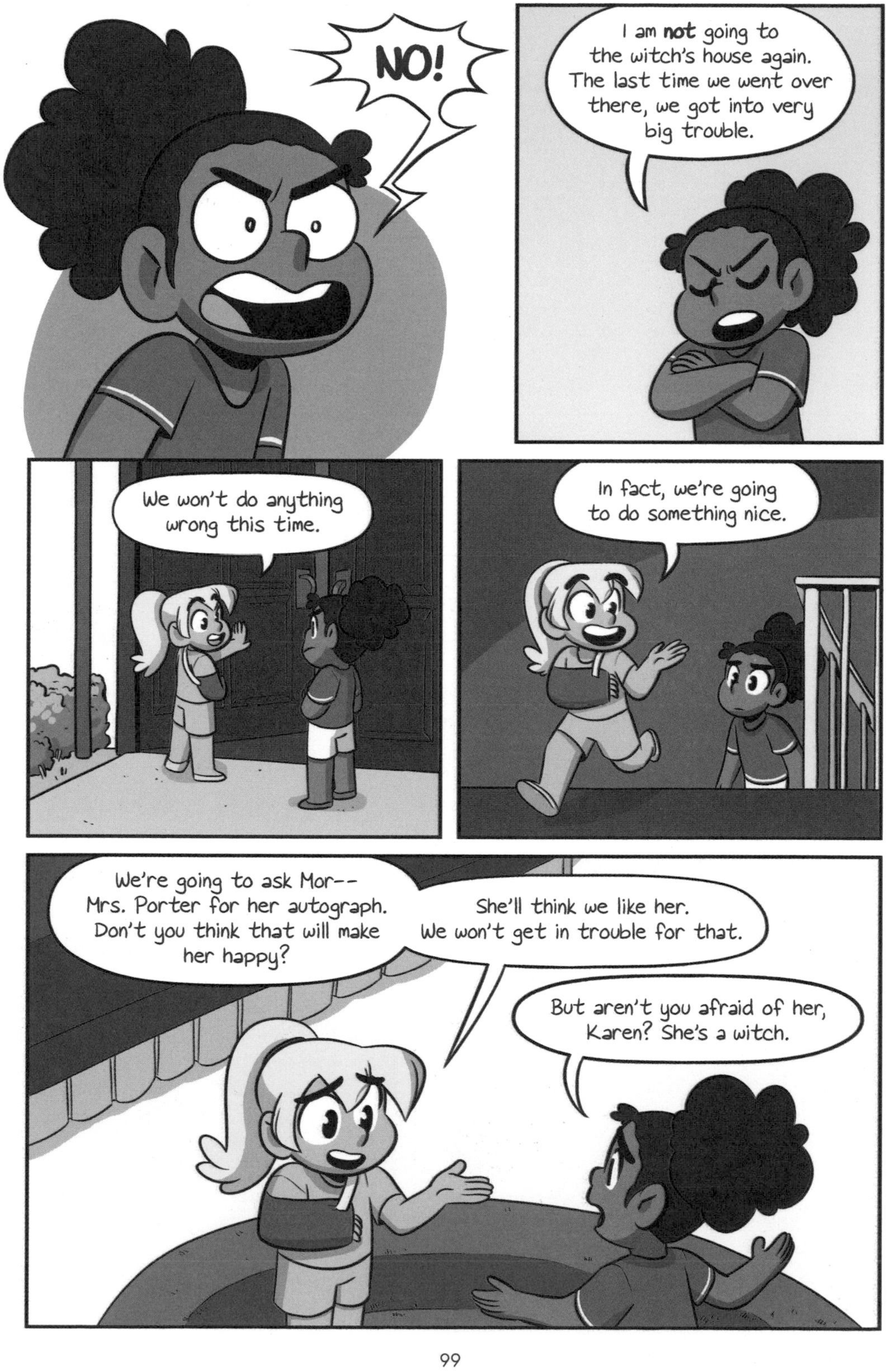
NO!
I am **not** going to the witch's house again. The last time we went over there, we got into very big trouble.
We won't do anything wrong this time.
In fact, we're going to do something nice.
We're going to ask Mor-- Mrs. Porter for her autograph. Don't you think that will make her happy?
She'll think we like her. We won't get in trouble for that.
But aren't you afraid of her, Karen? She's a witch.

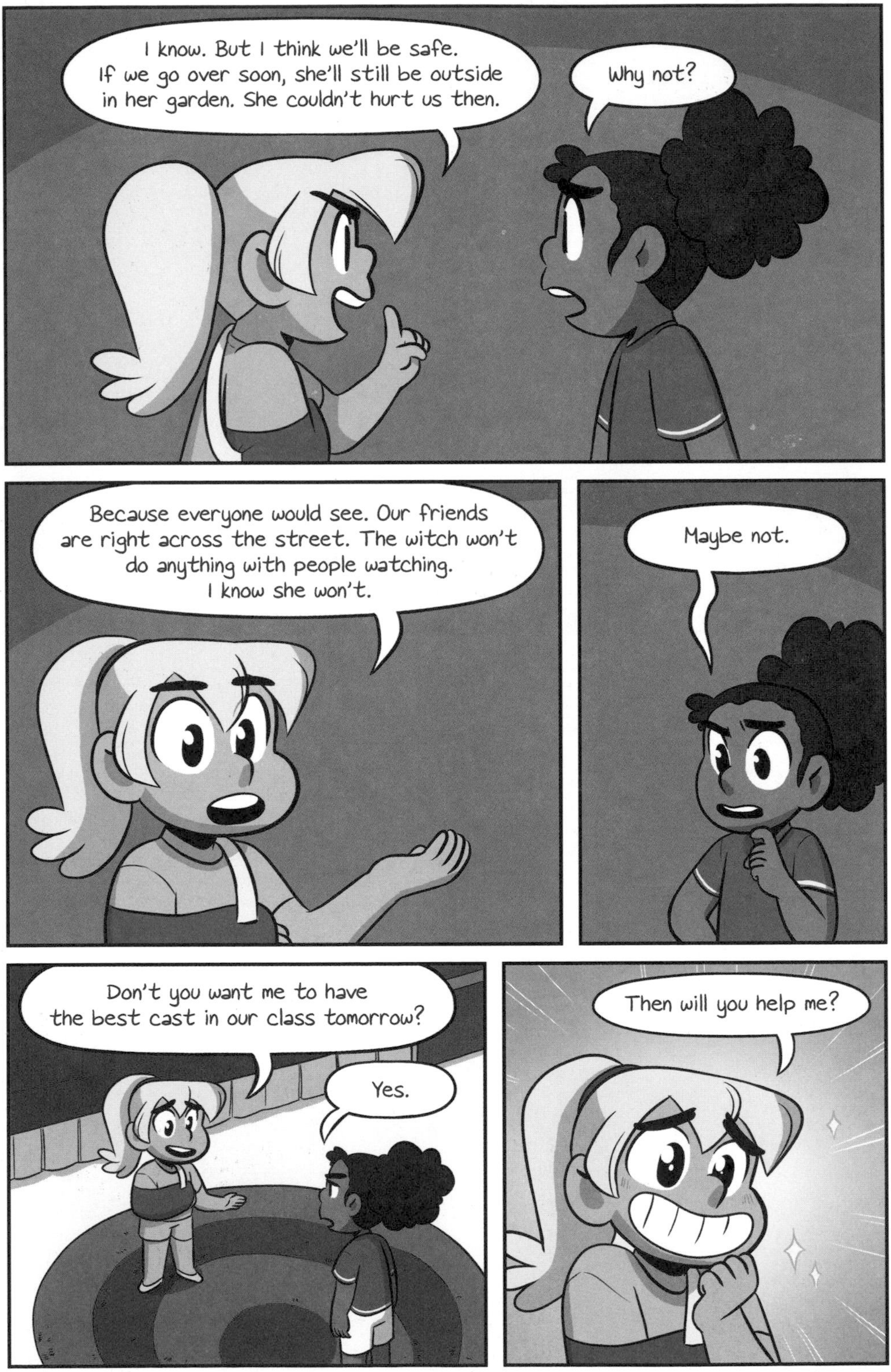
I know. But I think we'll be safe. If we go over soon, she'll still be outside in her garden. She couldn't hurt us then.
Why not?
Because everyone would see. Our friends are right across the street. The witch won't do anything with people watching. I know she won't.
Maybe not.
Don't you want me to have the best cast in our class tomorrow?
Yes.
Then will you help me?

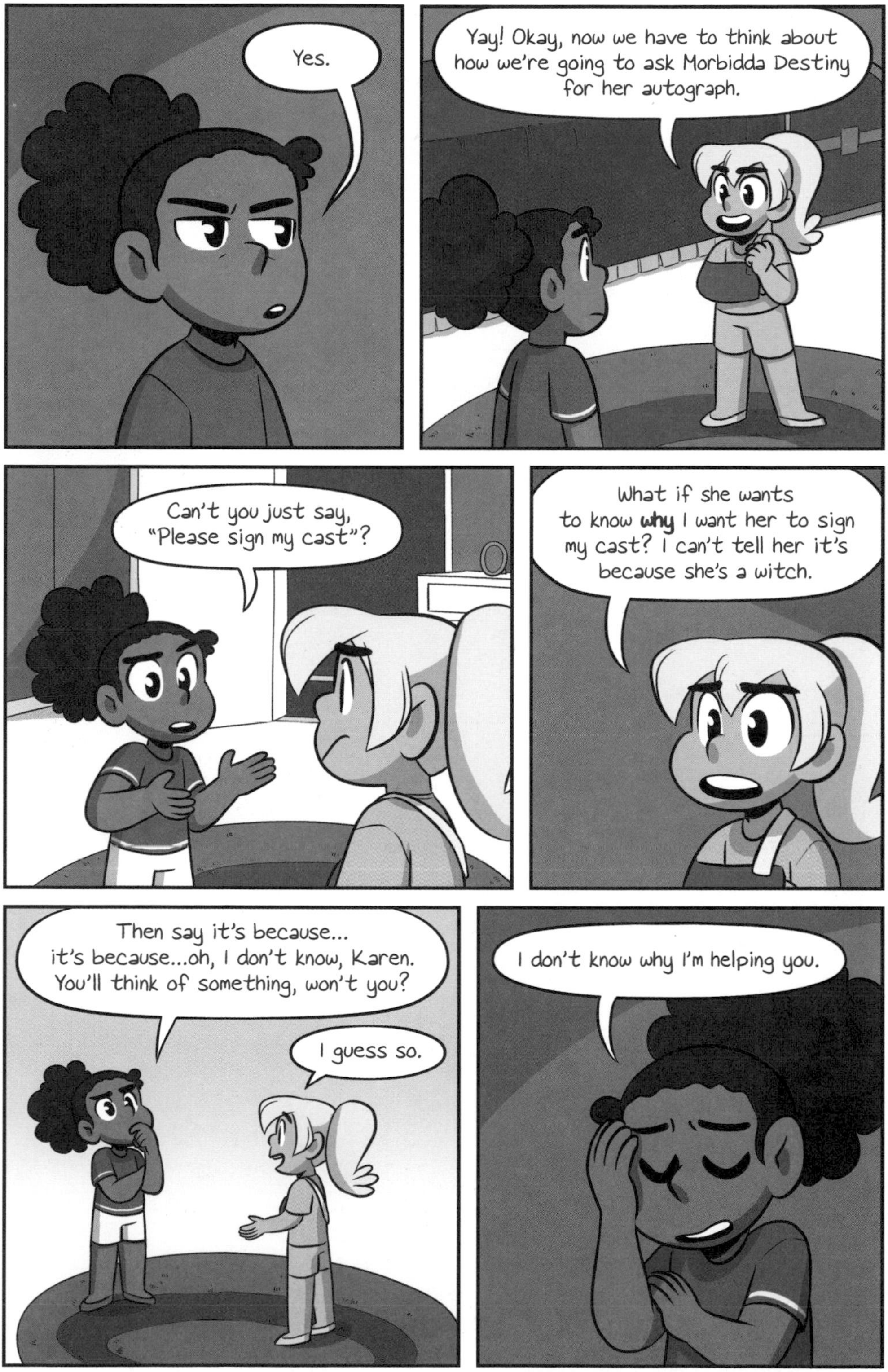
Yes.
Yay! Okay, now we have to think about how we're going to ask Morbidda Destiny for her autograph.
Can't you just say, "Please sign my cast"?
What if she wants to know **why** I want her to sign my cast? I can't tell her it's because she's a witch.
Then say it's because... it's because...oh, I don't know, Karen. You'll think of something, won't you?
I guess so.
I don't know why I'm helping you.

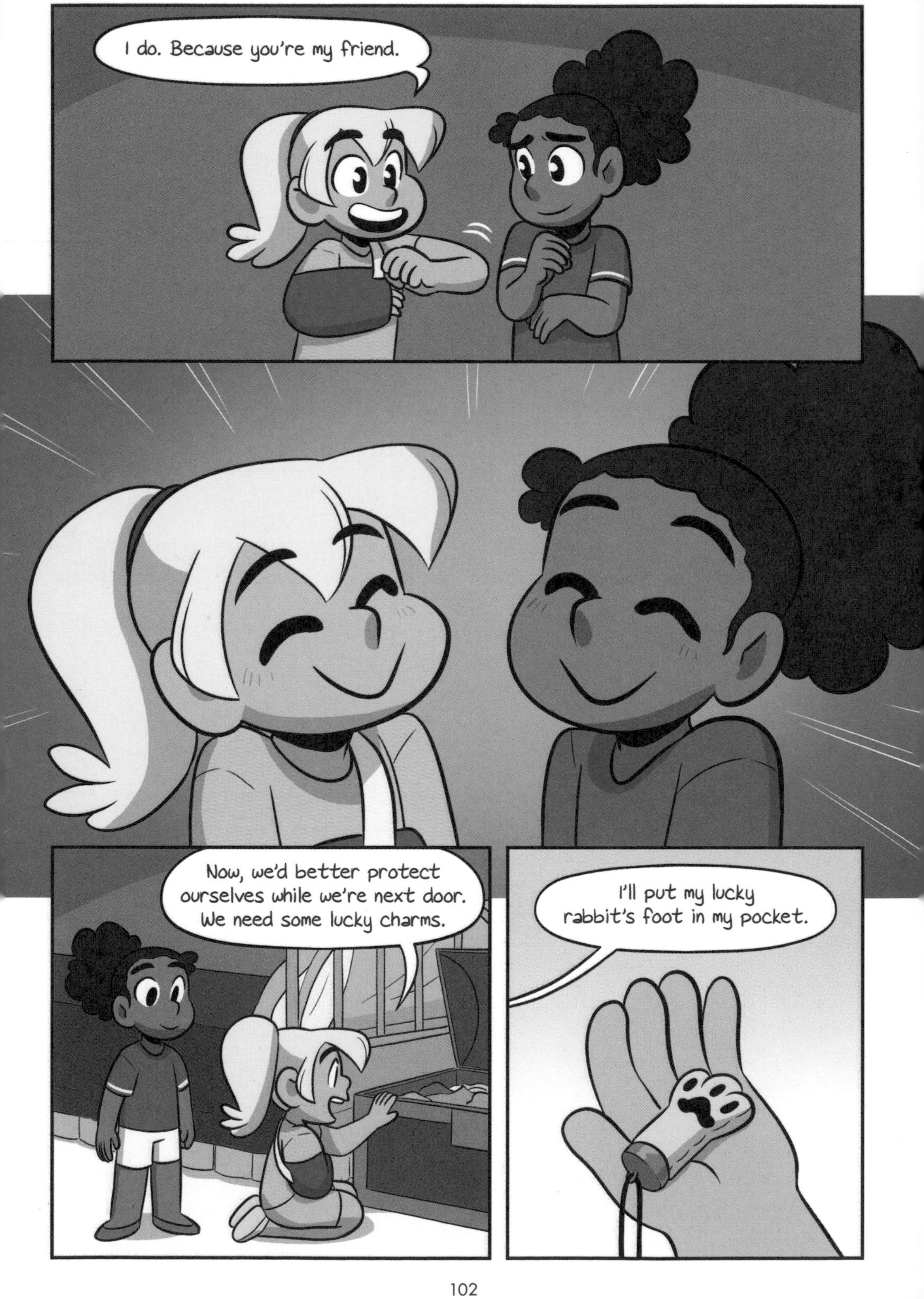
I do. Because you're my friend.
Now, we'd better protect ourselves while we're next door. We need some lucky charms.
I'll put my lucky rabbit's foot in my pocket.

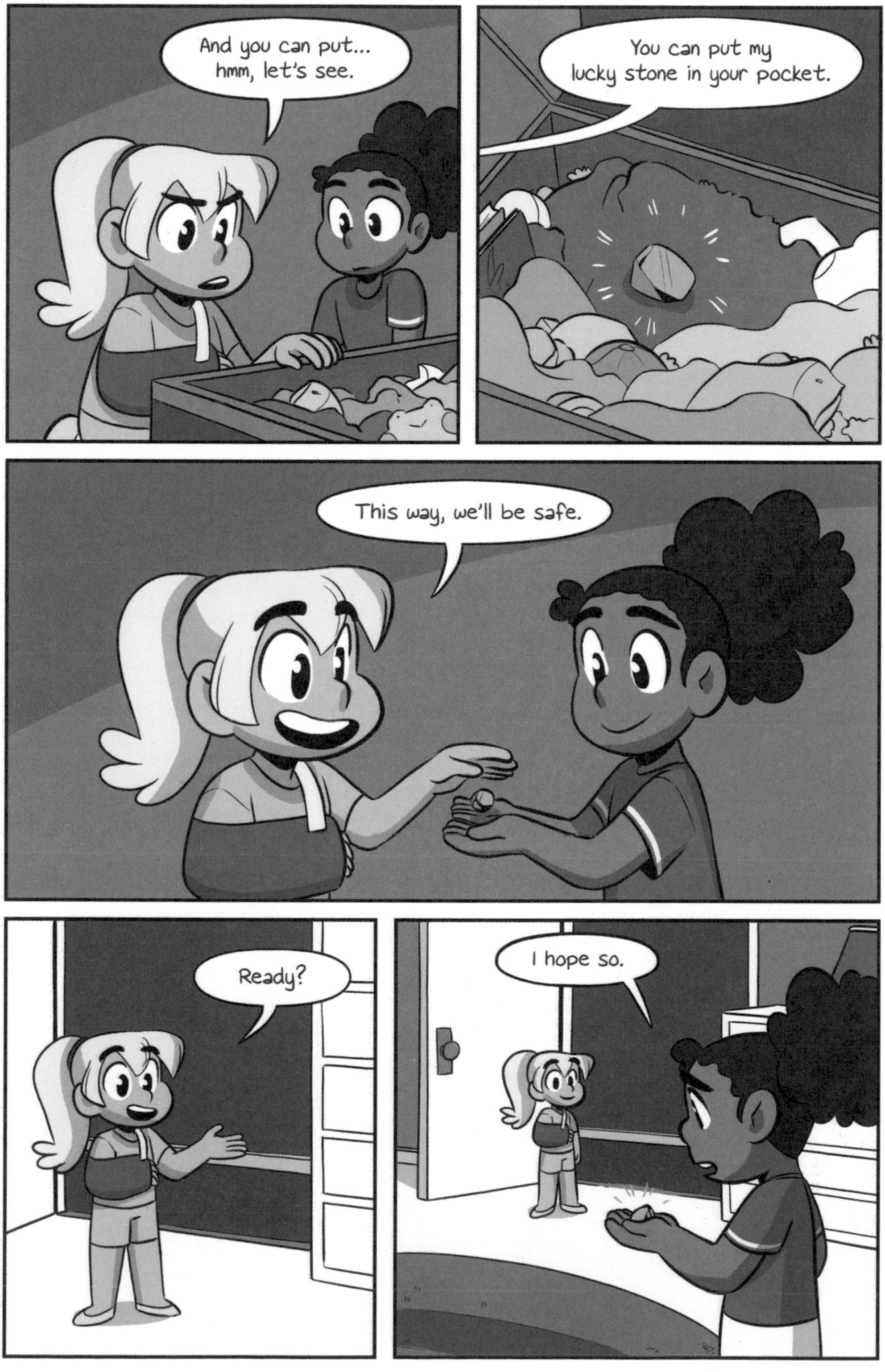
And you can put...
hmm, let's see.
You can put my
lucky stone in your pocket.
This way, we'll be safe.
Ready?
I hope so.

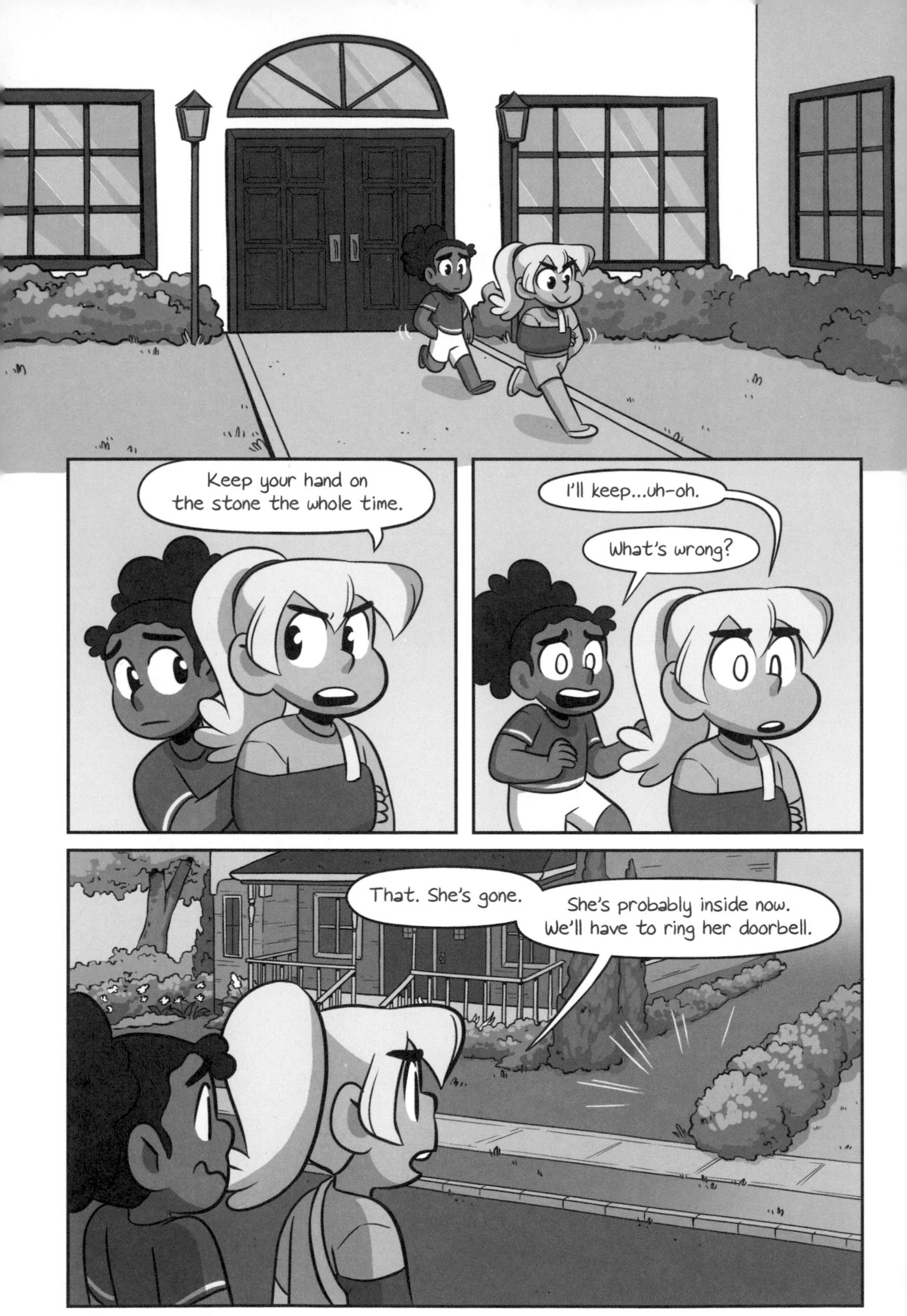
Keep your hand on
the stone the whole time.
I'll keep...uh-oh.
What's wrong?
That. She's gone.
She's probably inside now.
We'll have to ring her doorbell.

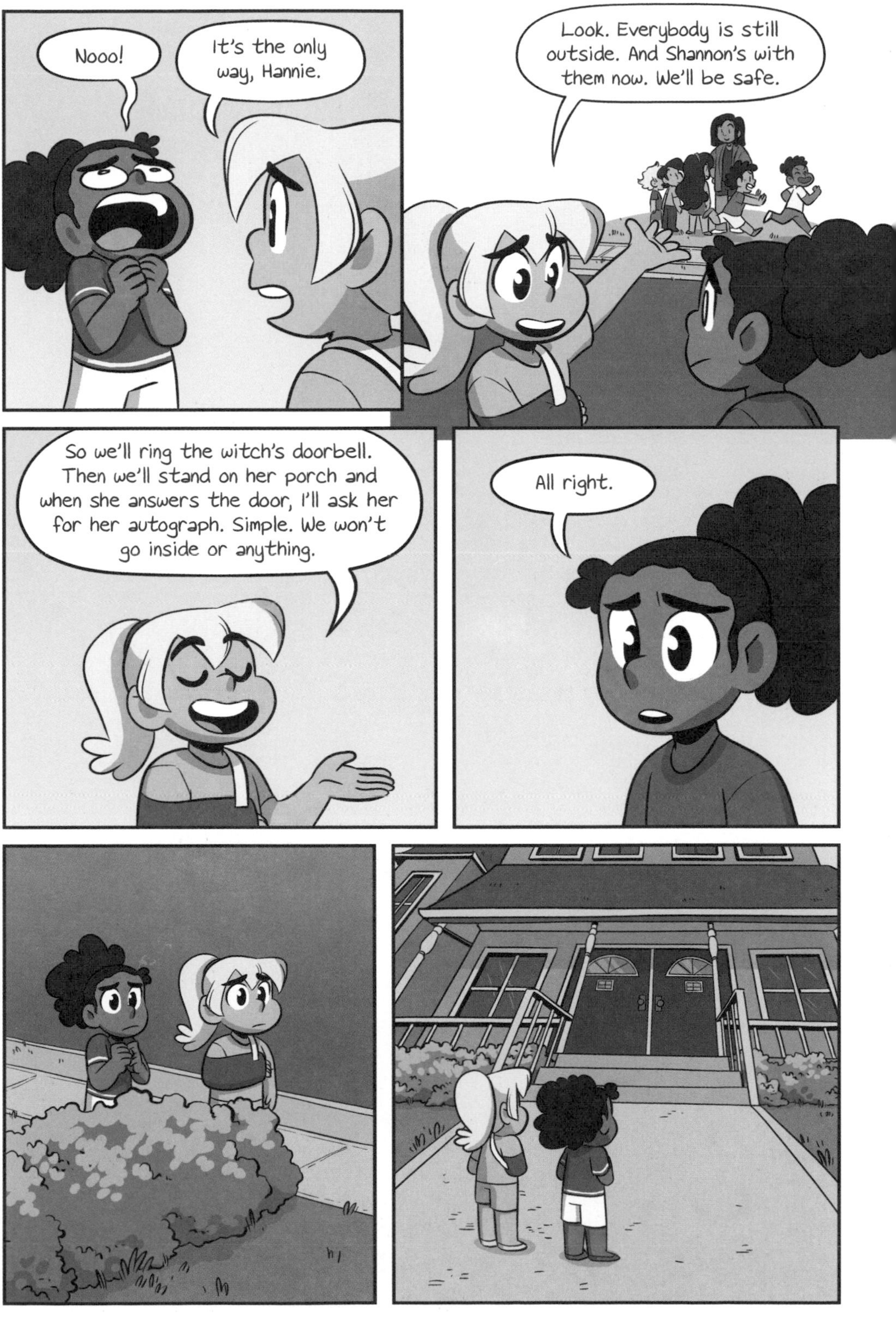
Nooo!
It's the only way, Hannie.
Look. Everybody is still outside. And Shannon's with them now. We'll be safe.
So we'll ring the witch's doorbell. Then we'll stand on her porch and when she answers the door, I'll ask her for her autograph. Simple. We won't go inside or anything.
All right.

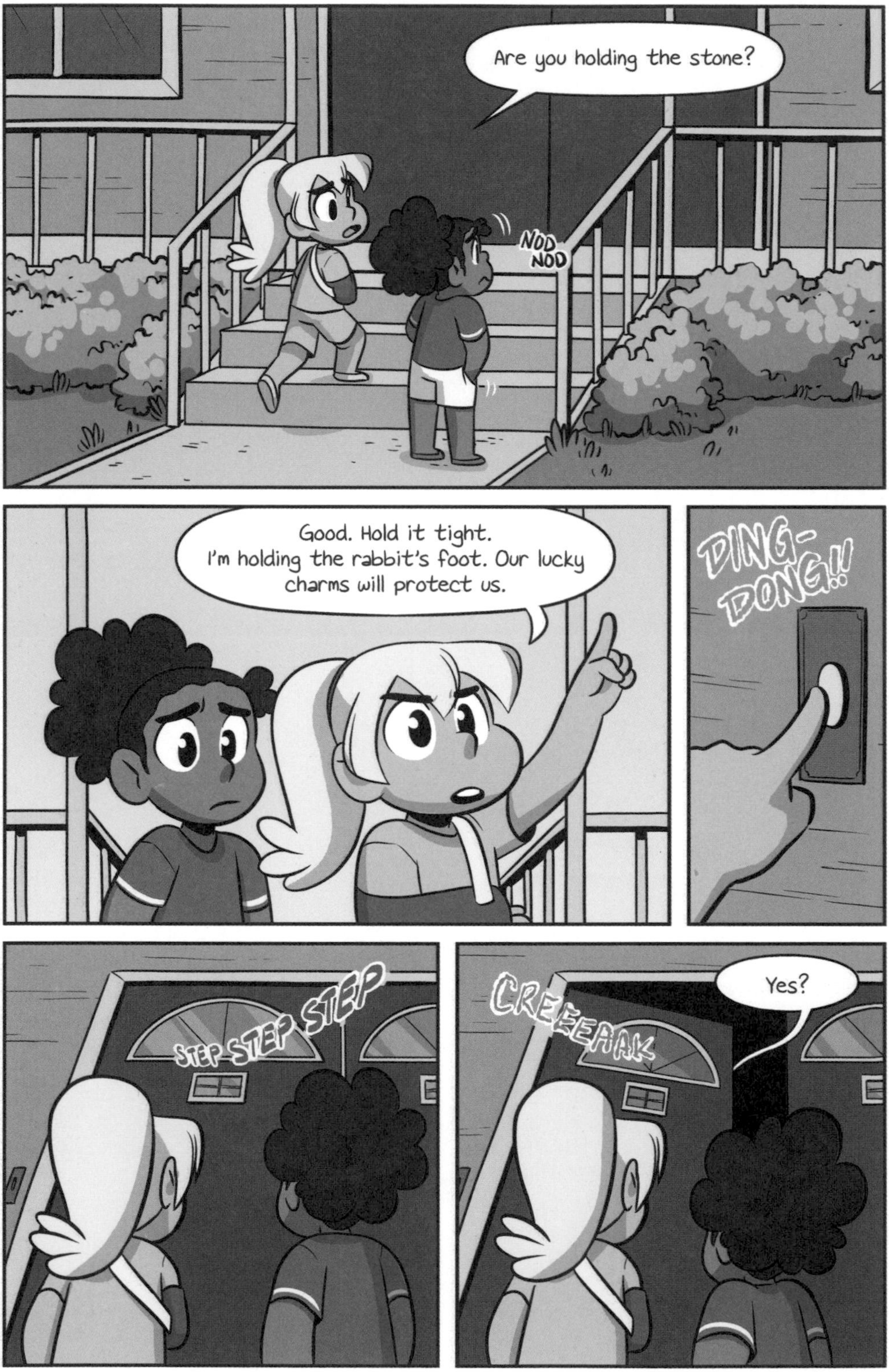

Are you holding the stone?
NOD NOD
Good. Hold it tight.
I'm holding the rabbit's foot. Our lucky charms will protect us.
DING-DONG!!
STEP STEP STEP
CREEEAAK
Yes?

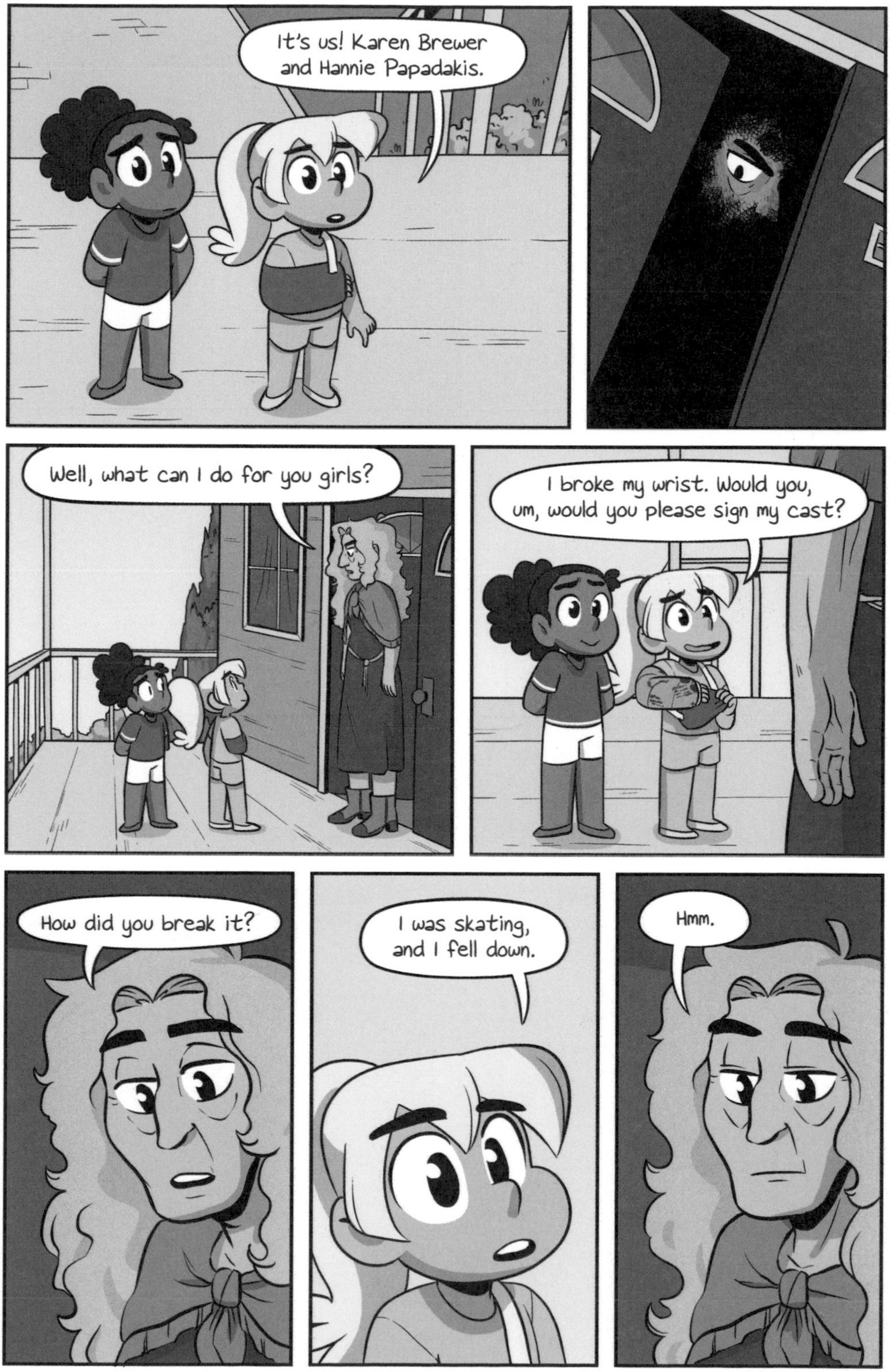
It's us! Karen Brewer and Hannie Papadakis.
Well, what can I do for you girls?
I broke my wrist. Would you, um, would you please sign my cast?
How did you break it?
I was skating, and I fell down.
Hmm.

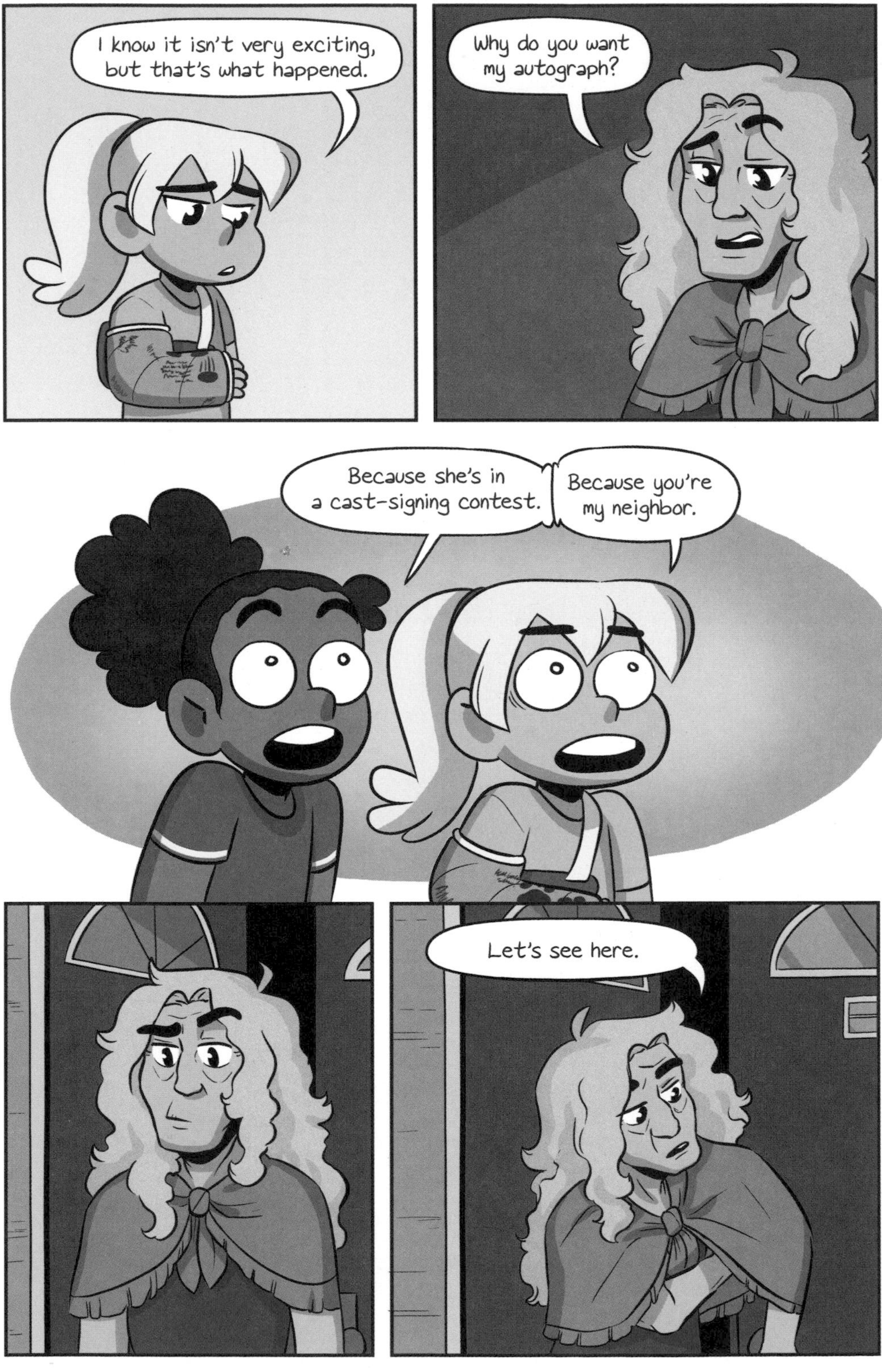
I know it isn't very exciting, but that's what happened.
Why do you want my autograph?
Because she's in a cast-signing contest.
Because you're my neighbor.
Let's see here.

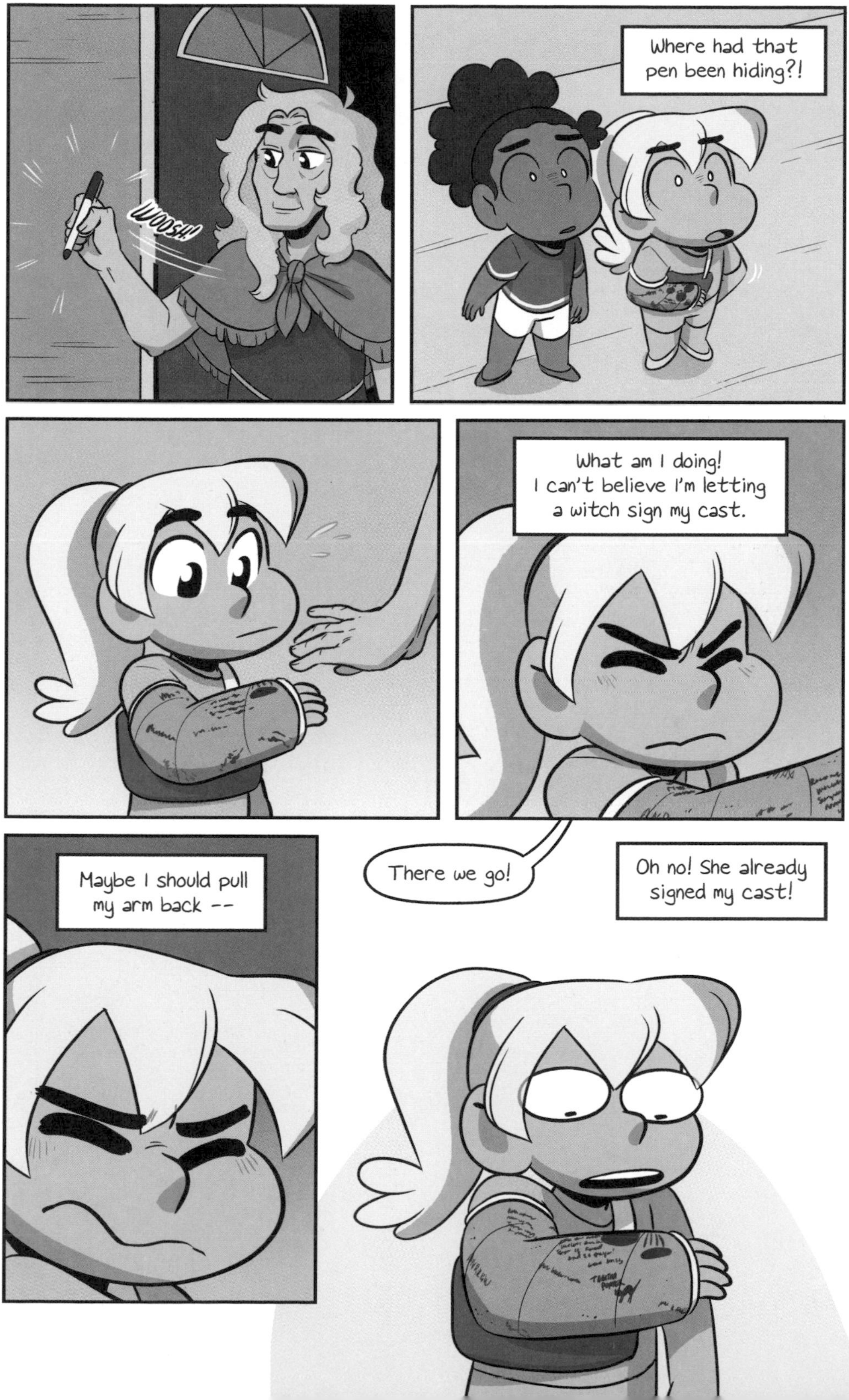
WOOSH!
Where had that pen been hiding?!
What am I doing!
I can't believe I'm letting a witch sign my cast.
Maybe I should pull my arm back --
There we go!
Oh no! She already signed my cast!

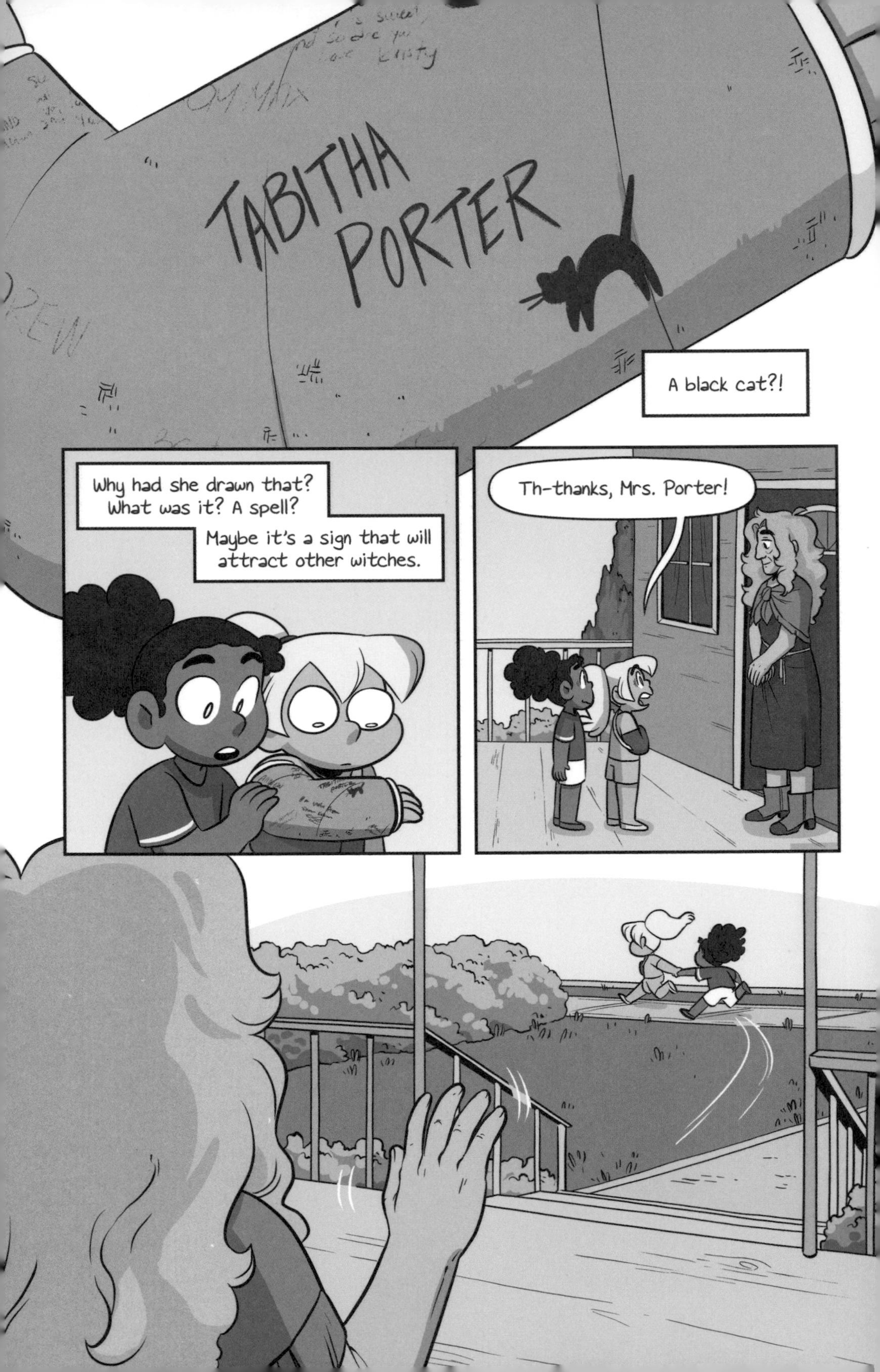
TABITHA PORTER
A black cat?!
Why had she drawn that? What was it? A spell?
Maybe it's a sign that will attract other witches.
Th-thanks, Mrs. Porter!

CHAPTER 9

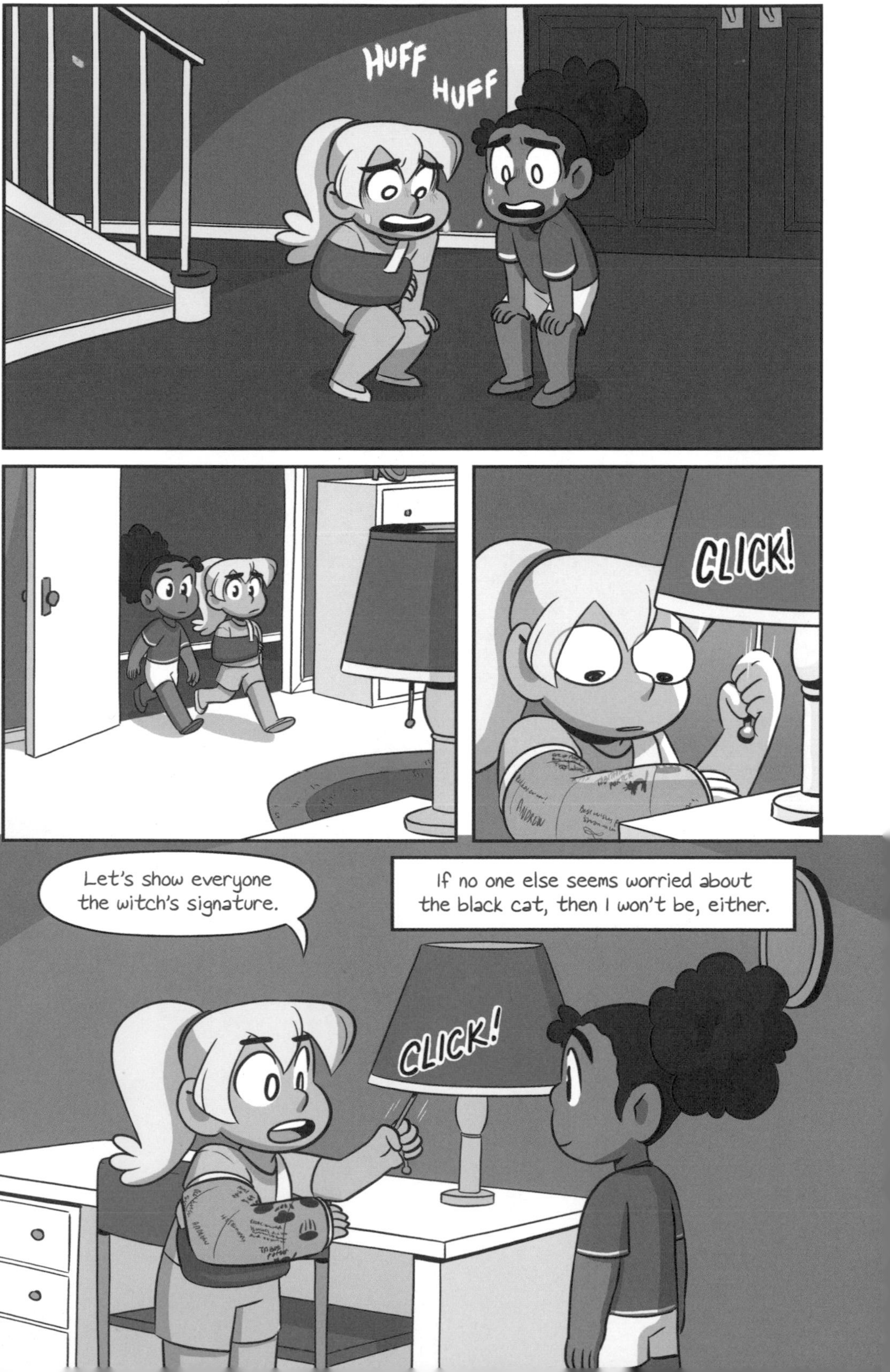
HUFF
HUFF
CLICK!
Let's show everyone the witch's signature.
If no one else seems worried about the black cat, then I won't be, either.
CLICK!

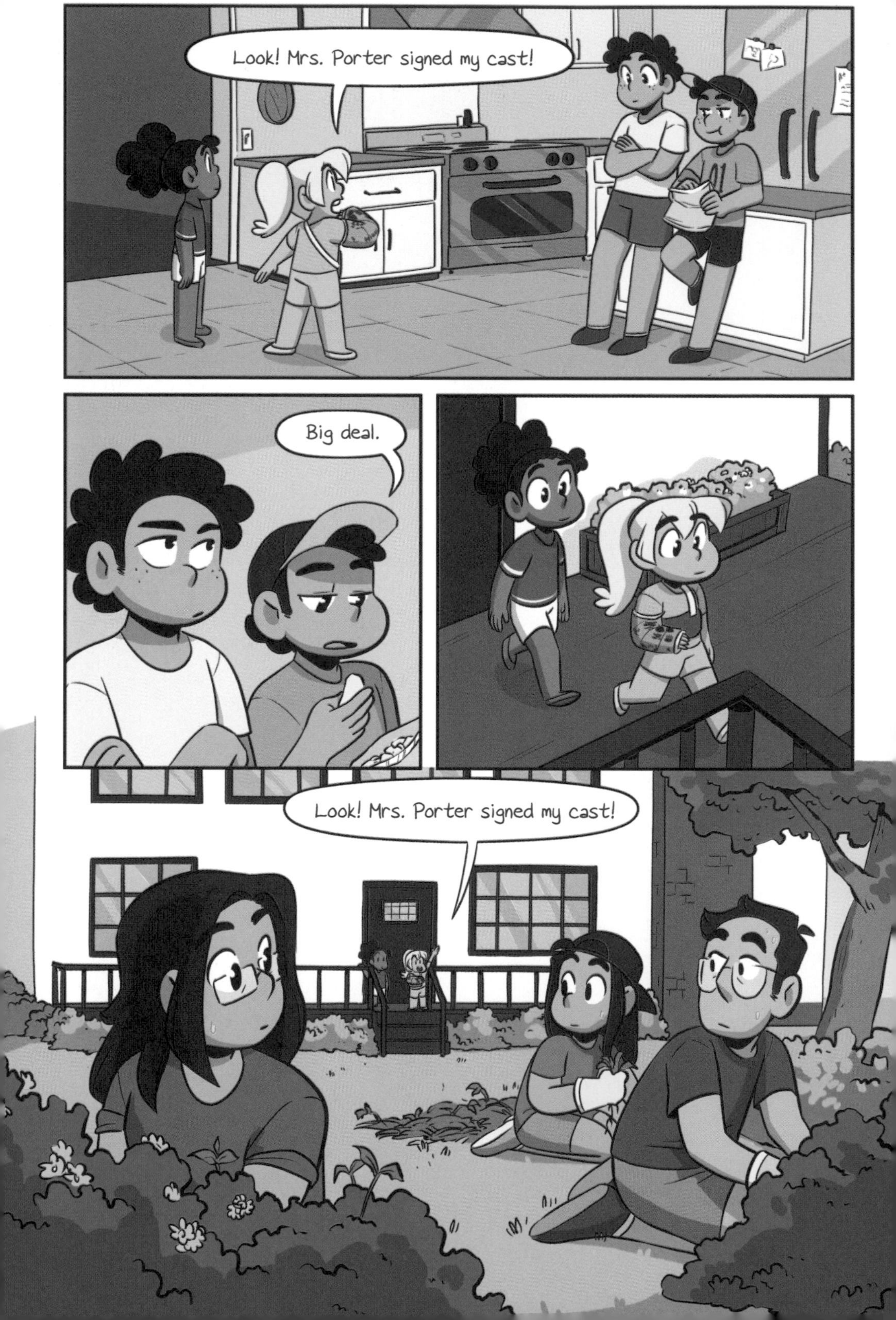
Look! Mrs. Porter signed my cast!
Big deal.
Look! Mrs. Porter signed my cast!

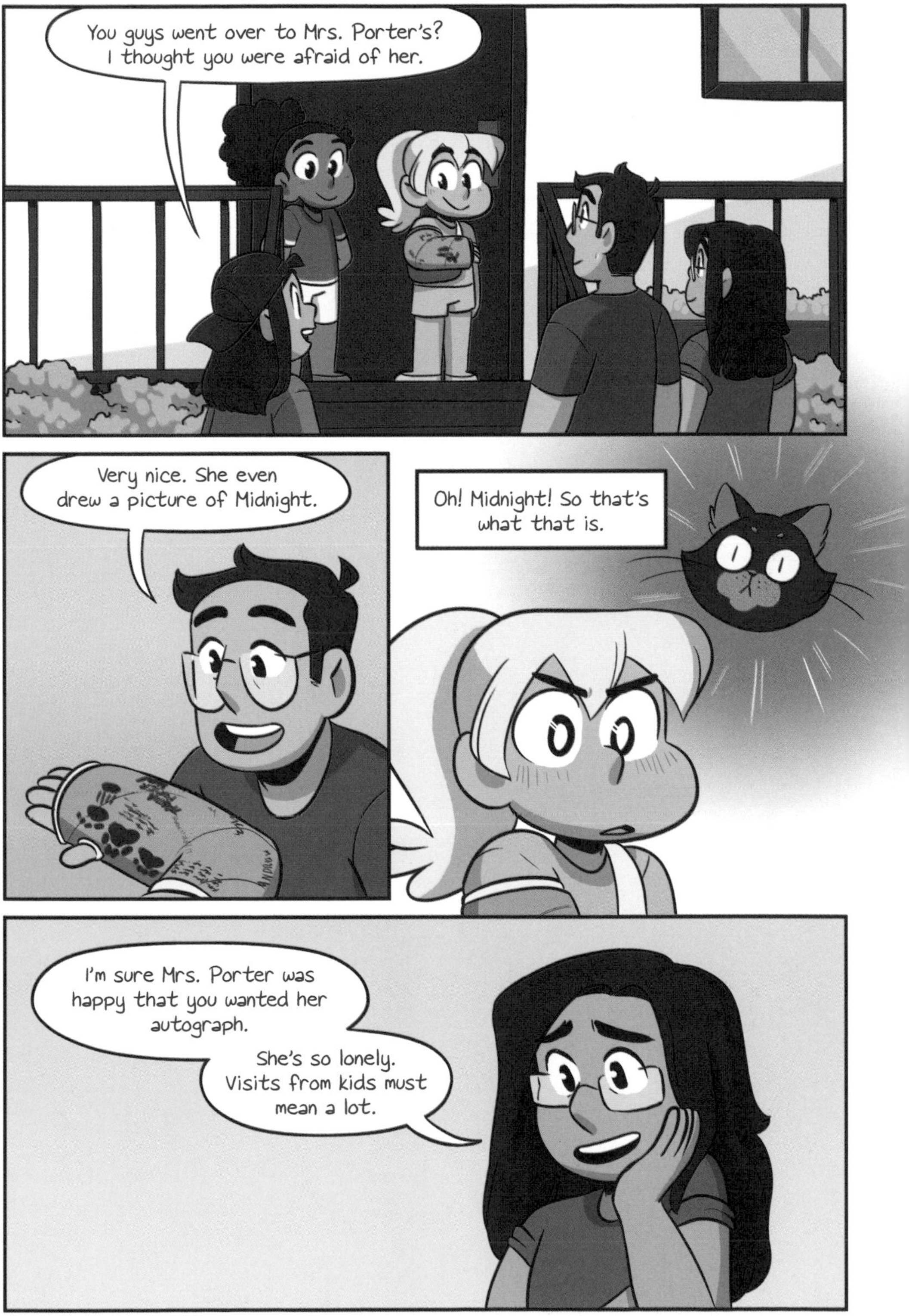
You guys went over to Mrs. Porter's? I thought you were afraid of her.
Very nice. She even drew a picture of Midnight.
Oh! Midnight! So that's what that is.
I'm sure Mrs. Porter was happy that you wanted her autograph.
She's so lonely. Visits from kids must mean a lot.

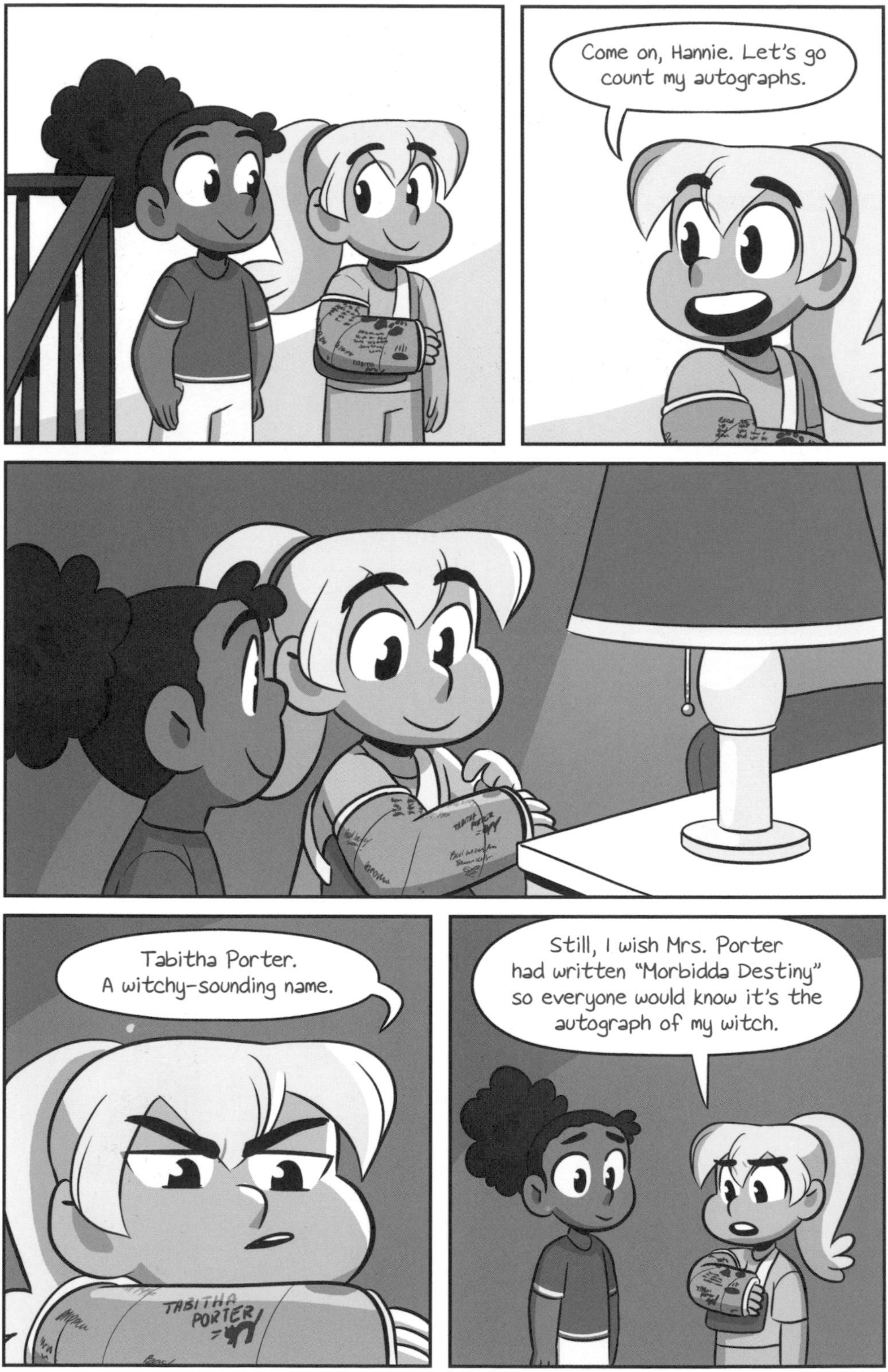
Come on, Hannie. Let's go count my autographs.
Tabitha Porter.
A witchy-sounding name.
TABITHA PORTER
Still, I wish Mrs. Porter had written "Morbidda Destiny" so everyone would know it's the autograph of my witch.

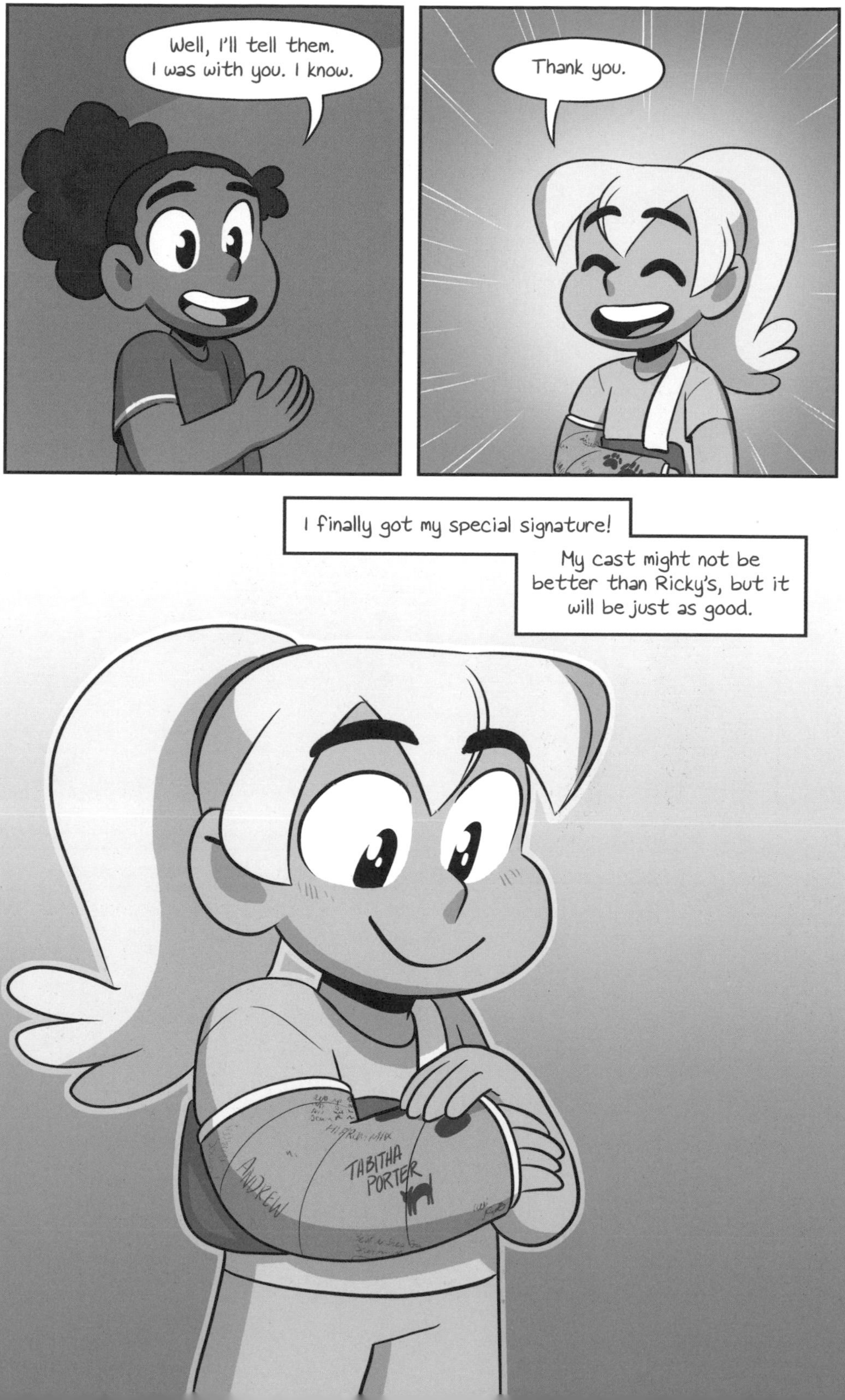
Well, I'll tell them. I was with you. I know.
Thank you.
I finally got my special signature!
My cast might not be better than Ricky's, but it will be just as good.
ANDREW
TABITHA PORTER

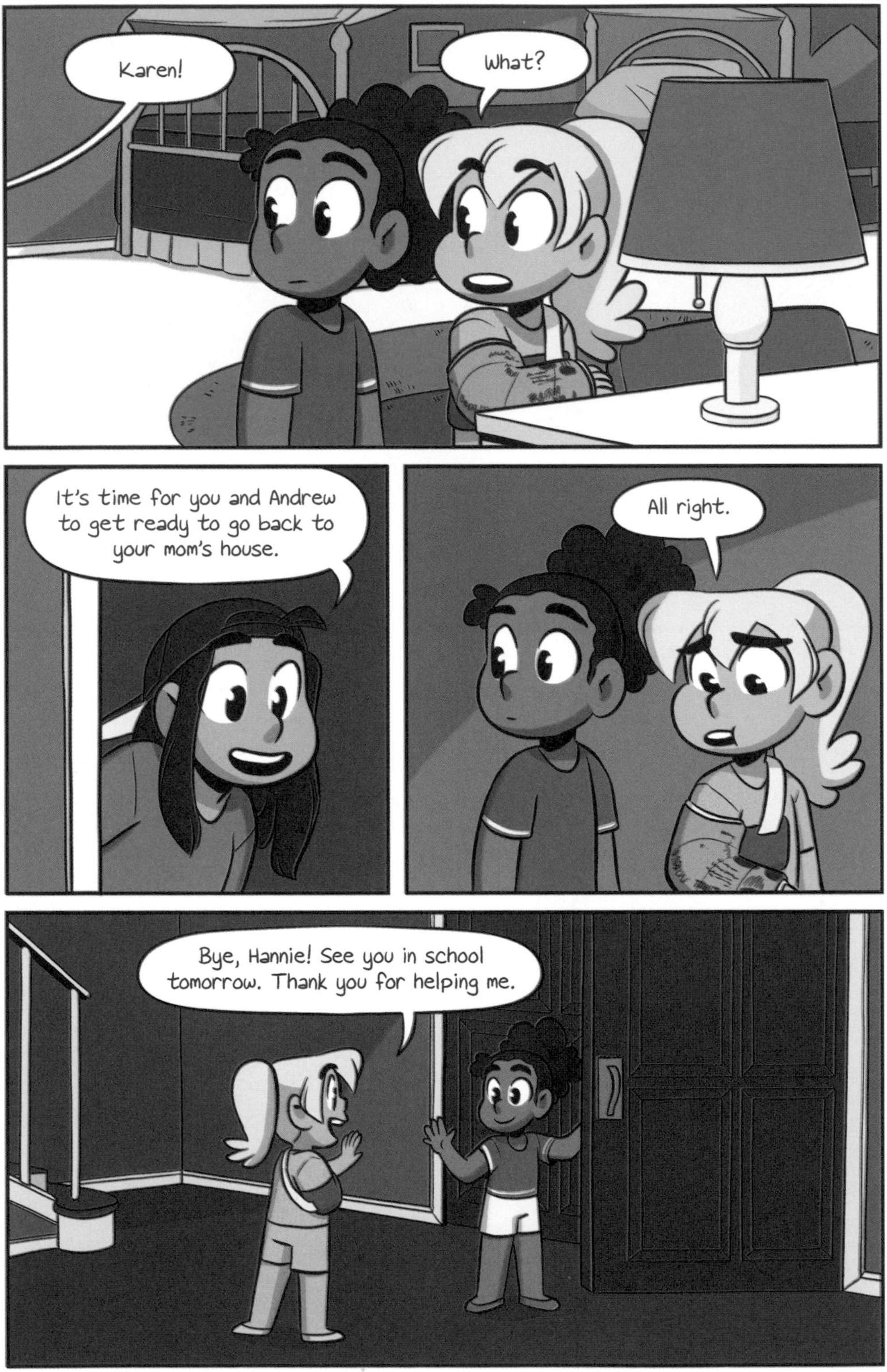
Karen!
What?
It's time for you and Andrew to get ready to go back to your mom's house.
All right.
Bye, Hannie! See you in school tomorrow. Thank you for helping me.

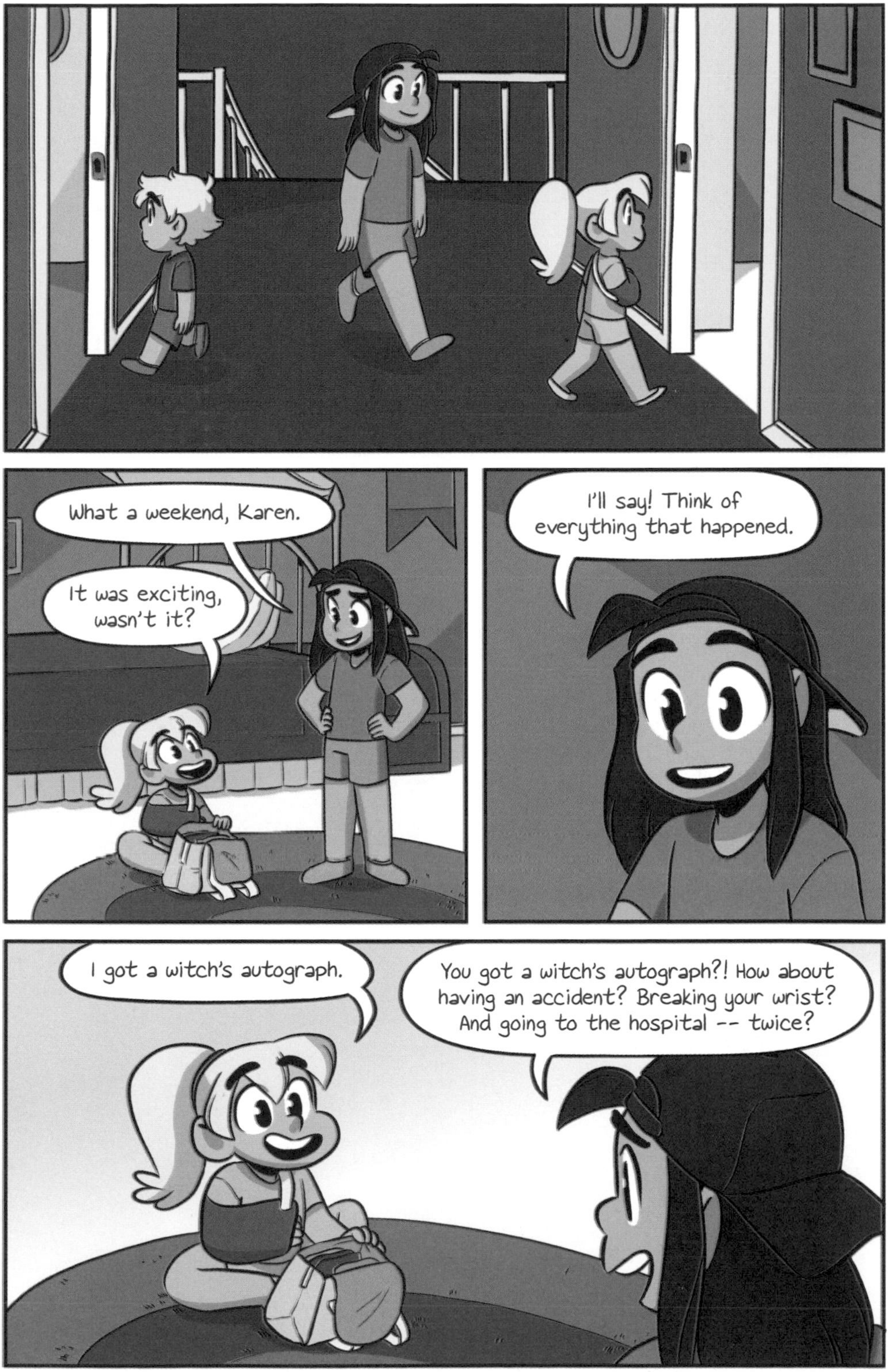
What a weekend, Karen.
It was exciting, wasn't it?
I'll say! Think of everything that happened.
I got a witch's autograph.
You got a witch's autograph?! How about having an accident? Breaking your wrist? And going to the hospital -- twice?

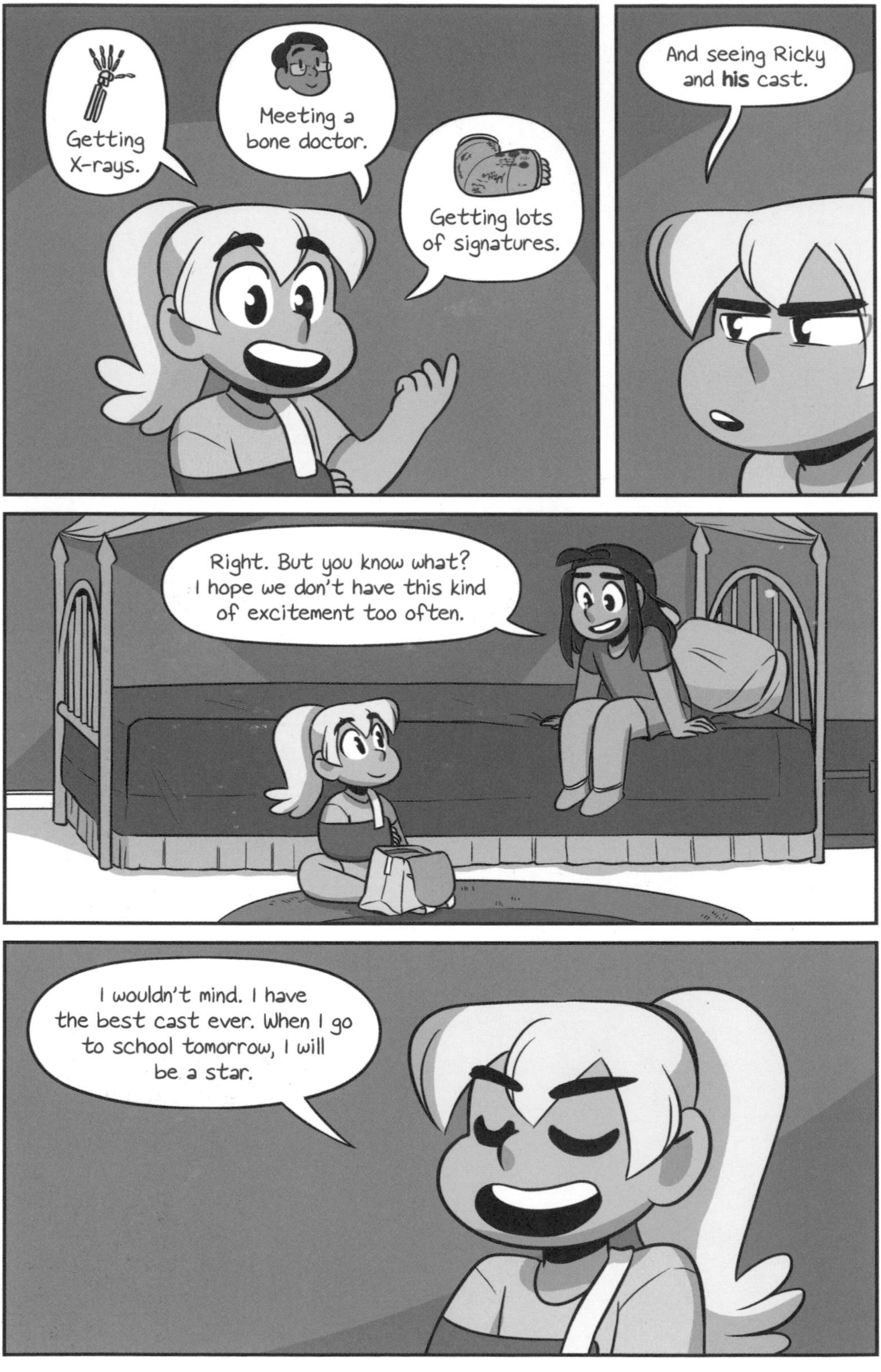
Getting X-rays.
Meeting a bone doctor.
Getting lots of signatures.
And seeing Ricky and **his** cast.
Right. But you know what? I hope we don't have this kind of excitement too often.
I wouldn't mind. I have the best cast ever. When I go to school tomorrow, I will be a star.

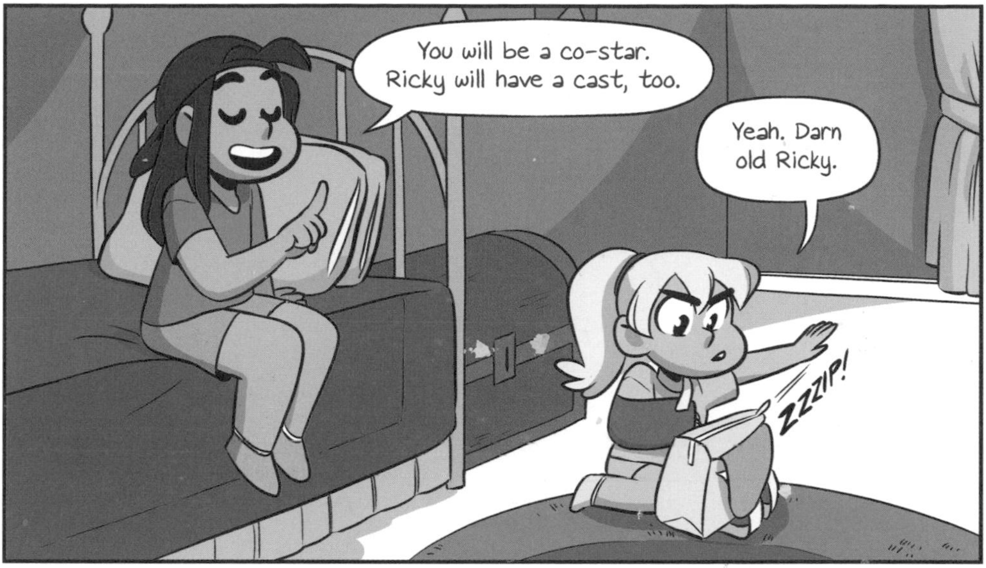
You will be a co-star. Ricky will have a cast, too.
Yeah. Darn old Ricky.
ZZZIP!

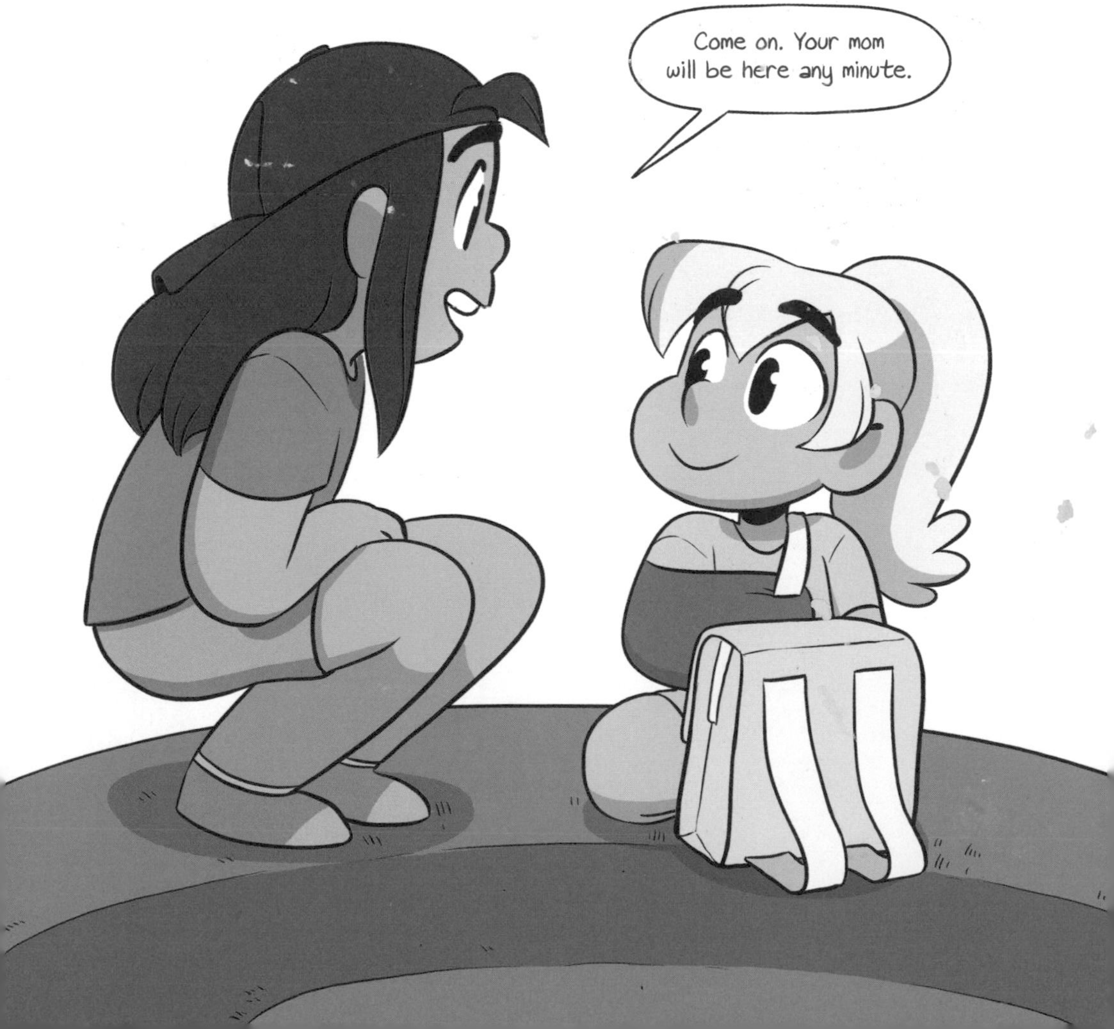
Come on. Your mom will be here any minute.

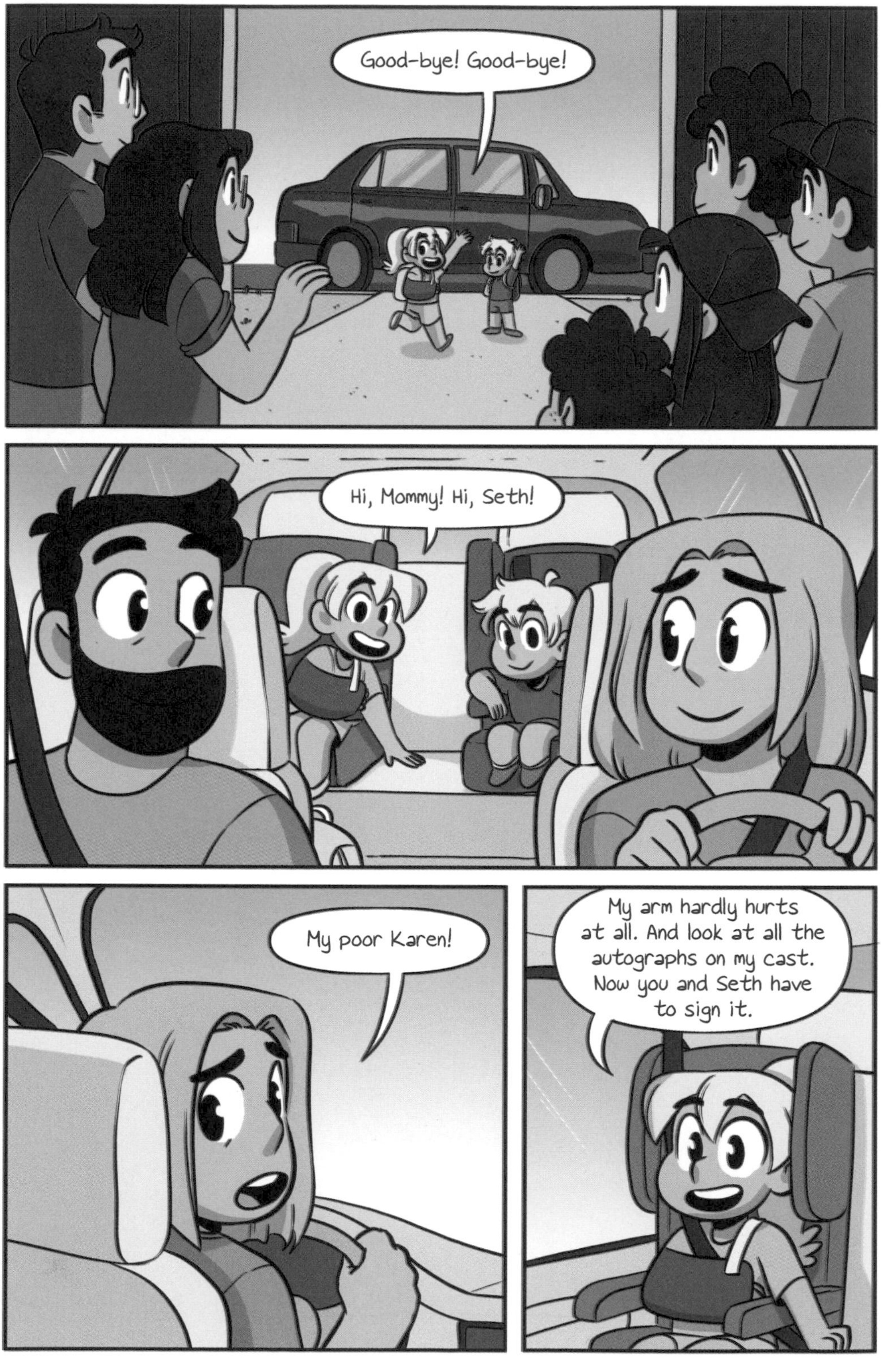
Good-bye! Good-bye!
Hi, Mommy! Hi, Seth!
My poor Karen!
My arm hardly hurts at all. And look at all the autographs on my cast. Now you and Seth have to sign it.

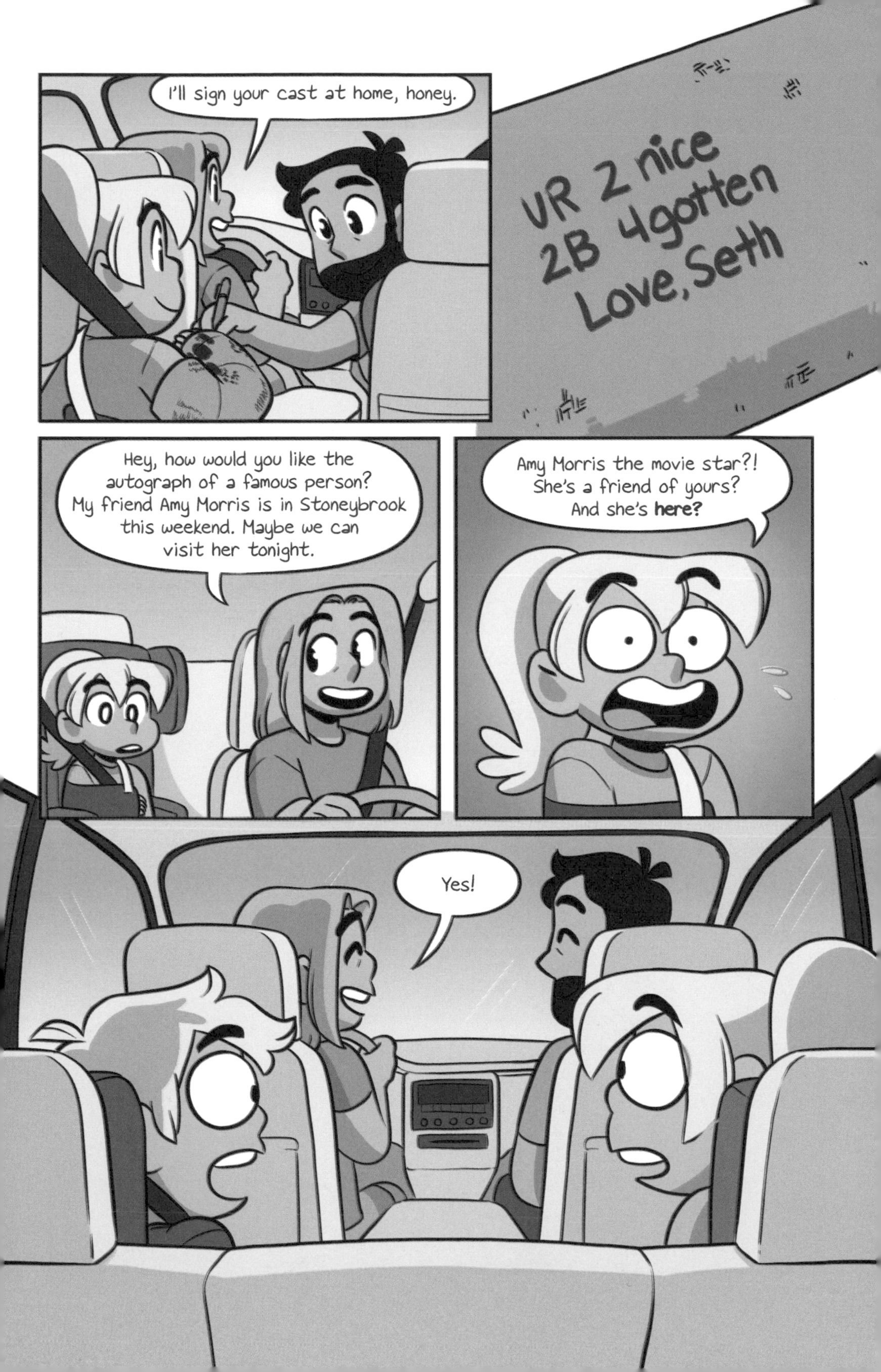
I'll sign your cast at home, honey.
VR 2 nice
2B 4gotten
Love, Seth
Hey, how would you like the autograph of a famous person? My friend Amy Morris is in Stoneybrook this weekend. Maybe we can visit her tonight.
Amy Morris the movie star?! She's a friend of yours? And she's **here?**
Yes!

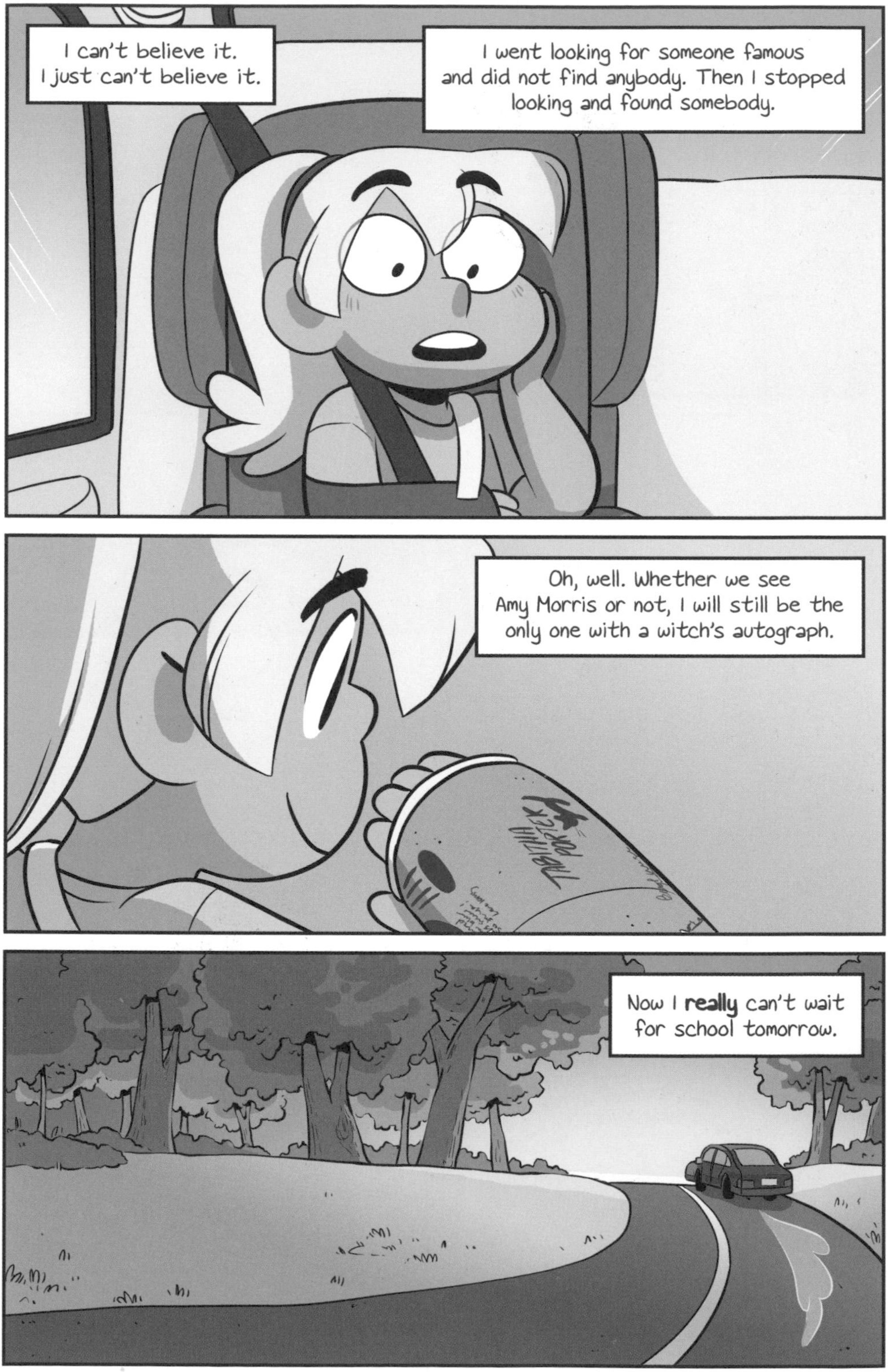
I can't believe it.
I just can't believe it.
I went looking for someone famous and did not find anybody. Then I stopped looking and found somebody.
Oh, well. Whether we see Amy Morris or not, I will still be the only one with a witch's autograph.
Now I **really** can't wait for school tomorrow.

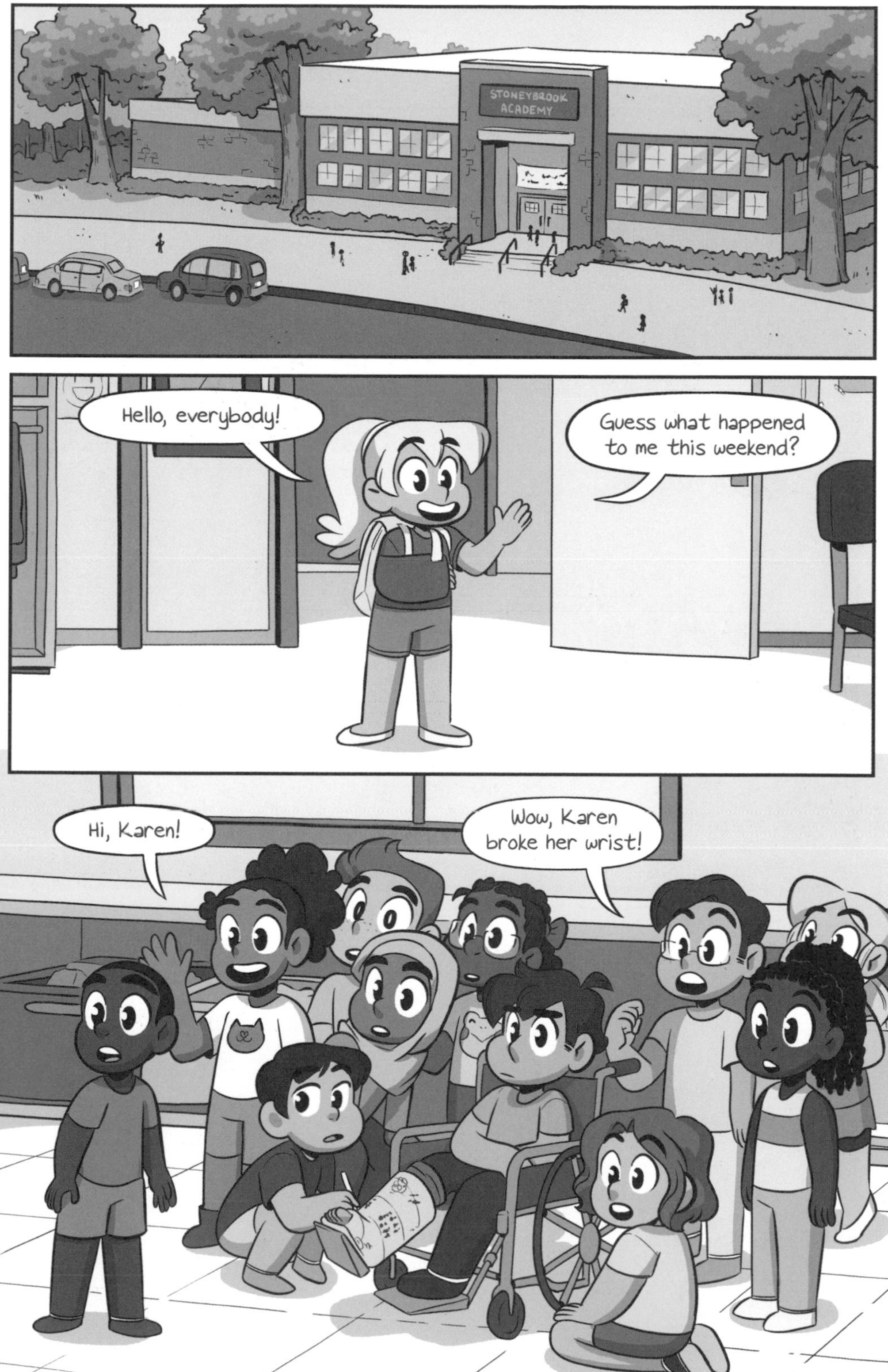
STONEYBROOK ACADEMY
Hello, everybody!
Guess what happened to me this weekend?
Hi, Karen!
Wow, Karen broke her wrist!

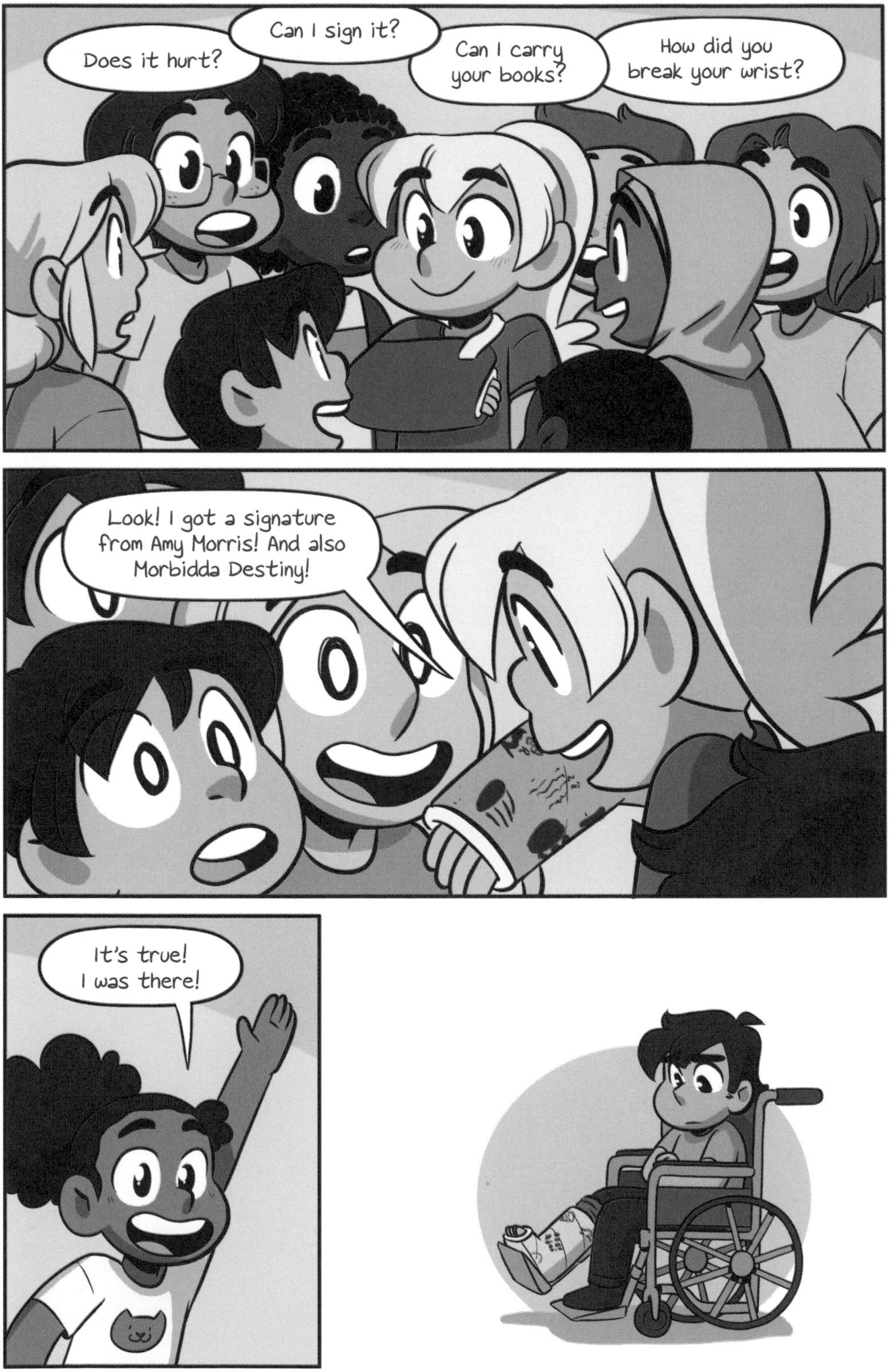
Does it hurt?
Can I sign it?
Can I carry your books?
How did you break your wrist?
Look! I got a signature from Amy Morris! And also Morbidda Destiny!
It's true! I was there!

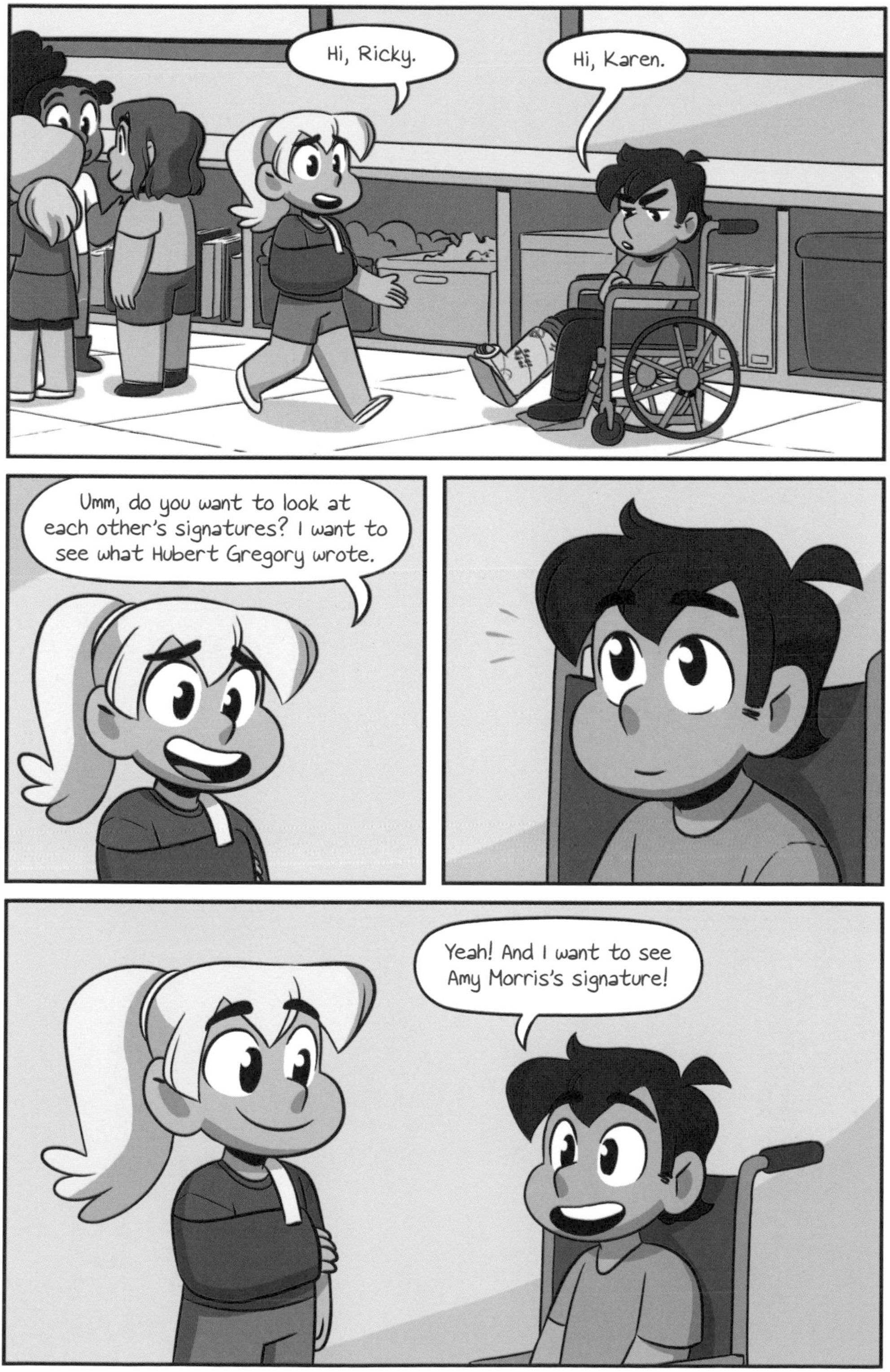
Hi, Ricky.
Hi, Karen.
Umm, do you want to look at each other's signatures? I want to see what Hubert Gregory wrote.
Yeah! And I want to see Amy Morris's signature!